The Same Chill, the Same Funny Feeling in My Fingers . . .

as when I was a foot-patrolman and entering an alley with a sense of danger, knowing something was there but not knowing what or where . . .

I have the same sense of danger now as I step out into the backyard. Something is wrong despite the greeting I get from the green wet of morning, the grass, the stuff hanging out of the rock garden, the leaves of the lilac bushes and young trees. I whistle for the dog and hear him behind me. He appears nervously from under the steps. Then I see his nose and flinch from the sight of it. A slice is missing, as if from a razor, a quick pink opening right around the edges where it has bled and coagulated. I try to hold his heavy head for a closer inspection of his nose but he won't stay still. The sun burns the back of my neck. I let the dog go and rise slowly. All is quiet. Then I hear something, a breaking or fluttering of leaves, and I wheel around, my revolver half out of the holster. . . .

Books by Andrew Coburn

The Babysitter
The Trespassers

Published by POCKET BOOKS

THE
TRESPASSERS

Andrew Coburn

PUBLISHED BY POCKET BOOKS NEW YORK

POCKET BOOKS, a Simon & Schuster division of
GULF & WESTERN CORPORATION
1230 Avenue of the Americas, New York, N.Y. 10020

Published by arrangement with Houghton Mifflin Company
Library of Congress Catalog Card Number: 74-10942

ISBN: 0-671-83048-1

First Pocket Books printing June, 1980

10 9 8 7 6 5 4 3 2 1

POCKET and colophon are trademarks of Simon & Schuster.

Printed in the U.S.A.

To Bernadine Casey Coburn

THE
TRESPASSERS

1

SLEEPING FITFULLY, A BIG MAN BULGING out of T-shirt and shorts, I wander through a dream where I'm a stranger seeking some palpable reality, a cry on my lips: *Where the hell am I?*

Sweat rills down my cheeks. I'm suspicious of the terrain. I sense danger, as if this place were inside the hundred-square-mile hunting ground of wolves. My feet are thick. I can't run. My strengthless hands hold nothing, which is all right. I have nothing to carry, not even my gun, which in sleep I neglected to take along. Some cop!

Outside is the black of night. Everything at peace. The breathing locked in their sleep, the dead in their abyss. And here am I wandering on strange ground and hoping for a gift of energy, an inner man taking steps that don't show and making murmurs that don't leave the lips. With birds flapping overhead. I have just noticed them. They may be skua gulls. A skua is disreputable, a cannibal among other things, and he will purposely crap on your head. He will also claw it.

There is little peace in my sleep, and little privacy, though I certainly don't want the utter seclusion of death, which to my mind is a vulgar detail of life, a dirty cobweb at the end of it, something my sister chooses to ignore. When President Kennedy was killed, she pretended he hadn't been. While others of her political temperament wept, raged, penned elegies, my sister smiled therapeutically, claimed it was all a mistake, and wrote him a letter. She knew she was acting irrationally, but said it was the proper thing to do at such a time. But when Martin Luther King and another Kennedy were killed, she shrugged and said, "Nothing surprises me, or at least it shouldn't." Now, facing a danger of her own, she is again shrugging and saying: "Really, Bobby, it's too stupid even to be talking about."

I want to wake up. I feel that I should. I want to touch my wife, who sleeps with her back to me and dreams her own dreams. They are completely her own. She will not share them. Our daughter Darcie is asleep in the next room, which is papered with photographs of rock singers, movie stars, and white-suited astronauts reaching for the moon. When Darcie was younger and we lived in a housing project, I held her hand in the early morning dark of a parking lot and pointed skyward to the speck of light that was Sputnik. She thought it was a star.

My dog is sleeping outdoors. He resembles a wolf. His place is on the side steps guarding this old high house of mine, this property which lies against a river, the river the width of a country road where it passes my property and winds around the Lincoln Apartments. My brother-in-law, if he is not home, is asleep in one of the Lincoln's luxury units. He is a thirty-five-year-old problem child full of maladaptive habits, a case not only for behaviorists but for a grand jury, conspiracy to murder my sister.

I haven't time to think about this. I must keep my mind on the birds, which are acting like spy planes taking evasive action. My revolver would come in handy, a blast to keep the birds at bay. Though I frequently examine the revolver, a snub-nosed thirty-eight, rub my thuhb over the surfaces, I seldom fuss with its inner workings. I should clean it and check the firing power, but I treat it more or less as I do my car, the hood of which I have never lifted. I can't find

10

the latch. According to the guy at the gas station, it's in a tricky spot.

Except for circling birds and unfamiliar terrain, this dream isn't as upsetting as some I've had, ones where I keep running into a bowler-hatted man, someone I've never seen before, a walking stick in his gloved hand, ice in his eyes, a touch of madness on his smiling lips. Look out for the stick! Pure melodrama from a British mystery novel I can't remember reading, but unnerving nevertheless, because the stick suddenly strikes me, a whack across the face, and the man assumes the bloodless demeanor of an undertaker. Indeed, he is an undertaker, hovering over my sister and me as we sit talking in the plastic-flowered waiting room of his parlor, with each of us wondering what we're doing here, my sister speaking in her Radcliffe accent and casting a slender and shapely shadow when she rises to snuff out a half-smoked cigarette in an oversized ashtray. Then it happens: the sudden arrival in the airtight room of our father. He totters toward me with a joyous smile as my sister gives a little gasp, for it's the first time she has seen him since his death a number of years ago. My father draws up a chair next to mine and talks five, maybe ten minutes, while never uttering a word to Joan, who, with a fresh cigarette, views him in the manner of a newspaper reporter who sees a dark plot in everything. Then slowly she realizes the truth, which is tragic to her. He doesn't recognize her. She pulls my sleeve, but I can't help her. We are subject to sleep which, through dreams, rearranges reality the way a winter wind carves snow into any shape it wants and, in doing so, remakes the landscape. "Help me," my sister says. She doesn't understand. "Tell him," she says. He wouldn't understand. He was victim of a bullet from a small-caliber pistol. The bullet must have had a hard time getting through his skull, but it did, and it reached the brain and killed him.

The birds scatter. Coming this way are six or so

women grouped as if for military purposes. Nothing to worry about. Despite their formation they appear peaceable. It's possible I've encountered them in another dream, or that they're in this one by error. I raise my eyes. The birds are gone, but their absence means nothing. A grass fire will hide, or act dead, and then leap up when you turn your back. The women draw near, all in step, and I drop my eyes. I pretend I'm busy, a man doing chores. I study the reddish ground as if contemplating planting corn. At the same time, from the corner of my eye, I wait for their glances to stray my way and stay awhile. But they scarcely notice me. Dressed in short garments of classical cut, they are husky and fresh-smelling and obviously untamed and ungirdled, inexorable maidens not of this era but dating back when sturdy legs were admired and female fighters famous. I have an urge to join them. Their march has the hard and relentless beat of rain. There are certain complexities in their gait, in the sway of their garments, in the short curly cut of their hair, like the mathematics in music, the calculated ambiguities in poetry, like the frills and curves and spikes of elaborate seashells. They aren't fantasies, these hearty women, but timeless warriors wandering through history to answer the exigencies of battle. In the direction they head, I can hear horses on a wooden bridge, drums, calls, commands. Then a bloody shriek.

In the instant I know what it's like to have a bullet in the brain: the sudden snapping of strings and the whistling away of life, the fast and fanatic situation in which nothing matters.

The shriek is not human, and it is not bird. It is from the real world, from the dark outside my house. It is from my dog.

My sleep is sucked away as if through a straw.

2

POGGIO AND PRIMACK EMERGE FROM NATE'S
diner where my father used to make book with the
fervor of an old scientist who has outlived family and
friends and still has projects to complete. A smart man
my father, warm and honest despite the illegality of
his work, gentle in his conversations and sensitive, not
cold and crass like these two. They are parasites, and
the little one, Poggio, is probably insane. In the streetlight and in the neon glow of Nate's they show off new
suits, new shoes, new leases on life. If they haven't
gambled it away, they have money in their pockets,
or rather in Poggio's pocket, a bulge of bills next to
a knife I know he used in a chance encounter some
years back with a gang of suburban youths bent on
adventure. Rowdy, smart-mouthed, ready for rough
sport, they were misled by Poggio's effete face, pink
hands and marionette walk and figured him for a fairy.
One boy lost his lower lip. Another boy threw up his
hands in surrender and lost his surprisingly flimsy hold
on life. A jury found Poggio, represented by a Boston
lawyer, innocent of murder and guilty only of pro-
tecting himself against brutal teen-aged thugs from
nice homes.

Primack towers over him. Primack, swaying as if
his new shoes hurt, has the appearance of a country
bumpkin. The seersucker jacket is too tight around
the shoulders and too short in the arms. His brown
slicked-down hair sticks up in back. His face is mawk-

ish, his eyes close together. His huge hands are damaged but still formidable. A former Golden Gloves boxer, he fought more effectively outside the ring. He once beat a bartender into an unconsciousness that lasted for weeks. The bartender's body survived, but his mind didn't.

Poggio glances toward my car without seeing it. His eyesight is not good. He hitches up his slim trousers, tugs at his suitcoat and tightens his tie. He grew up an orphan with a name that wasn't his and that doesn't seem to suit him. He is blond and pink, delicate and diminutive, unwell and unfit. He dreams of being noticed by organized crime. He imagines himself traveling to great ports of the world to oversee heroin shipments. A diamond on his pinkie and a numbered bank account in Switzerland. A pretty person from a distance but unclean up close. The feminine mouth is a dirty remark and the pink face an ache. The hair needs washing and the scalp scrubbing. He gives the impression that he has no function as a male, that he is no begetter, that he is merely a stunning little creature with a fast but unfertile brain. He is about forty but could pass for twenty-five. It is probable he shaves no more than once a week. He has a lengthy juvenile arrest record and spent time in a training school where he knifed a guard who mistreated him. His adult record includes arrests for forging checks, peddling pornography, pushing drugs, selling stolen cars and swindling the unsuspecting. His only jail sentences have been for assaults on women, a pink fist in the mouth, a quick knife slash down the face.

Primack studies my car. It is possible he knows it. He is smarter than he looks, more subtle than he appears. My car, a Chevrolet, five years old and rusted at the edges, is out of place in this part of the city, the Lower End, where the big bookies drive Thunderbirds and Cadillacs and where those not so big maneuver second-hand Lincolns and Chryslers. Primack leans against Nate's with a toothpick in his mouth. He protects Poggio. There's a little love thing between them, or something close to it, something soggy. Primack rearranges himself against Nate's, shifts his feet. That toothpick: a splinter in his face. He is the sort who breaks bones.

My hands are sticking to each other, not from fear but from simple anxiety. I haven't truly formulated a plan of action. I have only been waiting for them to step out of Nate's, and now here they are! I don't know whether to act as a police officer or as a private citizen whose sister's life has been toyed with without her knowledge, whether to shout to them from my car or face them on the sidewalk in front of Nate's, where they loll like character actors, their eyes straying insinuatingly to passers-by and their ears tuned to the street traffic which suddenly is heavy, as if piling up against some impending disaster. Too many headlights painting my car. Poggio is squinting. Primack picks his teeth and watches a woman across the street. He nudges Poggio. The woman is straining her eyes toward me.

There is a pig-squeal of brakes as she steps into the traffic with her hips swinging as if to bump away the cars. Her face is totally made up but on the verge of falling off, yet still attractive, still girlish. Corn hair, piddly blue eyes and overwhelming Polack tits. The wife of a fellow cop and the intense mother of six. Some years ago, following the birth of her last, she suffered a breakdown from which she has never fully recovered. Every so often she sneaks down here to the Lower End, to Alekel's where she sits with her legs crossed, a smile for whoever wants to buy her a drink. She simply wants to be treated decently and to laugh a little, except that after she has had a couple, men misinterpret the sharpness of her laugh and use their hands on her, sometimes their fists. Most men, however, avoid her—those who know that her husband, a sport shirt hanging over the waist of his police pants, will come looking for her, and God help the man with her!

"Southy," she says, and her hand slips through the

open window, and I squeeze her fingers because that is what she wants. "Wait," she says and withdraws her hand and hurries to the other side of the car. I lean over and open the door, an eye on Poggio and Primack who are giving us their full attention, one with an agonizing squint that makes a bunch out of his little face. She crowds into the front seat. Rose Mulligan. She has gained weight. She is puffy around the eyes, slack around the mouth, but still pretty. I remember when she was beautiful. She wears her yellow hair long and straight, the way she always has. She kisses me.

"God!" she says. "How long has it been?"

I'm not sure. Maybe it was a year ago I saw her in a supermarket. I was at the end of an aisle when I saw her. I left the carriage where it was, half-filled with groceries, sneaked down another aisle and left. It has been at least ten years since we have been in a car together.

"Oh, Southy," she says with distress. "You've lost some of your hair."

I run a hand over my head and wince. "I didn't think it showed that much. I'll have to comb more carefully."

"But you haven't got like Roscoe. He's all gray."

Kinky and wiry gray, and black eyebrows that meet over a pug nose. Her husband. A career patrolman who won't take promotional exams because he fears the stigma of flunking. His leather accessories are the glossiest. His revolver smells of bore cleaner and has something close to a hair trigger. It never misses its mark. The only cop on the force to kill more than once. A bully with a nightstick, which he once shoved up a woman's ass, hurting her badly. He nearly lost his badge. I have forgotten how he got out of it. The woman, I guess, wasn't much good, a bad reputation.

"Where is he?" I ask.

"Bowling. I hope he gets a hernia."

"You're taking a chance, aren't you?"

"On love, Southy. And that's a real old song, don't you know?"

"Don't push him, Rose."

"Why not? He pushed me into a nuthouse."

I squeeze one of her hands. I don't want her to get worked up over what she is saying, thinking, remembering. I don't want her on my hands. On my conscience. I don't want her husband after me. She pushes a heavy thigh against me.

"Southy, talk to me. You waiting for someone?"

I shake my head.

"Then what are you doing? Are you on a stakeout?" She leans forward and peers through the windshield and notices Primack and Poggio. "I know those two," she says.

"Forget them."

"OK. Let's get out of here. After all these years you can at least buy me a drink. Maybe some place nice."

"I'd like to Rose, really, but I can't."

She lifts her chin. "One drink. byou're afraid to buy me that?"

"Yes."

"Southy, don't make me beg."

"I was just about to leave. That's the truth."

"Southy." Her hand reaches for my face. "Not even for old times' sake? We used to have quite a time."

"We were younger then."

Her smile is softer than her face as she shakes her head. "I wasn't young, not with six kids, and you looked old because you were sour when you came home from the army. You expected too much from Libby."

"That was a long time ago. I don't remember."

"You remember," she says.

I shrug. Of course I do. I was an over-aged college student in dyed-blue army pants and, two or three nights a week, a working reserve cop with a wife and

17

child and academic problems and bills to pay and a
junk car stalled in downtown traffic which itself was
stalled in a rain storm that wanted to wash away the
city. She, Rose, whom I'd been screwing and now
was avoiding, appeared on foot in the traffic. A wild
woman in the rain, soaked to the skin. She pounded
her fists on the hood of my car. Risky. It could have
fallen apart. "Let me in!" she hollered. I opened the
door and she flopped in like a drowned cow, no raincoat and no underwear under her sopping dress. On
her breath was a mixture of liquor and medication.
"I'm drunk," she said. "I'm freezing to death." It
was a shopping night, a Friday. The traffic shoved
forward. By a small miracle I got my car going, but
I had trouble navigating. Great flapping waves of rain
inundated the windshield. The car slow-moving, sea-
swimming, a turtle. Rose shouted, "Look out!" and
shut her eyes as we got horn-blasted on three sides:
two taxis and a truck. "It's all right," I said. I had
milk and bread on the back seat and a wife and daughter waiting for them. Rose wanted me to take her
somewhere, anywhere. I was looking for a place to
dump her, peering through the miserable windshield,
the wipers half working because the rubber blades
were ragged. In the downpour people scurried against
store windows, glass doors, mortared walls—a struggling bas-relief. Caught in a flash of lightning, a brute
of a man appeared superadded to the substance of a
building. It was Mulligan, with the eyesight of a hawk.

At Ramsey High Libby and I had been sophomores
when Rose Wysocky and Roscoe Mulligan were sen-
iors. Rose and Roscoe. He the broad-shouldered and
handsome athlete over whom girls fawned, and she
the tight sweatered golden-haired honor student over
whom boys abused themselves. He the foul-mouthed
Roman Catholic who blessed himself before each play
on the field and then used his thumb in the eyes of
opponents, Roscoe who had no business on the team
because his grades were miserable. She was straight-
A with a half-dozen scholarships to choose from, none

of which she could accept because she was pregnant. A fast marriage at diploma time to Roscoe and a baby every year. He turned beefy and brutal and drove a laundry truck days and tended bar nights for three or four years until he found a place on the police force. With each pregnancy she swore she wouldn't have another. She clapped her hands when she had miscarriages. Drunk at a policemen's ball, she screamed she was losing her looks and her sanity because Roscoe wouldn't use a rubber. At home he beat her with his open hands, knocking her from one part of the house to another and once, according to Rose, drove her to her knees and forced the point of his service revolver into her mouth and threatened to pull the trigger. She claimed she tried to pull it for him. She was two months in the state hospital where, she said, she was assaulted by a Negro psychiatric aide whose hatred and outrage were so great that while humping her he cursed sky, land and water, as if they were of white man's doing, and later he tried to pull the blond hair out of her head and the tongue out of her mouth. That was what cured her, she said. Someone whose outrage and frustration were deeper and darker than hers.

Mulligan was waiting for me in the project parking lot, concealed in his car by the rain. He approached me as I climbed out of my car. His wiry black hair was taking in the rain like a sponge. I didn't recognize him until he knocked the bread and milk from my hands. He had only one question, to be answered yes or no, and God help me if I lied: Was that Rose he saw in my car? It was my sister, I told him. He hit me. I was on the pavement beside my car with pain in every one of my teeth and a fear that my jaw was unhinged. I saw the toe of his shoe coming at me and rolled under the car. He got on his belly and came after me, blood on his breath. He got a piece of my jacket but not enough to hang on to. He couldn't maneuver well. He got stuck. I rolled out the other side. I don't know what Rose said to him later, what lies she told that he chose to believe, but he phoned me that next evening at the police station and said he had come to realize that I was not the sort to take advantage of a woman not long out of a mental institution, a woman with children. I accepted his apology, which seemed to anger him. I didn't ask why.

She crowds against me. "Come on," she says. "We always did look good together."

I give her a grin. "We'd have every eye on us. That dress of yours scarcely covers your ass."

"That's the way they *wear* them today!"

"What kind of stockings are those?"

She raises a knee. "Fishnet. Don't you like them?"

"They're pretty. They're pink."

"What about the leg?"

"Still nice."

"Southy." A wide smile as she reaches for my hands. "And I like these. You know how to lay them on a bar so they look like something. They're good hands. They were always nice to me."

Gently I try to push her away. Poggio and Primack have moved into the shadows. Their faces are invisible except when Poggio draws on a cigarette. Rose reaches for the radio dial. I stop her hand.

"What's the matter? Southy, be a little bit glad to see me. I'm glad to see you."

Then her eyes follow mine to where Poggio and Primack are standing. In the glow of his cigarette, Poggio's face is a red plum.

"Oh God, Southy." She claps her hands together. "I think I understand. I heard something horribly juicy about your brother-in-law, and you're watching those two. They're the ones, aren't they?"

"Who's been filling your ear?"

"Roscoe says it's all over the station. Southy, be careful. The little one's crazy. That's what Roscoe says."

"What else does he say?"

"Your brother-in-law paid them money, but he wasn't serious. He was drunk or something. But now they want more money. They're squeezing him."

"That's gossip. You know how much truth is in gossip."

"No, Southy. Tell me."

"There's nothing to tell. It's an absurd situation."

"Your sister should leave him, or throw him in jail. *You* throw him in jail."

I smile and place a hand on her cheek. Immediately she presses her hand over mine. I was, she says, good to her once, and she doesn't forget that. I was kind and considerate and gentle, she says. I don't remember myself being that way, but maybe I was.

"They know you're here," she says. "They keep looking this way."

"I want them to know I'm here, and that's all. Nothing more."

"It's like a game, you mean. Can I play?"

I reach for the ignition key. "I'm going to drive you home."

"No!" Sudden violence in her voice. "I'll raise holy hell. I mean it!"

She glares at me. I sit back, and she relaxes. She smiles.

"I want to help you."

"I don't want you to."

"And you don't even want to buy me a drink."

"Another time."

"That might be years from now. You realize I could become very ugly now. But I won't. I'd rather help you."

"You mind your business. I mean that, Rose."

"I know what you're up to. You want to throw a scare into those two. Right? Get them off your brother-in-law's back. I'll help you."

"You'll do nothing!"

"Really."

In the instant I know what's on her mind, but she is out of the car before I can stop her. With swinging hips, with a violent smile over her shoulder in the direction of Poggio and Primack, her smile coming loose like a split sea urchin, she ambles down the side-

21

walk. She is all ass and legs. Flashing headlights catch her, hold her, and then let her go.

They saunter out of the shadows. Poggio snaps his cigarette away. He has a queer little step. Primack, for a big man, has an agile one, that of a dancer, a boxer. They're cracked, they're cuckoo, but they have me where they want me, because I don't know what to do. Primack, in passing, peers through the open window of my car and says, "Fuck you."

3

I DON'T MOVE. TORN FROM SLEEP, I CAN never immediately retrieve the pieces. I'm soft and flaky and farty, a bundle of feelings not yet bound, not yet fitted with bones and dipped in blood and wrapped in flesh.

The echo of my dog's shriek remains in my ears. No sound comes from the outside. It's still dark. I have at least another hour or two to sleep.

I touch Libby to see whether she's awake. She isn't. She's a worm in a leaf. I won't wake her. Roused suddenly or lightly or lovingly, she would stay for the most part unawake, unrelieved, unready and unwilling. I'm not so foolish to think that after sixteen years of marriage things will suddenly jitterbug into place.

We married young, Libby and I, and wanted to be a nice couple, a Dagwood and Blondie with fine children and lots of little dogs. We have one child, a daughter born too soon, and we have a handsome silver-streaked German shepherd. Darcie is growing, growing. An adolescent. Soon she will be gone. The dog, a replacement for one slaughtered on the highway, is still a pup, ten months old, a lovable slob to me but already an awesome animal to strangers. The possibility that he is dead is considered only for a moment.

Without moving, almost without breathing, I become alert and ready and involved with myself. Pleasantly and achingly I feel myself being thrust into shape, a large man stretched out in his underwear under warm covers, a vigorous person with large hands and feet that begin to move, a considerate husband careful not to disturb his wife whose sleep has always been important to her.

The rugless floor is cold. Squatting on bare feet and pressing my nose against the screen on the window, I strain to catch sight of my dog or at least a sound from him. Gray clouds conceal the moon. My property—my trees and shrubs and bushes and rough rock gardens—is three stories down because of the lay of the land. It's a little valley, a pocket, with parts of it, such as the driveway, built up with landfill long before I came here. On the far side of the driveway the land runs level for a short distance until it reaches the river bank where it slopes into the dark water, into which sticks, stones and the corpses of small animals disappear forever. The front of my house, almost flush with the sidewalk, is situated on solid ground and the rest of it rises up on a brick foundation. An old barn-red house, with a gable here and there, built maybe seventy years ago and nudged on either side by an unmortared stone wall shared by other houses up the street, in the opposite direction from the apartments. On the highway side the wall is only hip-high, but on my side, because of the land drop, sheer on each side of the house, it's ten feet high. When I'm in my yard, when the leaves are on the trees, I'm sealed off from the world, which rumbles by on the highway. I like it that way. So does Libby, if only because of the memory of the housing project where everything was exposed.

The moon remains hidden. It was lying on the river before I went to bed, a seemingly perfect circle, a fallen discus I suspected I could have lifted if I waded into the water. The trees across the river, great greening shapes, hide the dozen handsome brick buildings of the Lincoln Apartments. The buildings that front the highway have the luxury units. Only when the

24

trees are naked, when the world becomes wood and then white, can the buildings be seen from my property.

Last winter I walked onto the river to the middle where the ice was not perfectly safe and experienced the nightmare of a skater who sees faces beneath the surface. I saw mine as the ice began to crack. A woman on the sidewalk leaned forward against the stone wall, gesticulated in my direction, and shouted to the others, "There's a man in trouble! Call a cop!"

"For Christ's sake, I am a cop!" I hollered up to her, and baby-stepped to safety.

That was in the dead of winter. People with freezing faces, steaming mouths, bitten noses and raw knuckles. I slipped lightly over the ice to where the river had stolen soil from my property and formed a shallow inlet, a frog pond that in the summer smears itself with dot weed and grows high with reeds. The inlet was frozen solid, fine for skating. A gust of white wind nearly knocked me down. I scrambled up the snow-crusted bank and viewed the apartments like an explorer sighting a lost city. What I really wanted to do was travel. I wanted to reach warm countries and dig into sand and unearth secrets on stones, blocks of black basalt with mysterious messages. I wanted to find pottery and tools with fingerprints of the primitive people who used them. At the same time I wanted to chisel my own history in a dozen languages on the face of towering rock. I know only English and a few soiled words in German, the kind soldiers pick up.

In the spring I dug into the bank of the inlet and uncovered rusted cans, broken bottles, pieces of crockery, dumped there by the former owners of the house, an elderly man and his wife. Scots. I must have dug up a hundred cold-cream jars, the large economy-size, and as many bottles of Geritol, indicating a furious fight by the old couple to keep their faces smooth and their hearts pumping. The old man dropped dead by the river of a cerebral hemorrhage. His wife couldn't keep up with the taxes. That was when Libby and I bought the house, ten years ago, a G.I. loan, nothing down.

On another part of the property, near pine trees where I park my car, I fought poison ivy, struggling with the tough bright-brown roots which, stabbed with a shovel, broke, spurted juice, and yielded wet white meat. I tore up the ground because one root led to another, and each was haired with rootlets. Fighting a losing battle, I ripped roots up with my bare hands and poisoned my skin. My hands bubbled up and, where the blisters leaked, my fingers stuck together. I couldn't manipulate a pencil, let alone my revolver.

I phoned the station, said I was sick, and stayed home with a bunch of books. In one book I cut through the print and sneaked inside the paper where the people were. I fooled around with a character named Forbush, an ornithologist, going along with the guy to, of all places, the Antarctic to study, of all things, the mating of penguins, to poke among their precious eggs, to shake my freezing fist beside Forbush's at savage skua gulls with faces like those of demented old men. I saw the wind wrench the sea, and I saw the sea turn chaotic and cruel. I saw poor Forbush's frostbitten fingers and later, chapters later, I saw the man, apparently mad, make music to the midnight sun. I fled. I repropped my pillow, chose another book, and basked in a warm country.

I like the brilliance of the sun and the heat of good memories (clearly I remember inspecting Darcie's baby teeth and finding a cookie crumb I thought was a cavity). I like the green cool of spring and the burning of summer, and sometimes I like the salt warmth of myself, of my sleep, of my dreams. My name is Robert Southwark.

I am, however, in the wrong business. Certainly I'm not cut out for violence, for nut cases and maniacal murderers. I knew it years ago when, still a reserve, I saw a man knock a woman to the pavement and then hit her with an ax so hard that a part of her sat up. Hello. Alive, dead, dying? I didn't know. I was raw, a rookie. I didn't wait around. I blew my whistle.

Ramsey isn't a big city, only ten or eleven square miles, but there's a lot in it. A population of eighty thousand (more than that before the textile mills moved south), street after street of triple-decker tenements (my father and I lived in one), and sections where the houses are grand and old (where my aunt lives), and streets where the houses are long low ranches with swimming pools (such as where my sister lives). A city heavy now with electronic companies and minimum-wage sweat shops in the old mill buildings, and too many barrooms and package stores, especially in the Lower End, a piece of which is giving way to urban renewal, tall tenements and Lebanese coffee houses and small bakeries and smoke shops abandoned to plans for a shopping plaza, bigger than the one on the far side of the Lincoln Apartments. The Lower End is where the violence is.

I was still new on the force. A woman with a triangular face and the hard hot complexion of candle-grease answered my rap. In a cracked voice she called from the bed of her one-room apartment. She appeared ill not from sickness but from indignities. She smiled fiercely. Stains around her tight mouth. She was leaking oil. My God, what had she taken! Anything lethal? Yes. Iodine. I was thumbs and tripping feet, an awkward clod in an illfitting uniform. Hello, hello! The phone wouldn't work. In a voice no longer human, she said, Take your time, officer. But there was no time! I lifted her from the bed, and a bare blue-veined titty fell out of her robe. I dropped her! Christ, she could've got me on criminal assault. It was easier to face a drunk in an alley, his skull open and his brain battered out of its pan.

This crazy human turmoil, this unnatural fury. How do you deal with it without succumbing? How do you keep your strength while fighting the fatigue of greasy days, the screeches of unhinged women, the monotony of adolescent hoodlums whose white faces caught in an explosion of cruiser headlights look like a pack of albino rats? How does one face a weapon and remain steady on the feet?

A hopped-up guy with a rifle was holed up in a room above a vacant store. He had a child with him, one he'd pulled off the street. I charged up the stairs with drawn revolver, not the stubby one I have now but the long-barreled one I later got rid of. On the heel of my right shoe was a scrap of newspaper smeared with dogshit. I stopped to kick it off and nearly got shot. Wham! The rifle bullet tore open the wall, powdering me with stinking tooth-yellow plaster. Bang! Bang! Bang! My shots went into the ceiling which nearly collapsed on me. Callap! The rifleman threw down his piece and threw up his hands. I give up! Christ, so do I, I said.

Just as I never knew why my father became a bookmaker (I never asked why and he never said), I don't know why I became a cop. No, that's not entirely true. I have inklings. The uniform and the stick weren't factors, but the revolver probably was. In the army, peaceful service as a military policeman, I felt on top of things with a Colt forty-five semi-automatic pistol holstered to my hip, even though I had never drawn it to kill or even to threaten. But it was company. It was visible, and it was primitive in one way and sophisticated in another. Holstered, it was quiet authority behind which I tended to my own business, viewed the passing world and counted the days to my honorable discharge.

On the other hand, if I hadn't bought this house I might have finished college, and if I had finished college I might not have become a cop.

But the fact remains that, despite bumbling beginnings, I haven't done badly, because otherwise I would not have become a detective-sergeant authorized to carry a snubnosed revolver under my arm inside the dark blazer Libby bought for me two summers ago at an end-of-the-season sale, and otherwise Libby (she stirs in bed, and I press my nose deeper into the screen and whistle softly for my dog) would not have stuck by me all these years despite an apparent lack of love on her part attributable to no one reason but ground up in the many things we don't say to each other.

From the dark of outside comes the tinkle of dog-tags, a new one and an old one. My dog is alive!

Yes, and otherwise my daughter Darcie would not come to me in times of teen-age stress despite an obvious impatience with me. She is dating now. Boredom boys, I call them. They don't know what to do with themselves. They wear sherbet-colored shirts and ass-splitting pants and pointed shoes with hard heels. Darcie, where's your taste? She's growing, growing. A couple of weeks ago I intruded into the bathroom where she was sitting in a tub of steaming water and wearing new dungarees. A shrink job. Otherwise she was naked. What a pair of knockers for a fifteen-year-old, as proud and perfect as kamikaze pilots preparing for a takeoff. Damn it, Darcie, lock the door when you're like that. And she with a raised face and quick voice: For God's sake, Daddy, we're the same flesh and blood! Later, her long honey hair hanging over her shoulders, she appeared in a short iridescent dress, a mini. The boy who called for her was tall, acned, and taciturn—a good-looking kid in a flippant way. Where had I seen him before? He had bunchy sideburns and the start of an unhealthy moustache. His name meant nothing to me, but my suspicions wouldn't let go. He avoided my eyes, kept his own on Darcie, and hurriedly ushered her out of the house. I reached the front window as his car sped off, the rear tires spitting pebbles. In the next instant I was tearing out of the house and running for my beat-up Chevy. I remembered where I had seen him. He had been one of slobbering many, the cruiser lights hitting them and scattering them. Beer cans and condoms on the ground. A gangbang, the girl an unfor-

29

tunate creature with bursts of ugly speech. She claimed rape but had no case. I spun the Chevy onto the road. Where was he? I was Pelops, a great charioteer driving a tortuous trail for the sake of a princess. I caught sight of the kid's speeding car. It had bald tires. Darcie! Darcie!

Yes, and otherwise Rose Mulligan would not find something stabilizing in me, something solid, something gentle; and otherwise Evelyn Abbot, my lawyer friend, aloof and dissociated, frosty-haired and forty, attractive and untouchable, would not accept my company over coffee across the street from the courthouse in Diadati's cafeteria and render free advice. About the way I hug my intricate acre of land: Some men, she said, shouldn't own property; they defend it like animals. They fly flags and kill in the name of it. They become soldiers. You know what a soldier is, Southy. He's a caged animal trained and then let loose to do battle. About my daughter, Darcie: Let your wife handle her. Girls grow up fast today and become sisters to their mothers. About Libby whom she scarcely knows: Appreciate what you have, Southy, and you'll be appreciated. About my sister whom Evelyn knows better: Her husband's her problem, not yours, and if she still sleeps with him he can't be all that monstrous, now can he, Southy?

I think of my brother-in-law as a clumsy criminal with a fascination for the scene of his crime; he must return to it: my sister, who, for all I know, may be amused when he doesn't come home at night and may be annoyed when he does, or she may feel excitement when he slips into bed with her, a man who paid money to have her murdered.

I told Joan what he wanted to have done to her, but she already knew. Auntie Wren had quietly phoned her and told her as much as she wanted to know. She didn't want to hear any more about it from me. She spoke of unsupported stresses in his life. She spoke of the thing itself, what he wanted done, and wrote it off as an accident of time and place. And the girl with

30

him couldn't be blamed, because she was looking after her own interests. My sister pictured the whole thing lightly. He, David, was in that club, Alekel's, a little tight, a little horny. Surely, my sister said, I could understand that. Yes, I could, I said, but not the murderous plot on her life, the intricate and gruesome arrangements to feed her remains to pigs at a farm outside the city. The man's mental, I told her, and she stiffened. He's a child, she retorted, and nothing more, nothing less. At the very least, I told her, he has a slight crack in his psyche. Who doesn't? she said.

Yes, and otherwise her husband would not seek my help, and Auntie Wren would not offer me money (though doing so as if I were her handyman, the fellow who mows her lawn and washes her windows and runs errands), and otherwise the district attorney, who ordinarily brushes by me with a nod, if that, would not stop for a chat. Alderman Jimmy O'Rourke, who appointed me and promoted me, pulls me to one side— the most powerful man in the city, with the mayor only a figurehead and the D.A. a drunk. Jimmy has a warm spot for me because of my father who, he has said many times, was a gentleman and a man of honor. Jimmy puts an arm around me. He's a big man with a massive grandeur about him from the top of his great balding head to the tips of his mica-bright black shoes. His voice, however, is raspy and rotten; he has throat trouble and a cigarette perpetually between yellow fingers. He's in his early sixties but the pictures on the campaign posters are those of a man in his thirties. Another election is coming up. He wants to discuss my brother-in-law. Too much loose talk, he says, which isn't good. The last thing he wants, he says, is a scandal smearing Parker's name and the department store which that name represents. The store—Parker, Inc.—is controlled by Ramsey National Bank where Jimmy, through a relative who's a director, has an interest. On the other hand, he says, as public safety director of this city, he has to protect himself if things get out of hand, which they shouldn't if handled right. His arm tightens. He knows, he says, I'll take care of what amounts to family business in a manner that's both efficient and quiet.

Evelyn, who can be cold-blooded in court, who can cut a police officer's testimony to pieces, lets me off easy in my weak testimony against her client, a diminutive Puerto Rican charged with receiving stolen property, a color TV. My sister, expecting friends, members of the Ramsey Citizens for Equal Opportunities, of which she has long been chairman, speaks to me about love as if it were candy, a Lifesaver, something to suck. The D.A. jokes about his spinster sister who moved into his house when she was twenty-four and now at age fifty-six is a lifetime fixture. Auntie Wren offers me a thousand dollars to pull Parker out of his mess. Jimmy O'Rourke, licking his dry lips like a lusty priest, mentions the girl Parker is mixed up with. Then, as we begin to walk together, he reminisces about the old days when my father was a big book, a gross exaggeration. My father was never big. He made a living. That was all.

Again I hear the jingling dogtags. The dark is thinning. I strain my eyes. I don't know what I expect to see—robins who peck the ground and pull out worms.

Behind me the bed creaks, and Libby says, "What are you doing?" Still in a squat, I spin around on bare heels. She's not really awake. She's already dropping back to sleep. Her face is sour but will turn sweet with the first splash of cold water. She will brush her teeth and her words will be peppermints. A small woman except when her clothes are off. Freckles on her nose and shoulders. Her hair is short, thick, and rusty. Except for stretch marks, the color of old iodine, which have never faded from her belly, her body is still snug. According to my sister, who would like to know Libby better but has never found time, Libby will look ten years younger than she is until age seventy and then

32

turn white-haired and quaint and Darcie's daughters will tell their friends their grandmother is adorable, a little doll.

I brush my feet and climb into bed. Libby is curled up again, her back to me. I touch her under the covers. I move against her and mold myself to her. Her nighty is snagged above her hips. Her rump is a lifeless mouth.

"Don't!" she says, coming awake again. Only in the morning is she unready and unwilling. All the same, aroused I cling to her. She fights me. Any other time she'd twist around and accept it readily. "Don't!" she says again, and I pull away from her and lie quietly on my back.

Drifting into sleep, I'm a series of double-exposures, a person superimposed on himself. I'm a blur, a blob, a big fellow and a frantic father hunting for his daughter's red ball lost in some roadside bog. I'll never find it, but inexplicably it's essential that I look.

I remember peering from the window of the bedroom at the housing project and seeing Darcie scamper down the driveway of the asphalt parking lot after her runaway doll carriage. I shouted to her and struggled with the closed window. The nearness of death with cars squealing to a stop. The possibility of tragedy slashed me like a razor. How could I carry through life the memory of a dead child?

She was just about to be born when I went away not to Korea where the fighting was but to Germany. Two years and a month. Frankfurt, a fine city. When I returned, Darcie defiantly had a thumb in her mouth, and Libby, prim in a white blouse and dark skirt, her voice not at all as I remembered it, welcomed me. I kissed Darcie first because Libby thrust her into my soldier arms. She was stiff and unyielding, her shoes tiny white hooves kicking me. Afterwards I tried to embrace Libby, but she said wait because there was something I should know first. As she talked I shook my head. What she was saying was indigestible. She told me everything except the man's name, which didn't matter, she said, because I didn't know him and neither did she anymore.

I come awake and remold myself to her, and this time pay no attention when she says, "Don't!"

4

"WHO'S THERE?" PARKER CALLS OUT. WHEN I don't answer he bounds out of the bathroom in a ridiculous little shave-'n-shower coat with a towel around his neck and shaving fluff hanging from his jaws and a small razor in his hand. Bare feet and naked legs. He stops at the doorway of the living room and peers past me without seeing me. Inside the shaving fluff his mouth is the color of blood that has gone brown. His eyes, which jiggle, are the artificial green of frozen peas. He stands stiff as a bird-dog, as if ready to use the little razor as a weapon. Then he spots me.

"Jesus," he says and steps onto the living room rug. With a tail of the towel hanging from his neck, he wipes the razor clean. The fluff on his face is dripping. With a mixture of relief and annoyance, he says, "Why didn't you ring the bell?"

"I did, twice, and I knocked."

"So you just walked in."

"As anybody could."

He shrugs, and then he grins. He apologizes. "I'm jumpy," he says. "Look, sit down." He gestures with his razor hand to a blond piece of furniture, but I don't move. He jerks out a laugh and says, "Don't worry. She left a half-hour ago, zoomed away in her T-Bird. Didn't you hear her go by your house?"

I point to the rug. "You're dripping."

"Story of my life. The rug's Bokhara. The furniture's Swedish. Not bad, huh?"

35

"She must be worth it."

He shrugs. "How did you know I was here?"

"It wasn't hard to figure out."

He smiles sheepishly, while standing tilted in the silly little terry-cloth coat that hangs open at the chest and resembles a toga and probably is one of the latest items at Parker, Inc., Ramsey's oldest and largest downtown department store. He's a woman-chaser, a Don Juan with high cheekbones and compelling eyes. The fluff drying on his jaws is starting to resemble semen.

"Go on," I tell him. "Go finish shaving."

I roam the white-walled living room and touch furniture that is probably handcarved. It smells of polish. The walls curve into a nook containing a reclining chair, an ashtray stand, potted plants, books, magazines, newspapers, a large window, much sunshine. His young woman may sit here with the window open and darken herself. This is my first time in one of the Lincoln's luxury units. Evelyn lives in one of the rear buildings, and her apartment is much smaller and has no nook.

I stand at the bathroom door and watch Parker pat aftershave on his face. The bathroom is fluorescent and steamy, and the mirror is hot-looking. Two piles of towels and underclothes are on the tile floor near the shower—his stuff and hers. The pink wastebasket under the sink has been tipped over. At the base of the john is a spilled box of sanitary sticks. I had pictured her as more tidy, if only because my sister is not. My sister is careless in keeping house and forgetful about arranging meals. Parker gives me a grin.

I push the bedroom door open. The shades are still drawn. The room is dark and disarrayed, sheets and blue blanket trailing on the floor, one pillow at the head of the bed and another at the foot. Immediately I have a horny image of him and her, and I can feel her sexual presence, warm in one way, mocking in another—heavy, distinctive and pervasive, like the smell of cat piss.

I know her only in pieces and scraps. Glimpses of her high-heeling out of Parker, Inc., with an armful of parcels. Glimpses of her from my front window when she speeds by in her Thunderbird, her long Lebanese hair black as printer's ink. Enchanting and dark-eyed and scarcely past twenty. A college dropout working now and then as a secretary or receptionist. I have no idea how she and Parker met. It could have been anywhere downtown. Maybe she was lunching with her boss, and Parker joined them and moved in on her because she provided the opening. The Thunderbird came from one of her ex-bosses with whom she had spent part of winter in Florida. She drives the Thunderbird fast, sometimes with her father beside her, an old man who lives above the Lower End store where for years, until all his customers died, he sold pipes and tobacco and booked on the side. Now he is retired, and the store is boarded up, with obscenities chalked by children on the wood.

"Excuse me," says Parker, and I step aside to let him into the bedroom. He opens a closet that holds her clothes and some of his. The closet is spacious. I can see at least three of his suits and some of his shirts, Hathaways. He never wears the same suit two days in a row and seldom keeps his suits more than a few months. When I was slimmer, my sister collected them and sent them to me. Now she mails them to black people in Mississippi. She sends her own discarded clothes there too, even though Libby, and even Darcie now, could certainly use them.

"I hope you've got something good to tell me," says Parker, poking into the closet for something to wear. Instead of answering, I leave to let him dress.

The kitchen is cluttered and messy. A cigarette is floating in a glass of ginger ale. Her lipstick on the tip. I saw her once in a playsuit with rings that connected the shoulder straps to the low front, which zippered down the middle. I had a fantasy about the zipper. Near the ginger ale glass is a number of unopened

37

letters that look like bills. They bear her name, but they must be for Parker.

"Where is she?" I ask as Parker comes into the kitchen, wearing a dark suit and blue shirt and a tie with tiny designs. He feels the coffee pot and then turns on the gas.

"Her life's her own. That's the way we work it."

"That's not what I heard."

"Then you must've heard wrong," he says, and sets out two cups.

"I don't want any."

"I do," he says, but then changes his mind and turns off the gas.

We don't stay in the kitchen, maybe because he doesn't want to get his suit soiled. We go to the living room, and he sits on a low couch. He slumps in it and crosses his legs.

"Fuck me," he says, and for a moment looks miserable.

I can picture him as a child with his nose snotty and his voice affected by it. I'm staring at him hard.

"Please," he says. "Don't third-degree me. I can see it coming."

"You have good foresight."

"But no foreskin. How about you?"

"You're good at jokes."

"Only horrible ones. I know that now."

He had told me that not for a single second, even while drunk, did he seriously consider arranging my sister's death. He viewed Poggio and Primack as two creeps and led them on for the fun of it, and when they talked "hit" and "contract" he pretended he had use for a couple of operators like them. What he didn't realize, he said, was that while he was playing, they were not, and that was the reason he had to give them money, to get them off his back. And they started threatening him, and he had to give them more money. It was crazy, he said. He says it again.

"Crazy. Honest to God."

I feel a whistling inside my skull. I remember a

young mother at the housing project who accidentally scalded her baby to death with a kettle of soup, and I remember a father in another part of the city who blasted his son's head off showing the boy the mechanics of a shotgun. Greek tragedies. Absurdities. Apollo, without meaning to, dropped his best friend with a discus. Forbush nearly lost his life through a careless step in a white wasteland.

"Please," he says. "Don't stand over me. Can't you sit down?"

I do, in a chair facing him, my eyes clamped on him.

"I don't intend to question you, even though there are holes in your story."

"What do you mean?" he says, indignant.

"The money you told me you paid them conflicts with what I understand they got."

"Explain. I don't know what you mean."

"The money came from Auntie Wren. You conned her. You skimmed some off the top in each instance."

"So what. You know damn well what that bitch did to my father. Any money she's got should be mine."

"Then there's the question of why you took out extra life insurance on Joan."

"That was months ago!" He throws a finger at me. "And that was Joan's idea. You ask her!"

"Then there are the fine details of the thing. Everything worked out so precisely. Poggio was to use his knife, so that it would look like some civil-rights druggie turned on her. But Primack has a better idea. Just let her vanish. Feed the body to enormous pigs at some farm they said they knew about. The pigs would eat everything except the skull and the bigger bones."

"Who told you that?" he says in a voice I nearly don't hear because it sinks.

"They have big mouths. They joked about it."

"I know, you ass! I told you, it was a joke!"

"The district attorney might not laugh."

"He doesn't have to know."

"But he does. I've already told you that. You conveniently forget things."

"I know what you're trying to do to me, Southy, and I can't blame you. You want me to squirm. I'm squirming—see!"

He moves his ass around on the couch. Theatrically. He has made his point, but he keeps it up. His face has no color except for the tiny razor nicks on his chin and near his mouth. I think of Joan who enjoys people, causes, cruises, parties, flirtations that may or may not lead to anything.

"I know you resent me, Southy, and for reasons I probably don't even know about. Am I right?"

While I was standing guard and sucking in the raw morning air at the main gate of Drake Kaserne in Frankfurt, Germany, sundered from wife and infant, he, Parker, was flunking out of Dartmouth, nipping about in a siren-red convertible, and drawing an unearned salary at Parker, Inc. And I, as a junior in high school, had sweated at that store, pushing around boxes and cartons in the shipping department for fifty cents an hour.

"Listen," he says. "You know the game room I've got at home? Well, *your* sister once threw a steel dart at me. I ducked. Good thing. Should we tell the district attorney about that?"

I don't bother to respond. I stare at his ghastly white face.

"You were paid to straighten things out," he says.

I slowly shake my head. "I haven't been paid anything yet, and if I'm doing anything, it's not for Auntie Wren or for you. It's for Joan."

"All right. I'm sorry." He runs a hand over his mouth. "It's just that I'm upset. I'm scared, for Christ's sake. Those guys aren't normal. You've got to get them off my back. They're bloodsuckers. They think because I'm president of the store, I'm loaded. *You* know I'm not. *You* were supposed to tell them."

"They don't listen."

"You said you'd make them listen."

"I said I'd try."

"You said you'd use muscle."

"No, I didn't say that. But as a matter of fact, I did use muscle. I hit Poggio in the mouth. I got one of his teeth in my knuckles. That was a funny sensation."

"You're lying to me. Jesus Christ, Southy!"

I make a fist and show him a tiny injury between two knuckles, and he lets out an angry cry.

"That could be from anything!" He shudders. "You don't care."

The forlorn sound of his voice reminds me of a kid who a couple of years ago clutched my arm. A school dropout. I knew him vaguely. I must have done something for him once. He had bad teeth, bad breath and poor posture. He swept the floor in some machine shop. He collected metal shavings and at the end of the week a meager paycheck that he spent on beer and a mentally retarded girl with whom he lived. The girl, pregnant again, was about to be committed to an institution. Could I help them—please! What could I do. Except to pretend.

Parker stands up. "I don't sleep right anymore, and I don't eat. That's the truth, Southy."

"I'm sure it is."

"Tell them you'll arrest them if they don't leave me alone."

"They figure I can't do that without implicating you."

"I can't give them any more money."

"Then don't."

"But they want more!"

I lean forward in my chair, and get a pleasant sensation—I don't know from what. I tell Parker that he has been just a patsy, that Poggio and Primack were never actually going to harm Joan, that all that talk about a contract was so much shit, that all they wanted from him was money—eight hundred he gave them as down-payment and eight thousand he gave them later to kill a contract that was never made, only feigned. Parker is shaking his head.

"You're wrong, Southy. They were going through with it all right. There were others involved."

"No others."

"Guys from Boston."

"No one from Boston. Only Poggio and Primack."

"Are you sure?"

"I'm sure."

"But they're crazy, you know that."

"We're all crazy."

"I'm not. I want to live. I don't want to get beaten up. I don't want to get mutilated. That's what they said they'd do to me."

"I bet they're bluffing."

"But we don't know!"

"You're right. Not for sure. The way Joan will never be sure about you."

He sinks back. "So that's the way you're going to play it. Thanks, Southy. Thanks a lot."

I rise. I have a sudden headache, which came from nowhere. I used to get them in Germany, wondering about my wife.

"Where are you going?" he says.

"Aspirins. I'll find them."

With the cold water tap on, I rummage through the medicine cabinet, inspect little bottles and tubes, a comb with long black hairs in it, some pills packaged in cellophane. Parker appears, and I slam the cabinet door shut.

"No aspirins!" I glare at him. "What kind of woman is she? Have you considered she might have set you up? She was talking marriage, wasn't she? She was the one who brought you there, right? She picked the table near theirs and got you drunk and horny and then left you."

"No, she wanted me to leave."

"She's good, really good. You couldn't walk."

"Yes, she is good, Southy. Is that what's eating you?"

"A lot of things are eating me. I should make a list."

"Later, Southy. Christ, help me first."

I wash my face in the cold tap water I didn't turn

42

off, and hug my face in a used towel that smells, which makes me want to be home. Libby's towels are always clean.

I brush by Parker.

"Where are you going?" Panic in his voice. He's following me. "Southy, I'm breaking up with her, you know. I plan to tell her."

I put my fingers to my forehead where the pain is. I think of my father. The desire to live, I suppose, decreases with the pain of the bullet.

5

THE SAME CHILL, THE SAME FUNNY FEELING in my fingers when I was a foot patrolman and entering an alley with a sense of danger, knowing something was there but not knowing what or where, and moving cautiously past the stench of garbage and the dank smell of motor oil, studying empty quart-cans, Texaco, yellow-stained where they had been punctured and drained. Creeping, glancing left and right, holding my breath and then nearly jumping out of my skin when a rat, oversized and red-eyed and with mess around its mouth, leaped out of a barrel and streaked between my shoes.

I have the same sense of danger now as I step out into the back yard. Something is wrong despite the greeting I get from the green wet morning, the grass, the stuff hanging out of the rock garden, the leaves of lilac bushes and young trees. I whistle for the dog and hear him behind me. He appears nervously from under the steps. Then I see his nose and flinch from the sight of it. A slice is missing, as if from a razor, a quick pink opening rigid around the edges where it has bled and coagulated. His nervous paws claw my clean blazer. He cries in whistling needle noise, as if apologizing for waking me in the night and disturbing me now. I try to hold his heavy head for a closer inspection of his nose but he won't stay still. He feigns biting me and laps my chin. He's hot and drooly, victim of a pre-dawn attack. The sun burns the back of my neck.

I let the dog go and rise slowly. All is quiet. Then I hear something, a breaking or fluttering of leaves, and I wheel around, my revolver half out of the holster.

It's nothing, merely a bluejay ripping through the pear tree on the far side of the house. Usually crows attack that tree. They gobble the fruit like panthers devouring their kill. When I hurl stones at them they caw to high heaven and fly over my head and across the river to roost in the big trees. They rob me of fruit. They hack away at the pears, many of which drop to the ground and in the sun turn to swill.

The jay flies away, and I stand motionless, staring toward the river, whose current is sluggish and whose color is affected by the shadows of the big trees. My dog is alert, his ears cocked for voiceless things—fish, fleas, snakes in the grass, worms in the earth. The only sound is the work-bound traffic on the road. The cars flash by in the opening of the stone wall. In the wintertime snowblind cars curb-crawl and hang in front of my house as though the drivers wanted to come in.

I move and the dog follows, each of us sniffing the sunshiny air. I move in a crouch toward my car which is dripping with dew, parked where once stood a small garage that had to be razed. I can remember the dust and dry rot, the squeal of boards clinging for life to their nails, the enraged but feeble honeybees flying fatly at my hands, the skinny wasps flittering sideways, the remains of bird nests hanging like children's mittens from the beams. Hundreds of tiny cocoon clots were glued as if by a child's hand to the brittle tarpaper behind the clapboards. When I pulled away strategic supporting beams, the roof slanted slowly the wrong way and collapsed on a tree I had planted the past season.

Cautiously I approach my car, which I figure is a logical hiding place for intruders, including tramps. The rear window is thick with sunspray. My reflection resembles someone else's. I'm not sure whose. A heavy shaved face. A flint-flash of eyes and a tight

45

mouth. A glimpse of myself as a madman. I unbutton my blazer, rest my hand on the butt of my revolver, and peer in the side windows. The car is as I left it, with litter on the front floor and rings from a coffee cup on the seat. Occasionally I drink while I drive. When I turn corners the coffee invariably spills.

Darcie, when she's in the mood, cleans the car. She washes, sweeps and vacuums it. She's dying for the day she can have a car of her own, one without rust spots. She wants lessons now. It's illegal for a fifteen-year-old to operate on a public way, so she sits in my car and practices starting it up. She backs it up and races the motor and toots the horn and plays the radio loud. Some of her friends, older than she, already have cars.

My dog, as I move away from the car, trots back to the porch steps. I slap my thigh for him to come to me, but he quickens his ears, thumps his tail, and acts as if he'd like to obey but his place is on the porch. He's a handsome beast. I bought him in New Hampshire for thirty-five dollars, without papers. He was six weeks old, a rank ball of dust huddling with his brothers and sisters in a barn bin. I saw his father in the field, a huge handsome stud whose teeth glinted like pistol shots. According to the farmer's wife, a bulky and breasty young woman who smelled of the barn, I got the pick of the litter. She lifted him up and spread the fur to prove he was male.

A small catalpa is growing nicely in a circle of soil that's watered weekly. I spotted it downriver last fall, watched it during its winter nakedness, and carefully transplanted it in the spring before the buds burst into floppy heart-shaped leaves. I check the leaves for bug bites. Toward the top of the tree the leaves are shattered as if from machine-gun fire. Jungle warfare.

If something is amiss I can't see it. There's only the fat of my land and the river that touches it. The massive swamp maple throws its shadow but misses me by a mile. Not far from it is a hole. I've seen the woodchuck that lives in it. He looks like a teddy bear.

Near the hole are four dead trees that cast shadows like men assembled at a grave.

The gravel driveway resembles a country road. It splits my property in half. Years ago it was a backyard right-of-way for somebody with a house farther up the street. The grass is wild on the river side of the driveway. I don't mow here. I like the wildness, the wide prickly plants, the milkweeds, the raspberry bushes, the wildflowers that have no sense of direction, no aim, no goal. I've worn a path to the river bank and laid stones for steps down the bank to the inlet, beside which is an aluminum chair and an upended box on which to rest a coffee cup.

I stand at the top of the bank. Already the sun is hot-blooded. By noon it will scream. These swollen days. But already summer is slipping away. Already the raspberries are rotting on the bush. Some trees have leaves yellowing at the edges or bleeding through the green, a presage of shorter days that in time will become brisk and brittle, the fire in the sky taking to the trees and flaring up while the grass grays and the sunshine hardens.

I shiver. There's something deadly about the approach of winter, something sinister about the bark of birch that looks as if it were composed of smoke, something maddening about bare maple twigs that put together pictograms but reveal no messages, something weird about milkweeds that split their pods and hang wild white hair in the air. The winter wind veering toward me. The burlap ground whitening before my eyes. I don't like the snow, the frozen slush, the job of maneuvering my car up the steep driveway to the highway where the traffic is packed and salted. The river freezes and the wind whips across it and shakes my high house. The pointed air chips Libby's mouth and hurts her throat. Darcie and her friends skate on the inlet. The blades on their feet flash and scrape, and Darcie and a boy try to use the silver gleam of their mingled breath as a mirror. Then more snow. The wind attacks a vulnerable pine and tears

47

off an upper branch which plunges through other branches and explodes into pins and needles on the ground. Icy rain. Trees turn to glass and twigs to fancy bottles. Some branches snap in two in mid-air.

Unhappy Albert DiSalvo. Why should I think of him, a name in a dead newspaper, a psychotic I never met? He claimed he was the Boston strangler. A little man with a big nose hooking the air, catching fuzz, and boiling over in cold weather. He claimed he raped thousands of women while soldiering in Germany. He was committed to Bridgewater following charges of assault on women around Boston, the assaults unrelated to the stranglings. The assault victims testified that among other things he milked his penis in front of them. With two others he escaped from Bridgewater, which has dungeon-like cells with HELP scratched on the walls. His two friends spent the day in a Waltham bar where they drank whiskey and eventually gave themselves up. And little Albert, his brothers dumped him into the fierce February weather in Lynn where he slept in a cellar and emerged in the morning in a sailorsuit that didn't fit. He surrendered saying, "I didn't harm nobody."

I didn't harm nobody.

My brother-in-law says the same thing in better English. My sister stands as living evidence. I open my mouth and taste the sunshine like a boy at an altar rail sticking out his tongue for a wafer. My sister has twin boys. I can't remember when I've last seen them. They're big now, I'm sure. In the summer they're at a camp somewhere high in New Hampshire near a town, my sister says, where nearly everybody speaks Canadian-French. The rest of the year the boys are in a private school in the western part of this state. My sister isn't maternal-minded and has never pretended to be. She drifts over her property as I do mine, except that she opens hers up to others, young persons with evangelical fervor. Once she had a group up from New York, boys and girls wearing berets. Some berets were black, some blue, some red, the colors representing different organizations. Sweat-shirts. Those also stood for something. The girls wore jeans and the boys chinos. The boys wore short heavy boots. They stayed a weekend and were not invited back because they broke furniture in the house and one of them, in the words of my sister, "shat in the swimming pool."

I close my eyes and stumble in a raspberry bush. At the same time there is a shuffling noise, a crackling of dry grass, a sort of lifting-up sound that raises the hair on the back of my neck. My thought is for my gun. Instead I freeze.

6

A SNAPPING TURTLE WITH A HEAD LIKE A hard-on, flies flicking around it, with eyes hidden, with a shell like ancient crude pottery, a good foot in diameter, with stubby legs that sprawl jointlessly out of folded skin. The skin is putty-like and scum-gray. The snapper looks like the oldest creature on earth. It looks dug-up, dead, as if it emerged stillborn from the depths of the prehistoric past. Its claws are clamped to the ground, claiming it. The head is pointed my way. I nearly stepped on it. The jaws, razors, would have cut my ankle to the bone, and for a moment I wouldn't have known. I wouldn't have felt pain till I took a step; then the weight of the wound would've brought me to the ground.

My dog is in the driveway, ears erect. In the sunlight, his sliced nose is fiery. He's lucky. He must have met the snapper in the night and merely got nipped. I pat him as I pass him, and he follows me to the cellar porch, beneath which I find a weapon, a bladeless hoe handle, old and weathered, Revolutionary-War-looking. It was here when I moved in, half-buried under the porch. The first time I used it the blade fell off. The staff is solid, heavy enough to be oak.

The dog follows me as far as where the grass begins and then stops. Ignores a command to follow. The sun greases the inlet. Grass cracks underfoot. The snapper's head is higher, and one eye has slipped open into a glistening bead. A primeval monster with an ancient and burdensome shape, with a monotonous hump and jagged tail, with a repulsive head. When I shift ground and parry with the hoe handle, the snapper's other eye pops into a bead. I can see its lost world. I can smell the muck, the scum, and I know now what the river would smell like if it dried up. I keep an eye on the head which can snap open. The sun is a blast. I wipe the melt from my forehead. Everything is silent, as in a world that doesn't work anymore, the key turned off and rusting. A moment to glance at a passing cloud and wonder whether it will ever return this way. I parry once more with the hoe handle. The snapper's head dips, snake-like. It is geared for battle. So am I.

I jab. The head shoots forth and the jaws flash in a white froth, crack like a rifle-shot, and whack the hoe handle out of my hands.

I'm conscious of a thumping heart and of crows screeching across the river; except for their blackness the crows could be gulls waiting to scavenge a beach. I'm conscious of landscape, of the sharpness of trees, every bough a bow and every leaf an arrowhead. The snapper's head hangs in the air. The rigidity of some things, their unshakeableness, as if they had a path to follow and if you were in the way and wouldn't move, they wouldn't either!

I retrieve the hoe handle. This is a question of territorial rights, even though time and place seem out of joint. The snapper moves toward me an inch or two, as if something had pushed it. The color of its shell reminds me of gray leaves that have weathered a winter and now are ready to be mulched into the earth. I whistle for my dog who doesn't come, and I steal a glance at the house to see whether Libby is watching, whether she's aware of this battle which began in the pre-dawn dark when my dog made a patrol of the property. When I rolled away from her, with the sun creeping into our room, she rose without a word and pattered away on bare feet. I gave her a few minutes before following her into the bathroom where she was rinsing her breasts, which were fish-cold. "Don't!" she said, knocking away my hands which were intended as apologies and facing me wearily, like a teacher burdened with a pupil who must be told the same thing over and over. "You'll never learn, will you," she said, her voice flat and heavy and deliberate. "I don't like doing it in the morning."

She's not at any of the windows. She has no idea of what has come out of the river and is on our land, the same way that when I tramp over the property I have little knowledge of the chemical warfare among the trees and plants.

I raise the hoe handle above my shoulder, raise it higher, feel the sun against my neck, and with all my might slam the handle against the snapper's hump; its head flies forth, almost flies away, and this time the jaws crack naked air. I raise the handle again. The sunshine is straight and tall, like an immense amount of liquor. *Slam! Slam!* Like a cannibal trying to break a skull to get at the brain—and again the enlarged but futile snapping of jaws, a monster under attack and fighting for its life, its attacker swaying with sweat hanging off his eyebrows. I nearly stumble from the weight of the staff. I'm dizzy and remembering myself in remnants of an army uniform, the snow falling against the project windows like heavy paper and my fingers pawing Libby's belongings and finding stationery resembling tinted toilet paper, a letter never mailed to a man not named . . . *I like it when you* . . . I didn't want to read on but of course I did. A vertigo of laughter. December, the dark month, the nadir. I remember disbelieving the laughter was mine and wheeling around to see who else was in the bedroom. How that winter lagged. Snow glistening in Libby's hair like slivers of glass, as if someone had broken a bottle over her head. My ungloved hand holding her arm because of the icy walk nippled from drippings. A treacherous path to my car in the project parking lot. She never should have told me anything in the first place. Knowing, I never should have opened the bureau drawer and pried into its depths. Blind, I could have listened forever without ever hearing the snow fall.

With sudden strategy, with a sudden memory of clever primitive devices like the pulley, the lever, the hinge. I make a flanking movement and thrust the hoe handle under the snapper's bottom plate. With fury the turtle's claws grip the ground and its tail thrashes grass. But I have leverage, and wrists and arms of steel, and I plop the thing over on its shell where it rocks and reacts with frantic head and tail action, its head rearing and rooting into the ground and cutting sideways and its tail knifing and sawing; with a heavy heave it rights itself, a silent creature full of evolutionary fury, a monster no longer sure of its ground, a crusted creature rising like bread, floating up on its claws and coming at me in a ludicrous but frightening slow-motion charge, the shell tipping from side to side and the grass breaking. Before my eyes the color-sprinkled wings of a butterfly, the kind I used to watch Darcie chase when she was four or five in the play-ground behind the project. Things seen through a window-pane, remembered through a mist. How smoothly I draw my revolver, which I've seldom aimed, seldom fired. How surprisingly steady my hand is. Across the river a woodpecker is drumming on a moribund tree, which in time, five to ten years, will topple into the river. I aim. What difference will one turtle make? The fall of the great reptiles was eons ago. Slowly, as taught, I squeeze. The revolver twangs like a bow letting loose an arrow, and the head of the snapper jumps away in sparkling pieces.

7

I GRAB THE PHONE IN THE MIDST OF A RING and listen to the rock-hard sound of my name. *Robert? Robert!* Yes, go ahead, I tell her. Her speech is clipped and broad-A'd, as if she, my aunt, and not my sister, had gone to Radcliffe. Her tone is cold and professional, as if she were still running Parker, Inc. My infrequent contact with her is by phone. Only twice in my life have I talked with her face to face, once when I was sixteen applying for an after-school job at the store. She assigned me to the shipping room, a dungeon, where she never stepped foot. The second time was a year later when I passed through the gates of her property and entered her house to see my sister. Auntie Wren stopped me and said I had no business there.

She understands, she says, that I saw David Parker this morning. I tell her that that's correct. "You upset him," she says sternly.

"Yes, I did."

"And for no good reason," she says. "You had nothing definite to tell him. And when you do have something definite, it's I, not David, you report to. Do you understand?"

"Not quite. I haven't been paid anything."

"You haven't done anything."

"Just a moment," I say with mock seriousness and explain that though I have little to report right now, I'm nurturing a plan of action, hiding it in my heart, holding it in my hand at night, and waiting for the proper time to spring it. She tells me to talk straight, and gives me no chance. She wants those men, she says, out of David's life, and she doesn't want them to bother him again.

"*Ever*, Robert. Do I make myself clear?"

I whistle softly. "Should I murder them?"

"Don't be asinine."

"You had me worried."

She sighs sharply. "Don't waste my time and your own if you don't know what to do. As a policeman, you should know ways to get them out of town or put in prison where they belong. I can't tell you how to do that."

"It's a tricky situation." I clear my throat. "It's Joan's safety I'm concerned with."

"We have each agreed she is in no danger. They are merely extorting David."

"Who can say for sure? They're not rational men, and I wouldn't want to gamble on Joan's life."

Auntie Wren makes an unpleasant sound. "Is this your attempt to extort me?"

"No. You've already been extorted. David didn't pay those guys what he said he did. Each time he kept some for himself. That woman he has is expensive."

She is silent for a moment. Then she says, "I'm not interested in that, and it's none of your business either. I gave him two loans. I'm not interested in how he used them. What counts is keeping David intact. He's not used to pressure. He's younger than you."

"He's a year younger, and he's a grown man, and he's president of Parker, Inc."

"Exactly," she says, and I let out pent-up laughter, and I can tell by her silence that she is angry at herself for letting the conversation get out of hand.

"Finished?" she says.

And now I'm angry, because I was laughing at myself and have just realized it.

"Finished," I say.

"Fine," she says.

I wait.

"When you have something concrete to tell me," she says, "call. Otherwise I don't expect to hear from you."

She clicks off, which is her way, never a goodbye, as if she were still at the store giving orders to underlings. Everyone there was her underling because David's father, Honey (his nickname, what everyone called him, including the help), abdicated his authority to her. The stories about Honey. He was pudding, a misfit who as a young married man worked the necktie counter. Honey's father had founded the store and made it big, a humorless old man with no use for incompetence. He terrified Honey, who hid from him. Honey moved from neckties to billing and fouled up accounts. Honey became a junior buyer and made worse mistakes, and to escape his father's wrath hid behind unopened cases of clothes he shouldn't have purchased. Sometimes he hid in the lingerie department where my aunt, nineteen or twenty at the time, was a sales clerk. An antiseptically attractive girl, according to a dog-eared photo of her that my sister once showed me, she kept Honey on his feet. She steadied him, calmed him, whispered sympathy to him, flattered him, at times scolded him, and at the close of each day sent him home to his wife who had a baby to play with, David, and no time for another, Honey. When Honey's father died unexpectedly, a heart attack, Auntie Wren literally led Honey by the hand to the old man's desk and seated him in the big leather chair which at first he was afraid to sit in, because that was where his father had suffered the heart attack, slumping into the chair as if he were asleep rather than dead. Auntie Wren made Honey sit there and overcome the fear, and they took the old man's picture down from the wall, because Honey had the impression the old man was watching him. Auntie Wren became personnel manager and head buyer and then, because he needed her, she became Honey's personal assistant and shielded him from all decisions because

56

decisions upset him, sometimes to the point of hysterics. When he showed signs of cracking, Auntie Wren tipped him back in the leather chair, smoothed his thinning hair, loosened his trousers and, according to store gossip, jerked him off with an impersonal hand. According to my sister, that was probably true and the extent of their sexual relationship, since apparently it was all that he required. His wife was a frail shadow seldom seen in the store and rarely recognized when she was. Through tears she kissed Auntie Wren's cheek when Auntie Wren announced my sister's engagement to David, and she wept through the wedding and swooned during the reception. My aunt, who had maneuvered the marriage, never sought one for herself. She was busy at other things.

For years she took kickbacks on merchandise which kept the store overstocked, merchandise that shouldn't have been bought because it couldn't be sold, not even on dollar days when clerks hauled the stuff out of storage. Drygoods such as chintzy curtains and gaudy bedspreads after twenty or twenty-five years rotted at the folds in the cartons they came in and were deposited at the city dump. Some merchandise arrived and was immediately shipped out again, and only Auntie Wren knew where. She fired those who questioned her too closely. She used company money to buy a fine old house in the city's staid section, and she used money from the same source to make investments for herself and to put my sister through two years at Abbot Academy and four at Radcliffe. She had safe deposit boxes in at least two Boston banks. When the store's financial picture began to rip she persuaded Honey to sell real estate that was in his and his wife's name, and Auntie Wren used the proceeds to temporarily patch the picture. Later she had him borrow heavily and annually from Ramsey National Bank where he had inherited a directorship from his father.

The irony is that for years officials at the bank knew that Auntie Wren was wheeling and dealing, but none was prepared for the enormity of her manipulations which had put the store on the brink of bankruptcy. Following audits and investigations, the bank people wanted her prosecuted, but Honey, his world bursting, pleaded for her. He pretended that everything she'd done had been with his knowledge and consent. He frightened the bank people with his hysterics. Like a child he pulled a tantrum and hit his head against the wall. They considered him insane. He couldn't bear to sit behind his desk, and he couldn't bear to go home where his wife, wasted to seventy pounds, was dying slowly of cancer under the eye of a practical nurse. He entered a convalescent home, and Auntie Wren, imperially aloof and answering none of the charges, resigned before the bank could fire her. In a desperate effort to hide the scandal and to recoup losses, the bank gave David his father's title, a reasonable salary and no authority, and installed its own personnel in key positions. The store endured. Honey didn't.

He wept for Auntie Wren. She never went near him. He suffered a mild stroke, wailed her name, and mistook nurses for her. Then he suffered another stroke and lost the power of speech and the use of an arm. At the same time he caught pneumonia and within two weeks was dead. His wife died a few days later. Auntie Wren, a recluse in her home, attended neither funeral.

I try to ring her back, but the line's busy. I dial my sister's number and get the same sort of sound. I want to be one of those bureaucrats for whom things are always "going according to plan," even though nothing ever happens.

I dial Auntie Wren's number again; she answers. Coldly she says, "You're becoming more trouble than help."

I say nothing. Before my mind's eye is a blown-up picture of myself, a boy of sixteen overnourished on food from a diner carted home in greasy quart-sized containers with wire handles: fish and chips, clams, onion rings. My father and I guzzling milk with our food, wiping grease from our mouths. The silent glances we exchanged. If there was nothing to talk about we didn't say anything. Our common supply of knotted neckties hung from the handle on the refrigerator door. A radio on the shelf. The solid security I felt inside that cluttered and unclean three-room flat and the uneasiness I felt outside.

"Don't start making a nuisance of yourself," my aunt says, and in her voice is all the harshness of years, all the terrible drafts that can develop in an old house. For no reason I mumble something about my father.

"What did you say?"

I can't answer because my dry throat contains a knot the size of a baby's fist. I carry the phone to the window and peer through the screen at the sky. The sun is setting, and the air is green-red and cushiony. Clouds are galloping off like proud spotted stallions; trees are marching away with their colors.

"It's possible," my aunt says, "you have nothing to say, nothing whatsoever."

I kneel with my face in the screen and catch the rev and roar of traffic. The sun's battle against the coming darkness is a bloodbath, into which the headlights of cars are intruding. Gently, before my aunt does so, I hang up the phone.

My father went a bit at a time. A disease in his eyes eroded his spirit. When he learned his blindness was permanent he killed himself. Auntie Wren, who never had any use for him, who said my mother's marriage was beneath her and her death was because of it, called him a coward for putting the little gun to his head. He wasn't. Active all his life, he simply couldn't be bothered with a crippling affliction.

I was in Germany when he committed suicide at the kitchen table. My sister, home with my aunt during a week's recess at Radcliffe, wired the message: *Our father Joseph W Southwark is dead.*

Such stiffness! I recoiled when I read it, and only afterwards felt grief. It wasn't Joan's fault. She never knew him properly. I was five and she was two when our mother died. Auntie Wren took my sister. I stayed with my father.

I placed a transatlantic call that cost twelve dollars a minute. Joan's voice was weak. I could hardly hear her, but she complained I was shouting. As if sitting in her ear, she said.

"If you'd told me he was dying," I said, "I somehow would've got home."

"Bobby, he *shot* himself! He had an operation and it wasn't successful and he was blind as a bat. It was permanent!"

I was loathing my sister and her long Radcliffe hair and the Shetland sweaters she wore, and was angry over the allowance she received from Auntie Wren and over her relationship with David Parker which my aunt was fostering. In all my months in Germany Joan had written to me only once, but that letter was a package, book-size, with an address label that promoted me from sergeant to colonel. Written over a period of months, it said nothing to me. It began as notes to herself, random thoughts, mood pieces, and it widened into a stream-of-consciousness sort of thing, and not all of it in her hand but in several, those of her classmates, sophomoric fantasies of love and adventures, put-ons, puns, obscenities, the language fatuous and pretentious or simply crude, little drawings, little poems, little jokes, a snobbish exercise (*Soldier boy, I bet you're better than my Harvard stud*) and an insult to me. I threw it away. I should have tried to peddle it.

"Bobby, did you hear me? Auntie Wren is taking care of everything. There's no insurance, you see. The funeral will be private. It's today."

My father. A body in a box. A salmon homing to its area of origin. The ground, the river, the trees. The sinuous windings of a country road that for miles follows a stone wall and heavy woods and then bursts upon a house, a barn, an endless cornfield. Crows, I heard crows!

"What about his things?" I was thinking of nothing

specific, except maybe the neckties we had shared on the refrigerator door and of the radio on the shelf. Then I remembered the radio had a crack in the shell.

"Bobby, there was just junk. Auntie Wren had a man dispose of it." I don't remember how the conversation went on from there. It didn't last long. I wanted to speak to Auntie Wren, but Joan said she had stepped out, which I knew was a lie.

When I was seventeen, Auntie Wren cornered me in her big house where I never had an invitation; it was my sister I was seeking, but Auntie Wren in her cold and cultivated voice said, "You have no business here, and you are *not* to bother her. She is different from you. She is not used to you. Nor to your father. You're not to come here again." I turned to leave, but she wasn't finished. She had some advice which she considered long overdue. "Your mother didn't turn out to be a very good person. Do you understand? I say that so you won't ever think it necessary to moan her."

"Moan her?" I said with sudden laughter. "You mean *mourn* her, don't you?" And it took her a second to react. Then she slapped my face and pointed to the door.

Yet, when I graduated from high school, she mailed a five-dollar bill to me. My father gave me a wrist watch and he gave one to Libby who graduated with me, but her parents ordered her to return it, and they refused to let her wear my identification bracelet. Her father, a worker at Western Electric, considered me unfit company and my father a gangster. I suspect that if he and his wife (I remember her legs, shaped like giant flashlight batteries) hadn't been so fierce in their opposition to me, Libby would have eventually broken up with me on her own. Instead, at eighteen I enlisted in the army and for a while was stationed close enough to Ramsey to see Libby every other weekend and to get her pregnant.

I found my father in Nate's diner. He'd been having

trouble with his eyes for some time, but the condition had worsened. His appearance was potty. His suit was rumpled and his necktie stained. He was eating a hot chicken sandwich surrounded by a scoop of potato, a slice of cranberry sauce and a sprinkling of peas. He was eating carelessly, leaving this and nibbling that. When I slid into the booth to face him, he glanced up with the cold curiosity I've seen from bullfrogs in the inlet. Then his belated recognition and embarrassment:

"Bobby! The uniform fooled me."

His eyes were hazy, full of strains and tiny breaks. Violet scratches in the whites, as if put there with a pen. His face was abnormally serene. I told him I was home for thirty days and that Libby and I were getting married.

"That's great!" he said and reached across the table and pumped my hand. "Your mother, God rest her soul, would've loved that piece of news. Have you eaten?"

I nodded and spoke to him about his eyes and asked why he at least wasn't wearing glasses. He laughed.

"They don't make 'em thick enough for what I need. Fact is I need an operation, but I'm in no hurry. When I start trippin' over things I'll head for the hospital. There ain't no rush, Bobby. That's a fact. The doctor said I could take my time makin' up my mind."

He pushed away his plate which still had much food. He had touched neither peas nor potatoes and had only poked at the chicken meat. He instead viewed me with blinking pride.

"You look swell in that uniform. You've slimmed down. You've got your mother's looks, thank God. Tell me about it, Bobby. I was never in no army. What's it like?"

I shrugged. What was there to say? As long as one kept busy it wasn't bad. For a married man, which I'd soon be, it had special drawbacks. Nothing more lonely than a partially deserted army camp on a drizzly

Sunday afternoon. No wife, no children, no home. Only a bunk and a bag and a fit of depression.

"But you learn discipline, Bobby. You become a man in fast order."

He reached across the table to touch me again, as if casually considering the day he might have to use his hands instead of his eyes, a day I couldn't imagine and, as it turned out, a day he couldn't face.

"You learn to conduct yourself," he said. "Something I should've helped you with but didn't know how. But you're officer material, I can tell. All you gotta do is listen and learn."

I smiled thinly. I was learning to hurry up and to wait and to stand perfectly still in emulation of the starched-khaki stance of a drill sergeant with a sucked-in stomach and spit-polished boots, the kind of soldier recruits called a dumb bastard among themselves but secretly feared and respected and maybe even loved.

My father said, "And you learn to use a weapon. You a marksman?"

I laughed. "I'm afraid not. How about you? You still carry that little cap pistol?"

My father laughed. "With my eyes I'm afraid of what I might hit. Besides I don't carry the dough I used to. I don't even drive now."

"Aren't you booking?"

"Sure, but not like before."

He napkined his mouth. For a moment he appeared twenty years older. His eyes fluttered. Then he was all smiles again, the lines in his forehead racing about like hastily scrawled bets, except my father never wrote down a bet in his life. Everything was in his brain, even complicated parlays.

"Anybody crowding you?" I asked quietly.

"Naw, Bobby. I just don't get around like I used to."

"You've always got Jimmy O'Rourke's protection in case someone does try to edge in on you or shake you down."

My father snorted. "You know Jimmy. With him money talks. I can't pay off to him like I used to." Then he chuckled and rapped the table with his fingertips. "Course if anybody pushes me I'll birdcall for LeBoeuf."

We shared a chuckle. LeBoeuf. A fearsome-looking man who divided his time between civilization and wilderness, raised in the backwoods of Maine where as a youth he lost half his hand to a buzzsaw. A tall scarecrow of a rummy who could sleep through a winter night in an alley and not freeze to death. With his jagged face, hollow eyes, long yellow teeth and one good hand, horny and animal-speckled, he looked like the first hunting hominid to appear on earth. Mild enough when sober but murderous when drunk. He liked Ramsey. He liked the bars and taverns in the Lower End, and he liked the food at Nate's, but never for too long because the woods would call him and he'd vanish. But during those times he was in Ramsey he was available to the bookies, including my father whom he liked and respected: one-handedly he collected from chiseling horseplayers, not one of whom ever dared to stand up to him.

"Where's he now?" I asked.

"The woods. But it's gettin' cold. He'll show up soon."

The waitress placed a cup of coffee in front of me, no charge. A fair and pointed-nosed woman who remembered when I breakfasted there with school books beside me. She asked whether I wanted anything to eat, and my father said, "Yes, he does." I ordered a hot dog. We fell into a silence until it arrived. It had a queer taste. I chewed the roll and left the dog.

My father said, "I like your girl. Libby—right? You're gettin' yourself a fine wife. You tell her I said that."

"It'll be a quick wedding. Nothing elaborate. We're eloping. A justice of the peace."

"That's how your mother and I got married. Best way to do it."

64

"Libby's pregnant."

My father napkined his mouth again. "Nothin' to be ashamed of," he said. "Lots of marriages start off that way. Hell, most do."

"I have a thirty-day leave. It's to get married on, and also because I think I'll be sent overseas soon."

"Korea?"

"I don't know. I imagine so."

"I'm scared for you, Bobby."

"I don't plan to be a hero. I might have a chance to be an M.P."

My father reached into his pocket.

"No," I said. "I don't want it. I don't need it."

"It's not much. Ten bucks. I wish I could give you more."

As I tucked away the ten, the waitress asked what was wrong with the hot dog. "Nothing," I told her. "Just me." She wrote out two checks. My father grabbed them.

Outside the air was cold. My father raised his face to it. Early November air. I was thinking of what lay ahead for my father. The enormousness of white winter. A snowblind world.

In Germany, at twelve dollars a minute, I got my sister back on the line. It had taken four hours. I was incoherent, and she said, "Listen to me! You've got to be philosophical about this. *He* certainly was. Every man must face decline and death, except those who choose to shoot themselves. That's what he chose. It's what he wanted."

At the main gate of Drake Kaserne I watched the winter wind climb the trees and rattle the branches. Thin trees banged against one another like people bumping heads. There was seldom much snow in Frankfurt, just enough to coat the ground. Pink-cheeked and blue-eyed women waited near the gate. They segregated themselves into two groups. One waited for white soldiers, the other for black. Firm and tall I stood, arms crossed, and I viewed both groups like a killer unhaunted by the recollection of his victims.

Asleep on my bunk, my boots still on, I was dreaming. Nightmaring. A telegram arrived. *Our father Joseph W Southwark is dead.* My father was the bearer. My sister appeared beside me and snatched the telegram out of my hand. She read it and slowly looked up at my father and shuddered as his hand groped between her and me with a receipt book that needed to be signed. "What's the matter with him?" my sister whispered, stepping back. "He can't see you," I said, signing the receipt and returning it to him. "He's blind," I told her. She screamed. He had his pistol out and was putting the barrel to his temple.

8

I STUDY THE PHOTOGRAPHS OUTSIDE ALE-kel's, a series of glossies behind glass stained by mouths and fingers. A full-breasted brunette with a ballet face and shimmering legs. A fast caption repeated under each still: *Tansy bares her soul.*

The entrance is a dark corridor that leads to a coat-less cloakroom, where a cigarette is suddenly sucked, the glow illuminating the unmistakable monkey-face of a small wiry woman with towering platinum hair. I know her. Gertrude, a waitress and a whore, who at one time or another has worked in every joint in the Lower End. She is taking a break from the noise, a quiet cigarette. Her face is wired with wrinkles, as if she were a hundred years old, a white woman with skin the color of old tobacco. I know she isn't much more than fifty. I know her better than she suspects. I've seen her soiled foam-rubber breasts on her dresser. I and another cop once dragged a crazy boy-friend from her room. I don't think she remembers the incident. It was some time ago, and she was drunk.

I smile, and she nods, but I doubt that she recognizes me. She doesn't have her glasses on. I pass through padded swinging doors and stand at the edge of the noise. Every table appears taken, though it's hard to tell. There's too much smoke and not enough light.

Alekel greets me with a grimace. He is paunchy and bald and has a bad heart and a friendship with Jimmy

67

O'Rourke that goes back to Prohibition when Jimmy dealt in bootleg liquor and Alekel ran this place as a speak-easy—facts I heard from my father who watched Alekel become the biggest bookmaker in the city. That was before Alekel's heart attack. Now he's the quiet operator of a noisy club and a winter visitor to Florida where he owns beach property and throws parties that Jimmy attends. He grabs my arms and says, "Let's have no trouble!"

I look at him wide-eyed, which annoys him. But his grip is not unfriendly.

"Jimmy know you're here?" he says.

With a smile, I tell him Jimmy has too much on his mind to keep track of me.

"Mulligan's wife is here," he says. "I don't like that."

I try to show surprise and crane my neck to catch sight of her.

"Look," he says, closing in on me, "you know she's here, and you've got a God-damn good idea who she's sitting with. You're using her, ain't you? I've already told Jimmy I don't want no trouble, and your brother-in-law ain't welcomed here. We don't need pigeons flying in."

"Has he been back?" I ask casually.

"Once was enough."

"What about the girl he came in with that time? Oma Tarshi, is it? Something like that, anyway. Was she ever in here before?"

"Don't play cute," he says, and his hand on my arm becomes a steel claw. In the old days, according to my father, he had a punch that could maim a man, and he used the punch more than once. Now it would hurt him to do so. I smile at him. I like him. I know he was friendly with my father and respected him.

"Some quick advice," he says. "Get her out of here. I don't know what kind of game you've got her playing, but those two guys don't fool around. They're cracked, and the little one's a cocksucker. He'll cut her up. You know that."

"I tried to stop her."

"You didn't try hard enough. Give her a kick in the ass. Go lay her. You used to, I hear. Just get her home before her husband comes looking for her. I don't want that sonofabitch here."

He drops his hand, and I shrug and move into the noise and right away see Rose's yellow hair and Poggio's pink face. They're at a table, and Poggio's on one side of her, Primack on the other. She appears smashed on gin-tonics, which means she's been drinking too fast. Primack's hand in on the back of her chair, and his fingers keep blundering into her hair. Poggio sits primly like a choirboy with a dirty picture in his pocket. He gives no evidence that he has seen me, but I'm almost certain he has. At any rate, I squeeze into a table where none of them can miss me.

It's too noisy here. Young welfare mothers shriek when they talk, and gamblers grin at them, nodding knowingly among themselves, a lot of easy scores. Clean-cut couples are here for kicks, quick breaths of atmosphere. Puerto Ricans segregate themselves to one side and chatter like jungle birds. Some old men sit at back tables and kiss their empty shot glasses and rub their mouths around the rims, sticking their tongues into the sucked-dry sockets. Nondescript men, mostly under thirty, line the bar and assume postures that aren't theirs. They are womanless beer-drinkers with quarters and creased dollar bills on the bar, change from slightly larger denominations with which they started the evening. They are waiting for Tansy.

I signal to Gertrude who, brightly bespectacled, is back on duty. She brings a shot of whiskey and a glass of water and mixes the two. Her monkey-face seems shrunken behind her spectacles.

"Can you sit down for a second?" I ask.

"I'm not answering any questions," she says.

"Just one."

"About your brother-in-law?" She shakes her platinum head. "Don't ask, and I've got no time to sit."

"Just let me get something straight in my mind about the night he was here. The Tarshi girl was with him. He got tight, and she didn't, and she went off to the ladies' room or somewhere, and those two guys sitting over there with Mrs. Mulligan moved in on him. Am I right so far?"

"I wouldn't know," she says. "I didn't work that night."

"What night was that?"

"I don't know."

"I did you a favor once, Gert. I wonder if you remember."

"I don't remember anything. That way I don't get in trouble."

I nurse the whiskey-and-water. I shouldn't drink at all. Even a little affects me. I stare over some greasy heads and catch Poggio's eye for a second. Primack is engrossed with Rose and has an arm curled around her. I can't catch her eye. I have a horrible picture of her floating in the river, arms moving as if alive. Jesus Christ, Rose!

She gets up. She glances toward the ladies' room and heads that way. Then she detours toward me. Unsteady steps. I motion to her.

"What the Christ are you doing?" I ask.

"Telling them how tough you are," she says, leaning toward me, showing her breasts.

I can't detain her. She scoots away, bumping between tables in a crooked path to the ladies' room, where she misjudges her steps and nearly bangs her nose on the door. Suddenly I have Gertrude in my ear. I catch a whiff of her platinum hair which looks like cotton candy.

"I'll tell you this much," she says out of the corner of a pie-crusted mouth. "They were arguing, and that's when she got up and left, and those two guys didn't move in on him. They were at the next table, and he invited them over for a round, like he was a big shot with money to throw around. That's all I know."

70

"Wait a minute."

"No. I don't know anything more."

Alekel keeps a filthy men's room. It stinks. I stand before the mirror, which has a lot of face in it, a lot of jaw, a lot of capped and crowned teeth that keep my mouth intact, a lot of root canal work that nearly killed me. A couple of deep lines in the forehead. A firm and hard nose. A solid Yankee face. Southwark. The name has a British slap to it. A long street in Liverpool. My mother's name was Wren. Jews once were the chosen people. Now Americans are. As I hold my head up and widen my smile, the door opens behind me.

Poggio stands beside me at the mirror, a doll-man with a feminine face and an unclean scalp. The vanity of a girl and the pouting lips of one as he pats his hair and touches it with a comb whose teeth have never been brushed. He tips past me. I join him at the urinal, a trough littered with cigarette butts, scraps of paper, and slimy hairs. For a moment he stares at me, a forty-year-old boy-man with long lashes and blackheads in his nose. A glint of sharp teeth. A deviate. Don't make fun of him. An addict. Watch out for a knife. I zip up and stand behind him. He's urinating indefinitely, like a drunk, except he's sober.

"Hurry up," I say. "I want to talk with you."

He shakes his penis, makes a production out of it.

"Come on. We've got a few things to discuss about my brother-in-law."

Suddenly he's pissing again. How the hell can anyone do that? "See my lawyer," he says and farts.

I hit him between the shoulders hard enough to make him wet on himself. He whirls around and hits my blazer with a fast hot spray. I throw a fist at him.

He's on the floor and making sounds like a bird that a cat has clawed, and he's holding a bloody mouth. He screeches when he realizes he's missing a tooth. He smears his fingers on the floor in search of it. I clutch my fist, which is chipped between two knuckles. He springs into a crouch.

"Don't!" I tell him, and whip back my blazer to reveal my revolver. His knife is half drawn. "Don't try it," I warn him. "Look, I didn't mean to hit you like that. I'm sorry."

Blood is dripping off his chin and staining his shirt and suit. His knife is fully drawn. So is my revolver.

"Jesus Christ, I don't want to shoot you."

His prick is still out. There's blood on it. He looks at it and screams.

I get the hell out of there.

A fierce round of applause, and hoots and cheers. Everything is dark except on the small square dance floor where Tansy stands motionless in a nude white light that burns her bare parts and fastens itself to her glittering bra and spangled crotch cloth. Long slippery legs which are stalks of silence anchored by silver slippers. Disinterestedly she flings her hand toward vague men with horns and drums. The music is muted. Her movements are gradual. The quiet music quickens, and so does she.

I stumble in the dark. I look for Rose's yellow hair and instead find a pair of pink legs that aren't hers. They belong to a young Puerto Rican woman sitting with a runt of a man who tears his eyes from the hot light on the dance floor and shows his teeth.

The music becomes jerky with sudden blasts and bends and rolls, and Tansy's dance is random and sullenly autoerotic. I grope to the bar to get my bearings, and somebody jabs an elbow into my ribs. I'm in his way. Sorry. Tansy is treating the music as if it were a snake curling around her waist. The man who jabbed me shudders, as if someone had stepped on his grave, and he glares at me as if I had been the one. With the music coiled around her, Tansy sways toward the tables and the darkness between them where, if men are fast enough, liberties may be taken. Here at the bar little urgencies are breaking out, and the man who jabbed me and others like him are shifting their feet like restless horses and whistling through their noses and biting into their beers. Across the way a streak of light appears as the men's room door opens. A flash of Poggio's Cupid face with a raw mouth. I search for Rose.

Tansy is back in the white light and pulling the sound of a horn toward her. She arches her back, butterflies her arms behind her, and frees her bra straps. She drops her eyes and shakes her breasts. The bra falls off. In the hush, I holler, "Rose!" Tansy scrapes her fingers down her body to the spangled crotch cloth, which is half off. Midst the roll of a drum, she brushes it away, exposing that which has its own life, its own cruelty, smug and snug and quaintly curving and—sprayed with something—brightly hairy, like a Christmas thing.

Rose is near me. She touches me. "What's wrong?" she says.

"We're getting out of here."

"Don't worry about a thing. I've got them believing you're a tiger, a killer-cop like Roscoe."

Tansy in the hot light half-squats with her knees spread and her head thrown back, as if to perform some supreme function, every muscle ready, which brings to mind the way whole bodies of certain snakes are geared for one predominant act, to eat an egg. Tansy makes a sound as if she were going to lay one. That is when the light wrapped around her flicks off, and other lights blast into existence.

"Rose!" I grab her arm and push her toward the swinging doors. She bumps against me and nearly slips. I'm hurting her.

"Southy, cut it out! I can't leave them like this. The big guy thinks I'm coming back. At least let me tell him I'm not."

I shove her through the doors and down the corridor and use my shoulder against the outside door and stand her still for a moment on the sidewalk. She gulps the street air, chews it and goes into a fit of coughing. I slap her back.

73

"Stop it," she says.

"You're coming with me."

"Make it someplace nice then."

I hurry her along. She's not up to quick-time and complains of a pain. "I'm a little drunk," she says.

A maddening journey to my car. I push her inside. She's all over me when I slip in behind the wheel.

"You can't take me home yet," she says. "Not in this condition."

I drive away from the lights, away from the traffic, down a narrow street marked for urban renewal. Condemned houses rise up on either side, some with families still living in them.

"Like old times, Southy," she says and draws up a leg so that her knee is practically in the pit of my stomach. "Where are we going?"

"I'll get you coffee."

"I want a Coke. Get it from a machine, so we can drink it in the car. Are you going to fuck me?"

I turn left at an intersection, cruise slowly and then nose the car between two rows of pumps at a darkened gas station with a night-light burning in the window. I search my pockets for change.

We share a king-size Coke. The motor is off and the headlights killed. The gas pumps cast wide shadows. Rose slumps in the seat and swigs from the bottle.

"You didn't answer my question," she says.

I reach for a cigarette and come up with an empty package. I take the Coke bottle and drink deeply.

"Am I an old bag now, is that it?"

"You know exactly what you are. A good-looking woman, despite all the trouble you've had. But you're Roscoe's wife, and I can't fight him. I don't have the strength, and I don't have the time."

"You used to go down on me. I bet you wouldn't anymore."

I give her the Coke bottle. She takes the last long swig and tosses the empty in the back seat. It makes a soft thud, a little bounce. I check my watch.

74

"Don't brush me off!" she says. "We were good to each other once. We're not even friends now. Kiss me."

I do, and she starts to cry, small sick tears. I stroke her hair, which is as soft as I remember it. There is too much moonlight shining on us, and the night-light in the station seems brighter, as if someone had turned it up.

"Don't be nervous," she says.

There is a wind now, a cool one. It shows up in the big solitary tree across the street. The shadow of the tree is smashed against the moonlit sky, which is jumping with hundreds of excessive gestures. Rose slips a hand inside my shirt and tells me what I've heard before, a long time ago, that she made a fierce mistake in marrying Roscoe, a man who became careless about himself, about his breath, his underwear; a man ignorant and proud, deeply superstitious, forever blessing himself, reading his horoscope, that kind of depressing crap. A man with no ability to talk soft, with a hand ready to hit, a brutal face, zigzag hair gone gray.

"And I'm losing mine," I remind her, running a hand through it.

"But it's nice hair. I like the way it doesn't stay in place. Don't you understand? You're special to me. What am I to you? Not much!"

I put a hand on her face. "In high school I used to jerk off thinking of you."

"You did really! Why didn't you ever tell me? You're not lying?"

"No."

"In high school I was skinny as that stripper. Do you remember?"

"Of course."

"And Roscoe was beautiful. He really was, then." She laughs. "No he wasn't. I'm kidding myself."

She pulls my shirt out of my pants and unbuckles the belt and yanks the zipper and gives a little cry as her hand clenches certainty, logic, circumcised symmetry. She stares at me with a face white and blue in the moonlight. I glance around because no one had declared us invisible.

"May I, Southy?"

I can hear the scrape of the wind against the stiffness of the night, the tender teeth of leaves that float by from the tree across the street. I can hear myself, my heart beating, maybe bleeding, my feet readjusting themselves. I hear the sound from what she is doing, but I don't hear the cruiser, and I don't see the brilliant spotlight until it burns my eyes open.

"Don't move," I whisper, my fingertips resting on Rose's head. "And don't stop."

I hear the scrunch of footsteps that stop suddenly on my side of the car and turn away, and I hear the muttering of disgust from a young cop whom I don't know but who apparently knows me.

9

A PIECE OF TOAST, COFFEE, A CIGARETTE burning between us. Darcie is upstairs. Her electric toothbrush sounds like the distant drilling of a dentist. The dog lies beside the table with his chin flat on the floor and his eyes half-closed. Libby tried to wash the ugly wound on his nose, but he wouldn't let her. She was afraid of infection.

She bites toast, and I puff a cigarette. She glances at the wall clock because I am more than an hour late for work. I'm seldom punctual, but I've never been this late before. I sip coffee.

"Why did you shoot it?" she says. "You could have got rid of it some other way."

A hunch of the shoulders. "I didn't know of any other way. You saw the size of it. A monster."

She makes a vague face and takes a last bite of toast. Freckles on her nose. Her rusty hair is dry and curly. The sound of my gun, she told me, ricocheted through the house. To me, standing in the sunshine, the shot was no more than a whistling that hurt my dog's ears but not mine and didn't wake Darcie but brought Libby to the porch rail, where she clamped a hand over her mouth because, from the way I stood, tilted to one side and digging a winged insect out of my ear, she thought I had shot myself. I buried the snapper's remains in the river. I left my revolver in the car because Libby didn't want it in the house. After it had been fired, it smells like fried chicken for twenty-four hours.

I pour another cup of coffee.

"You're late," she says, annoyed.

She clears the table while I remain at it. She has on a loose striped shirt and white shorts. The sound of Darcie's movements comes through the ceiling. She is exercising, sit-ups and push-ups, an occasional stationary run.

"Why is she up so early?" I ask.

"It's not early," says Libby. She stands with her back to me. I study her shoulders and the fall of her shirt over her shorts which are filled out nicely. No broken veins on the backs of her legs. Her calves are slightly muscular, as if they were expecting a heavier person in time. She runs water over dishes and rinses out a cup. I pick up yesterday's paper and read.

Later I find Libby on the porch with her hands on the rail and her hair full of sunspray. She drifted from the kitchen without my knowing it. She is peering down at the yard, my jungle.

"What's down there?" I ask, catching sight of small brown birds pecking in the grass.

"Bread. I threw it."

I'm more than an hour and a half late for work. Libby sighs. She wants the house to herself. I understand the feeling. I flip my cigarette over the rail and the birds vanish. I stare at a distant cloud mass that looks like a thousand pounds of white bombs about to be dropped. By whom? Good question. God gazing down. The Big Bombardier. Never misses.

"Go to work," says Libby.

"I'm waiting around in case my sister calls, or David."

"Why should they?"

Libby's voice is sharp. My sister and Parker, as far as she is concerned, live in another world. Their lives, except in condescending ways, don't touch ours, she says. Because of circumstances, because of the business brain of Parker's grandfather which gave my aunt a store to play in, my sister lives loftily. Their friends are not ours. For that matter, Libby and I have no

78

friends unless I count Evelyn Abbot, who is my friend, not Libby's. My sister and Parker vacation in Bermuda, and every couple of years Joan tours Europe. Libby has never been out of New England. And I haven't been out of it since the army. Our lives are anchored. My sister has hot beliefs in humanity, fraternity and equality, and she disregards what I consider human lessons to be learned from the territorial behavior of plants and animals: they want only what's theirs, and the right to rule it, guard it, protect it from intruders. Libby and I live in a fortress. We even have a wall. Our house is high enough to be a tower. In the event of hurricane we can hide in the sub-cellar, and we would have at least a slim chance of survival down there during a nuclear attack. In case of fire we could run to the river. We could even live off our property: berries from the bush and fish from the water. We regard our property with secret knowledge knotted like dimes and quarters in a handkerchief. Little bunches too tight to clink.

Libby and I move from the rail to that part of the porch which is roofed and screened and extends itself to the back of the house and the far side. On sultry nights we have slept out here on cots and made love to the tune of crickets.

Briskly, for the first time, I mention my aunt's offer of money in return for helping Parker, and Libby says, "Why tell me now?"

"A thousand dollars," I say.

"I'm sorry. I'm not impressed."

Nor is she impressed with details of Parker's troubles which I told her about a few days ago, and which I expand on now. She stops me.

"That's their business," she says, "not ours."

"But a fast thousand wouldn't hurt, would it? The shingles are sliding off the roof, and the chimney needs fixing."

Libby says nothing, but the irony in her eyes is obvious, and it stirs a memory in me. Home from the army. I didn't want to remain in Ramsey. I wanted to live in some Vermont or New Hampshire village with houses growing out of the landscape like vegetables. "Fine," said Libby, with a plastic clothes basket in her arms and little Darcie at her skirts. "And what will you do for work? Be a handyman? A gardener?" She wanted me to see Auntie Wren because she felt I was entitled to some of my aunt's money, at least enough to give us a start. But I couldn't bring myself to ask Auntie Wren for money. The request would have been useless and humiliating to boot. Instead Libby and I stayed in the project where her mother and father wouldn't set foot because of screaming children and dirty words scratched on brick walls and the whole stigma of project life into which Libby and I and Darcie were tooled. "I can't blame them," said Libby, blocking her ears against the wrath of the woman next door. Paper-thin walls. The woman, a restless divorcee, left her small children alone at night and in the morning she sent the oldest, a second-grader, to school with dry soda-crackers for lunch. One winter I watched her children, their hands mittenless, make a milk-white man out of snow, no nose but pebbles for teeth and thumbholes for eyes, and twigs for fingers and toes. I remember the winter well because it was our last at the project. We bought this house by the river. When we passed papers, Libby cried convulsively. The tears came without warning. When we moved in, she vowed she'd never leave.

We are loners, Libby and I. Queer ducks, Jimmy O'Rourke has called us. Jimmy promoted me to sergeant and appointed me to the detective division. In return I plaster bumper stickers on my car each time he runs for re-election, though usually he has no opposition, and I peddle tickets to fund-raising events for him, outings and dinners and dances. His people give me a list of bars, taverns and clubs, and at each I toss a thick roll of tickets to the proprietor and hold out my hand for the money. Sometimes they squawk, a means to get rid of their anger. Then they pay. At the outings Libby and I sit away from the crowd and eat hotdogs and drink root beers. I play softball and she waits in the car and reads a magazine. After the softball game there's a crap game behind the backstop. I lose a few dollars right away and leave. Each April I distribute tickets to the dance sponsored by the O'Rourke Associates, a drunken affair in the auditorium of St. Patrick's High School. Libby and I don't stay long. I don't dance. Libby dances one dance with O'Rourke who never fails to get cute, usually with a pinch which, despite Libby's tough elastic girdle, gets through to the skin and marks her.

Libby would like me to become a lieutenant and eventually a captain. She doesn't figure much beyond that. I'd like the promotions. I wouldn't mind at all taking over Captain Kilcoyne's job as head of the detective division. Maybe as a detective-captain I could make some outstanding arrests, get my name in the papers regularly, and run for Jimmy's job. I wouldn't like politicking, barreling through crowds, pumping hands, but I could do it if I had to. Certainly Libby wouldn't mind my having a desk in city hall, a cop to act as my executive secretary and another one to chauffeur me around in a black Chrysler. Alderman Southwark. With a voice and vote at city council meetings. With a bagman to collect from the bookies. With a constant roll in my pocket.

Libby has gone down to the yard. I move back to the open porch to watch her walk beside day-lilies in full bloom, a sharp orange against her light-colored shirt and white shorts. Then she crosses the driveway to where I shot the turtle and stares toward the river where I buried it. Then her gaze crosses the river to the great mute rush of trees which gives me the impression of giant soldiers carrying their dead, because among the live trees are gray barkless ones, some broken in half.

Darcie's voice: "Daddy, what are you doing?"

She's behind me on the porch. She has a spoon and a bowl of cereal in her hands, and she's wearing a greenish wrap called a cooler, a sheer short-sleeved thing not meant to be worn outdoors, except she has under it the two slim pieces of a bikini bathing suit. Unlike Libby and me, she tans easily. Her face, arms and legs are copper. Her eyebrows are white and her honey hair faded, as if she were from a parched place, Algiers or Jerusalem.

"Why aren't you at work?" she asks.

"I should be," I tell her. "I'm leaving shortly. You look like you're going somewhere."

Her mouth is too full of cereal to give out words. She nods. I have nightmares of some boy with dirty fingernails tinkering with her as if she were the souped-up motor of his car, guaranteed to fly on the open highway. She opens her mouth as if for a dentist's finger and says, "Beach."

"In that?"

"Why not? Bikinis aren't bad." And she laughs because she doesn't want to argue. She steps to the rail to wave to her mother who is walking back toward the driveway. Darcie rests the cereal bowl on the rail. I have occasional and reassuring fantasies of her finding a quiet scholarly boy, a non-drinker and non-smoker, owlish with his hornrims and gentle with hands that have held nothing more threatening than pencils and pens and his own penis.

"Who are you going with?" I ask.

"Bunch of kids."

"Boys?"

"Girls."

"You don't mind my asking, do you?"

She grins. Such beautiful teeth. "I'd think something was wrong if you didn't."

"Whose car?"

"Sarah Goodman's."

Sarah Goodman has a long lovely face and seems much older than Darcie. "Who is your boyfriend now?" I ask.

"No one. I'm in a lull."

"Who is Sarah going out with?"

"She's in a lull too."

The phone is ringing. Darcie says it's for her and runs into the house, leaving the cereal bowl behind. Libby is at the far end of the driveway. The dog is with her. She is waiting for me to leave so that she may have her house back. She will do the housework with a businessman's efficiency and have everything done by noon. Then time to watch a TV talk show or maybe a ball game. Once I knew the players. Now she does.

Darcie's voice comes through the screened living-room window: "It was for you. They want you down to the station right away."

"Who was it?"

"Officer Bennett."

"What did you tell him?"

"You were on your way."

"Good."

I meet Libby in the driveway, and I scratch the dog's ears. Libby picks lint off my blue blazer. "You're lucky," she says, smiling a little, "you didn't get the turtle all over you."

"I nearly did. Darcie tell you she's going to the beach today?"

Libby nods. "With Sarah Goodman. Anything wrong?"

I hunch my shoulders. The girl has too much money to spend and drives one of three station wagons the family has. She was once friendly with a boy arrested for having pot in his possession. I know. I was one of the arresting officers. I remind Libby of that fact.

"Do you know where the boy is now?" she says. "Fort Riley in Kansas. That's a way station to Vietnam. He may not be back."

"You miss my point."

"I don't think so," she says, and we walk toward my car under the pines. Darcie reappears on the porch.

"That was the station again," she hollers. "Mr. Jordan, this time. I told him what I told Officer Bennett."

I wave a thank-you, and my hand stays in the air,

83

as if stuck. I want to gesture Darcie to come down. I don't want her to go to the beach. The hot breeze is stirring her honey hair and opening her cooler. She belongs here in the green of my property or in the countryside setting of farmers garnering their crops, of horses the color of wheat, of white cows splotched with black. I drop my hand. I have a dark picture of Darcie in a speeding station wagon, of rain glittering off leaves and polishing rocks, of the hysterical dance of trees in a thunderstorm that is violent and then more violent.

"What beach are you going to?" I cry out.

"Rye," she shouts.

Rye, Hampton, Salisbury: they're all alike. Scenes of tricky undertows. How would I ever find her?

Libby hollers out: "Take your cereal bowl in."

The boy the Goodman girl knew was a sad soppy fellow who left his parents' home and lived in a rented Lower End room with pots on the windowsill, home-grown grass. A sound way of saving money because otherwise he would have had to buy it. That was what he told me with a smart-ass grin. I remind Libby of that.

"From what I understand," says Libby, "Sarah went out with him only once. Look, Robert, if you're that worried, if it really bothers you, tell Darcie she can't go."

I shake my head. I climb into my car, pick up the revolver from the seat and holster it. I don't understand boys today with their heavy hair and bearded faces. They look like codgers, like mountain men who have lived a lifetime and learned little. Fifty miles to Rye where the Atlantic rushes the rocks and breaks into the sand. The road is fast. Route 495, unless they take the old road where passing is dangerous. Sarah Goodman will exceed the speed limit. I have helped haul broken bodies out of smashed cars. I have seen faces with noses wiped off. Bodies laid out in the shadow of a serpentine wall.

I get out of the car and run up into the house. Libby

is washing her hands at the kitchen sink. Darcie is at the window waiting for her friends. Her beach bag and towel and floppy straw hat are on a chair.

"What's the matter?" says Darcie, and I stare at her feet. An old coarse blade of grass is caught in one of her sneakers. She and her friends adrift on the burning beach, their charms held in by the flimsiest of bathing suits, their damp footsteps dogged by mongrel packs of boys, their every movement scrutinized by bored young husbands with their wedding rings off and their eyes searching for something fresh, rapists contemplating peaceful persuasion. The sea drying and dying on Darcie's sunburned shoulders and sand sticking to her legs.

"Be careful," I tell her.

10

MASSIVELY GOTHIC AND STAINED BY NEARLY a century of pigeons, the police station rises three stone stories inside the rattle of downtown Ramsey. Blue-domed cruisers are squeezed in the alley which horseshoes the building. A new station was supposed to have been built years ago. Heavy stone steps lead up to double doors which are difficult to open. I always resent the effort. Inside I resent the odor of decay, the grime and grit of the surroundings, the dim lighting, the dirty windows that reflect institutional gloom. Officer Bennett, who looks older than he is, mans the main desk. He is losing his hair, his teeth, his color, his substance, possibly the result of years of Irish whiskey. He sees me and gives a cautious wave. His face is full of hollows. His eyes are painfully blue behind glasses rimmed in pink plastic. When he dies, my father, who knew him well, will scarcely recognize him because he's smaller now, less there, as if he'd abridged himself.

He points to the ceiling and makes a gesture with his eyes to let me know I'm in trouble. I gesture back to let him know I appreciate the warning.

Young cops, many of whom I don't know, some still reserves, are loitering around the Coke machine. They swagger, swear and chew gum. They wear their gun belts slung low and their caps cocked over their eyes. They use rabbit punches on drunks and billyclubs on the city's relatively small population of Negroes and Puerto Ricans, and when they participate in drug raids they plant evidence on suspects who, they say, are guilty anyway, so what's the difference. They root for the Red Sox, bruit about the secrets of women they've known in the line of duty, and support a fortress America with cannons to erase Europe and all of Russia and China and any other un-American place, including Vietnam where a couple of them have fought. One nods to me. My plainclothes status impresses him. The others exchange little smiles.

The detective division is on the second floor. It's one long room crowded with old desks and chairs and other pieces of institutional furniture, most of it in disrepair. A long row of unwashed windows overlooks downtown. Once a man we were questioning about a criminal assault on a high school girl tried to hurl himself through one of the windows. I grabbed him by the back of his belt and Sergeant Paul Jordan by the sparse hair on his head, ripping some of it out. He butchered his hands and face on the jagged glass. A loser, which we should have known right away when we began interrogating him and he impaled himself on one lie after the other. He was under twenty-five and looked middle-aged. Balding head and sunken mouth and ears like broken egg shells. His appearance made Paul and me want to do something for him, a glass of water, a cigarette. He was dispensing toothless smiles like a machine full of red gum balls, one for me, one for Paul, two for me, two for Paul. An idiot's game. Paul and I glanced at each other. That was when he leaped for the window.

Paul, sitting at one of the desks, is keeping current with a newspaper, the *Record-American*. He reads the race results even though he doesn't play the horses. He's Jimmy O'Rourke's bagman. Weekly he visits the bookies and for his trouble skims a percentage off the top and socks it away. Except for driving a large quiet car and owning a color TV, he and his wife live frugally. A second-floor tenement not far from where my father and I lived. My blazer cost more

87

than his suit, an acetate material he wears winter and summer. His shoes are cracked. He's a quiet man. Like me he distributes tickets to O'Rourke's fund-raising affairs, but he and his wife never attend them. I've never met his wife to speak to, but I've seen her downtown now and then on bargain days, a wiry woman with a tight squirrel-face. Like me, Paul is a loner in the department. O'Rourke likes loners. He figures they keep their mouths shut and do what they have to do without stirring attention.

Paul glances up from his paper. A sympathetic frown. We work together once in a while. We don't try to outshine each other. And sometimes we do some good detective work. In a low voice he says, "I tried to cover for you, but the Cap'n knew you weren't in."

"Is he upset?"

"Yeah. Jimmy's with him. I guess it's Jimmy who wants to see you."

Automatically I glance down to the far end of the room. The door down there is the side entrance to Captain Kilcoyne's office. "How long's he been waiting?"

"Too long, Southy. You'd better get in there."

I knock first and then open the door. O'Rourke isn't in there, only Kilcoyne behind his desk, a slight man in a gray suit, a grandfather with a neat moustache the color of cigarette ash. Like Bennett down at the main desk and Paul in the next room, he reminds me of a fading character actor. He smokes a pipe which gives out virtually no smell. On cloudy days or in a mist or rain he becomes a gentle apparition. I can picture him easily as an unassuming police inspector in a British movie. I told him so a couple of years ago, and he smiled. He was having trouble at the time. A purplish spot, the size of a dime, appeared on his face. He ignored it, even when it started to grow, until finally his wife forced him to visit the family doctor, who took one look at it and surgically removed it in his office. Malignant. Now he has a spot on his left wrist, same purplish color but quite small. Benign. The doctor is keeping an eye on it.

Because he doesn't speak or even look up at me, which is his way when he's angry, I finally take a seat in an old leather chair that squirts air under my weight. I cross my arms and then my legs. Kilcoyne puts aside the piece of paper he was reading and looks toward the other door. I start to speak, and he says, "Wait till Jimmy gets back."

I uncross my arms and study my fingers like a gambler checking out the combinational possibilities of a poker hand. Kilcoyne doesn't like idle conversation, and he likes arguments reduced to their simplest terms, a carry-over from the days he was police prosecutor at district court.

The other door opens, and Jimmy comes in. He shuts the door so that the frosted glass rattles. His beefy face is scraped from a shave. It's almost raw. He's sucking cough drops, his tongue clicking them against his teeth. He glares at me.

I had something prepared. Now I've forgotten it. Jimmy twists a chair beside Kilcoyne's desk and sits in it. His suit is a slippery blue color. He wears a diamond on his right hand, the resale of which would put my daughter through a year at one of the smaller colleges. With a rasping voice, he says, "I could dismiss you from the force right now."

"I don't understand," I say, my eyes widening. "I'm late because I had trouble with my car."

"Don't play dumb," Kilcoyne says quietly. He has been watching me like a cat from a windowsill.

I say to Jimmy: "I think I know what you may be referring to, but it's not quite what you think."

"You think those cruiser cops didn't have eyes!" he says. "You think what they saw doesn't get around! You're an asshole, Southy."

"I don't think so."

"I do!" He wipes his mouth. He had spittle there. "What the hell's the matter with you! She's a nutcase, wife of a brother-officer, and you take her to a gas station so she can go down on you. What are you, for Christ's sake, a degenerate!"

I say nothing. There's nothing to say. I had a blow-job which was good. I must have needed it. Jimmy places a cigarette between his lips and lights up.

Kilcoyne says, "Maybe you haven't heard the worst."

I give him a blank look and feel a sharp draft in one of my back teeth. I shift the blank look to Jimmy. His addiction to cigarettes shows on his fingers.

"She's in the hospital," says Kilcoyne.

"No, she's home now," says Jimmy. "She should've stayed. She wouldn't."

My voice says, "What did he do to her?"

"What did *who* do to her," snaps Jimmy. Then his voice smoothes out, the rasp almost nonexistent. "Mulligan? He didn't do nothing to her. It was the two guys *you* were going to take care of."

Kilcoyne says, "We know you took her to Alekel's. She—"

"I didn't take her there. I met her there and I took her out of there when I saw who she was sitting with."

"She went back the next night." He pauses and glances at Jimmy.

Jimmy says, "Go on, tell him."

"They got her drunk and took her to that same gas station. One of them used a knife on her. Stuck the point up her nose and slit it open from the inside. A clean cut. And somehow or other she lost two teeth. I guess it was two."

Jimmy says, "Her nose is stitched up. It's the teeth she ain't got."

"Have you seen her?" says Kilcoyne.

Jimmy shakes his heavy head streaked with a few slicked-back hairs. "I don't go near that broad," he says out of the side of his mouth.

He was friendly with her once. It didn't last long. She didn't like him. He was all grunt, she told me. Jimmy crushes out his cigarette in the ashtray on Kilcoyne's desk. He says something to Kilcoyne that I don't catch. Their conversation is private. It's as if I were not there. I wish I weren't. I wish I were home and it were winter. Last winter I shoveled paths through the snow that led to nowhere. Then by design I shoveled one down to the river, and at the edge I cracked the ice and pulled dead fish out of the water. I carried the fish to high ground, buried them in the snow, and in a few weeks, springtime, used them for fertilizer. The cold spring days. I remember watching a bird perched on a stray sheet of ice on the inlet. The bird would jerk his head this way and that way and then grab a quick drink of water. Not a thought in my head except of those birds returning from wherever they had spent the winter.

Kilcoyne's voice, which is suddenly sharp: "Jimmy's talking to you, Southy."

"I'm sorry. I missed the question."

With sarcasm Jimmy says, "I understand you hit the little fag in the mouth. That's what Alekel tells me."

"There was a scuffle, nothing much. No one saw it. I don't know how Alekel found out."

"Maybe somebody was taking a shit. Maybe that's how."

"I don't know."

"What are you getting red for? You mad? Good!" He takes out a box of cough drops, shakes a few into his hand, and throws them into his mouth. I steal a glance at Kilcoyne who stares at me with a faint expression of sympathy.

Kilcoyne says, "Jimmy made a commitment the store wouldn't be bothered by any scandal from your brother-in-law. That's what you were supposed to take care of. Instead people are getting hurt."

I shake my head and remind each that this is not the first time Rose has been beaten up. She goes on rampages, as they very well know. She gets tanked up and things happen.

"But," I point out, "this last incident seems to solve everything. All we have to do is arrest Poggio and Primack for assault with a dangerous weapon."

Jimmy clicks the cough drops around in his mouth, as if positioning them to spit at me.

Kilcoyne, patiently, says, "She wouldn't make a good witness, Southy."

Jimmy says, "She's a slut."

"And more importantly," says Kilcoyne, "she's a police officer's wife. We don't intend to smear the department."

"Do you understand, Southy?" says Jimmy. "Those bastards might just be a little bit smarter than you. They just might know that we don't want to smear the department."

I point a finger at Jimmy, something I usually don't do, and disagree with him. "I think you're wrong. Smart guys never worry me. They're not hard to handle. But the dumb ones scare me. No brains, which means they act without rhyme or reason."

"Jesus Christ," says Jimmy with too much sarcasm. "That's a hell of a good theory. You oughta come over to my office sometime so we can discuss it. Will you do that?"

I can feel Kilcoyne's eyes. I think he is embarrassed for me. Jimmy is on his feet. He's leaving. Kilcoyne hurries out of his chair to walk him to the door and exchange a few hushed words. They are related through their wives, who are sisters, quite attractive in their day.

Kilcoyne returns to his desk and, sitting back, stares at his pipe, which lies dead in the ashtray.

"Jimmy's not well," he says. "He sounds and looks terrible."

Once, I remember, I came upon a dead cat in the snow and sidestepped it. I wonder whether I would do the same with Jimmy. And I remember another cat, a white one with black spots. It was creeping over hard snow and at times was invisible. Only its spots were seen. Only its spots moved.

"Jimmy," says Kilcoyne, "could go any minute. You see, among other things, it's his heart."

"Like Alekel."

"Yeah, like Alekel." For a time, Kilcoyne stares at me, somewhat disgustedly, I think. "You know," he says, "Jimmy thought a lot of your father. He took care of him in ways you don't know about, and he took his death hard. And I think you know when your father was alive, he loved and respected Jimmy. If it wasn't for that relationship, you wouldn't be where you are now. Plenty of men on the force would have put themselves in hock for what you have. You never had to pay a dime."

"I peddle tickets like everyone else for him."

"You just don't understand, do you?"

I give that some thought. Maybe I don't. Kilcoyne picks up his pipe. When I was much younger, I once had a fantasy of planting a kiss on the soft underbelly of his wife. That was when she still had her beauty.

"What do you really know about Jimmy?" says Kilcoyne, sucking the dead pipe. I don't think that is the question he meant to ask, but I try to answer it anyway.

"Well, in regard to the numbers game, I've heard collectors come into Ramsey from Boston or Revere and deal in some way with Jimmy. I mean, that's what I've heard. All I know or want to know."

Kilcoyne is flushing from an anger he seldom shows. What the hell am I doing?

"I'll disregard that," he says, "and get back to the point. This is probably Jimmy's last re-election. I don't want to see him lose. Nobody does. Right?"

I nod, and remind him that no one is running against Jimmy.

"You never know," he says. "You never make that assumption. You never leave yourself open. That's why Jimmy's decided to wash his hands of your brother-in-law. If the D.A. has to prosecute him, if it comes to that, he will."

I sit up. "But it won't come to that. I've already

made it clear to Poggio and Primack that they've gotten all they're going to get from Parker. They know. They're not dumb."

"A while ago you said they were."

"Dumb like foxes."

"I see. Well, anyway, Jimmy would like you to take some time off, a varation. You have any compensatory time coming?"

I don't answer right away. I don't know what I have coming.

"I'll fix it if you don't," he says kindly.

"How much time am I supposed to take off?"

"I'm not sure. Let's say at least a couple of weeks."

I feel as if I have just eaten a heavy meal. I have to push myself to my feet.

11

THE FACES IN THE SIDEWALK CROWD ARE fat, and their voices are scalding splashes in the air. The heat of the sun is terrific. Each windshield from the traffic is a blinding throb of light that creates spots in front of my eyes, like the quick shadows of fish. I feel my awkward posture in the squeeze of the crowd which is mostly women. The August sales. Women with lips that open fiercely and fingers that point; their bodies slant desperately to where they are going, with their facial muscles agonized when somebody gets in their way. My feet get tripped over. There's also the lunch-time crowd to contend with. My back is padded with sweat which leaks into the seat of my pants. Pains in my legs. Then the sudden hard suspicion that someone has his eye on me. A quick turn. Paul Jordan. Automatically we weave toward the curb and squint at each other.

"Why didn't you tell me what happened to Mulligan's wife?" I ask.

"I thought you knew."

"How come Jimmy's so worried about the election?"

"He always worries."

"You know of course about my brother-in-law."

"I've heard talk," he says tonelessly. No blood in him. We are each unlikely cops. We once saw an old woman jump from a fourth-floor window. We turned our heads before she hit the ground. She didn't kill herself. The ground was soft. She sank in it, her two legs broken and her neck out of joint. He took out a quarter to flip to see who would have to wait with her while the other phoned for an ambulance.

"I've got two weeks off to do nothing."

He nods. He already knows. He says, "Look, I was told to keep an eye on you, but I don't have to, do I?"

"You certainly don't. What's the matter—they afraid of me?"

"You didn't look well when you left the station. The Cap'n thought I could give you a ride home."

"I've got a car."

I straighten my blazer and hitch up my pants, and Paul takes a handkerchief out of his back pocket and mops his face. A man and a woman step between us off the curb between two parked cars and wait for a break in the traffic so they can cross the street. The woman is built like a thick strong bottle, and the man has a head of lank hair. Paul wipes the back of his neck with his handkerchief.

"It's hot," he says.

"You must have things to do," I say.

"I do."

"You don't have to worry," I tell him. "I'm going to spend the afternoon in my back yard. It's good out there. You and your wife ought to come over sometime. I'll show you around."

"I'd like to," he says. "Sometime."

He steps away from me, and the sunshine grabs him. He leans into the whining traffic. Poisonous exhaust fumes encircle him like soiled silk. He glances back at me with a choked expression and gives a little wave. Then, as the traffic stalls, he glides away.

I follow the edge of the sidewalk. Ahead a Plymouth is pulling out a parking place, and a Thunderbird is sliding into it, the driver immediately recognizable— her long black hair, and the attention she gets as she steps out of the car and walks around to the sidewalk, her clean brown face and her legs as sleek and shapely as those of the dancer Tansy. A glance my way as she pauses at the parking meter. We've never met, but we know each other's faces. I've seen her in her car and sometimes in Parker's, and I've seen her at the shopping plaza on the far side of the apartments, passed her silently in the aisle in the supermarket and stood behind her in the drugstore where she bought cigarettes or a magazine or batteries for a transistor radio. And she, I've been told, has seen me by the inlet. Early last spring and late last fall when the trees were bare. From her apartment, in the nook where she reads, she looked out the window and saw me dig and rip and shift earth; perhaps saw me carry on imaginary dialogues with myself, my face changing to answer myself; saw me, I'm sure, swing a sturdy stick like a baseball bat to hit pebbles over the river, home runs if they reached the trees, grand-slams if they sailed over them. I wonder whether she kept score. I did. A grown man slugging stones.

I lose her. Her step is faster than mine, not hurried, simply quick and sure. She has a path through the crowd. I'm rubber-legged. Fish-shaped spots in front of my eyes. Faces that bump by are sour—men robbed of their salt, women of their charms. I've no breath, and I'm staggering and dealing redundantly with myself. I'm slipping.

All my inner hands work to hold me up. My toes grip my shoes. My mouth sucks in the hot trafficky air. The crowd slows but doesn't stop, and I glare at those who look as if they might. I feel my chest for a pain that may or may not be there. I smoke too much, and I eat irregularly and bowel the same way. Dreams corrupt my sleep and rob me of rest. I'm at one with those persons who never learn to relax and burn themselves out.

"No!" I say to somebody who wants to help me, and grope for support against a plate glass window. Parker, Inc. Behind the glass is another crowd. A bevy of female mannequins viewing me without interest, superbly impassive, prematurely dressed for autumn. Their heavy jewelry—earrings, bracelets, pins, chains and lockets—looks as if it were made in a machine shop. Their short coats have massive zippers. Their gloves could be worn by workmen who scale girders and handle blowtorches. They carry cobra-skin bags. Their hair is fierce scroll-work. One mannequin, her price tag in her fingers, ungloved, smiles icily. A frozen invitation to pass through the glass to talk with her. The way a man and his wife will sometimes sit down and try to figure out precisely when and why they started hating each other.

I assume the stance of a window-shopper stopped for a weak spell brought on by heat. I'm no different from an overwrought executive with his defenses down, his dandruff showing and his gums bleeding. I head for the high glassy doorway of Parker, Inc.

A sudden breath of ice. The store is blue and vast, with carpeting that muffles footfalls, with fragrances from perfumes and lotions, with women whose shopping is desultory. Some, Libby's age, have summer-bruised legs, women used to running their hands over fine fabrics, wives of doctors and dentists and lawyers, women whose movements resemble my sister's, whose fingers instantly and expertly touch only valuable things, like miners who take from the earth, rob it of its mercury, its lead and zinc, nickel and iron, silver and gold. Many of the clerks are high school girls, sultry as the mannequins in the window. A middle-aged clerk, who appears to be a boss of sorts, casts a cryptic glance my way. A name tag on her blouse. *Ruth L.*

"Ruth L., excuse me."

The sound of her name startles her, but only for a moment. She stands tall, having been raised to the dignity of a section chief or whatever you call her position. Her blouse, lacy and pure white, is the kind my aunt wears, or used to.

"I'm looking for somebody who may have just stepped into the store. You couldn't have missed her.

Striking young woman with black hair and short skirt and long legs."

Ruth L. doesn't answer. She is thoroughly sizing me up, the way I, as a police officer, often do to others. I wonder whether she knows that she and I are more alike than different.

"She's the young woman sometimes seen with Mr. Parker. My name is Southwark. I'm Mr. Parker's brother-in-law."

Ruth L. is suspicious, but her face doesn't alter an iota, a perfect professional with waiting eyes.

"I don't come into the store that much," I explain. "I worked here years ago, when my aunt ran the place. You remember her, I'm sure, or you've at least heard of her. Wren."

"I'm sorry. I can't help you," she says.

I can easily picture her with a sneer on her face. One is nearly there now. She is, on the surface, as much like my aunt as anyone could be, and attractive for her years, and she probably was much more intimidating as a younger woman, the sort whom men wanted to screw if only to take the starch out of her.

"I suppose Mr. Parker's office is in the same place." And I point to the ceiling, leave her, pass shoppers. I don't need the elevator, not with my breath back and strength in my legs. One step, and I stop. She is descending the stairs. With sun-glasses on, with her long legs dropping effortlessly, with her head tilted to one side and her black hair flowing in that direction. The stairway is narrow, with a rail on one side. I take four quick steps up, and she stops because we are not that far apart, and I'm blocking her, and smiling.

"We've never met, but I think we know each other."

"Yes," she says easily. "You're the man who prefers plants to people."

"Yes, and flowers and butterflies and birds, and I

99

dig a lot in the ground. But neighbors can't hide anything, can they?"

"I guess not, Sergeant. I never really thought about
it."

"I'm on my way to see David."

"Let me save you a trip. He just stepped out."

"That's too bad. I wonder when he'll be back."

"I don't know, Sergeant."

Her use of my rank makes me feel like an enlisted
man. and I think she knows it. There is a slight show
of impatience as she shifts her weight on the stairs,
and peers down at me through her dark glasses.

"Can you spare a minute?" I ask. "I need to talk
to you."

She glances at her watch, a delicate sprinkle of silver around her wrist. "Sorry. I have an appointment."

"It's important."

She removes her glasses. Her eyes are black and
brilliant, with greenish hues, like hyacinths creeping
out of cold ground. She is waiting. I wish we were at
her place, drinking good bourbon with a little water.
Then I could give her some alternatives.

"Funny," I say, "but you look even younger than
I know you are."

"What is it you want to talk to me about?"

I cough, fist to my mouth, the other hand clutching
the rail. "Do you know David could be charged with
conspiracy to commit murder?"

That doesn't shake her. I figured it would. I let go
of the rail, stand straight, and pull my blazer together
to conceal a flutter in my stomach. I fear another weak
spell, and that scares me.

"And you could be charged with the same thing,"
I tell her.

She puts her dark glasses back on. Her face has a
faint flush.

"That's slanderous, what you just said Sergeant."

"But it's a possibility. I'm sure you know that."

"I know nothing of the sort."

"Then you ought to give it some thought."

My thoughts have returned to her apartment, to the imagined sweetness of our showering together, soaping each other, enjoying slippery kisses. With her hair sopping, she would look like a teen-ager.

"Look, I know it's awkward to talk here. Let's go some place where we can sit down. Maybe a ride."

"I have an appointment, and nothing to say to you."

"I'm trying to help, and I can understand certain things. You're a beautiful woman. I can see why David went off the deep end."

"Can you?" she says, with a twist of her mouth, as if to make herself unbeautiful. I could love this woman, I'm sure of it. I smile at her, and feel long-armed, like an ape.

"In terms of years," she says suddenly, "David is an adult, but in other ways he's not. I think that explains the whole situation."

"Not quite. You pushed him."

"What the hell do you mean?"

"You were pushing marriage. Are you pregnant?"

For a moment she appears on the verge of laughter, but she merely smiles with her teeth shut and then quietly says, "No, Sergeant, I'm not."

"I asked that as a friend."

"Oh, I'm sure, but maybe I had better get myself a lawyer. Would you suggest that?"

"I'm not suggesting anything."

"Oh, yes, you are," and her laughter is a ripple, as I lean against the wall with my arms hanging like long cloth tubes. "But," she says, "as long as you're here, blocking my way, which seems to be violating my rights, I'll tell you something. I had the lock changed on my apartment. Do you understand what I'm saying? That is what I came to tell David, but since he's not in, maybe you can pass on that information when you see him, along with the full implication of it."

She is trying to push by me. "Wait. It's not that easy. Things have got out of hand. They intend to bleed him dry, and there's going to be no one to help him. This could all backfire in his face, in yours too."

"Look out!"

I grab her arm, and at once am conscious of her smoke and breath and moisture, of her female facts of life, aware of the woman with her hair and warm blood and milk—as her arm resists my determined hand. With leg and chest, with penis stiff and prominent, I press against her and breathe in her smell, which is soap and water, and she says, "Sergeant, guess why kids call you guys pigs?"

My strengthless hands.

"Go home," she says. "Go play in your yard."

Her whole body shrugs, as if to wipe away my presence. Her black hair and long legs leave me, a swift departure. I try to follow and fail, descending those few stairs heavily and bumping into a crowd that has lined up at the elevator door, and feeling a pain in my chest, a pain that is faint at first but seems to grow. I don't want to die. Who knows the dangers that must be faced when that happens? The one-way groping down dark corridors. The deplorable traffic along the way. Voices of strangers bleating in both ears. Ruth L.'s face appears near mine.

"I want you to leave," she says.

"I'm looking for Parker's whore. She must have just run by."

Ruth L. points to the door, actually shoves me toward it, to the heat of the sidewalk where, my hand on my chest, I bump into a man fresh from a barber shop. His head is pruned. I grab hold of it.

"Jesus Christ!" he says, leaping away from me.

I slide along the glass that shields the mannequins, whose faces all belong to her, Oma. I have sweat in my eyes and hear a morbid discharge of sound from either my nose or my mouth. At the same time I'm at one with myself and not in the least upset that when I die, I won't leave anything, that after my death it will be as if I never existed.

I lean against the glass and wait.

12

FOUR DOORS AWAY FROM PARKER, INC., I take refuge in a drugstore and have a quick Bromo Seltzer. On impulse, I get a chocolate ice-cream soda, but I can't finish it. "Forget it," says the clerk, who knows me, but I pay him, anyway, and leave a tip. The phone booth is in back. I dial my sister's number while checking the coin-return. Bonanza! A dime rubs my finger the wrong way. A quick mental picture of a bird pecking a raspberry and finding a gift inside— a worm. The dime is mutilated, a hole drilled through the center. My sister's voice is smooth and soothing, but I've caught her at an awkward time.

"Bobby, just a minute," she says, and tells somebody the way to the bathroom. "Sorry," she says to me, laughing.

"Sounds like a convention there."

"Practically," she says.

She is entertaining members of the Ramsey Citizens for Equal Opportunities. Crustless sandwiches and speeches. My sister has peace-marched around the Boston Common. She has carried a sign into Ramsey City Hall protesting housing discrimination against blacks and Puerto Ricans, and waved her fist at a police officer who told her and her friends to get out. But she has never been Maced or tear-gassed and awaits the pleasure.

I ask for David.

"Bobby, I can hardly hear you."

I raise my voice and get through to her, and she tells me David's not in and has no idea where he is if he's not at the store. He's not at the store, I tell her.

"Then, I don't know—really. What's the matter?"

"I think he needs a lawyer. There's a good chance the case will go to a grand jury."

After a pause, she says, "What case? There isn't any case. This is a private matter. Besides, who's going to testify against David? Certainly I'm not going to. And those two men aren't going to cut their own throats. Bobby, I can't talk about this right now."

"Those two men you spoke of aren't going to let him alone. That's pretty certain."

"Wait a minute," she says.

I can hear her talking to someone. I can easily picture the faces there. Four years ago, uniformed and uncomfortable, I was slated to address the group at her house. My speech, memorized, was tentatively entitled "A Police Officer Is More Than a Cop." I had spent a week agonizing it into shape. Quotes plucked from authoritative books. My own words weightily written and staked with heavy punctuation, especially exclamation points, sometimes clusters of them. I gave a draft to my sister, who frowned as she read and said, "This is fine. I mean, I really like it, but couldn't you be more natural, use your own language. It would be much more interesting." I was one of two scheduled speakers. The other speaker's headgear was on the hall table when I arrived—a red conk rag. His hair was a jagged bush that looked as if it would cut your hands if you touched it. He was an enormous black with beads, bangles and a goatee, one earring, gold in his teeth, a slur in his voice. He stood head and shoulders above the crowd, a teacup in his massive hand, my sister at times on tiptoes to put words into his ear. "Your people are self-hating," I could hear her saying. "That means they're suicidal. We must stop that." I waited for him to pat her head. He didn't. I edged away, aware of my bright blue uniform and a woman staring at it with amusement. Her hair was black and her face supremely white, finely chiseled and sullenly classic, traceable, I was sure, to ancient Jews, Babylonians, Egyptians. I could visualize her toting water jugs to workers slaving at the construction site of a pyramid, and I could hear her criticizing the colossal egotism of the pharaoh and sneering at his women. The brooding crotch of a female liberationist. I started to speak to her, but her eyes turned to someone else. She had nothing to say to me. I fled the room and left my undelivered speech next to the red rag on the hall table.

My sister finally comes back on the line. "I'm sorry," she says, "but I just can't talk now. I think you're making too much of this—you and David both. And something else: you don't owe Auntie Wren anything, and you don't have to prove anything to her. So, please, drop it. All right?"

"You don't seem to understand."

"No, *you* don't. Bobby, I really do have to ring off."

And she does. I step out of the phone booth. A great surprise waiting for me. Evelyn Abbot is drinking a lemon-and-lime at the fountain, her briefcase on the floor at her feet. She is impeccably dressed in a linen jacket and skirt and engrossed in her thoughts. Her face is moist. I lean against the fountain and stare at her hair, which went silver when she was still a young woman. She moves her arm, exposing a perspiration stain, and I acknowledge a long-standing desire to break her reserve, to crack her professional facade. My fantasies of sometime sneaking into her apartment and catching her at something terribly private, such as cutting her toenails or examining herself—her apartment where she lives alone, now that her father is in a nursing home. I dig up an old makebelieve picture of her ass, wide and waiting.

She notices me. A sudden smile as her eyes tumble into mine. "Southy." Then a serious tone: "Anything wrong?"

I realize I'm clutching my chest. Still a little pain

there. I drop my hand, and point with the other one at her drink.

"Is that your lunch?"

"It's going to have to be today. I have to visit my father and then get back to court."

"Anything exciting?"

"A divorce, but kind of messy." She pauses. "You sure you're all right? You don't have any color in your face."

I shrug, smiling. I'd love to go to her apartment, stretch out and wait for her to come home. The last time I was there was when she thought I was interested in law school, a cop with ambition. Her irascible little father, however, hovering near her like a sulking sexual partner, knew well why I was there, knew with the intuition of a jealous child that I harbored the hope that, given enough time in an appropriate place, Evelyn and I would eventually make love. It never happened. He never left her side and never had two words for me.

She finishes the lemon-and-lime. I pay for it. "Come on now," she says, just a little annoyed, and tries to force a quarter on me.

"I'm getting out of it cheap," I tell her. "I was going to ask you to go to Diadati's with me."

We leave the drugstore. I like being seen with her. I like it when we have our irregular cruller-and-coffee conversations in Diadati's. The last time we talked about heart transplants, and I told her why I was against them. Heart, soul, life, breath, spirit, shadow— all synonymous, all intrinsically identical. And she, with certain reservations, agreed.

Her car is in a paid parking lot one street from the police station. Mine is near there, at an unfed meter. She is walking too fast for me and, realizing it, slows up.

I laugh. "I'm not in very good shape today."

She stops, and we move to one side to let people by. "What's the matter with you?" she says.

"I'm not sure," I say, lighting a cigarette.

"That will certainly help," she says. Her mother had been a chain-smoker and victim of angina pectoris, choking of the chest, terrific pains, never without nitroglycerin handy. She died relatively young with, according to Evelyn, a cigarette in her hand.

I'm smiling at her. Her hair is glistening in the sun like fall frost. I'd give anything to feel her up.

"Do you want me to drive you home?" she says. "I can swing by that way, but we've got to hurry."

"No, it's all right."

"Where's your car?"

I tell her.

"Can you make it to it?"

"Of course." And I'm smiling again, maybe a little idiotically. She shifts her briefcase from one hand to the other.

"Look," she says. "I know something's wrong. Would you care to tell me about it fast?"

"No, I'd stumble around, and it would take too long. You're in a hurry."

"Is it about your brother-in-law?"

"That has a little to do with it. He could probably use a lawyer. May I recommend you?"

She squints at me. "No way. I try to avoid criminal cases, except for little ones. Wills, torts, deeds, divorces—those do me nicely."

"You're good in cross-examination."

"Not that good, and if he's really in trouble he'll want the best. But look, Southy, is it possible you're making too much of this because it's close to home? I don't know Parker that well, but I have the feeling he acts more on whimsy than anything else."

We are walking again—at a pace she wishes were faster. She glances at her watch. Crossing the street, we pause for a Volkswagen bus filled with children. As far as I know, she has never had the desire for any. A self-contained woman, whose child is her father. Or maybe I'm wrong. Maybe there are men I don't know about.

We reach the parking lot. She tells me to go home,

get some rest, take care of myself. I try to tell her things with my eyes, but she ignores the messages, or perhaps they're illegible. I watch her hurry toward her car. She glances back with a shrug. I was hoping for a sigh.

I drive my car cautiously, lightly touching the brake as the traffic bucks and jolts. I mop my face. The heat hangs in my car. The traffic becomes free-flowing, winding out of downtown and spanning railroad tracks by a crusty bridge, passing the abandoned Boston and Maine station and taverns where the regulars file in at nine in the morning, slipping through green lights at one intersection and then another, tenements giving way to two-family houses and the street widening to four swift lanes while sloping toward another set of traffic lights. The traffic stalls again.

I drop an arm out of the window and let it hang down the door. The woman in the car in front of mine sounds the horn, and sounds it again before realizing the holdup is a red light. With an impatient face, she turns to her passenger, another woman, and they shake their misty heads at the situation. They are each elderly, seventy, maybe eighty, and their car, an old Pontiac, gleams as if it were brand-new.

The traffic-wait increases. I haul in my arm and light a cigarette. Two little girls come out of a variety store, one with a bottle of Coke and the other with Fresca. The one with the Fresca, pigtailed and dirty-kneed and cute in a saucy way, her dress too big for her, turns toward the traffic and catches sight of me. My eyes are fastened to her cold drink. As if mocking me, she throws her stiff little pigtails back and guzzles from the tall green bottle.

I lean forward on the steering wheel and gaze through the dusty windshield at the sky, which suddenly is wrinkled, and just as suddenly the air is cooler and a pleasure to taste. The traffic crawls ahead and then stops because of a jam in the intersection. The old woman in the Pontiac sounds the horn again, and a man in a webbed T-shirt comes out of the variety store to see what's up, a belly on him like the burlap bag of beer a fisherman hangs from the rear of his rowboat. The girl with the Fresca says something to the man, something apparently not nice, because he sneers out of the side of his mouth at both girls, and they laugh. He glances in my direction. I'm still tasting the air—like a snake.

The traffic light has changed from red to green, but the jam remains. The old women in the Pontiac turn their attention to the girls swigging their soft drinks. The man with the beer belly returns to his store. The traffic inches forward, stops. A woman is sitting in a lawn chair between two houses. She is chubby and wearing a green one-piece bathing suit with a cutout midriff, from which her belly protrudes like a medicine ball. She appears asleep. The old women—I can tell— are clucking about her. And the children are making faces at the old women.

The traffic inches forward and then jumps away fast. A long line of it shoots through the intersection. The old women are caught unawares, their attention still on the woman in the bathing suit, who has risen from her chair and is shaking her hair. I tap my horn, which angers the woman driving the Pontiac. She twists her head around and gives me an indignant look. Then she hits the gas pedal.

It's as if I had seen it all before and didn't need to watch. The little girls are running beside a high wrought-iron fence, and the one with the pigtails is clinking her empty Fresca bottle against the bars. A terrible noise. The Pontiac races toward the intersection, but the light has changed. Cross traffic is moving. No screech of brakes from the Pontiac. Instead it swerves toward the children, jumping the curb.

I not only close my eyes, but block my ears. The crash seems a redundancy. I've already heard it, the smack of metal and glass, as if a giant sack of junk had dropped from the sky. Then the screams.

The woman in the bathing suit is racing barefooted down the hot sidewalk, and cars are squealing to a stop, and people are appearing from nowhere.

I don't need to get out of my car, but I do, with a face lifted to the sky, sensing the approach of rain, walking stiff-legged and knowing instinctively there is no need to rush. Everything has been settled. So I stop and wait and hunch my shoulders at those who throw questions at me as they run by. Then I listen to the distant wail of sirens that slowly draw near. I count the cruisers, two arriving almost simultaneously and then another. I sit on the curbstone. The ambulance arrives next. There is no fire, but a fire truck is coming.

I get up and begin walking stiff-legged again. The two old women are standing side by side. The one who was driving is holding her arm and wailing. She thinks it's broken. Her companion has a gash in her forehead and has lost her eye-glasses. Cops are hollering at onlookers and trying to push them back. A tow truck arrives.

"My God!" says the woman in the bathing suit. "I've never seen nothing like this." She is talking to me. She is older than I thought, fifty-five perhaps. A tough, puffy face and veins in her legs, which from a distance hadn't looked bad. "Do you have a cigarette, please?" she says. I give her one and strike a match for her. She's Hungarian, she says with a slight accent to prove it. As a child, over there, she tended chickens. Now she's a grandmother with a son-in-law who works in a bank in Boston. She has granddaughters, she says, just like those two little girls. "I can't look," she says, with a retching sound.

The man from the variety store says, "Jesus, they were just in my place. I know them."

The woman, crossing her arms to cover her belly, says, "Old people shouldn't drive."

The tow truck is removing the wrecked Pontiac. The ambulance has already left, and another has taken its place. The attendants, aided by firemen, are using rubber sheets. Another fireman is working a hose on the sidewalk and another is sweeping away glass and metal. Two cops are at the caved-in wrought-iron fence where flesh clings stubbornly to the bars. I look away. I've seen the blood. I don't want to see the bone.

The man from the variety store says, "Did you hear what that old lady said, the one that was driving? That it was the kids' fault, they should've gotten out of the way."

Suddenly I'm holding onto the man. I'm holding onto both of them—him and the woman. The woman's bare shoulder is greasy.

"What's the matter?" they say in one voice.

I'm trying not to faint.

13

I FALL IN AND OUT OF SLEEP. I DREAM AND redream. Without waking I know when Libby changes the cold cloth on my forehead, and I know when the rain begins, a wild rain, as if the world had split, a huge rain that bends trees and squashes bushes.

I dream that strangers are in the bedroom, standing in a pear-shaped formation, as if readying themselves for a hunt. Who the hell are they? I try to slip out of bed but Libby holds me back. Her hands are heavily veined and her face is different. It's too old. And, a mirror tells me, mine isn't mine. The hair, what's there, is white, and mouth is flabby. The pain in my chest is from advanced age. One of the strangers, a youngish man with a vacant military face and a rhythmed walk, approaches the bed (Libby seems to know him) and hands a document to me to sign. I don't want it. He commands me to take it.

I know when the rain lessens, a slow steady spray, like insects cracking against the screen. The room is filled with the cool breath of the river. The young man, a soldier despite his civilian clothes, an officer no less, hands a pen to me, and I sign my name jaggedly and a little extravagantly. The document's a death certificate. Libby is a witness. Darcie is gone, grown; she's married, a grandmother herself, and she's here in the room, one of the strangers, and the soldier in civvies is her son. He has two other documents. With a stiff upper lip he tells me that they're for his two daughters,

Darcie's grandchildren killed that very afternoon by two old women in a car in which the gas pedal was stomped instead of the brake. I start to weep for them. Weep for yourself, he says. I ask whether my sister is still living. I don't know your sister, he says.

A cold cloth replaces the hot one on my forehead. I open my eyes. The room is dark, and Libby's face is white, her eyes approaching me like two boats moving silently through still water.

"What time is is?" I ask.

"After nine," she says, turning on the reading lamp whose light is dim. "You've slept a long time, but you thrashed around a lot. How do you feel?"

"Better. It's still raining."

"That's only drippings from the trees."

"What time did Darcie get home?"

Libby's eyes float away. "She isn't home yet."

I sit up. Libby props a pillow behind me. There's a pounding in my head. A geologist whacking and chipping at boulders. I keep the cold cloth clamped to my forehead. "She should've been home before dark."

"Don't worry about her, Robert. When it started raining they probably drove from Rye to Hampton and they're on the boardwalk now gabbing with bozs."

I toss away the cloth. I feel rough and loose and unhinged, a soldier with too many bloody victories, subject of too many hoarse calls to arms. I'm hungry.

"I'll get you something," Libby says.

"Have you had the radio on? Did you hear about the two little girls who got killed today?"

She shakes her head and I tell her details.

"O God," she says.

"The most the driver will get will be a fine. Operating to endanger."

"It's not fair."

"It seldom is."

She leaves. I can hear the downstairs drone of the television. She returns with a tray. Tomato juice, coffee, a sandwich. She arranges the tray on my lap. "You watching anything important?" I ask.

"No," she says.

"Then sit for a while."

She sits on the edge of the bed and watches me drink the juice and bite into the sandwich. Pressed ham. I tell her that I've decided to take some compensatory time off from work and that the fact of the matter is that I'm growing a little tired of being a cop. I tell her that while I like being a detective, a good detective is one who can rattle a man into confessing crimes that aren't his, and that's not my style. She, with no expression, agrees. I tell her that tomorrow, for kicks, I may glance at the want-ads and even mail out an application or two. I'll be blunt. I'll write that I'm God-damned industrious and will do a top-notch job no matter what it is. I'll tell them where I stand, firmly on middle ground. No nonsense about me.

I can't finish the sandwich. I'm no longer hungry. I light a cigarette to go with my coffee. Libby is sitting as if she were in a moving car and preoccupied with repetitious roadside images and things that puff out of sight, distant trees, barns, stacks of hay.

"I've often wondered," I say, protruding a smile.

"Wondered what?"

"Whether we'd have married if Darcie hadn't come along."

"Who knows?" she says, removing the tray from my lap and standing up.

"I guess we'll never know," I say. "But I think if I hadn't gone into the army we would have had a better start. I was away too long. It wasn't fair to either of us."

No expression from her. A dead issue being discussed, but exciting all the same, the way, under certain circumstances, such as sexual confession, the coldness of a woman's voice can heat a man.

"Do you mind my talking about it?" I ask, patting the bed for her to sit down again.

"Talk about what, Robert?" she says, still standing.

I smile. "I've never wanted to know who he was."

At first the question doesn't seem to register with

her. Then it becomes clear, and she says, "Now you do."

"No, I don't. He was nobody. I wouldn't recognize his name if you told me."

"That's right."

"He was just somebody who happened along at the right time. Who was it, a delivery man, or maybe the project manager? No, don't tell me. I worked it out in my mind long ago. It was like a meeting between two sexless creatures. A contact, yes, but nothing shared. Nothing produced."

For a moment she says nothing. Then with a chilly voice she says, "Is that what you think?"

"Yes, that's what I think. That's what I hope. Have you ever seen him again?"

"No."

"Do you ever think about him?"

"No."

"It was just one of those things."

"Yes," she says.

She leaves with the tray and I lie alone in the room, the light off, the darkness snuggled next to me like a friend. It's raining again, drizzling; I listen to the sizzling fry-pan sound of traffic on the highway. The drone of the TV. Darcie is growing, growing. Trenchcoat and rainboots in her closet. A bra bigger than Libby's. I was in Germany when she suffered colic and croup, but I was home to help Libby nurse her through chickenpox, mumps and measles. I pasted her first scribbly drawings in a scrapbook and, when she was in second or third grade, I glowed over one of her watercolors. a lilac-colored elephant with feet that looked like faces because the toes she made became eyes and noses. I still have the picture. Somewhere. I took her to see the swans in the pool behind the Bulfinch courthouse in Newburyport, and she was convinced that from the neck up the swans were snakes because of the way they curled, curved, lolled, twisted, wiggled, dipped and struck. She was highly indignant when, right in front of her, they threw their long soiled necks around their snowy bodies and pecked at their bumholes.

The soft rain-ride of sleep with its dry roof. I'm in a prison that has a hospital-like atmosphere, flat-white walls, rails, slick floors, elevators, tall doors and no sane way out, and at my side dull Paul Jordan who would like to help me but doesn't know how. I show him. I drop to the floor, make my eyes awry, hang out my tongue, and play dead. And Paul comes alive. He grabs me under the arms and drags me down a corridor to a door which opens suddenly. A guard wearing starched baker's whites confronts us while I fight to maintain the fixed stare of a dead man. Paul, red from pulling my weight, takes charge. "This creep's dead!" And the guard steps back gingerly, wanting nothing to do with stiffs. Paul drags me through the open door and down a flight of stairs. The journey is too rough. I lose a shoe. He drags me toward an elevator but not in time. Two nurses, young and husky, step in front of us. Each has blue eyes and a clenched mouth. "Dead man!" shouts Paul, but this time it doesn't work. One nurse swears and the other pushes Paul back, and he loses his grip on me. My head strikes the floor. Blue eyes peering into mine as I fight back a blink and keep my tongue loose. The nurses grab me by the ankles and drag me, my head banging on the floor, down another corridor to an open room where, shouting for Paul's help, they lift me onto an examining table. "How long's he been dead?" one nurse barks at Paul who says, "Just croaked, not ten minutes ago. I'm supposed to put him in the basement." The nurse who barked rips apart my shirt, thumps my chest, and throws a hand over my heart. A massage. The other nurse, her fingers long and pink, tears open my pants. Right away my peter comes alive with her touch. "Dead my eye!" she shouts, and Paul jumps between them. "That's just a muscle moving. I told you he just croaked." He yanks me off the table and with a strength neither of us knew he had he throws me over his shoulder. We are running. Doors wing open for us. Guards grab for us and miss. Dividing walls disappear. With me over his shoulder he's running down stairs four and five at a time, and at the bottom and extending out of the hospital and onto turf are cheering crowds. Go, Paul, go! I'm a jockey spurring a horse, then terrifying it, anything to win. I have a million bets on me.

Libby is in the room undressing. I can see her shadow. She moves to the window and gets a breath of air on her ass. I sit up, and she says, "Don't turn on the light."

"I wasn't going to." I get out of bed and stand on shaky legs. She moves to her closet and slips on something. "I fell right back to sleep," I say. "What time is it?"

"Midnight."

"Where's the dog? In or out?"

"Out."

"And Darcie's still not home."

"Yes, she is. She's in bed. She was home an hour ago."

"She all right?"

"Of course."

"Was there anything good on television?"

"Nothing."

I relieve myself in the bathroom, and wash my face and brush my teeth, and for a while sit on the edge of the bathtub. I look in on Darcie and see only a shape.

Libby is crawling into bed. The sheets have been changed. I crawl in next to her and we lie on our backs. I tap my chest. "The heart's here, right? The pain I had was there."

She props herself up on an elbow and touches my chest. "This is where your heart is. Where'd you have the pain?"

"Right here. It might've been a muscle spasm."

She lies back with her elbows up and her hands behind her head. My eyes are accustomed to the dark. I can see her clearly. Her short thick hair and her pert nose, her softly sprouting mouth. A nighty on, the same one she wore to bed last night. She turns her eyes to me.

"I'm going to tell you something, Robert, and the reason I didn't tell you before is not because I'm brave or anything but because I find the whole thing boring and a little repulsive. Two men for a good half hour today, beginning around noon, kept driving back and forth in front of the house. Each time they slowed up and looked at the windows and down the driveway."

"A big man and a little one, right? Which one was driving?"

"Never mind, I don't know, and you don't have to tell me who they are because I can guess. I don't want that sort of thing going on in front of my house. Either you should arrest them, or arrest David, or arrest them all, or you should step out of the situation completely, because apparently you haven't frightened them away. I don't know *what* you've done."

"And you don't want to know."

"That's right. I don't. And I shouldn't have to. This business with David isn't police business. It's something else, something stupid. You don't have a right to involve this house, our property."

"I feel the same way," I say and move against her, an arm over her. "That's why I'm taking time off from the department. I'm going to dig up the ground. I've got an idea for some fall planting. I'm going to put in evergreens along the riverbank, the kind with little red berries. I want to see more green during the winter."

"And I don't want to see those two men in front of the house again. I mean that."

"They won't have any more reason," I say, and take the bulk of her head into my arms and kiss her hair. We are two individuals who have never really enhanced each other through conversation, idle or otherwise, which is too bad. There's much we could have learned about ourselves that way. Her eyes are closed and her lips are full, like a flower, one that I've picked and placed in water. My wife. We reach each other only in bed, sharing an unspoken conviction that sex has beauty and that beauty, like all precious things, lasts for mere moments, sometimes not even that. I lift her nighty to feel her hips and belly, and I kiss her breasts through the filmy material.

"Do you mind?" I ask.

"You know the only times I do."

"Sometimes I forget."

"No you don't."

I get up on my knees and snap open my shorts and reveal where I'm beginning to run to fat. The belly. I try to keep it sucked in, the way a woman tries to keep herself cunningly polished to look new. She removes the nighty, and I dip over her and around her and down her and taste her salt and sweet and sour. Words mouthed on her and and in her. By now, a doctrinaire approach. "Come on up here," she says, and we clench together. Between us are these assumptions, these coughs, these starts, these angers, these circles. The contest of coitus. She meets each thrust with one of her own. In the struggle she uses her nails. Christ! She always lets me know when she's coming. She spits that information into my ear, as if she were absent without leave from herself and were now returning, more substantial than ever, more female than before, more woman than wife.

With a robe on she deserts the bedroom for the bathroom. With nothing on I step to the window and squat by the sill. Moonlight clinging to the trees. A breeze sweeping over the murky river and making marks that look like serpents with human heads. And high above the river, toward dark baggy puffs of clouds, my thoughts are flying single file like pelicans. they'll be long gone by daylight.

She's back in bed before I am. She has folded herself up for sleep, on her side with her arms tucked in and her knees drawn up. I arrange myself away from her.

Through my sleep I hear the bark of my dog and fast jingle of his dogtags. I wait for a screech. It comes as if I had willed it.

119

14

HIS BODY IS NEAR THE RIVER BANK. SOME-
body patted his head and then swiftly slit his throat.

Libby, gasping, grabs her own throat.

She should not have come out. She was eating
breakfast. I excused myself. I didn't know she followed me.

"Go back, please," I tell her. "We don't want Darcie to know."

The grass is bloodsoaked. The eyes are staring. He
is no longer my animal. He is counterfeit, a poor fac-
simile. He looks stuffed, artificial, a replica of something, not a shepherd, and not even a dog. Lupine,
vulpine, but not canine. He looks smaller, but from
another position he looks larger. Yesterday's slash on
his nose appears as an old wound, a brave scar from
a past battle, his jaws slightly open, his eye-teeth
showing, as if his brain recalled the battle.

"You knew!" says Libby.

"Easy," I tell her. "No, I had a feeling."

She starts to stumble. I hold her up. "It's because
of that God-damned David!" she says.

"It could be. I don't know."

"They could still be here!"

"No. It's broad daylight."

She is biting a knuckle and holding in a scream.
"Good God!" she says. "What kind of people are
they?"

"They made one mistake. They stepped on my
property."

She gives me an agonized and uncomprehending look. I try to help her along, but she breaks away and runs into the house.

I emerge from the house in my old clothes and with my revolver shoved into the top of my pants. I have a shovel. Fast glances to the far corners of my property. I'm closing ranks and digging in. The dog, mine, not mine, already has an affinity for the ground. The body is stiffly impatient for the hole to be dug, and the paws are pointing the way.

Sweat flies as I dig. Through it I can see the quick knife and the surprise in my dog's eyes, utter surprise because he'd never expect harm to be done him, and I have a distant sensing of the outrage to his body, with the pain too preposterous and stupendous to be fully felt. The total mutilation of flesh and breath. Through the good graces of death the inner pandemonium becomes external, foreign, fading, gone.

I rest a bit. I don't have the breath I used to. The morning is a perfect mix of warmth and wind. The late summer wind blows off the river. There's no trace of the night rain except on my car whose body dust is streaked and rearranged. Bees and hornets are attacking the goldenrod which, when Libby and I first viewed the house, covered nearly half of the landscape. After we bought the house I went after the goldenrod with shears and sickle and suffered blisters, itchy arms, a bitten neck and an atrocious infection in one eye that discolored, closed up, squeezed out and oozed into a cruel microcosm of a misplaced smile. I remember the showery day the real estate agent showed us the property. A peppery woman wearing a raincoat and sneakers, she danced about because the tall grass wetted and tickled her bare legs. At one point she squealed and at another grabbed my arm to catch her balance as I was losing mine, for I could see the river and all the places to hide which would be mine. Libby was already in the house, moving through the rooms, making them hers.

The hole is dug. I wait for the dog to sneak into it.

The earth is rich and worms clean and pink, as if just born. I figure if I look away the dog will do what he has to do, if only to escape the flies he and his blood have attracted. The inlet water is skimmed with green dust which is here today and gone tomorrow. Sometimes the water is clear enough to distinguish the catfish that swim around with the whiskered faces of old Chinamen. Earlier in the summer a long orange fish, probably a carp, appeared in the inlet and stayed a week. Even when the water was murky the fish stayed visible, a slender glow of fire.

The dog hasn't moved an inch. I'm afraid to touch him because his head may fall off. High in the sky is an airplane, the size of a toy, the sun melting it into the blue. Suddenly the sunshine is dreadfully hot. The wind has died. With the dog at my feet, I stare at the terror of reality: the bursting trees, the burning sun, the blazing blue sky with an airplane stuck in it, extricable only by a blow torch. I drop the shovel.

I wash my hands and arms at the kitchen sink and dry them in a towel that smells of furniture polish. Libby snaps at me:

"You didn't bury him!"

"I can't. I will later."

"Darcie's up."

"She won't see him. I threw a burlap bag over him."

Libby's arms are tightly crossed, as if she were cold. She has a hard blank expression on her face.

"It's very simple," I tell her. "We simply keep Darcie out of the yard. Why should she go out there anyway?"

"I'll bury him myself," she says.

"Yes, or you can wait and I'll do it very soon. I just want to get my breath."

She doesn't wait. She goes into a closet in search of her garden gloves.

The dog's death. Maybe a mistake, maybe a warning, maybe a clue. He had a good life here, good food, a good place to romp. When I brought him home he was no bigger than my foot. He grew so fast, as if to catch up to the shepherd that preceded him, the one killed on the road.

Libby comes out of the closet with the gloves. "No more dogs," she says.

Which is what we said the last time. This time we mean it.

"Wait, will you—I'll bury him in a minute."

No. She's gone. The heavy work has been done; the delicate remains. I figure if the dead really rise from their graves the dog will be back, if only to sniff along the river.

Nate's number is easy to remember, even though I haven't dialed it in years. Three threes and two twos. Nate answers. He's an old man now and seldom worries about the business, which remains good even through the food has become bad. I tell him who I want and what I want.

"They ain't here," he says with a rusty voice, which brings back a memory of my father, his face, that's all. "You hear me?" says Nate. "They ain't here."

"Then just tell them what I said."

He sighs. "Let me give you some advice. If you ain't got enough to bag 'em on, leave 'em alone. People are sick you stay away from 'em. They're sick."

"Just pass on the message."

"No, Southy. I ain't passin' on nothin'. You do it yourself."

I put the phone down and immediately it rings. A woman tells me to hold on please. The call is from the store. I can hear Parker's voice. He's on another phone and, from what he's saying, apparently talking to my sister who obviously isn't taking him seriously because he's becoming more excited. I have a mental picture of an injudicious swimmer in the surf, who could be myself. A slow journey in uncharted waters. I remember my father's friend LeBoeuf who, when cold sober, had a tendency toward mysticism. Times my father would be talking to him but would know

LeBoeuf was off on a flight, except LeBoeuf called it a swim, because, he said, he always had this feeling of moving his arms, as in a breast-stroke, his sweeping hands unfolding the distance, parting it, placing it to one side, as if he were always entering something but never leaving anything. My father would call LeBoeuf crazy without meaning it, without even half meaning it.

"Southy!"

I've got Parker now and the voice that sounds younger than the man. I suspect it grates on my sister, whose voice has a hoarse and hollow sound.

"Did they do anything to you?" he says.

"Who?"

"Poggio and Primack! They were here, not ten minutes ago! They said they took care of you."

"Impossible. Here I am."

"They want fifty thousand dollars. They say that's it. That kills the contract forever and I don't have to worry any more."

"Talk about your brass balls, huh, Dave? What did you tell them?"

"I said I didn't have that kind of money. They said I'd change my mind fast."

"Who did the talking?"

"The Jew, smiling all the time like it was legitimate business."

"Like he practiced it in front of a mirror. What did the other one say?"

"He didn't open his mouth. He just stood there like a kid."

"Like a wind-up toy."

"Yeah."

"Probably all doped up."

"I wouldn't doubt it, Southy."

"What did Joan say to do?"

"She told me to tell them to go to hell. But she doesn't understand. They've got their minds made up I've got that kind of money."

"The store's impressive, Dave, but don't worry. I think I can take 'em."

"What do you mean, Southy? How come you've changed your mind?"

I clear my throat, like someone not used to making speeches. "Let's just say I've had a call."

I go out into the yard. The dog is in the hole but Libby hasn't buried him. Libby is standing near my car and looking up at the pine trees which form a little grove and a natural garage. Among the pines is a dead maple where a woodpecker lives. That's where Libby is looking. Her garden gloves are at her feet. I pick them up.

"I'll finish it."

She nods.

"The keys are in the car. Why don't you take a drive?"

She shakes her head. She says, "I don't want Darcie to know. When she misses him you tell her he wandered off."

I bury the dog and then I mulch the mound to disguise it. Libby is still under the pines. She is full of cold reserve, as if all familiar things had been removed and she were in hostile surroundings.

"His head cameoff," she says.

"I was afraid it would."

"It just about came off."

"He's buried now."

With a disdainful glance she moves to the driveway. Her reddish-brown hair is alive and wet in the sun. She has on a short-sleeved jersey, bermudas and sneakers. She looks like a child, as young as her daughter.

"Where are you going?"

She doesn't answer. I follow her up the driveway to the opening in the wall where she watches cars in fast pursuit of one another. For a moment I see her schoolgirl face, round and freckled and frowning. The seriousness of the high school student she used to be, except that I was a better student than she. She tried too hard. Her shyness matching mine until we were alone, and then she said I became impossible. My ardor, as if to nail her down in the event she was waiting for a better boy to come along. My arms around her. I had a few invisible things to say, and she had to close her eyes to listen.

She turns from the traffic and assesses me too hard. "You're standing out here with your gun in your pants."

I glance down and step back. She grimaces.

"You think you're a big policeman-brother to them. What do they care for you?" Two tears roll down her face. She savagely wipes them away. "I'm crying for the dog!" she says.

And I remember now that it was she who fed him, brushed him, needled tics out of his hidden skin, and pulled chicken bones out of his throat, bones I had mistakenly fed him, and they came out bloody, as small burning sticks.

She wants to take a solitary walk. She says. "I'll be all right. Just leave me alone." I give a gesture that says go ahead, and she steps away smartly, but without a purse or a bag she cuts an odd figure. I want her to come back to me. I try to will her to, but it doesn't work. She's walking in the direction of the city, past the houses of neighbors we don't know.

Darcie is still in the bathroom and may be in there for another hour. I go into her room. Her bed, in need of a new mattress, is unmade. When she sleeps she does so as she did as a child, with a hand under her cheek, a habit that comes from the time she had an ache in a baby tooth and found that the pressure of her face against the palm of her hand brought a certain relief. The two pieces of her bikini bathing suit, thrown on a chair, are slightly damp. Hersneakers have been tossed under a chair, grains of beach sand in each. She has big feet. Certainly they're not her mother's. They're mine. Posters of rock singers and

126

astronauts on the wall. Her transistor radio with its dying batteries and her small Japanese tape recorder that contains rough renditions of her voice singing, reciting, mirror-acting, whispering. Her chess set. Neither Libby nor I know how to play. Her diary, which a long time ago I took a private oath never to read. On her bureau are combs and brushes and little bottles and vials and tubes. I don't like it when she uses makeup. Her face becomes fussy, as if caricaturing an older woman nervously fighting to save her looks. Darcie needs none of that smear-stuff. I have a color photograph of her as a sticky-mouthed child with candy eyes that look as if they could be edged out and eaten. And I have a more recent picture of her in which she looks like the daughter of someone much more substantial than a policeman.

She's out of the bathroom. I hear her go down the stairs, and follow. She has washed her hair which is turbaned in a towel, and she has on a blouse that belongs to her mother and tight shorts that make her behind a quick hand-clap. Pouring orange juice, she is only slightly surprised to see me home at this time of day, perhaps because I've never been one to let my sick-time slip by unused. Her nose is burnt from her day at the beach. The nose is Libby's, the mouth is big like mine, and the eyes, heavy and handsome and slightly gloomy, are my sister's.

We sit at the kitchen table, she with her orange juice and I with my cigarette, the smoke from which saunters between us. I express concern over the hour she came home, and she apologizes because it was late, she knows. She inserts bread into the toaster.

"You must have had a good time," I say. The things I would like to ask I seldom do. "I figured you'd head home when it started to rain."

She grins.

So do I. "Boys?"

She shrugs. Boys they met on the beach when the sand was full of fire from the sun. Darcie with long strands of honey hair straying down the front of her face, the nose burning up. Boys who weren't so great, she says.

"Boys who smoke pot?" I ask.

She shakes her toweled head. "Nothing like that."

"Beer-drinkers," I offer.

"No, they were just sticky." She pulls out hot slices of toast that burn her fingers. She dots the toast with hard chunks of butter which will melt and be easier to spread. It's the way I do it. Then I use peanut butter. She skips that.

"Where's Mom?" she says.

"Outdoors. But I think she took a walk to the shopping plaza. The dog's with her. At least I hope he is. I haven't seen him."

She bites into the toast, the noise denoting teeth that are hard and healthy. Her tongue wipes away crumbs on the outside of her mouth. She leans forward.

"Why are you wearing your gun that way?"

"I want to clean it. I never do."

"When are you going to teach me to shoot it?"

"When I learn myself."

She laughs. She offers me a slice of toast, which I decline and she tears in two for herself. She catches my hard eye and says, "What's the matter?"

I'm thinking of those sticky boys about whom she hasn't elaborated and I haven't inquired. I'm thinking about the Goodman girl's car and rain clattering against it, thousands of shiny fingers trying to get in, but all breaking, snapping, popping. All that drool on the windows. Boys in the car, and a wet road that doesn't know where it's going.

"Your mother and I were worried about you."

"I know. I said I was sorry." No annoyance in her voice. She's merely reminding me. I don't believe for a moment she has experimented with drugs, but if she has I don't want to know about it. We have other things to consider. I must learn to live with her and be prepared for that terrible time (which, I've read,

128

comes to all parents) when her understanding of things is different from mine, when hers enters directions I can't follow because of twenty-foot fences. "Last chance," she says, holding up the last torn piece of toast. I must consider the fact that she's no longer the child who used to follow me out to the yard to inspect sunsets which after a bitter winter day could possess all the soft blues and pinks of a baby's blanket and yet in the gentle springtime be fierce and bloody. To be near the river at that time when, frozen for weeks, it would begin to break, strips of ice peeling away like old skin and clotted water springing loose. The joy of seeing it and sharing it. In spring when things caught in the winter ice float free down the river—boards and branches, bottles and cans, large rubber balls, baggy from loss of air. Now when she goes out into the yard it's because she wants to be alone.

She grins, as she adjusts the towel on her head. A little wickedness in her, for she says, "May I ask you something?"—and I know exactly what it is she wants to ask, or at least I have a very good idea. "Aunt Joan," she says. I nod. I know. "Does she really still sleep in the same room with him? How can she?"

"I know your mother hasn't mentioned any of this to you, and I haven't, so who's filling your head with gossip? The Goodman girl? Where has she picked it up? Let me tell you something. Usually a story by the time you hear it has been drained of most of its truth. People twist and they never subtract, they always add on."

"Didn't Uncle David want somebody to kill Aunt Joan?"

"Do you really believe that?"

"It does sound fantastic."

"Exactly."

"But he does like women."

"What man doesn't?"

"But you don't do the things he does."

"I don't have his money."

Suddenly her hand comes across the table and touches mine, and she says, "Even if you did, you're not that kind of person."

My hand overturns hers and gives it a quick squeeze, which provides an instant memory of the two of us peering up at Sputnik. My jaw jutting and my finger pointing and my other hand wrapped around hers. Such a steep place the sky!

I carry a cup of coffee up to the bedroom and pull a chair near the window where, at a glance, I can see the river and the traffic on the road and, when she returns, Libby. The revolver is on the windowsill. Darcie is in the driveway. She has taken the towel off her head and is shaking her hair in the sun. As a child she's played out. As a child she's down and going under. She's nearly sixteen, not a woman, but not a child. Strength and dignity in those long legs. In the shock of sunlight her hands are skinned fish. She sees me in the screen and waves.

There's a mixup on the road, a horn blast because some driver is attempting a U-turn and snarling traffic both ways, and I don't see Darcie when she strolls to the river bank and looks at the mulch pile. I see her when she turns away from it with no apparent curiosity. She stands overlooking the inlet which is dusty green and drowsy, though every so often something in the water disturbs the surface. The soil around the inlet is rich, almost blue. The clouds are small and fat, cows put out to pasture.

Birdsongs in the pines. My eyes are away from her when she decides to move in that direction. I'm watching the traffic untangle itself and the driver who disrupted it speed his vehicle away. I'm watching for Libby. I don't see Darcie when she opens the door of the car. When my eyes turn back to her she's already sitting behind the wheel. I lean my face into the screen and call to her, but the road traffic, heavier now and swift, gobbles up my voice. I can't remember whether the keys are in the ignition. I know what she wants to do. Move the car forward and then back it up, wheel it halfway up the driveway and then down again.

The explosion, red one moment and yellow the next, is deafening and total and my first thought is not of my daughter or of my house, which seems to be rising out of the ground, but of a memory of myself burning old trousers in the trash barrel, the trousers not of cloth but of a chemical material that sizzled and bubbled like bacon, the stench stunning and the sight sinister, as if the material were living and fighting and dying.

Some of the car is in the pines and the rest of it is full of fire, and all traffic on the highway has stopped. I no longer have a daughter.

15

THIS MORNING THE HOT SEPTEMBER RAIN didn't last. Quickly the sun popped back into sight. Puddles were scald-marks. Clouds had shrunk, resembling boiled potatoes. Yesterday I didn't turn on the television. I reread the novel about Forbush, which took most of the morning, and then I read a magazine about organic gardening, and about one o'clock or so I fell asleep on the couch and didn't wake till early evening. Then I went upstairs and lay next to Libby, who had dozed away the day and was set to do the same with the night. "What time is it?" she said, even though it didn't matter to her. I moved against her and ran a hand under her rumpled skirt and over her belly slump. She didn't mind.

Today I watched television, beginning with the *Today* show, and then reruns of situation comedies and the dating and mating games and the news, and in the afternoon the chilling soap operas which didn't need to be watched, only listened to, because they were all dialogue revealing plots and counterplots. In the evening, switching from one channel to another, I watched two hours of news and then *Gunsmoke*, the characters from which seemed like old friends, for the program has been on for years and I've watched the actors age but in other ways never change, never marry, never die. Then I watched part of a movie and turned the set off, and the lights.

The dark draws everything near, as if the furniture

were animals at my feet. The windows are half open and the outside creeps in, carrying in the taste of the river and the glow of trees whose leaves have turned early, some brilliantly. The house creaks.

Libby and I have been living uncounted days, as if the last few weeks were never on any calendar but were something extra and inexplicable, a period in which everything that had been done could be undone. Fire-fighting equipment was used to get the metal out of the pines. Directing the operation was a brittle and inflammable mite of a man with a fang-like face who for a moment I thought was Attorney Evelyn Abbot's father. Police gagged the mouth of the driveway so that the curious couldn't slip through. They did, anyway, through other places, as if a big movie were being made and they were extras seeking parts. Captain Kilcoyne and Paul Jordan and the Chief himself were putting questions to me. I sat at the window. The curious were standing on the top of the wall and cops were trying to knock them off. Fire equipment and men were crushing my property, trampling flowers and bruising shrubs. The air was stinking. Killer air. And brick-red faces. Gone was a windbreak of poplars I had planted five or six years ago. Kilcoyne shook my shoulder and slapped my face. I raised my fist. "Don't!" he said. He wanted to know where Libby was. We spotted her from the window. She was at the mouth of the driveway. She couldn't get through. Then, with horror on her face, she turned sharply and walked onto the highway. Paul Jordan went after her.

The next day they dug up my dog. I protested at first and then walked away. A cardinal was in the broken pines, his redness a screech. Kilcoyne followed me, his face nebulous, almost spiritual, his moustache an ash mark.

"Go in the house," he said.

I did. I couldn't find Libby. Sometimes she was in one room, sometimes in another, or in the bathroom with the door locked.

They took away my dog in two pieces in a plastic bag which, in the sun's glare, looked like liquid steel. An FBI agent and two overfed detectives from the district attorney's office conferred near the catalpa tree with Kilcoyne and Paul Jordan. The FBI agent did not stay long. Jimmy O'Rourke arrived, but he didn't get out of his car, and he didn't stay long either. Later nearly a dozen uniformed police officers arrived, all of whom I knew, at least by sight, and they reconnoitered the property with heads bowed, as if looking for lost money. I watched from the window and then went outside. Kilcoyne asked whether I thought Libby would be all right. I said that her emotions were pushing into one another, and that she no longer had a single one she could lean against.

"Let her lean on you," Kilcoyne said.

We made our way down the stone steps to the inlet, where a big bullfrog surveyed us. Kilcoyne was surprised it did not jump away.

"The way we've pieced it together and from what we've heard," he said, "it was supposed to have been only a little charge, just enough to scare you. But they didn't know what they were doing."

I was only half-hearing him, so he stopped talking.

"They in custody?" I asked.

"They have a woman alibiing for them; she claims they were with her the night and day before. She's a Canuck, a weirdo. She might not be hard to break. We're working on it."

He waited for me to say something; instead I stared at the bullfrog, not the sort of fellow you could get chummy with.

Kilcoyne said, "Any help you give us we'd appreciate."

That evening the district attorney came to the house. His pink pudginess was lost in a chair. He didn't look well. His liver. In the fourteen years he had been D.A. he had never personally prosecuted a case. He has able assistants, particularly a fat fellow whose name I can't remember. He sipped the coffee

134

I gave him and puffed a Chesterfield. He talked about his sister, a fixture in his home, a deep-rooted annoyance to his wife. He spoke of his son who recently passed the bar, an occasion for celebration, and became engaged to a Jewish girl from Andover, a matter of gloom. He asked where Libby was. Sleeping. He asked whether I was Catholic and remembered I wasn't, remembered there had been no formal funeral, only a burial. He spoke of religion just the same and compared it with something overpowering, like the span of a bridge. Then he held up his right hand and said, "They'll pay. You have my word."

Unofficially I'm on an indefinite leave of absence. Officially, per order of Jimmy O'Rourke, I'm on the sick list and drawing full pay, along with certain group insurance benefits. Financially I'm doing better than if I were working. Emotionally, I'm light, like a Styrofoam ball, but I've been a positive help to Libby who is still on sedatives. She has lost weight. Indeed, she has shrunk, grown shorter, turned child-size, abridged herself in a way that reminds me of Officer Bennett. A week and a half ago she suffered tremendous cramps that doubled her up. She bit into a laxative that TV claimed was better than prunes and two hours later began boweling in ten-minute intervals. By evening, hardly able to flush the john, she was sure she had shot away her soul. She thought she was dead. I nursed her back to life. I spoon-fed her and bathed her and read to her. I took her outdoors and placed her in a lawn chair where she could watch me plant evergreens on the far side of the house near the pear tree which crows were attacking. I did what I could with the shrubs and bushes that had been damaged.

I'm serene because with no trouble at all I can imagine Darcie is at the home of some girlfriend, perhaps the Goodman girl, and I need only to find transportation to reach her. Or I may simply pick up the phone, dial the right number, which I haven't found yet, and hear her voice. Sometimes I imagine she has gone sailing into space, each day many more miles away from me, the distance steadily growing inconceivable and therefore not worth bothering my brain with. Other times I imagine she is in the yard and I need only go to a window. I don't see her because of the fine film of somebody's breath on the glass.

My sister and brother-in-law have been to the house. Sort of by appointment, because Libby till then wasn't up to seeing anyone, even though my sister offered to hire a nurse or be one herself. When they arrived I felt a little ashamed of the greasy couch and the frayed carpet and the curtains that hang obliquely because the slim short nails holding the rods are loose. Neither of us is handy with a hammer. I lack the patience and she lacks the skill, or vice versa. Under the circumstances my sister and I didn't know exactly how to greet each other. We've never had a relationship we could tear apart. She has hands one cannot clasp, and I have an awkwardness that puts people off. She embraced Libby. Parker avoided my eyes as we pumped hands. He and I moved out of the room to stand near the radiator in the hall. "I'll do whatever you say," he said, his green eyes jiggling. He had on an olive blazer with a striped shirt and bright tie. He held out his right hand. "I'll cut it off if you want. I'll . . ." His voice faltered and he turned his eyes away. "What can I do, Southy? Tell me!"

"What can you do?" I said with a gentleness that seemed to frighten him. "It was a fight that suddenly became lethal. We didn't expect it. Have they tried to contact you?"

"No," he said with a shudder. "I don't think they will. They can't now!" He punched me; he actually did, but without meaning to. "Southy, what are *you* going to do?"

I tried to convey to him that for the present I had no incentive and no luster, that at the moment I had too many things to pull together. "And I'll tell you, David, the old woman may have had no business behind the wheel of a car, being stupid or senile, but she certainly didn't mean to kill those two kids. A horrible accident."

"What are you talking about?" he said and then stepped back. He wanted to get away from me. Libby cut between us. She clambered up the stairs. She didn't have time to shut the door. A frantic tearing of paper tissue, then a half flush of the john.

My sister and I drifted out of the house to a spot under the pear tree. She was pleasant to look at, slender and gloomy-eyed and dressed in light wool that may have come from Ireland or England. We sat on the grass, in a clean spot away from the squashed fruit that the crows had dropped and that the ants had eaten, the ants like miners, digging into the pit of the pear. She spoke of Parker, calling him poor David, and said she knew when she married him that she was getting someone who could give her everything she didn't need. She married him, she said, because of Auntie Wren, to whom she owed much, her upbringing, her education, her monthly allowance that David knew nothing about. Auntie Wren, she said, felt no love for Parker but much responsibility, as if he had been a child Auntie Wren had had too late in life, too late to love.

"When I married him," she said, "I assumed her responsibility, but I never meant you to."

I gave a cigarette to her and lit hers and mine. We gazed at each other. Her ambiguous face seemed to glow and gloom at the same time. She leaned back on her hands and crossed her legs.

"You've held up very well, Bobby. Libby looks like hell, but you look good." She viewed me as if I were someone tragedy embellished rather than withered. "Bobby, why aren't those men in prison? Why haven't they been arrested?"

Something flashed through my mind—a picture of myself with no gun, merely a simple stick, sturdy and symbolic. Symbolic of what? "Certain procedures have to be followed," I said. "Evidential aspects of the thing must be considered. Besides, they have an alibi.''

"David's been questioned. He hasn't said anything, but he'll do whatever you want. But I'll tell you, Bobby, he could never go to prison. He'd never survive. He wouldn't even survive a trial. He'd go to pieces.''

"There's no need for him to do anything.''

She leaned forward, as if she were an idea-person to an executive and about to whisper something really great. "You're a good person, Bobby. You're a good brother. You're a good policeman.''

"I keep my eye out for idle people, bums and drunks.''

"You're a detective and a first-rate one.''

"I've made a few good pinches, though offhand I can't remember them.''

"You will, Bobby. In time you'll remember everything, and I'll be here to help if you want me to.''

We stood up holding hands like two plants connected in growth. She was trembling, which surprised me. She wanted to know whether she and David were in danger. The other night, she said, she had a nightmare in which a man came to her with a bent bar that made a zig-zag shadow on the wall. David, she said, had a worse nightmare, one which brought him into her arms like a baby. She, she said, took on the guilt of a woman who drops her infant, the fall cracking his skull.

She didn't want to go back into the house. We walked up the driveway and around the stone wall to the car, hers, a Falcon. David was sitting on the passenger side. I opened the door on the driver's side for my sister, who spread two fingers, the peace sign, and kissed my cheek. I kissed hers.

I remembered the kiss the next day when I was riding in Paul Jordan's car and we saw a boy and girl on the side of the road, each with a rucksack, each with a thumb out. Even though they knew we weren't

138

going to stop and pick them up, they made the peace sign and the girl blew a kiss. The boy was bearded and the girl had long coarse hair, as if the only care it got was sun and rain. Their faces were sexless and soulful, and I thought that if I could join them I'd be able to feel the future and move within it.

Paul and I exchanged no words. The sun was a small perfectly round white-hot coin, a dime or a nickel. I felt as if I were paying for my ride. Paul could've driven into the yard of the city garages but he didn't. We left the car at the gate of the chain-link fence and we walked into the yard past open stalls where mechanics had the animated faces of children playing in the mud. They appeared from under trucks and around heavy doors and peered at us. The tools, the things they worked with, cast shadows like heavy caliber weapons perched on tripods. Jimmy O'Rourke's car was parked near the end stall, and he was standing in the sun with a cigarette, his florid face shining like overripe fruit in a basket. Captain Kilcoyne, blurred by the sun, was scarcely discernible.

A part of my car was reassembled in the stall. Other pieces were laid out on the hard grease-streaked floor. Kilcoyne went into the stall and returned with a paper bag which he emptied on the fender of Jimmy's car. "We want to make sure these are yours," Kilcoyne said and ran his hand over a soiled road map for which I never had any use, a corrugated packet of salt the size of a match book, a ballpoint pen I knew didn't write, a chunk of hard candy, and a penny. I said that probably the penny was mine and certainly the other things were. Suddenly, surprising us all, Jimmy hit the fender with his fist and the pen and the piece of candy jumped into space.

I waited for him to speak, knowing his voice would be rough and rotten, but it was worse than that, yellow and cracked, and he put a hand to his throat, and his face was as big as a board, vibrating, as if a nail had been pulled from it. He spoke to Kilcoyne, not to me.

"I want somebody arrested, you hear! I don't want no more reporters on my ass. I want somebody arrested and I don't care who."

He got into the back seat of his car. Kilcoyne motioned me to one side. He put a pipe in his mouth and said, "If we could put them anywhere near the scene . . . but we can't. Maybe you saw them."

"You know I didn't."

"There was a lot of moonlight that night, and maybe you happened to glance out the window and saw two faces, or maybe one face and recognized it."

"I'd rather do it right, Cap'n."

"What have you got in mind?"

"Nothing at the moment."

"People are horrified, Southy, like this was Chicago or something. It hasn't been easy for Jimmy. Help us."

"Something will break. Maybe the woman, their alibi."

He took the pipe out of his mouth. "Maybe your brother-in-law will break. That wouldn't be nice, would it?"

I squinted into the September sunshine. According to the calendar summer would end in a day or two. Kilcoyne said a few more things, his voice dry, like the ashes in his unlit pipe. He ended his words with a question: "You understand, don't you?" I nodded and he gave me a sympathetic look before he got into the car with Jimmy. I heard Jimmy say, "Well?" and Kilcoyne hunched his shoulders.

Grease monkeys stared at Paul and me from their stalls as we walked back to the gate. Paul kept his eyes on the ground. I kept mine high. I had a fantasy: if there were trouble I'd drop to the ground, roll over and come up firing.

On the ride back, Paul took streets I wouldn't have. We passed the bright brick of an elderly housing project, newly constructed. On the porch of the front building was an old woman with a shoulder slump and a helpless drooping of one hand. I put an elbow out

140

of the window. A nurse about my age was climbing out of a Volkswagen near a variety store. The sunshine greased her hard white uniform. She had her nose in the air, a woman used to sticking thinos into a man.

"Anything wrong, Southy?"

I shook my head. Everything was fine: the balance of buildings, the upright crash of trees against the sky, the scarcely disturbed clouds. We skirted the urban renewal area and the Lower End. The car rattled on a torn piece of road. We took a wrong street. Dead end. He had to back up. A bum on a corner stared at us; he was shabby and gray and abnormally tall, possessor of a fierce nose and flabby lip and dagger-like chin, curmudgeon in his expression. For a bright moment I thought it was my father's lost friend LeBoeuf. A resurrection of him.

Back on a straight street, Paul said, "Jimmy's worried about the election. That's why he yelled. He didn't mean it. He knows what you're going through."

"I don't see why he's worried. He's got no opposition."

"He does. That young lawyer Fredette."

"A Frenchman couldn't win in this city."

"The city's upset. People think it's full of gangsters. Did you read that street interview thing in the paper?"

I shook my head. Paul drove faster, too fast, and was surprised by the sudden appearance of cross traffic released by signals he'd forgotten were there. Horns. Hollers. I sat calmly, glimpsing two small stores, antiques and dry-goods, that had faced each other for years. Demolish one and the other wouldn't be the same.

"Jimmy's been good to us," said Paul.

"You're his bagman. He's been good to you."

"To all of us, Southy."

They were still on the road, the boy and girl with rucksacks, but heading in the opposite direction. They must have hitched a ride that took them where they didn't want to go and now they were hoofing it back.

Maybe they tasted the future and didn't like it. They gestured to us, this time not so pleasantly, and Paul snorted quietly.

"People don't act like they used to," he said. "What used to mean a lot is being ripped apart. Kids, Southy. They scare me. Too much has gone to hell."

I chill down one cheek. I was thinking with satisfaction that my daughter would never need to endure the ferocity of a rock festival with its interminable ear-splitting music and tedious talk and wild and outrageous faces. She'd never need to bathe bare-naked in a pond while boys idiot-eyed from drugs watched her. She'd never need to—

"And they call us pigs. Oink. Oink. That's their kind of joke. Who needs it, huh, Southy?"

We pulled up in front of my house. The sour smell of explosion was still in the air, in my nose at least. Paul turned to me as if he had something to say, but he didn't say anything. I got out of the car, unsure of my step, unsure of myself. Like a spy who had too many years living under false identities to be himself anymore.

"If I can do anything . . ." Paul said.

I thanked him.

Before going into the house I stood at the stone wall and looked down at my property. Where a man could sustain himself if he had to. Patches of land where a man could plant and raise food, pick pears and berries, shoot ducks, pheasants and rabbits; where in spring, summer and fall a man, like a squirrel gathering nuts, could prepare for winter.

The house creaks, and the upstairs floor does. Libby is up. Her movements are slow and heavy, as if she were a much bigger woman. I close the windows so she won't be cold, and I pull the shades and snap on a light. Her footsteps down the stairs are solid. She has shoes on. She appears in the doorway dressed to go out. "I need some air," she says, and comes over to me for inspection. She has scratched away a circle of hair on the top of her head. She had dug it into a scaly red hole, but it's not noticeable if she brushes her hair properly. She has on a sweater. I give her a coat.

The night sky is full of stars and has a heavy moon. Libby and I stroll as if nothing in the world were scheduled for us, as if we were vacationing on the outskirts of some strange city. We walk without speaking, passing the kind of houses where the women cook, the children help, and the men wait. Traffic is occasional.

Never before has she been interested in police work, in what I've done and seen, in the people I've encountered. Now she is. We begin the conversation gradually, and I tell her about a man, a vicious son-ofabitch, who blackened his wife's eyes and stomped on her foot, breaking all the toes, including the little one. Pitiful. I responded to the call, carried her to the cruiser, and drove her to the hospital, but I couldn't get her to file a complaint.

"What's her name?" Libby asks.

"I don't remember. It was a long time ago, when I was on cruiser duty."

I tell her about a young hoodlum who in a jealous rage beat his girlfriend to death with his fists and feet, pummeling her, kicking her, stomping on her and finally jumping up and down on her, as his friends watched. His name was Flynn or Flannigan, I forget which.

"Where is he now?"

"Walpole. Life sentence."

"Will he stay?"

"Hard to say."

I tell her about another hoodlum who, the day he was released from Walpole, followed two attractive black girls from a bar, caught up with them as they entered a dark parking lot, and smashed their heads together. He raped the one who remained conscious.

"Did the girls recover?"

143

"I guess so. I know they didn't die. They were from out of town. There was no conviction. The girls didn't show up to testify."

"So he's free."

"Last I knew."

Libby shrugs. Her mind seems to be drifting. We pass some thick bushes and hear a small scuttling in the dark, some animal, most likely wild. Protectively I clench Libby's hand, which scarcely seems there. She asks whether it would have been better if I had stayed a patrolman walking a beat. She says I looked "real good" in the uniform. I remind her that I was trimmer then and had all my hair.

"You had a good beat," she says.

I didn't think she remembered, but that's true, I did have a good beat, with a number of nice stops: the drugstore where I browsed the latest paperbacks, the back room of the barbershop where I read them, the cab stand where I helped the dispatcher with his crossword puzzle, the social club where I chatted with old Italians sitting at tables with cards and drinks. I never went to the club's bar in back because that was where booking was done. I never went out of my way to hassle anyone and never had my hand out for anything. I regarded my beat as peaceful personal property, where I could stroll in the sunshine and hole up in the winter.

"You were well liked," Libby says.

"Yes, I was."

I didn't care much for the transfer to cruiser duty because it was nighttime and much of the world was blotted out, and what was left was neon and fluorescent. I didn't like responding to accident calls, with the siren's crazy yowl in my ears. The fear that I would hit somebody, and I know cops who did. I didn't like handling drunks. The fear that I would catch something. I didn't like busting up fights between savagely married couples. The fear that both sides would turn on me. I didn't like leaving the safety

144

of the cruiser to prowl an alley. The fear that I wouldn't come out.

I tell Libby about the time I was inspecting an alley and stumbled over the body of a derelict dead of natural causes. In fact, I fell right on him. His skin was the color of boiled cabbage, and a lot of stinking gas was coming out of him. I got up and ran, left my beat, went home and washed.

"Do you remember that?" I ask, smiling through the dark.

"I'm tired," she says. "Oh God, am I tired!"

"We'll go home."

"I've got to sit first."

I guide her across the street, through the intersection where, at this time of evening, lights flash yellow one way and red the other. We pass the wrought-iron fence where the two little girls were crushed by an old woman's car. The fence is still caved in. A bus bench is up ahead, vandalized, but usable.

"Chilly?" I ask and slide an arm around her when she sits firmly against me. The bench is hard, but it's as if we were lolling together in a big comfortable chair. I twist toward her, and we share a nice kiss with our tongues running together. I put my arms around her and squeeze. We kiss again. I edge a hand between her legs. The crotch of her panties has a hole.

"Don't," she says.

I tell her that we should get away for a while, if only for a weekend, though longer if she likes, maybe to the woods of New Hampshire. We could go hiking. We could go like cowboys with a couple of horse-blankets and a bag of cornbread and dried beef. Really rough it.

One of her hands slips up from nowhere and smooths hair from her forehead. I kiss her forehead.

"Can we get another dog?" she says.

I look away. "I'd rather not."

Two cars pass by, one immediately after the other, a station wagon and a Ford convertible.

"It's not too late," says Libby, "for us to have another child."

I stare at the male moon, a high and hard pocked ball.

"I wouldn't be afraid," she says, as if her body were tough and her spirit elastic.

I don't mean to be cruel. I don't mean to laugh, but I can't help it. And I can't stop.

16

LIKE HADES WITH AN INVISIBLE CAP I SLIP through the blazing daylight. October and it's still hot. Yellow leaves from a beech flutter to the sidewalk, which has been chalked by children. Their names and little games.

A fat Irishman who dates back to my father's day stands in front of a barber shop with a paper cup of coffee. He's a gentleman bookie now, semi-retired, conducting business only when he feels like it and then only big bets for friends, pals like Jimmy O'Rourke. He finishes off the coffee and crumples the cup and tosses it into the gutter. He's sunning himself. He wants some color. Each winter he disappears and each spring he reappears, though apparently not from Florida or any other warm place, for he never has a tan. Instead he reappears pale, groggy, drained, as if from a hateful hibernation. He glances my way and fails to see me.

Nobody does. It's broad daylight and I'm stealing through streets. My steps are spears, my fists stones. I have on my blazer, newly dry-cleaned, and I have a shine on my shoes, a high gloss. I did it myself. Made a paste by spitting into the polish and buffed the toes with one of Libby's old nylons.

For moments in the midst of crossing the street I stand islanded in traffic. Lines of force whiz by on each side. A hot breeze. What I have set out to do is as simple as building a box. No elaborate plans are necessary. A simple frame with no picture is all that is required. No details.

I reach the other side of the street while blowing my nose into the sick-sweetness of a perfumed hankie that was long entombed in Libby's handbag. I had put money in the bag in the event she took a stroll, tired along the way, and needed a taxi. A pack-rat, I had dropped the money and swiped the hankie.

A solid stretch of dead buildings, abandoned and vandalized, burned in places and pulled apart in others. I stop short. Men are up ahead, a bevy of politicians pointing at buildings and inspecting things with swift eyes. The portly mayor is there and Jimmy O'Rourke and the other aldermen and a baldheaded state senator and some people I think are federal, and among them, easy to miss, is the local urban renewal director, a relative of Jimmy's. Jimmy spots me and does a double-take. What the hell am I doing here? He is too far away to ask, and I'm not advancing. He touches his ear as if to tune me in. Impossible. No device, no matter how sophisticated, can pick up a man's secret stuff, his inner music, his invisible strings. In this respect man cannot be bugged. I throw Jimmy a thin smile and change direction.

One alley leads to another which drifts into a junk-yard owned by two disreputable brothers, one equine, the other asinine, both criminal. A vast immobile concourse of cars, a beaten generation of old automobiles with empty sockets and no tires and with grillwork pulled off or bashed in and with doors removed or hanging and with roofs bloated and indented. A harsh metal maze, a queer rusty silence. I stop near a battered Oldsmobile, and a voice jumps out.

"What d'you want?"

The voice is full of grit and tight feeling. The man it belongs to blinks from the back seat of the car. I move closer. He's thin except in the belly where he's fat. He's one of the brothers, horse-faced and snorting, and he's concealing something in his hand which he's been jerking. I step back so that he can put it away.

"I'm taking a shortcut," I say with a little gesture.

"This ain't no public way," he says with a snort. "It's private." He deals in these junk cars and in drugs, and in stolen radios and TVs that are in a shack somewhere in the yard. He has dead eyes, black hair and connections; he has never served time. He's the brains. His brother's the idiot.

"Do you know who I am?" I say.

"Yeah, I know who you are. You used to be a cop."

"I still am."

"That ain't what I hear."

"Watch yourself."

"Fuck off. You don't scare me."

I continue on, the shortcut. A man with no wheels must take the quick route. He's an adventurer looking for fast waters. He must beware of the sharpening of frost and the growing of night. Weather for those on foot is an important consideration, the same as for seamen. My father's friend LeBoeuf, when he wasn't in the woods, slept in places like this, in junk cars, an empty pint bottle on his chest and the head of a cigarette smoldering in the cushion. The smoke or the fire would wake him up and he'd move to another junk car.

I stop in mid-step because a shattered Ford that once was maybe green and now is no color is shaking and squeaking, a rhythm. I step closer, with the memory of investigating a complaint of a boy and girl doing it in broad daylight in a car parked on a downtown side street. "Get out of there, for Christ's sake," I said to them, rapping on the window, and they scampered out in disarrayed clothes. "Take your shoes!" I said to the girl and nearly brained her with them. "Get out of here, the both of you!" I hollered. "Don't let me see you again!" I wanted to cry. The girl was so young, thirteen or fourteen.

I peer into the Ford, expecting to see the other

brother. Instead it's someone else, a youth with a shock of red hair and shut eyes and features that make him look like a callicebus monkey, someone I don't know but may have seen around, too old for high school and too erratic for a job, lying on the front seat with a busy right hand, doing what the horse-faced brother was doing, but doing it openly and faster. I strike the windshield with the soft part of my fist; he springs up with eyes that don't focus.

I motion to him. "Zip up. Get out." He begins to cry. "Out, I said!" He comes out of the car decent and trembling and stumbling and stands with his head turned to one side. "Look at me!" He has tears in his eyes and snot on his lip. A face on which life has written nothing of importance and never will. I tell him to pull up his sleeves and hold out his arms. Which he does. "You've been shooting, haven't you? And you bought it here, didn't you?" He's afraid to lie and afraid to tell the truth. He's afraid even to make a sound, or maybe he's just sick. "Go on, get out of here," I say, and he doesn't need to be told twice. And I don't need to be told that somebody's been watching from the rear of a burned-out pickup truck. I let him know that I know.

It's the other brother, the idiot, harmless except when frightened and then criminally dangerous with fists that strike without rhyme or reason. He doesn't know whether I'm friend or foe. He needs to be told. He has a brain that at one misty point in his life didn't get enough oxygen and sugar. I give him a "Hi" with my hand, and after a moment he returns it, like a puppy ready to come to me, but I back off, with a smile. I get out of there.

The junkscape becomes vacant-lot thistle, brown burrs and scraggly grass. I'm invisible again. In the distance is a clump of trees that soon will bare themselves to one another. Frost in their holes. I test the air. Soon the clouds will become too cumbersome for a sky streaked with birds, the branches of great autumn-torn trees floating after them like fishermen's nets. I will panic at the first hint of ice flashing from a puddle.

What was once a brake-lining factory lies ahead. Now it's abandoned and its windows are boarded. In the rear is a small garden of love concealed by stunted beech trees and sumac. High school couples nest there. I find their leavings on the ground, tissues and skins and mottled pieces of Saran Wrap and a few flattened cigarette packs. I stand and wait.

Leaves and twigs are breaking. He has a heavy foot. He never could sneak up on anybody, least of all me. I turn around. He's uniformed. I didn't expect that. I figured he'd be a little less conspicuous. He's uniformed and armed, and his leather glitters and smells of what he uses on it. His visored cap, because of his big kinky hair, looks ready to pop off his head.

"Thanks for coming," I say, and he says nothing, cocksure of himself, the big man, even though I outrank him and am smarter than he and can pass exams he's afraid even to take. "No sympathy for me?" I ask.

"I'm sorry about what happened to your kid," he says. "If you'd had a funeral for her we could have all told you so."

"What was there to bury, Roscoe? She was driven out of her bones."

He looks away. As if for her.

"We both have a score to settle, haven't we?" I say, and he says nothing. "I'm sorry about what happened to your wife." His face flattens out. Deadpan. He doesn't like men to mention his wife. "You must know," I say, "whether she told you or not, Poggio and Primack did the job on her. I hear she's all right. I'm glad."

He says something I don't hear because his voice is hoarse and spitless, and he's tugging at his visor and his hand is in front of his mouth.

"Maybe we can help each other," I say.

"You got me down here to say that?"

I nod. "I think we can team up this once and do

something will benefit us both. You want to hear about it?"

He laughs, but almost without sound, and runs a hand over his jaw. "Who needs you? Southy? Think about it for a minute. Who does? You were never much of a cop. Why pretend to be one now?"

We stare at each other without expression. He hooks his thumbs inside his gun belt. His jaw is dark as tree bark. There is, hidden in the growth around us, the smell of rot. Clouds are dimming the sky.

He says, "Cuttin' up with my wife again?"

What's there to say? I say nothing.

"You armed?" he asks too innocently.

"Yes," I say.

He cocks his head to one side, as if putting it on a pillow. He half smiles. "You can get away with something once, Southy, but not twice. Not with me, baby!"

I scratch dirt with the toe of one shoe. "At least listen to what I've got to say."

He lifts his chin and straightens his position. Suddenly, strong sunlight sifts through the beech trees and sumac. Tattered shadows nick his face.

"We both have scores to settle," I say, and outline a plan that is quick and may sound almost too easy, a course of action involving his gun with mine behind it, a situation where he would come out a hero with me behind the scenes, fast police-play disarmingly simple. Bang. Bang.

"You're out of your mind," he says.

"No," I tell him. "Listen, will you! They'll be resisting arrest with heroin on them."

"Some fucking plan! Do it yourself."

"There are two of them. There should be two of us."

"Fuck you. You're nothing."

"Those two kills of yours, Roscoe. They were a long time ago, and they were just kids running away from a break."

His face tightens, and the rest of him seems to rise. "They were over twenty-one," he says.

"One was," I remind him.

"They had guns."

"No guns. One had a screwdriver and the other had a crowbar which he dropped, though you claimed he came at you with it. You didn't give either a chance, and it can work the same way again, except I'll be there to back you up in case anything goes wrong."

His eyes weigh mine. Without hurry, his fingers pull open the flap of his holster. He draws his revolver, highly polished, and points it at me.

"You're under arrest. Conspiracy to commit murder."

I laugh at him. "Put it away. To conspire, I need a co-conspiritor. Shall I arrest you?"

"Try it."

"Don't be stupid."

"I don't like you, Southwark. I never have. Go ahead. Resist!"

I glance skyward, as if for a trap in the ceiling. He is grinning and aiming the revolver at my face.

"Run," he says.

I take a step forward. A fat arrogant step, and I say, "I understand. You're all fucked up because of Rose. But you're acting like I was the only one. There've been so many. Why pick on me?"

His outstretched arm is rigid, the revolver at the end of it. The weapon isn't frightening. Not even menacing. It is simply there.

"Keep talking," he says.

"Why tell what you already know?"

He is a dead shot. He fires point-blank and misses.

My revolver has never come so easily into my hand, despite the noise in my ears, the stench in my nose, the water in my eyes. I fire point-blank, and the bullet tears a patch of hair above his left ear, and his eyes go wide because he thinks he has been hit in the head.

A noise comes out of the sumac, and we spin in that direction, our guns smoking, his hair smoking.

The sumac moves. The face in it is stunned, and the eyes are glazed. The head has a shock of red hair.

Mulligan points his revolver at him.

"No!" I say. "He's a junkie."

"He's a witness!"

"No. Look at him. He's high as a kite. His fly's open. He's full of fantasies."

Mulligan's gun hand jumps, maybe without his wanting it to. No chance to stop it, despite my lunge. Noise. Stench of powder in my nose again. The bullet: a thrown grape against the kid's forehead.

I turn, stumble, hit my eyes with my hand and accidentally discharge my own revolver into the sky. I stare at Mulligan, wondering why his cap did not pop off during all this. He grabs my arm.

"We walk out of here, you hear? Like nothing happened!"

We are clever and swift-footed, acting with aplomb. Hard sunshine. I'm dribbling at the mouth. "Your bullet's in his head. I can arrest you."

"Shut up!"

We part near the junkyard. It is broad daylight, but we are invisible. At least I am.

17

THE CABBIE'S EYES AND THE BRIDGE OF HIS nose appear in the rearview mirror. I shift into a corner. Wrist up near my eyes to study the lines in my skin which resemble roads, rivers, rough traveling. Some lines are deeper than others—cuts, canyons. The cabbie takes a corner too sharply.

"Sorry," he says, his bald head bobbing on his shoulders, as if he were going to throw it at me. He becomes talkative and says he doesn't know whether his father is alive or dead because he ran away from the old man more than forty years ago in upstate Michigan. "Maybe he's buried, I don't know, or maybe he's in a place like where you're going. Your father there?"

"He would never consent," I say.

He speaks of doctors who think more of money than of medicine and maltreat patients with over-prescriptions. "You think that don't happen?" he says, and I tell him I'm sure it does. "I'm paying through the nose," he says, "to stay alive."

He coughs, clears his throat, and spits out of the window. "Let me ask you something," he says. I tell him to ask me any God-damn thing he wants. His eyes leap into the rearview. "What?" he says, and when he receives no reply he shuts his mouth. I roll down the window and gulp air.

The cab takes an incline and at the top rolls to an easy stop. I ask how much and he says, "For you, a dollar and a half." I give him two. "Look," he says, his chin is on the top of the seat. "I didn't recognize you at first. The paper had a picture of you in the uniform and cap. An old picture, that's why it took me awhile. I'm sorry for you. It was a horrible thing, what no father should have to go through." He gets out and opens the door for me and says, "Is it your mother in there?" The sun's in my eyes. He offers to wait. I tell him no.

A string of old people with shadows like coffled prisoners is shuffling across the lawn. The sun is a lenitive hand on their white heads. Those sitting in chairs on the porch have friendly smiles. The woman at the reception desk is another matter. Bespectacled and elaborately coiffured, she is my age and has a narrow nose, a cold professional air and a sheer blouse under which are high hidden breasts caged in a brassiere her husband may have watched her put on this morning. I wait to be recognized and am not. I ask whether Mr. Abbot's daughter is with him, and she says she doesn't keep track of the visitors, they come and go. Reluctantly (something about my manner doesn't strike her right) she gives me his room number.

Patients peer at me. They slink out of beds and from chairs and around corners. People without purpose. People putting off the task of collecting themselves. A shriveled woman, chaos in her eyes, wails from a bed. I have the strong impression she wants to go to the beach and gather stones and dig into the sand with a stick. If I still had my car I'd consider taking her.

I reach the right room, but I'm not sure I have the right man. He's sitting in a chair near the bed and moving his mouth and swaying his little head like a falcon pluming and eating. A fold of skin hangs from his throat. He's wrapped in a maroon robe which he opens so he can scratch himself. He has the meager body of a child and a tiny and cantankerous face. Abruptly he glances up and smiles, not at me but at some secret thought. A cold smile for a cold thought

156

that gives out all the ice of the winter months. It's Abbot all right; it just doesn't look like him, though of course it's been some time since I've seen him and that was when he was well. I make a sound to catch his attention, and he withdraws into his robe. He's on the defensive. Personnel here are caballing against him. He has proof of this which, with spittle flying, he relates to Evelyn each time she visits him, which is nearly every day. They're trying to poison him, he tells her, and he wraps his food in toilet tissue for her to take to a laboratory for analysis. He slips her a list of names scribbled in an unreadable hand, names he wants checked with the FBI, names of nurses and orderlies and doctors and patients, some of whom are dead. He has turned inward; he's dying, delaying it, telling Evelyn something one moment and denying it the next, an outrageous pain in the ass both to her and to those attending him. He messes himself on purpose and waits for some regenerative process to purify him, confident that all cemeteries are full, room for no more.

He's trying to figure out who I am. His mouth is open, revealing stray teeth that could be bullets of various colors and calibers. He doesn't have much of his sugar hair left. What's there is wispy and ghostlike. With my arms behind my back and without moving my feet, I bend toward him.

"Sir, do you remember me? I'm Robert Southwark."

His tiny eyes flicker and fingers slip out of his robe. His voice is a high cackle. "You've got no business here! You shouldn't have been let in!"

He is dying, and he'll be dead maybe not this minute and maybe not tomorrow but my next week or next month. His eyes say that much.

"You, you!" He is pointing a finger at me. "You sniffed around my daughter like a dog. I knew what you wanted. You never got it, did you!"

I have an idea that being dead isn't all that bad,

157

that it is simply a case where you cannot see—and you cannot hear and, among other things, you cannot move.

He's drooling. He can't control his saliva. "You're no better than your father. He was a bum. And your mother—" He wipes his mouth with the sleeve of his robe. "Everybody knows what she did. She robbed that store and sent a good man to his grave."

"That was my aunt, sir."

"A thief and a whore!"

He is using his tongue now to wipe his lips. A disgusting and dying old man going into a fit of coughing. He has a handkerchief out and is bunching it around his mouth.

I'm staring at him, smiling, frightening him.

The handkerchief is bunched in his mouth. He's trying to hold something in, a lie maybe, a horrible one that could send him straight to hell. He is trying to retreat into his robe.

I don't hear the footfalls behind me, not until they reach me and a hand touches my upper arm. A nurse says, "You'll have to leave."

She is fifty or so, the nurse, and has a broad waxy face and muscles under her uniform.

"Sir!" she says when I don't respond.

You can tell when a person doesn't like your looks. The nurse doesn't like mine. She escorts me out of the room, away from the old man and down the hall past patients who are leaking out of their rooms. I break away from her at a door marked MEN.

I stand at the urinal and give out the hard steady piss of a man who has ignored the demand of his bladder past a reasonable point. I take too long. The nurse opens the door. I zip up and wash my hands at the sink and dry them in paper.

"Sir!" she says.

The receptionist rises from her desk as we approach. She comes around her desk and steps in my way and exchanges a secret look with the nurse. The receptionist's glasses are tinted and stylish, and she doesn't have a hair out of place on her elaborate head.

"Are you a relative of Mr. Abbot's?" she asks.

"Simply a dear friend."

"I'm sorry, but I'll have to ask you not to come here again."

My eyes drop to her sheer blouse, long enough so that she knows what I'm looking at.

"Please leave."

"Of course." But I stay standing, smiling at her face. Her skin reminds me of eggshell. Were I to guess anything about her, I would say she had been the child of parents who hadn't got along, who may have been a source of shame to her. She looks at the nurse.

"Get him out of here." She starts to turn, then says, "Wait a minute. What's your name?"

I hold up three fingers which, for all she knows, could be in honor of the Trinity. Then I drop two fingers, leaving the middle finger erect.

"Move!" says the nurse, and she escorts me to the outer door, near which is a phone booth.

"I have to call a cab."

I'm in the booth before she can protest. She waits near the door. I call the station and get Bennett.

"Jesus, where are you?" he says. "We've been looking for you!"

"Something to tell you. Pass it on. Has anybody checked out that place behind the old brake-lining factory? Might be a good idea."

"We know. You hold on, the Cap'n wants to talk to you."

"No time. I'm looking for my lawyer."

"Don't hang up! Where are you?"

The nurse's face is close to the door. An old woman, a patient, wild-looking with a snowstorm of hair, stops to see what is going on. The nurse sharply shoos her away.

"Southy," says Bennett. "Don't do anything foolish. There's only a couple of guys who know anything about this. The Cap'n wants to keep it that way for right now. You hold on."

"Hold Mulligan instead. He's soft as a grape."

"Southy, that kid was no good. Got out of Bridge-water a week ago."

The nurse bangs the glass door. She jerks her thumb. She wants me. I give her the finger. She opens the door.

I walk briskly under the huge cloud-softened sky. Along the gutter of the road is a drift of leaves that no longer crackle when walked upon. When a car comes I hang out a thumb.

18

WOMEN, MOSTLY MIDDLE-AGED, FILE OUT OF the courthouse, their day done. Clerks with the years neatly typewritten under their eyes. It must be difficult for some of them to admit that come five o'clock their bosses cease to remember them. Women with headaches and unsteady insides and sore feet. It must be difficult for them to glance across the street near Diadati's where much younger women, chattering and silly and nicely dressed, some provocatively so, are emerging from the telephone company into the cars of boyfriends, guys who, with loose lower lips and no neckties, don't look good enough for them.

Leaning at the rail at the bottom step of the courthouse, I suck the late sunshine and nod to a clerk coming out of the registry of deeds office. She nods to somebody else. Captain Kilcoyne appears from nowhere. He runs a hand over his hair, which is powdery like dry rot. His moustache is scarcely there. His suit and shirt are the color of pepper.

"You waiting for someone, Southy?"

"My lawyer, but she hasn't shown up."

He takes his pipe out of a pocket. "Does she know you're here?"

"I was hoping I would run into her. She's not in her office."

He bites on the stem of the unlit pipe. "Thanks for being where I could find you."

Two gumshoes. We walk along as if we had nothing

to say and nowhere to go, as if our only interests were in a square meal and a place to nap. We are quiet men, the Captain and I, not given to enthusiasm. Our step is slow, and our likenesses show up in a window of a shoe store owned by two Jews, Samuel and Saul. The beautiful biblicalness of the names strikes me, and I have the hot desire to be home with a book and slipping through the barbed wire of print and tramping across the desert, past palms, dates and figs. A fig, not an apple, tempted Eve and damned Adam, and maybe not a fig but another kind of fruit, a boiling banana with the eye of the devil on the end of it.

"Watch where you're going," says Kilcoyne, laying an arm in front of me. I was about to step into traffic with a smirk on my face. We cross the street, the Captain and I, and he says, "You've been hit with too much too fast. It's not fair and it's too much to ask of any man."

I tip my head back and taste the dying sunshine. Beautiful October weather. Better than summer. No heavy heat, merely a warmth that's sweet in the mouth. The Captain heaves a couple of thoughtful sighs.

"I don't want you to get hurt from this," he says.

"I was only a witness."

The Captain shakes his head. "There's the question of why you were there, the fact that Mulligan was there because you arranged it. And then there's that business of what you wanted him to do. And you'd been messing around with his wife, which doesn't help matters."

"What's that got to do with a pure act of murder?"

"Murder by haphazard, Southy. Just the other day I was reading about some man in Utah who pointed his revolver at his wife. He didn't know it was loaded. He thought it wasn't. He pulled the trigger."

"This was different."

"But no great loss, Southy. Bennett told you about the kid, didn't he? Besides being a junkie and a pusher,

162

he was disgusting. A menace to children, to little girls.''

"Yeah, but not to my little girl," I say, and scratch my ear. Sounds of the street, the fast jazz of going-home traffic. Safe sounds, except that I tower over the Captain and a careless push from me would put him on his ass and a harder one would put him in the traffic.

"What Mulligan did," he says, "was brutal and stupid and stomach-turning, but there are other things to consider, like yourself, Southy. You've got to consider yourself. And your wife? How is she?"

"She's better."

"I'd say that more than ever in her life she needs you around. How could she stand alone now?"

A bright parade of young men and women are streaming out of an office building. We make way for them in the breeze they make. A man leaning against the building doubles the afternoon paper, quarters it, and reads a patch of print, his eyes snaring sentences as if with hooks.

Kilcoyne says, "Nobody knows anything about it yet. We're keeping it quiet until tomorrow, pending notification of next of kin."

"Jimmy must be upset. It must look like he's got a bunch of nuts performing public safety for him. That's not too good with that lawyer on the ballot now. It will give him some more campaign fodder."

Kilcoyne nods. "There are a lot of things to consider."

I nod. "Too many people will get hurt just for the satisfaction of shoving it up Mulligan's ass, as much as we might like to do that."

"That's what it amounts to, Southy." He bites on the unlit pipe, slows his steps, and adds with a public smile, "And of course the victim was scum."

Casually and confidentially I sway toward him. "You may already know I was seen in the area. I cut through the junkyard and spoke to both brothers."

163

He gestures with the pipe. "I'm sure we can handle that."

"What else can you do, Cap'n?"

"The kid was a junkie since he was fourteen. We figure he had an overdose, fell into a lousy state of depression, and somehow got hold of a gun. We suspect suicide. Depending on you, we might suspect it very strongly and I would be surprised if the medical examiner didn't rule that way."

"We don't want any more murders," I say too loudly, which makes the Captain jump, and he grabs my arm and steers me toward the inside of the sidewalk while all the time smiling. In a lower voice, I say, "I mean, it's terribly contagious."

We pick up our step and walk in silence, the Captain smiling and occasionally nodding to someone passing. What is left of the sun is crusting off the facade of the police station. I look forward to the cool weather and a bite in the air, the ground coming to a rest. I button my blazer.

We stop at the bottom of the stone steps rising into the station. We took a roundabout route getting here. It is nearly time for roll call for the early-night platoon, which the Captain, before he took over the detective division, commanded. Two uniformed cops brush past us, deferential to the Captain and me, especially to me, their greetings low, as if not to disturb my thought. The Captain takes me to one side and in a quick voice tells me to forget completely what I was after Mulligan to do, because that sort of business is pure insanity. He says that he is also wiping it from his mind because he knows I'm not myself. I need rest, he says. I'm still in shock. In good time, he says, Poggio and Primack will be taken care of, all nice and legal, the right way, not my way.

"You understand?"

"Yes," I say.

"Really?"

"Yes," I say.

"I want you to take care of your wife and yourself.

164

I'd like to see you get away from your house, take your wife away somewhere for a change of scenery. Can you do that?''

"I think so.''

"Are you listening to me?''

"Yes.''

His hands drifts to my shoulder, rising to get there.

"People are afraid to offer you sympathy,'' he says. "You're holding too much inside. You're like your father was. He never said much either. When he was going blind he never mentioned it, like it wasn't happening. Then, God rest his soul, he shot himself.''

"I have no intention of doing that.''

"I know you don't but you should still loosen up a little. I know you're not religious but at a time like this it might help.''

We shake hands and part more or less as father and son. I have an offer of a ride home in a cruiser, but I prefer to walk a bit. The sun is hanging, dripping, at the end of the city. It reminds me, all of a sudden, of my father's friend, LeBoeuf, of his sundered hand with tiny pink balls where fingers used to be.

On the sidewalk is a spark, a dime the silver size of the sun. I stoop for it. It's mine.

19

THE DIME BRINGS ABUSE. I'VE NEVER HEARD
fury so cold and controlled. "Were you trying to kill
him?" she asks, she who never loses control, never
raises her voice, even in a court of law where she's
chaste, cool and smileless among her fellow attorneys,
she whose mystery is her silvery and heavy remote-
ness. "Don't *ever* go near him again," she says, because naturally her allegiance and affection lie with
him, a dying man, and I, essentially, am no more than
someone with whom she occasionally has coffee.

"I was trying to find you," I say.

"No," she says. "There was no need for you to.
I'm not your lawyer, and I've told you that before.
You can't push yourself into someone else's life. It's
not right. It's not natural."

Harsh words. I cough. The phone booth is full of
smoke. I have a cigarette going. It's burning down to
the filter. I drop it and squash it with my shoe. She *is*
my lawyer. She passed papers on my house, made it
mine.

There's a silence between us. I let it persist until
finally she says, "For God's sake, Southy, go to a
minister or something. Somebody to help you. You
can't go on this way."

"What way? I don't follow you."

"Southy, what can I do for you?" I don't answer
fast enough and she says, "Don't you understand?
My father is helpless and he's dying. No matter what

166

it is you're going through, you had no right in the world to torment him. If you do, you and I have absolutely nothing more ever to say to each other."

"It won't happen. You have my word."

She sighs, perhaps because she feels she has been too hard on me, I can picture her shaking her silver head and running a hand through her hair. She's certainly not a cruel woman, but she has her own to think about, her father who is already part ghost.

"Where are you?" she says.

I look around. I'm in a glass phone booth on the corner of a darkening Lower End street. The directory has been vandalized. It hangs like a killed bird, its feathers ripped and shredded. It's amazing that the phone hasn't been crippled.

I tell her where I am and that I'm starving and I'd like her to have supper with me.

"No, Southy," she says with a perfect mix of firmness and kindness.

"Why not? If I had a car I'd come after you."

A couple of taxis rush by, as if in a race, and I miss what she says. A streak of dying sunlight in the middle of the street, like a faint ink doing its best to make a mark.

"Maybe coffee in Diadati's tomorrow," I say.

"Maybe," she says. "If I can," she adds. Right now she has supper to make for herself. She doesn't mind eating alone: that's her pleasure, that's when she catches up on reading newspapers and magazines and law reviews. Books she reads in bed. I don't know that. I suspect it. The pillows propped as I prop mine.

I whisper something into the phone. "What?" she says. It's just as well that she didn't hear it. We end the conversation on better terms than we began it, with a flexing of shoulders on my part and a softening of voice on hers.

I leave the booth for the stillness of darkening streets. The mindless thumping of my shoes is the only noise. No cars. They come in batches or not at all. I'm checking street numbers in the shadowed doorways. I intrude into one too deeply and run in to the unmistakable shape of an arm: someone trying to ward me off, a wide hand belonging to a man who is embracing a woman. "Sorry," I say, and he says, "Hey, wait a minute," and he and the woman move with me to the mouth of the doorway. "What are you lookin' for?" he says, an arm around the woman, who has seen better days. The man is gaunt and tough and unclean, but not unfriendly despite a suspicious assessment of me. I tell him what I'm looking for, and he says, "You've got the wrong street to begin with, but even if you had the right one you'd be at the wrong end. It's two over and up."

The woman says, "Don't I know you?"

"It's possible," I say. "I've lived here all my life."

The man says, "I know who you are." He has a slight smile. "But you don't remember me, do you?" I study him. He gives me the time, but I'm not getting anywhere. "You pinched me once," he says. "It was a long time ago, B and E in the nighttime. Don't worry. I don't hold grudges. Too much has happened since, especially to you."

Sympathy. Sadness. A little pool of each. The man's breath is hotly acquainted with cognac. His eyes and hers are shiny-bright. "Go on," he says gently. "Two over and up."

Arms swinging lightly, I move dully down the sidewalk, and then down another, my step beginning to quicken, because man unless he moves isn't alive. Across the street is a small boy with a stone in his fist, a paleolithic figure under lamplight, the light like a dawn scarcely breaking. The boy is cockeyed and stunted and pale and listless, as if he were part of a groggy pack of rats subjected to research. He reminds me of Poggio, who belongs behind mesh with other laboratory animals.

I turn down an alley not a second too soon, because the stone that was in the boy's hand bangs head-high against the brick of the building. The scamper of feet.

The blast of a horn. He probably almost got hit by a car in his hurry to put distance between us. I continue down the alley, which is long and rank and black in places. Somewhere water is dripping. At the end of the alley is a slightly swaying shadow which separates into four figures. Pleased and faintly smiling youths with their eyes on me, two boys and two girls, all with their hair the same length, down to the shoulders, a joint moving among them. One of the girls, Joan of Arc in jerkin and doublet, cups the cigarette in her hand, and one of the boys, the taller of the two, wearing an Army field jacket with corporal stripes and sporting a blond beard that looks wet, like the juicy ooze of boiled corn, stands up straight. they all do. Each stares me in the eye. The girl in the jerkin passes the cigarette to the other girl, who is dark-haired and smoke-eyed and pretty, too pretty; she has a restless chest, no bra under her sweat shirt. She leans against the bearded boy. The other boy is short and squat and has a kind of bowler hat in his hands. He gestures with it and says to me: "Friend or foe?"

"Neutral," I say, since I'm too old to be their friend and my face has too many shelves with things in the corners.

The boy with the bowler says, "Here. Try it on. It's my billycock."

I hold up a hand. I don't want it on my head. They all smile. They would be comfortable with my sister, not with me. With her they could talk about social injustices and about Negroes needing their rights and about the sadness in cities and the armies of women on welfare, and I, maybe merely for the sake of argument, would respond that welfare mothers are hot-blooded adulteresses whose paramours are mean little sponging men, among them gamblers, perverts and ruffians, and that—but they would interrupt me. *Shit!* they would say.

The boy in the bowler says, "He looks like he needs something," and the dark-haired girl offers me a puff

169

on the cigarette, which I decline. "Suit yourself," she says. The bearded boy, against whom she leans, says, "He's already high."

I shake my head. "No. But all of you are taking a chance. You're in a rough part of town for this sort of stuff. Open to assault. It's nighttime."

The bearded boy, his beard shining in the semi-dark, says, "We buy it here. We smoke it here." And he takes the cigarette from the dark-haired girl, whose heavy smoke-eyes start to reassess me and then lose interest, but the bearded boy nudges her and she says, "Can you lend us some money?"

"Lend or give?"

She smiles. They all do, but she smiles the slowest and the longest, and she glances at the bearded boy, to whom, in one way or another, she belongs. She says to me:

"Does it make a difference?"

The way she says this and the way her smile fades and her face turns solemn and the way her dark hair hangs remind me of the Goodman girl, who is growing into a beautiful creature, who will become a magnificent woman.

"Are you Jewish?" I ask.

She stiffens, and her friends do, as if I had taken my gun out, as if I were a Nazi. I'm not. I'm reasonable, sensible, hopefully sane.

"I ask only because you remind me of someone. How much money do you want?"

"How much can you give us?" she says.

"What do I get in return?"

The bearded boy whistles, and the other boy twirls his bowler. The girl in the jerkin mutters, "Filthy bastard." I'm not. I don't mean to be. The dark-haired girl with the smoke-eyes steps from the others so that she is half in streetlight that falls into the alley. I reach into my pocket and draw a bill. I want it to be a five but it's a ten. I hold it out for whoever wants to take it. The boy with the bowler does, and then offers me the hat. I don't want it. The bearded boy offers what is left of the joint, whose smoke is a kind of silk in which secrets could be wrapped. Ribboned. I don't want that. The girl in the jerkin mutters again, and the dark-haired girl steps fully into the light, as if with automatic consent of the others. She hikes up her sweat shirt and reveals bare free-swinging breasts with the darkest nipples I've ever seen, almost black. "OK?" she says and pulls the sweat shirt down.

I don't know what the matter is with me. The tears in my eyes are terribly belated. They should have come more than a month ago. They're too small and slow-appearing to mean much, and I doubt that they glisten. There's a pain in the pit of my stomach which hasn't received food for hours. A hunger that takes on the proportions of starvation. If you're starving you can eat anything. Earthworms, frogs, toads, mice, rats. You can easily become a cannibal. White man, to a savage at least, supposedly tastes like ripe banana. I don't know, I'm not a savage, merely a white man, a bumbling Anglo-Saxon, a jerk.

I'm looking for support and have only myself, only my two shaky legs and walls that seem too far away. They're gone, the children, leaving only the sweetness of their smoke which I slowly pull away from. Sentimentally I retrace my steps through the alley, which is black in more places than before. I need Nate's and the food that's there.

I'm grabbed from behind. Near the doorway where the man and woman had been embracing. Under the chin, an arm lock, a love lock, the grip of a heavy animal. I want to cry, but my breath has nowhere to go, no exit, my lips sealed as if from a solemn promise I never intended to make but have been sucked into keeping.

With my arms going limp like a rag doll's, I can see a bit of him, his jaw, the side of his mouth. By straining, I can see an eye which is slightly crazed. "Just listen," says the mouth, and I know the voice. "It wasn't meant to be total," he says. "You hear me. You can believe that or not. I'm just telling you." He loosens his grip slightly, not enough to bring relief. I feel the hint of a pain in my heart and something worse in my ears, something fleeting and fast like the black cries of the daily press, my whole life laid out in a flash of print, with no chance to correct typographical errors.

"It was supposed to have been a little bang with you in the car," he says. "Only to scare you. We didn't even know you had a kid. You should've minded your business on this. Christ, why didn't you!"

He is angry, nearly to the point of tears, which I can understand. Cars sweep by, their headlights on, some with high beams. We sway together, Primack and I, like lovers. I make a movement with my left hand, and he clenches it. He is hurting bones, and his arm tightens around my throat so that I can't cry out.

"Jesus, don't!" he says.

I don't want to.

"We didn't even know you had a dog," he says, and suddenly, despite his grip, I'm making terrible sounds. I'm puking. And I'm ashamed. Primack shoves me away. I can't blame him. I'm a mess. He pushes me against the building and fires a heavy finger at me.

"You never should've done that to my friend."

I raise my hand to wipe my mouth, and he knocks it down.

"I'm sick over what happened," he says. "I'm sick about thinkin' about you. You wanna get even with somebody, it ain't us!"

I drop to my knees with violent stomach cramps. I double up, and at the same time contemplate my revolver. "Don't!" he says, but daring me to. He has his foot ready. He could kill me with a kick. I think he would like to kill me to get me out of his head. His eyes blink that message. I try to rise, to stay on my feet, but I'm stooped over as if from something on my back, my headstone. I slip back to my knees.

"Help me. Get me a cab."

"There ain't any," he says, studying me. I think he's hoping that I'm dying without a mark on me.

"Who?" I ask. "Who planted it in my car?"

"What God-damned difference does it make?"

"In case I can only get one of you."

"You fuckface! I'm trying to help you. We don't want to hurt you. Just leave us alone so we don't have to. We've got something else going now—don't have nothin' to do with you—and we'll be out of town soon. You understand?"

I'm puking again, and I'm on my hands and knees, and Primack's voice, which seems gentle to me, is far away. I'm trying to grab a last look at him but can't raise my head. I'm not sure how much time is passing, the way in a winter storm you can't tell how much snow is dropping because it's everywhere. You wait for morning and then measure it. The pain in my chest remains, but it doesn't get worse. My heart is thumping, which I take for a good sign. All I need now is some strength in my hands.

Somebody is helping me to my feet. There's no talk from him, only grunts and gestures, as if he were trying not to exert himself too much, as if he had troubles and didn't want them worsened by mine. "Come on," he says. "Help a little." The voice is Alekel's. We wiggle against each other. His bald head beams yellow in the night. Never in my life have I sat inside a Cadillac. "Get in," he says, opening the door. This is a car I could learn to live with. Everything is pushbutton. Alekel slips in behind the wheel. I don't hear the motor. The Cad greases forward. I don't feel the road. Alekel doesn't have a hand on the wheel, merely a finger, and scarcely that except when he turns a corner.

"What are you doing to yourself, Southy?"

"Didn't you see what happened?"

He doesn't reply. He puts a fist to his mouth and belches. He pushbuttons open the window next to him to get some air. "Jesus, you stink," he says.

"I puked."

"No kidding."

He turns the Cadillac down a neon street, a bad beat for a cop, lined with beefburger joints and submarine shops and pizza parlors, quiet at the moment. It will be noisy later. He belches again. I have the strong heart. He has the weak one.

"I need some food and some sleep," I say.

"I'm taking you home."

"Take the long way. I want to talk. I know you saw what happend back there."

"You don't sound good. Why don't you shut up?"

"I'm weak as a rag. Otherwise I'm all right."

He reaches over and opens the glove compartment. There's a flask inside. "Go ahead," he says.

No, not with my stomach. I slap the compartment shut.

"Your father didn't drink either," he says. "Just made a living, that's all."

"I need a favor," I say.

"Ask," he says, smiling with thick lips, glad to be of help.

"I need the name of someone who will take care of two guys for me, one of whom you just saw."

He whistles and shakes his head sadly. "What are you asking something like that for? You asking for a hit-man? You crazy? I know what your kid meant to you, but don't ask something like that. They'll lock you up."

"Just give me a name. I'll make the contact."

"What name? There ain't no hit-men in Ramsey. And you don't get a hit-man just like that. You clear through channels."

"All I want is a name."

"Don't be a meathead. They'll laugh at you."

"It's a favor I'm asking of you."

"You don't give up, do you?" he says, and mentions a name, that of a misfit whose crimes are sexual, who periodically seizes a woman top-heavy with bun-

174

dles in a downtown parking lot, muffles her mouth, and for a few fast seconds feels her up.

"You're putting me on," I say, shoving a cigarette between my lips.

"Yeah, I am. What else can I do?" He glances at me. "You shouldn't smoke. It's no good for the lungs or the heart. Southy, what can I tell you?"

The Cadillac pulls up in front of my house, which is dark, even though I know Libby is in there, napping or simply sitting in a chair.

"I asked you to take the long way."

He turns my way with a finger still on the wheel. "Southy, what can I say to you? You know what I thought of your father, a gentleman, drank a beer now and then but never any of the hard stuff, and never any women in his life after your mother died. She was a fine woman. I didn't know her to speak to, but I used to see her with him. Good people, the both of 'em. I want to do something for you, not what you're asking because that's ragtime, right out of this world, but something so you can pull yourself together. You like this car of mine?"

"You going to give it to me?"

"You want to borrow it? You and your wife drive it down to Florida for me. I got a place down there. Actually you'll be doing me a favor because I don't like driving all that way. I'd rather fly down and have someone else drive the car down. You got the run of the place till the middle of January. That's when I'll be down. What do you say?"

"I don't know. That's awfully nice of you."

"Hey, what's the matter?" he says, giving me a light punch on the shoulder, maybe because there was a catch in my voice, maybe because when somebody wants to do something for me I feel very young, because I don't know how to accept things and I don't know how to refuse them. "Hey," he says, "you'll be missing most of the winter. Nothing but sunshine. If it rains, so what? It don't last."

175

What can I say? I'd have to leave my property. Trees emptying themselves of leaves and exposing my house. Thieves going from room to room in the dead of night.

"Al, I don't know, you know?"

He scoffs. "You worried because you're takin' my Cad? I got a T-Bird. I got anything I want. Don't worry about it." His expression is avuncular. "You get down there you might like it. I got a few connections, enough to get you a job, hotel dick or something. What d'you say?"

My brain is aching. Europeans dream of America, Australia, Africa, Asia. I have Florida in front of me, the sun, a glimpse of the Everglades. With a Cadillac I can be an explorer, an adventurer, a rover, with Florida only the beginning.

Alekel looks at his watch. He has somewhere to go. He has to get back to the club. "Talk it over with your wife," he says.

But I'm shaking my head, because I have a beautiful chill in my bones. I don't want Florida. I want winter, with its no noise at night, only the hard whiteness, the silent slabs of snow, the frozen-tight river. The short choppy days and long sleek nights. I've got birds to feed and paths to shovel.

"I don't want to go," I tell him.

20

THE HOUSE ISN'T LOCKED. IT NEVER IS, whether anybody is home or not. The bulb in the hall has burned out, but the streetlamp lays a little light in, mostly on the carpet and some on the wall. I edge into the living room where the dark is almost pure, and snap on a light which reveals the charm of the chair I expected Libby to be sitting in. I snap on another light, and the windows go wide. I appear in them. I'm everywhere. I'm on three sides of myself, and there I am, much clearer, in the wall mirror.

Libby's cigarette butts are in an ashtray, and her hair is in a brush left on the coffee table. She brushes her hair often, sometimes brutally, as if seeking a beautiful stroke of luck that will change everything. A blanket is on the couch. Sometimes she sleeps there. Her slippers and sweater are on the floor.

"Libby."

No reply, but I'm sure she's home. I move through the dining room into the kitchen where the fluorescent light blinks before it turns bright. A dirty cup is in the sink, along with the dumped insides, including the grounds, of the coffee pot which sits empty on the stove. The kitchen walls are orange and burnt brown, a relaxing combination. When we first moved in, the walls were bright enamel yellow, which made us feel as if we were in the yolk of an egg. The insides of the cupboards were painted red; a bloody yolk. They're still red. We never painted them over.

I check a closet. She's not in it . . . and she's not anywhere on this floor. She may be upstairs or down in the cellar or in the sub-cellar. There are many places to hide in this house, though I doubt Libby would be in the cellar, which is gloomy, or in the sub-cellar, where the dark is total. Upstairs is a better bet.

In our room I stand near the unmade bed. Our dirty clothes are heaped in a chair by the window. I throw my blazer there. There's a crowded bookcase in the corner. Forbush and his penguins are there.

"Libby."

The overhead light in Darcie's room fails to come on. It's the switch rather than the bulb. The lamp on her desk sheds a dull light over a pocket dictionary and a transistor radio. The astronauts and rock singers on the walls are grinning. I move away fast, as if I were a stranger and the real owners of the house, Pappa and Mamma Bear, were due back at any moment. Downstairs the phone is ringing.

My sister is on the line. She says, "We've got her."

"What do you mean, you've *got* her? Did you catch her or something?" I'm annoyed. This is my wife she's talking about.

"She's all right, Bobby. We've calmed her down."

"What was wrong with her?"

"Let me tell you when I see you."

"Tell me now."

A sigh. My sister has patience. She says, "She phoned. She wanted to talk to David. She became hysterical and said a lot of wild things to him."

"You mean she accused him."

"No, I don't think so. He couldn't understand half of what she said. We went right over. She was outside the house, standing on the stone wall. She wasn't dressed properly, and she was screaming at the cars going by."

"I don't believe that. What time was it?"

"About five o'clock. We tried to get you. We didn't know where. Bobby, she's very disturbed. She's snuggling. She's looking for a hollow."

178

"What does that mean?" I say, a curl to my voice.

"It means you shouldn't leave her alone so much. You could lose her forever in a way that would be horrible for both of you."

She's talking as if she were a full head taller than I. I don't like the tone of her voice, which is more professional than sisterly, as if she were a social worker and I the husband of a case.

"Do you want me to come over?"

"No, she's resting. She'll be sleeping soon. Come over tomorrow. Come for breakfast if you want."

"I'll be busy. I'll be over later. The afternoon maybe."

"I'd like to keep her for a few days."

"If she becomes a pain in the neck, send her home."

My sister says nothing. She doesn't know quite what to make of me. She could tell better if she could see my face. There'd be no problem if we had been closer as children.

"Listen," I say. "You're sure you've got her? I could swear she's here somewhere."

"I'll send her home if you want," my sister says stiffly.

"No. I've got a few things to figure out. This will be a good time to do it."

I return the house to darkness and lie on the couch with my revolver under the pillow. A glass of milk on the floor. I have drunk a little of it. It hasn't set well in my stomach. I pull the blanket around me, lie on my side, knees drawn up so that I can press my hands. I don't really sleep anymore. I doze into dreams that keep me awake so that I can watch myself. A private world that's sleepier than sleep. I'm slipping over the duff of a soundless forest where there are no little birds, no insects, no hanging larvae, only a pervasive odor as if from a swamp, that uncertain terrain where land and water battle to a draw. No winners, no losers. That vast period when the past was unrecorded and people weren't a part of it. And indeed there's a swamp before me, long and low-lying, a strange sun-gnawed brew thick with powerful reeds and platters of bright algae, with varieties of musk, eel grass, sago pondweed, a great peeling-off place for birds. Except there are none. There is, however, a small red round something floating motionlessly in the water. Slimed with mud but still distinguishable. A rubber ball. Found at last! I'm reeling from the discovery, not a recovery because I can't reach it, like knowledge you can't use but which nevertheless is exciting to have. The forest soars. It widens, and the ground becomes stonier and harsher. Ahead in a clear space is a weather sign stuck in a clump of rocks, words dug into the board: AGE OF REPTILES BEWARE. Instinctively I drop to a crouch, eyes and ears on the alert for a rustling, a crackling, a lifting-up, a flash of froth and a snap that can break bones. I'm on ground that isn't mine, that's eons away from being familiar. I'm ready however, to do battle, the return match of which, because of the relativity of time, because of sleep, because of dreams where man is more alert than alive, because of a dog's bark, has already been performed, has already been won. By me! A snarl twists out of my mouth. I want the blood of whatever I'm going to fight. My tongue's out and my ego's indecently exposed. I'm the savage who lives by his wits who hasn't appeared yet. I'm the brute with enough cunning to commit crimes.

"Southy."

I bolt up at the sound of my name, casting off sleep as if it were never there. "Jesus Christ," I say, "scare somebody!"

"Sorry," he says. Kilcoyne, standing in the October moonlight that has slipped into my house. "I don't think your bell works," he says. "I wanted to talk with you."

"Sit down." I make room on the couch, but he doesn't move. "Something wrong? Jimmy send you?"

"Jimmy sends his regards, that's all. Your wife all right now?"

"You heard about that, huh? She's at my sister's. She's fine."

"We heard she was distraught. We called your sister."

"Thank you."

He lets out a weary sigh. "If you don't settle down, Southy, things are going to go from bad to worse."

"Ah, you've been talking to Alekel. I can see he's told you things, though it's his word against mine."

"It's nobody's word, and some things I don't hear. Southy, why didn't you take him up on his offer? It's still open. It's something you can do for your wife. Christ, get her away from here."

His breath reaches me. He has had something to drink, which is unusual. I've heard he has a few highballs at home after dinner but never so that it would show. I notice now that his eyes are red, which makes them look doubly tired. He raises his hand to rub them, and I see the cancer stain on his wrist. Still the size of a dime. Skin cancer, his doctor has told him, is the easiest kind to take care of. You can at least see it. His wife keeps an eye on it, inspects it every morning. The last time that I saw her was at a policeman's ball, a scrawny gray-haired woman wearing a low-cut gown she wasn't used to. All I remember about her are her breasts, little lumps, as if someone without skill had made them for her by hand.

"Maybe I will sit," he says, and takes a chair facing me.

"What's the matter, Cap'n?"

"Nothing. I'm tired."

"You're troubled."

He smiles wearily. "No, Southy, tired."

"It must be hard, trying to keep everything clean for Jimmy."

"I've never had this much trouble before. It's taking a lot out of me."

"First time it's shown. You know, the way you slipped into the house here—if you were an assassin I'd be dead." I lift up the pillow and reveal the

181

revolver. "But I'd have got a shot off probably."

"Don't let your imagination run away with you," he says.

I drop the pillow. Suddenly I have a mental picture of the Captain and me in the dismal interior of a diner, not Nate's, but some place like it. Fast shuffles of food for people hunched against a counter, the Captain and me among them, anonymous men. My stomach growls. I had a hunger. Then it went. Now it's back.

"Everything out of hand," he says. "Unreal. That's what gets me down."

"Let me ask you something, Cap'n. Can you really make that kid's murder a suicide? Now that's unreal. Even the way he went down. The bullet hit him like a grape, you know. Splat! Like in war, Cap'n, like Mulligan and I were in the jungle."

The Captain points a slow finger. "Let me say something basic—and Jimmy O'Rourke doesn't enter into this, except he'd tell you the same thing. We try to look after our own. That's what it all adds up to. I know Mulligan's an asshole—hell, he might even go off his nut now and then. I don't know. I'm no doctor. But as a cop he's put his life on the line more times than not, which you tell me how many people appreciate. You yourself, you've had some close calls. We appreciate it. Count on one hand others who do. You might not even have to use fingers. The kid was scum, you know that, and no family except for a married sister. I've talked to her. She said the kid is better off dead. She's got two little daughters and she said he once tried to fool around with them the wrong way. Her husband's got a good job at Western Electric. They don't want any messy publicity. Can you blame them? Who needs it? Southy, admit something to yourself. Except for a couple of screwballs who killed a part of your life, this is a good city. Not many niggers and not that many spics, at least not yet, thank God. And when Jimmy's ready, we're going to take care of those two screwballs, nice and legal, because their alibi isn't going to hold up. So don't worry on that score. Worry about yourself. Think about Florida."

He rises from the chair, like a minister or a priest who has finished a visit, who may even be pleased with himself, having done a duty or a good deed, having left as a gift some damned good advice.

He put a hand to his mouth. Maybe he's feeling the couple of drinks he has had. "Go back to sleep," he says, and leaves as silently as he came in.

The night is mild and moonlit. I stand by the river. My approach frightened a beaver whose tail-slap on the water was as sharp as a rifle shot. The ripples remain. My dog used to bark at the beavers and plunge into the water after them, never getting anywhere near them.

The moon is like a hole in the sky, as if made by a giant finger, somebody trying to get into this world. It's not at all unreasonable to suppose the universe is a microscopic part of something billions of times vaster, to suppose we are micro-organisms, germs, that haven't been discovered yet. Undiscovered, we're uncontrolled.

In the moonlight the debris of the day is on the river: leaves, dust, scum, a Coca-Cola can. The current will wipe it away. Compared with other rivers, this one is clean. Some industrial waste shows up now and then but no raw sewage. Three or four years ago a rubber company accidentally dumped a tremendous amount of heavy fuel oil into the river. The inlet turned black, and so did the bullfrogs and mud turtles. The oil formed a rubbery skin on the water, through which the floundering young turtles couldn't break. I tried to help them with a pail and a net, and ruined shoes, socks, shirts and pants. After much squawking on my part, the rubber company hired a chemical company to flush out the inlet and throw sand around the bank, but to this day, whenever the bed of the inlet is disturbed, oil drifts to the surface and rainbows it. The effect is that of a sinister painting.

I've had some queer dreams about this river, big monster fish emerging from it, dog-like, wee-eyed and big-headed, as if I were getting a glimpse of the river and the way it used to be, God knows how long ago.

Regarding Mulligan and what he did: It was what you might call, at least almost, an honest murder. A gunfighter who reacts so fast his gun is emptied before he has a chance to think. I move back toward the house, throwing a long shadow on the silver ground.

The phone is ringing. I let it ring. I'm making something to eat, toast smeared thick with butter and peanut butter. Coffee is percolating, the aroma of it filling the kitchen. The ringing stops. Then it starts up again. Intuitively I know the caller is Libby. I almost don't bother to go to the phone, as if picking it up were a superfluous gesture, as if all I had to do was say hello and she'd hear me.

"Robert?"

I expected her voice to be punctured from sedatives. Instead it's merely crusty. I expected it to be full of rips and tears, as if a cat had been at it. Instead it's all of a piece.

"I might divorce you," she says. "It looks pretty much that way."

I expected her voice to be full of little things, like the bones of birds.

"Do you really think that would solve anything?" I ask.

"I don't know. I've got to give it thought."

"There's no rush, of course. We can do a lot of talking about it."

"Oh no," she says. "I'm sure I can come to a decision quicker than that."

"How's my sister treating you?"

"I'm comfortable."

"I'd rather have you home. Here. I miss you, Libby. Let me send a taxi for you."

"Oh no. I couldn't ever live there again."

There's a hot pain in my chest, as if something extraneous, like a bullet, were in it.

"Libby?"

She is no longer on the line.

21

FINE CRISP OCTOBER SUNSHINE AND A BOUNCE to my step and breakfast in my belly. I ate at Diadati's where I was waiting for Evelyn who didn't show up. I didn't expect her to because she didn't absolutely say she would. A number of other lawyers came in, briskly, like soldiers with their 201-files, but never files encased in such fine old leather briefcases, substantial enough to contain summaries of all the arguments in the world. Some of the lawyers nodded to me, men half-bald, half-handsome, certainly successful, somewhat admirable, with wives at home who were probably still pretty. I ate my breakfast, and a couple of cops came in. After split-second hesitations they decided against sitting with me.

I ate bacon and eggs and drank two cups of coffee and smoked three or four cigarettes. I read pages one and two of the *Boston Globe*. I could have read more but I had no interest in massacres in Vietnam and in students' riots on college campuses, none of which seemed particularly extraordinary. I rattled the rest of the paper and then put it to one side and chatted for a while with the busboy, a man of fifty who once was a client of Evelyn's. She got some money for him from an auto accident case. A shyster lawyer could have got him much more, particularly one with an arrangement with the investigating police officer who for a consideration would have altered his original report.

The sun brushing the tops of cars. A woman talking

to another, their language earthy and throbbing. A bounce to my step. Men leaning against storefronts, eyes on them the size of pigeon eggs. I'm passing places where I was yesterday, except then the sun was dying. Now it's rising.

The continuous facade of doors and windows, each pane of glass tossing out a nostalgic picture of myself, my puked-on blazer replaced by a camel's-hair jacket from another decade when shoulders were packed with padding. The street twists and narrows. There is a straggle of stubby trees and a few gaunt cars parked curbside near peeling tenement houses.

At first I choose the wrong house. The number on the door is wrong and the words chalked on it are obscene. Inside an old man opens his door, mistaking me for the mailman, deeply disappointed when he sees I'm not. All the same, recovering fast, he gives out a wealthy grin and an abundant hello. I ask for directions, and he says, "Two houses down, but watch out for the outside steps."

The steps creak and pull to one side; they bend with the tenement house which is old and rickety, too involved with itself, and marked for demolition under urban renewal. No dirty words on the door here, except that the door makes a nasty squeak when opened. It opens into a hallway that has been scrubbed, that shows that somebody has been on hands and knees with soap and water and disinfectant, at least on this landing. The stairs leading to other landings are filthy.

Courtemanche printed on a patch of white cardboard and thumbtacked to the door. I rap lightly. Gradually and then suddenly the door opens. The woman, on the stout side, has a moon-face and scratchy skin and briary gray-flecked hair and black eyes that pierce mine. Such a stare! As if all my secrets were known and always had been, as if *in utero* I had been psychoanalyzed and diagnosed and she had a record of the reading at her disposal.

"Come in," she says, as if we had met before.

A big threadbare room with doors leading off it,

with the same disinfectant smell that's in the hallway, with holy pictures clutching the wall, with a vase of plastic flowers planted on a table, with the shades lowered and the curtains closed so that one would think it were evening rather than morning.

"Sit down," she says with an accent that is Canuck. She snaps on a table lamp, and we sit facing each other in lopsided cushiony chairs. "Somewhere I know you," she says. Her words are quick, like her eyes whose blackness brings to mind the beginning of blizzards.

"My name is Southwark. Robert Southwark. I lost my daughter."

"Yes, yes, of course. I'm sorry for you. You have a suffering only a strong man can bear." At once I become ten times more interesting in her eyes. "Suffering can stalk you to the grave," she says. "You have to stand high."

"I'd like to talk to you about the two men who live upstairs."

She makes a deprecatory sound and drops back in her chair. "I'm tired of talking about those two." She tucks folded fingers under her chin. "You're a policeman. You know what I had to go through. Questions, questions! I told everything I knew. I don't lie." Suddenly she pulls her legs in and leans forward and puts her hands on her knees and her eyes pierce mine. "Do you want to listen to me? Troubles aren't with just one person. Give me that cigarette."

She tells me that she's an ex-nun born and raised in Canada, a product of the Provinces, a workhorse as a child, with parents and then nuns who beat her. She narrows her black eyes. "You think my life has been easy? Do you think locking yourself from the world is fun?" Puffing on the cigarette as if to get rid of it fast, she says that after leaving the convent and arriving in Ramsey—she has an aunt here who will have nothing to do with her—she spent a year looking for a suitable companion and then made a wrong choice, an unfeeling man of fifty, as cold and bone-chilling as the winds over the Provinces. With him, she says, it was as if she were back there. She describes his hard forehead, his tiny eyes ("Like this," she says, narrowing her eyes to slits), his massive and brutally clean-shaved jaw. He approached her in the way, she says, a Protestant minister probably approaches his wife, with no change of expression, no passion, no voice, just the stiff thing. She snaps her fingers. "That's how long it would take. He thought of just himself. What fun was that for me? He's gone now and I don't ever want to see him again."

"What's his name? Maybe I know him."

She shakes her finger. "Oh no. I don't tell you that."

"How long were you a nun?"

She laughs abruptly, opening her mouth and then snapping it shut. "Too long," she says.

"The two gentlemen upstairs. I don't suppose they're home."

"If they were you'd know it. The big one walks like an elephant."

"Then again I imagine they sometimes sleep late, so you wouldn't hear them."

"Most mornings they do. This morning they didn't. OK? Why don't you come right out and ask me what you want? I don't like to play games."

"Relax," I tell her. She has on a blouse that she must have ironed herself. It has a scorch mark. "Tell me some more about yourself."

"Uh-uh, there's nothing to say," she says, slumping in her chair and stretching her legs. But her eyes flash, and with a fluttering of lips she tells me her opinion of nuns. Women without looks, she says, without charm, without warmth, sanctimonious old bitches for the most part, each clutching God like a hen farmer holding a rooster by the neck, some of them batty, all with years of their lives wasted, shot to hell.

"But that's all over for you. You're beginning anew."

She gives out a short laugh, perhaps without meaning to. "I don't like the neighborhood here," she says and, while stretching her legs again, crosses them at the ankles. She doesn't like the young toughs who roam the streets and back yards at night, all of them sadistic. The grisly sight of cats that have been slaughtered with knives, ripped apart, chopped up, heads kicked to one side, or just as bad, garrotted with packing-case wire and left hanging on a clothes line. She doesn't like the derelicts who sleep on the outside steps at night, sick men all of them, death warmed over, all of them already more or less committed to the ground; so they have no business on her doorstep.

"Maybe in time you'll meet a good man."

Again the involuntary laugh as she grabs the arms of her chair and pulls herself to her feet. "I offer you a cup of coffee in the kitchen."

"I accept."

I sit at her heavy chrome-legged table and watch her scoop sugar from a bag to a bowl which is cracked. She pours heated-up coffee into mugs that look as if they were swiped from a diner. Nate's. I smile at her.

"This is nice of you."

"I don't mind," she says, taking a chair opposite me. She drops four spoonfuls of sugar into her coffee and stirs it cautiously, like a gravedigger fearful that the scrape of his shovel will rouse a body from its coffin. She sighs and then takes a sip of the coffee, the spoon still in the mug. As if completing a thought, she says, "None of us has it easy."

"That's true."

For the first time she smiles brightly and wide. The purpose is to show me her teeth which, she says, are false. Years of an improper Canadian diet, from which, she says, some of her brothers and sisters died, five in all, not including nephews and nieces and cousins.

"So you see," she says, "we've all had our tragedies."

She pulls something up from the floor, her pocket-book, and lays it on the table, opens it, and withdraws a soiled card with something written on it.

"Listen to this," she says, holding the card to one side to read it. "In 1830 the world's population was a thousand million and double that in 1930. In 1960 it reached three thousand and will be double that by the end of the century. What do you think of that?"

"There's no arguing with figures."

"That's right, and no arguing with those who don't marry do the world a service, huh?"

She waits for agreement. I nod.

"Women who don't marry," she says, "should receive stipends. What do you say about that?"

"I would think they should."

"Of course they should. The reverse was true in France after the war. Those who produced children were rewarded. That's not needed anymore."

She waits for me to respond. I merely smile. She takes something out of her pocketbook, a snapshot which she passes across the table. "That's him," she says. A man with a husk-like head, minature eyes, and a Neanderthal jaw.

"I don't know him," I say.

"I wish I never did," she says and takes the picture back. I point to the ceiling.

"When do you think they'll be back"

"Who knows?"

"Do they mean anything special to you?"

She takes her time answering. She closes her pocketbook and takes a sip of her coffee. "They never treated me bad," she says.

"They ever give you money?"

"What's that to you? I'm not a prostitute."

"I know you're not. I was just asking. I know they were friendly with you. They still are, I guess."

Suddenly she laughs. Suddenly, in a joking way, she tells me she had expected something much more between the legs from Primack. She whispers. A disappointing dink curled like a snail against his balls. She snorts. But not bad once he got going.

I smile and make a snorting sound myself. "What about Poggio?"

She throws up her right hand. "Never touched me. He just liked to watch."

We share the humor of that and sip our coffee. Then her smile fades.

"What's the matter?" she says. "You think I should still live like a nun? You think I don't have any blood in my veins?"

"I'm sure you do."

"What stipend do I get?"

"I don't know."

"When they wanted to give me money they just did it. I never asked. They weren't stingy, not like that whose picture you saw."

We sit looking at each other for a while. Her eyes are making some kind of assessment. She views my camel's-hair.

"That's a nice jacket," she says.

"It's an old one."

"But it must have cost a lot."

She exudes a smile, one I suppose she means to be fetching. She pushes herself away from the table and stands, brushing a wrinkle from her blouse and another out of her skirt. She steps near me so that I have to look up at her over her breasts. She makes a gesture with one finger.

"You wait a minute, all right?"

I know where she's going. I know what she's going to do. I give her a moment, only a moment, and then follow her as far as the doorway of the bedroom, which is in semi-darkness. The shades are drawn, but they're tattered and sunlight tears through. Trinkets glitter from the top of a bureau. There's a glow on the far wall: a miniature near-naked Christ as a beautiful man with a perfect body in an agonizing situation. The bedspread is quilted and rose-colored. She may have

191

made it herself. The closet door is open. She's behind it. She peeks around the edge.

"What's the matter?" she says lightly. "Can't you wait?"

"There's one thing I'd like to ask you. The morning it happened to my daughter, you were with them during the—"

"What? Yes. That's what I told the police."

"And you're absolutely certain of that."

"I don't want to be cross-examined."

"I'm sorry. You'll forgive me, won't you?"

"Yes," she says, and then steps from behind the door. I turn my eyes. "You're a strange one," she says.

A glint of pink. I've never seen a woman in a corset before. Hers shines like slippery armor. She has her hands over her breasts. Her face is becoming unreal; her hair is rougher, and her ears no longer match, and her eyes are gazing inward as if they'd flipped, and her nose is knotted. Her nostrils are like nailheads. Her mouth breaks open as if something forced it to.

"Come in," she says.

I have something in my eye. I have to rub it out.

"Come on," she says urgently. She's in bed. She's removing her corset under the covers.

I take a single step into the room, and she smiles from the pillow. Her mouth is like the flare of a large safety match. Her teeth are out. Uppers and lowers are on the nightstand beside the bed.

"I can't stay," I tell her. "But I want you to tell them I was here looking for them. Tell them I'll be back."

She says something I don't hear. I've turned away. "Wait!" she cries. "At leatht leave me thomething!"

She wants it in her hand. She wants to see how much it is. "Bathtard!" she says, thinking it's a dollar. It's a ten. "Thank you," she says.

Like a mouse I climb the stairs to the second landing. I couldn't pick a lock if my life depended on it. The door, however, opens as soon as I touch the knob. The same layout as downstairs, one large room with others leading off it. I squat and loosen the laces on my shoes. Carrying my shoes in one hand and holding my revolver in the other, I explore the tenement. One big bed. Blankets but no sheets and no pillows. Newspapers on the floor. Dirty laundry in a corner, the way my father and I used to throw ours. A few suits and sports jackets in the closet, some shirts and ties on a hook. A depressing untidiness about everything. A bathroom without toilet paper. Water dripping from the tub tap. Slivers of soap, two toothbrushes, and one razor on the edge of the sink. A magazine on the floor near the john—*Playboy,* its cover coarse and blistered where it has been pissed on. Coffee, Coffeemate and sugar are the only items in the kitchen cupboards. Dirty cups on the tables. Saucers used as ashtrays are overflowing. Nothing in the fridge, not even beer. They eat out of diners, out of Nate's.

Untidy, filthy in places, but absolutely clean of anything that could be used against them. Not even a firecracker.

22

CLOUDS APPEARED IN MID-AFTERNOON, AND ever since the sky has threatened rain. Now the sun is vanishing for good, and the sky every so often gives out a distant rumble, as if from a bass drum. It is that uncertain hour when headlights glow on some cars and not on others.

I'm behind the wheel of a parked car, sitting against the door, one leg stretched down the length of the seat. I walked a lot this afternoon, like a sailor trying to recapture the feel of land. A couple of times I heard the screech of sirens, a terrible sound, as if someone's head were being chopped off. I ate three hot dogs and drank two Cokes in a canteen operated by a Puerto Rican who understood English but couldn't speak it well. I did the talking, mostly about baseball, heroes of the past. He had heard of Ted Williams, naturally, but Bobby Doerr, Tex Hughson and Jim Tabor were strangers. "Who?" he'd say, and I'd say, "Who hell! Jim Tabor was a terror at third, a redneck, a boozer, ignorant as they come, but with one of the strongest arms in baseball." I was quoting my father who used to take me to Fenway on Sundays. Later I had a beer in a small tavern patronized by men out of work not for just a long time, but forever, like ten or fifteen years. A rank odor in the place, as if from a cat box.

I don't know who owns the car I'm in. It is a black Chevrolet, similar to the one I had, but not as old. I climbed into it because it's parked near Nate's. It may belong to the waitress. If so, I won't be bothered, because she won't be out until midnight.

Now nearly every car has headlights burning. An old man who looks as if he had many medical problems shuffles by, craning his neck. The sun is dead, the sky elegiac. A young pregnant woman approaches the car with sideway steps of a crab, her condition an obvious rotten piece of luck. Her hands are clenched. They are red, like rubber balls. She appears untouchable. Too many exposed wires. She glances back at Nate's, as if hungry, though not for food, and continues on.

Many years ago I took Libby to a fancy place in Boston where we dined against fiddle and pianoforte, against the soft discourse of other diners lost in muraled surroundings. Libby liked the feel of an ornate fork in her fingers and French food in her mouth. Neither of us had been in such a place before (and we haven't since). I left a tip that didn't please the waiter, who followed us quietly to the door and became insulting.

A young man with quick feet comes out of Nate's. He has the Ramsey *Gazette* under one arm. I've already read it. A small piece on page one about a youth's body being found. Bullet in the head. Self-inflicted, according to a preliminary report. The young man falters. He has spotted the pregnant girl down the street, and his face turns cold and haggard, as if struck by an unseasonable frost. Abruptly he walks away in the opposite direction.

The windshield is rain-flecked. The street glistens from a fine spray, and the occasional traffic hisses. Headlights cut wild pictures on the rain, as if the dark were a cave and the rain a paint. The door of Nate's swings open.

Poggio, one ballet step ahead of Primack, appears lost in rapid thought. In the neon of Nate's, his blond head appears blue. He squints my way, but he doesn't see anything because his thoughts are elsewhere. He's

195

elsewhere. The self-absorption of a singing canary that ignores everything around it, the shell of seed, the leaf of lettuce, the water, the egg biscuit. He doesn't see me, but his big friend does. Primack nudges Poggio from behind, and for a moment each stiffens.

I'm out of the car, and my feet are slipping on the wet sidewalk. A fear that I'm not going to make it, that I'm going to fall.

For safety's sake, I've slowed my step. Primack grunts and edges in front of Poggio, as if to give me a welcoming hand. His fists are weapons. I keep that in mind as I slog toward him as if through shin-deep snow.

His eyes hard and busy, he moves to meet me as my voice cries out like a garbled radio message and my revolver like an object for sale, one as substantial as the other is not. He is fast, but his fist becomes snared in the rain and in the single bang-sound of my gun, the shock of which shoots up my arm and threatens to burst my brain.

Primack stiffens to his full height and stands tall with a horrendous hangdog expression. I have a perfect picture of him as a boy standing firm for his mother to break a hairbrush over his head. I have no idea what part of him holds the bullet, but I hope it's high.

Poggio appears stunned and stands cornered in the rain. I stare at his face, which is too smooth, practically unlined, artificial-looking, neuter, theatrical.

"You prick!" he says and goes for his knife, and I remember that he knows how to cut skin and sinew. I squeeze the trigger. Impossible to bring a bullet back even if you wanted to.

Primack is lying on the sidewalk. I didn't know he had fallen. He is stretched out as if he had been examined and medicated and now were sleeping, except his eyes are wide open, disbelief in being dead.

Poggio is on his knees and clenching his head as if from a skullache, and he makes a small sound, as if

196

the child in him were reappearing. Gently he falls to one side.

I walk away rapidly, ignoring the slurping-up in my stomach. I figure that if I can make it to the alley, roughly the distance from home plate to first base, I'm safe.

23

THE FENCE IS EASY TO SCALE, BUT THE WOOD
is slippery from the rain, which is light and steady.
Nailheads I didn't know were there rip skin and
clothes as I drop to the ground on the other side.

The grass is slippery and the earth sloshy. The darkness is dug into the trees and into the house ahead.
All the curtains and shades are drawn and pulled.

In the dark the bulkhead appears solid, but as soon
as I yank at the handle screws, hinges, and other
pieces of metal tinkle, pop, and roll into the rain. The
hole leading into the basement is ink-black. No man's
land. The steps going down are steep. They're tricky.
I prevent a fall only by throwing out my hands and
grabbing a post which grinds my cuts. I cry out.

Shivering, I squat, rock on wet heels, cuddle myself, hold my belly and retch at gentle intervals. I kiss
and lick my cut hands. The plight of Albert DiSalvo.
I know it firsthand.

Eyes somewhat adjusted to the dark, I move toward
a hum, the abdominal sound of a boiler with warmth
seeping through it. Matchlight reveals shapes, shadows, elliptic lengths of overhead pipes, sheets of
something shiny and ghostlike against a wall. I reel a
little, as if caught in a cave, as if encountering geolog-
ical patterns of the mind: the silhouettes of dream-
scape, the peaks of elation, the gullies of depression,
fissures of madness. The flame burns my fingers and
I jam them into my mouth.

The ghostlike stuff is filthy plastic sheeting, like that which drapes drycleaning: it hangs in tatters from ceiling to floor. I light another match, careful of the flame, because the stuff could go up in a flash. It hides cardboard cartons stacked atop one another. I strike another match and inspect stenciled markings. RAINCOATS. OVERSHOES. CURTAINS. Dates dropping back twelve, fifteen years. PULLOVERS. CARDIGANS. SCATTER RUGS. A date eighteen years ago. PARKER INC ATTN WREN.

A door opens. Her voice: "Who's down there?"

She has no fear of me, whoever I am. She stands in the lighted doorway at the top of the stairs, her eyes straining to see where I am. She snaps on an overhead light. Rouge on her cheeks. In the old days she didn't wear any.

"I can see you," she says. "Get away from there."

Her ears are little shells. Her dress is severe but stylishly short. Her blue-gray hair is tight. Her stance is stiff.

"Get in the light where I can see you."

I do. I move to the bottom of the stairs and give her a half-grin.

It takes a moment or so for her to recognize me. The lid on her right eye is droopy, which it never was before. The skin around her neck is noticeably wrinkled. But she still has her imperial air.

"How did you get in?" she says.

"The bulkhead."

"Why?"

"That takes some explaining."

"What do you want?"

"I'm hurt."

I raise my hands which are in worse condition than I thought. Gouges in the palms. Messy skin and raw flesh. I climb a step and she shouts, "Hold it!" Some of her tight hair has come loose. "What's happened to you?" she says. "Why do you look that way?"

"I'm drenched. It's raining and I've been walking in it. No car."

"You have no business here."

"I know," I say and climb more steps. Her droopy eye twitches. Her face is lit. She has been drinking.

We stand in the living room. I tracked mud through her kitchen and am dripping it on the rug. "Let's see your hands," she says and asks how I hurt them. I tell her. On her fence. She gets a whiskey bottle, good stuff, V-O, and I hold out my hands and she splashes them. I don't flinch. "Brave, aren't you?" she says, her face flushed and for a moment funny. "Sit down," she says and we sit in opposite overstuffed chairs. She glances at her wrist watch. "I'll give you a few minutes, no more. Are you in trouble?"

"Probably, but it's too soon to tell."

She puts her hands together and interlaces her fingers. She has long nails. Still a very prim and proper woman with an airtight bearing, with legs that a younger woman wouldn't be ashamed of. She tilts her head and says, "It's unfortunate. You're one of those persons who goes from bad to worse, no matter what the circumstances. Where in God's name did you get that jacket?"

I glance down at my camel's-hair, which, from the rain, looks like a drowned animal. She has a glass in her hand. I don't know how it got there. It's not V-O. It's gin or vodka. Her dress has risen on her thigh. She is assessing me.

"You're losing your hair," she says.

"I guess I am, slowly. It shows when it's wet."

She rearranges herself in the chair, skinking deeper into it. Gently she sloshes her drink. "You've carried yourself well, Robert. Having your daughter's funeral absolutely private—just you and your wife—was exactly right. I thought well of you for it."

"You never really knew my Darcie, did you?"

"There are a lot of people I don't really know. She wasn't singled out."

"You know the twins. Joan's boys."

"I pay for their education, Robert. That's all." She

is smiling very slightly and her eye is no longer drooping. "What were you doing in my cellar?"

"It was the easiest way to get in."

"I think they call that breaking and entering in the
nighttime," she says.

"Why do you find me personally repugnant, Auntie?"

She sighs with a smile. "That's a funny way to put
it. No, the simple fact is I've never had any feeling
for you one way or another. Is that hard to understand? I brought your sister up, not you."

"I think I understand."

She shifts in her chair. I don't think she can get out
of it. I think she holds her liquor well but at the moment it's a weight on her. She smooths her dress
down.

"I think you'd better tell me why you're here." Her
eyes narrow. "Are you here to do me bodily harm?"

I smile. "That's a funny way to put it."

"Are you?"

"No."

She puts the empty liquor glass to one side and
crosses her legs. "Don't be ashamed," she says.
"Very few men can stand alone. They need a woman
or somebody to protect them. Your father had a
friend, a dirty man as I remember, who used to look
after him."

"LeBoeuf."

"I didn't know his name. I only heard about him.
He couldn't speak English."

"Yes, he could, it was merely broken."

"He had only one leg."

"One hand. He lost the other to a buzzsaw."

"I don't know about that. But maybe you ought to
look him up, if he's still alive."

"He's dead, I'm sure."

We stare at each other. Her right eye is drooping
again. She's tired. She's thinking of something else.
She says, "Your sister has been a disappointment.

201

orking with Negroes and that sort of thing. I understand from David she smokes marijuana."

"I think he lied to you."

"Well." She tries to sit up straighter and doesn't quite make it. I think she's sorry she said what she did, as if that were intimate information I had no business knowing. She looks at her watch. "I still don't know what you want here, Robert."

"I'm in an awkward situation that could be better explained in the morning. I wonder if you could put me up for the night."

Through what must be sheer will, because sweat pops out on her face, she rises from her chair and stands firmly sideways, sort of like a bayonet stuck in the ground. Her old self. She could very well be back in Parker, Inc.

She walks stiffly to another part of the room where she picks up a telephone and dials a digit, then another.

"Who are you calling?"

The finger pauses, poised in the instrument. "The police," she says, "unless you leave this instant."

I rise from my chair and we exchange a highly communicative stare which, in its own way, is very private, quite intimate. We are as close as we'll ever be.

I head for the front hallway.

"Uh-uh," she says, still holding the phone but her finger no longer in the dial. "Same way you came. Through the cellar."

I can't help smiling. It's all a game, an act, except she's serious. If we were sitting together I'd slap my knee and then hers. If we were friendlier I'd play the part of a hotshot, of a dramatically decisive fellow who'd get on her nerves after a while.

"There's one more thing, Auntie. I think you'll learn in the morning, or maybe even now if you turn on the TV and catch the late news, that you have a bill to settle with me. Some cold cash, Auntie. David's never going to be bothered by those two men again, and for that matter neither am I. I think I'm making myself clear."

She doesn't say anything. Nothing changes on her face. It's inertly unresponsive.

"You can settle the bill at your convenience, Auntie, but please don't take too long."

She appears to be clutching the telephone table for support, and I'm smiling. I can picture her twenty years from now, ancient and quivering and queer, bent and spoon-fed. At the same time I can picture her as an old man from coyote country, hair like sage, raw eyes, remorseless mouth, an Adam's apple like a little skull.

"A question, Auntie. In the web of history is man the spider or the struggling fly? You want to know something? Spiders masturbate. That's the truth. I read it."

"I think you'd better get out of here," she says in a voice that is cold sober.

"I have a long walk ahead of me."

"Leave by the front door."

"Yes, that's good, that's better, but I don't think I can scale that fence again, not with my hands."

"The gate unlatches from the inside."

She accompanies me to the door. There are locks to undo and a chain to slide. She watches me from the corner of her eye, fearful maybe that I'm going to do something to her, on guard because she may feel she's getting rid of me too easily.

"Are you going to get on the phone as soon as I leave, Auntie?"

With a cold reassuring look she says, "I never go out of my way to involve myself with the police."

"You hold your liquor well, Auntie, but you should've given me one for the road."

She would like to shut the door in my face, but she can't because I'm only halfway out. The rain is now

203

a drizzle. I pull up the collar of my camel's-hair and smile at her. Her eye is drooping.

"On the other hand, a hot cup of coffee would have been better, Auntie. We could have chatted some."

I'm smiling broadly, but I step backwards into the rain and let her close the door in my face.

24

As soon as you open the door you greet yourself, or scare yourself. There's a mirror. A tall rectangular piece of glass that's clean and stunning in the night-light. It's on the wall flanking the stairs that lead to the apartments. The walls and corners and stairs: simple and stark and fast, not elaborate as in the building where the Tarshi girl lives.

Beautiful stairs. No carpeting but no creaking either. Except I leave mud on them. In the mirror I appeared as a victim of something, my head battered from the rain, my camel's-hair stained and blotched. Legs giddy from a hike scarcely remembered. My house was black. I passed it from the opposite side of the street, inspecting it from the corner of my eye. A speeding taxi lit it up. A police cruiser was pulling out of the driveway. I leaped behind a bush, and stayed there long after I didn't have to.

I press the little buzzer once and wait.

The door opens, and her face is big from sleep that's been interrupted. The frosty hair is mussed, the curls scattered over her forehead and peeking out behind her ears and rising on the back of her head. She has on a robe, pajamas under it. Her feet are bare.

"You're not surprised," I say.

"Not in the least," she says with what amounts to sadness. At the same time she's wary.

"My appearance is deceiving," I say. "I'm not violent, no matter what you may have heard, taking for granted you've heard something."

"Come in," she says.

I lean against her kitchen table. She doesn't know quite what to do with me or with my smile, which is contrite.

"I'm sorry, Evelyn. I never in my life thought I'd become a pain in the ass to somebody."

"Do you want me to phone your sister?"

"No." I look at my watch. "This is horrible. Three in the morning. I'm sorry, really."

"I heard on the radio what happened," she says.

"I heard the same thing, but tell me about it."

"Those two men who bothered your brother-in-law were murdered. On the sidewalk in the Lower End. Am I telling you something you don't know?"

I smile understandingly. "You think I did it."

"I hope to God you didn't."

"I'm not sorry it happened. There's no way I could be. But I didn't do it. I did a lot of walking tonight but nowhere near the Lower End. I don't like the place."

"Is that the truth, Southy?" Her face is brightening. "You had nothing to do with it?"

I raise my right hand.

"But why have you been walking in the streets? And why are you here now?"

"Because I've become a pain in the ass even to myself."

I have the use of her father's bedroom to change into something warm. The camel's-hair goes on a hanger. The old man has a rugged knit sweater that must be too big for him because it fits me. I keep on my own pants but slip on a pair of his woolen fireman's stockings. He's a Mason. His little lapel pin is on the bureau. I wonder whether he has a diary which I could steal and read. Then at his bedside I could frighten him to death with inside information, as if I were God Almighty. If I were that sort of person.

Evelyn has slippers on now, and her hair is brushed, and her robe is more secure. We sit down to a pre-dawn breakfast of bacon and eggs, coffee from an electric perk. I have three eggs. She has one. I have several slices of bacon and toast. Starved, I eat like an animal. She watches me like one.

"Who do you think killed them?" she says.

"Anyone could have. They lived that kind of life."

Her face is settled and solid. "Southy, if you did it, maybe we'd better talk about it."

"Why? Do you want to be my lawyer now?"

"I'm not an experienced criminal lawyer but I can suggest those who are."

"I know who they are, and I plead not guilty."

"Why'd you walk the streets?"

"I told you."

She napkins her mouth. Her crayon-blue eyes don't leave me. I finish my breakfast.

"Southy, you had every good reason to want them dead. You more than anyone else in the world."

"But that's not evidence, and their being dead isn't changing anything, isn't helping anybody, except maybe my brother-in-law."

She pours coffee for us. She's a big person for a woman, but her wrists are slim. Small-boned. Soft-boned. She accepts a cigarette. This is more cozy than in Diadati's.

"Are you a saint now?" she says.

I can't tell whether she's being sarcastic or sympathetic. But I'm one up on her, I think. Trying to get information from me is like pulling meat from a lobster's claw. What does come out is tasty.

"I rather like that," I say. "Saint Southy."

"I like Sergeant Southy better, don't you?"

"I'm on an indefinite leave of absence."

"Southy, why in God's name did you ever let yourself get mixed up with David Parker's problems?"

I'm surprised at her and say so. "The question is pointless."

I lie on her father's bed. Her idea. She says she'll wake me before she leaves. I use her father's bathrobe as a blanket. It's an old one. He got all new stuff when he went into the nursing home, cash purchase by Evelyn at Parker, Inc. Leather slippers, all of that.

The sun is rising. I move to the window to watch it. The trees are picking up their colors. The clouds are small, like puffs from a pipe. I strip naked and put on the old man's robe.

The dishes are gone. The kitchen table is clear, as if I had never breakfasted at it. No clutter. No stains on the stove. A clean floor. A clean everything. She's showering.

She should have locked the bathroom door. She should have known I wouldn't sleep. As soon as I slip inside, the steam wraps around me like bunting. The spray-sound of the shower is terrific. Body-bruising. Her shadow rocks behind the plastic curtain. Her right hand works the soap. Her robe and pajamas are on a hook. On top of the hamper are my fetishes, her bra and panty-girdle, laid out for wear. She bumps the curtain with her behind and for a second it shows up bright and pink. It's much bigger than Libby's. Libby's is tight. Hers is fullblown. I call her name, and at once she screeches.

"Get out of here!" Her shadow is frantic as she tries to turn off the spray. "Get out of here I said!" Her voice is nearly hysterical and full of outrage. The spray is off. Her shadow is in a corner. My robe is open, and that thing of mine is hard, high and lopsided.

Tears in her outrage and another screech as, with a jagged swoop, a scraping of rings, I rip back the shower curtain. "Don't!" she says, her blue eyes blazing and her shoulders burning with water droplets and her breasts full and jellying. Her belly bulges and then curves into the triangle of messy wet hair which has scattered itself.

I extend a hand. "Come on."

The flush in her face is from outrage that originates in the marrow. Her indignation is total. No attempt to

208

cover herself as she ignores my hand and steps past me, my eyes on her breasts.

"What's the matter?" she says, her voice half breaking. "You've never seen them this size before? The Mulligan woman doesn't have them?"

I grab her and twist her to me and try to punch it to her, but she uses her fists like hammers against my face, methodically mad blows against nose, cheekbones and temples. I get nothing into her, but she receives something from me all the same, a deep shudder, as if my head were cleaved in half and both pieces were screaming to get back together. Also my hurt hands are aching. I let her go.

She has no breath with which to speak. She reaches for her robe, but I snatch it away from her. She reaches for her underwear, my fetishes, but I push her hand away. One step behind her, an eye on her rump, I follow her into her bedroom and head her off when she heads for the closet.

"You'll pay for this," she says, her voice clear and plastic.

I push her onto the bed, but without her help, with her head turned to one side and her eyes staring at nothing, it's impossible to penetrate. I work hard, but it's a dry useless hump. A bee burrowing into an artificial flower.

"Stop it," she says finally. Her voice has changed. The outrage is gone, along with the panic and the plastic. What's there is a woman's patience. "Stop it before you hurt yourself," she says.

I roll off her. She covers herself with the bedspread and lies staring at the ceiling. For many moments she is silent. Then she says, "Why, Southy?"

"It's something any man might have done," I say with a crust I can't scrape off my voice.

"Is it something you have against women, or is it me personally?"

"That's a rough question. I don't have an answer."

"You killed them, didn't you, Southy?"

"Yes."

She throws off the bedspread and stands, all bubbies and belly, her face drained of color, her legs trembling. She backs away from me. I'm afraid she's going to scream, really go out of her head. But her voice is solid. "You get out of here," she says. "You get out of here now."

She puts on some kind of wrap and follows me to her father's room and watches me dress, her hand on her forehead. Neither of us speaks. We could drown in our own silence. She takes me to the door. "Don't!" she says when I start to say something. "Just get out of here."

Husky sunlight after a night of rain, some of it reflected in the puddles. People are appearing out of the apartment buildings to the left and right, young marrieds, middle-aged school teachers with tenure and nothing to worry about, businessmen with slim briefcases. Cars pulling out of their places. A Buick touches a station wagon. No damage, but the drivers get out and look anyway. There's much inspection.

I notice I'm drawing attention because I'm walking with too much swagger. I spot the Tarshi girl.

She's with a new beau. He has a long head and springy hair and an electronic air about him, a plugged-in individual at Raytheon or Avco or Western Electric, one of those places. She hangs onto his arm. Something different about her. Her dress is too short and of a color that doesn't suit her, and her face is animalized with cosmetic paint and neon eye-shadow. She catches sight of me.

She hastens her step and that of her beau, and he's trying to find out why, his eyes darting this way and that. Over her shoulder she gives me a second look. Her beau has a Grand Prix, a long heavy car with a hood that reflects the falling leaves and with a door that opens wide and handsome. She leaps inside, and he hurries around to the driver's side, aware that something is wrong and that I'm the cause of it.

210

I position myself so that the car has to pass me. When it does I do nothing. I have no strength in my hands.

I follow the stone wall which, crumbling in places but quite solid up ahead, leads to my property. It's almost as if my property were coming to me, Birnam Wood marching toward Dunsinane.

25

PAUL JORDAN, SEEDY-LOOKING IN THE SUN-shine, waits at the top of the driveway. Captain Kilcoyne comes down it. He steps carefully down the stone steps to the inlet where my mind is taken up with the swamp maple which throws its massive shadow across the river. I remember watching the maple last fall when it dropped its first flaming feather.

"Your gun," says Kilcoyne, his hand extended, his arm a board.

"I don't have it." I open the camel's-hair and show an empty holster.

"Where is it? In the river? In the mud? It'll be messy to find but not that difficult."

"It was stolen, Cap'n. By a person or persons unknown. Peaceful here, isn't it?"

The whispering and falling of leaves from the swamp maple. Leaves from upriver trees float with the current, a colorful armada. Kilcoyne steps closer to the inlet. A water bug is sprawled on the surface like a corpse. A bullfrog squeaks like a stricken bird, leaps, and disappears into the mud.

"It's no use," says Kilcoyne.

The water bug is skimming along the surface now, like a hockey player who has stolen the puck and is racing down-ice with no one near him, except that the goalie is getting bigger, is ballooning!

"We can't help you," he says.

212

The water bug is gone. A frog bigger than the one that vanished got it.

"I don't need any help. I've done nothing wrong."

He sighs wearily and I smile. I feel safe. Here by the river I'm attuned to old rhythms and safe sounds.

"I'm convinced, Cap'n, if someone hadn't gotten them, they'd have gotten me."

"We'll never know now," he says and glances in the rising direction of Paul Jordan, who looks our way but pretends he doesn't see us. All the same, he moves halfway down the driveway, so that he's not so visible from the road.

"Maybe I ought to talk to Jimmy. What d'you think, Cap'n?"

He shakes his head. "Jimmy doesn't want to talk to you. Later maybe. Not now."

"Maybe I'll blow the whistle on what Mulligan did to that kid?"

"Who's going to hear it, Southy?"

I glance in Paul Jordan's direction. "He's got me covered, hasn't he, Cap'n?"

"In a manner of speaking."

"I'm not dangerous."

"If I thought you were, I wouldn't have come down here."

"I thought we took care of our own, Cap'n. What happened?"

"To a point, Southy. Then it's impossible."

He moves a step or so away from the water. The ground was sinking where he was standing. Dragonflies are flying around the dying stems of cattails.

"Do you want to tell me anything about it?" he says.

"I'm trying to forget things, Cap'n. I'm trying to shuffle images like cards. Besides, you haven't warned me about my rights."

"That's because you've got cards, Southy, maybe some you don't even know about. No jury is going to condemn you for what you did. Too many extenuating circumstances. You were bound to crack temporarily."

"I could get off with a few years, you mean."

"That's right, and be a bit of a hero to boot."

"You talk like you got witnesses."

"You were seen."

"But not identified."

"And we talked to the Courtemanche woman."

"With or without her teeth? She's suicidal, you know." I'm jingling coins in my pocket. I didn't know I had any. "We should never take a glum approach to life, Cap'n."

"I wish we had a choice, Southy. On your own you should come down to the station and make a statement. With your lawyer, of course."

"With my lawyer. Cap'n, I get a physical thrill just thinking about it. Look, can you give me a little time? Twenty-four hours. I've got to see my wife and explain things, and make sure she's going to be taken care of."

"Your sister owes you that much."

"She sure does. And I'd like to close my house, protect it against the elements. What d'you say?"

He doesn't say anything. The sunshine shows up the weaved fabric of his face and the paper appearance of his teeth. He's got mud on his shoes. I smile. I feel imprisoned only by the weight and bulk of my clothes. Stripped, I'm free.

"Twenty-four hours, Southy. But if you don't show up we'll have to come after you."

"Do me a favor. Send Mulligan. I think I could take him."

He stares hard.

"I'm only kiddin', Cap'n."

He joins Paul Jordan in the driveway and they walk to the top of it without looking back. Paul, I'm sure, feels lousy. We weren't buddies, but we were partners at times.

The leaves on the river are carried by a slow but steady current, each leaf available for a passenger. I climb the driveway. My dog used to run it and stop short at the opening. I trained him well in that respect.

A piece of traffic floating past my house comes loose. An unobtrusive car, color gray, settles at the curbless sidewalk. The driver, alone, waits for my approach and then shifts from the wheel to the passenger window where he rests an arm on the ledge. He has a bony hand, and his eyes are shielded with blue-tinted sunglasses.

"You got a second?" he says.

"Sure," I say, bending at the waist to see him better.

"You know who I am?"

"Sure. I've watched you work in court. You're a pretty good lawyer, but I don't think you've got a chance against Jimmy."

"My name will be on the ballot anyway. Personally I think I've got a good chance, otherwise I wouldn't be running. Those two murders last night aren't going to hurt me. The city's on the map again, and people are pretty uptight."

"Yes, I'd imagine they are."

"Why don't I get to the point," he says. His sunglasses have slipped down on his nose. He pushes them back. "I think you're in big need of a lawyer. Maybe I can help."

"In return for what?"

"Tell me what really happened behind the brakelining factory."

I straighten. My back hurts. "All I know is what I read in the paper. Some druggie shot himself."

"That's not the way I hear it."

"I guess you hear things I don't."

"Look," he says, shaking his head with mild sympathy. "Haven't you lost enough? You want to spend the rest of your life in prison?"

"You don't know how to bluff. Besides, I've got a lawyer in the event I need one."

"You won't help me? What you did last night, and I have no doubt you were the one, I can understand.

What happened behind the brake-lining factory makes my skin crawl."

"I wish I could help you, but I have no idea what you're talking about. Sorry."

No sooner does the gray car leave than a blue one arrives, with an old man behind the wheel. This car would be lucky to get to Boston. The old man gets out. He is wearing a thick checkered shirt and rough trousers with a broken fly. He has an envelope in his hand.

"Mr. Southwark? I'm Miss Wren's handyman. She said to give this to you." I take the envelope and reach into my pocket. He shakes his head. "She said not to take nothing from you."

"That's all right. It's only a quarter."

He takes it and gives me a little salute with one finger and returns to his car. There's nothing written on the outside of the envelope which, yellow around the edges, must have come years ago from the stationery department of Parker, Inc. I remember the stock and even the carton it came in.

Five one-hundred-dollar bills in a folded piece of blank paper. Which isn't fair. There should be five more of them.

26

PURE INTUITION, NOTHING ELSE, TELLS ME she's not inside my sister's house but somewhere behind it.

Two cars are in the driveway, the big one that Parker drives and the small one, a Falcon, that belongs to my sister. Keys dangling from each ignition.

The garden is stiff with debris, with flowers that have fallen apart, with stems that have split, with stalks that have become straw. Vines close to the ground have become messy. The used earth is drawing in on itself for a rest.

Intuition told me she'd be there, but it said nothing about Parker. He and she are in aluminum chairs, he with his long legs thrown out, she with her head turned toward him. He pulls his legs in as I approach and says something to her. She glances up.

"Hello," I say.

Parker starts to rise.

"No, stay there."

In his car coat, chinos and high suede shoes, he resembles a college boy. With his hatchet face and pea-green eyes, he'll stay young for a long time. He'll keep his hair, turn gray very gradually, and appear more interesting with each passing year.

Libby looks better than she has in a long time. Rested and relaxed, and there's color in her cheeks. My sister has outfitted her. She has on a bulky sweater warm enough to see her through a night on a mountain.

She has on a plaid woolen skirt and dark stockings that shape her legs nicely. The hard sunshine is protective. It covers her like a plastic bag. She starts to laugh.

"What's the matter?" I ask, and she points to my camel's-hair.

"Where did you get that?"

"Deep in the closet. A little out of style, I guess."

"A little," she says, as if I had provided the entertainment of the day.

Parker rises. This time I don't stop him. "Let me talk to you for a second," he says. We walk a few feet away from her. "She knows," he says.

"What does she know?"

"She heard it on the radio this morning. We all heard it at the same time. She didn't react one way or another."

"Does she think I did it?"

"She didn't say anything. You mean, you didn't do it?"

"You mean, you think I did?"

"Who did then?"

"I don't know. I'm on leave of absence."

I turn back to Libby. Her eyes are brighter than I've ever seen them. She smiles at Parker, and Parker smiles at her, as if he had a half-interest in her.

"Would you like to come home?" I ask her.

"I'm comfortable here," she says.

"She's no trouble," says Parker. He whispers in my ear: "Honest to God, Southy, you really didn't do it?"

I'm a little sharp with him. He backs off, nearer to Libby, who seems annoyed with my presence and almost embarrassed by it.

"You look better," I tell her.

"I feel better," she says.

Parker glances away, as if he were responsible but too modest to take credit.

"Here comes Joan," he says.

My sister approaches with a smile, with her skirt

shorter than usual and her slim legs still bearing a summer tan. She has on a sweater that's woollier than Libby's.

She embraces me briefly and Parker makes some kind of sign to her. "Bobby," she says and inspects me at arm's length. Her teeth are so white they're almost blue. "I'm glad you came," she says.

Parker helps Libby out of the chair. She's blushing. "It's all right," my sister says to her. "I'll explain to him."

I let that pass because my sister squeezes my hand. "Come on," she says, taking my arm. "Let's go in the house."

We stroll toward the house, Parker and Libby behind us. My sister whispers, "She's like a child, Bobby. This morning she crawled into bed with us."

I readjust my face because suddenly my head is packed with too much noise.

"She's off her rocker," I say.

"No, she isn't, Bobby, but she isn't functioning properly. Too much has hit her. She needs a lot of rest and attention."

"She looks doped up."

"Just some medication we gave her."

I glance back at them. Parker is helping her along, though she doesn't appear to need the help.

"I'm taking her home," I tell my sister.

"At this time it might be disastrous, Bobby. She's comfortable here and she's getting her strength back. Think it over first."

We reach the back porch, but Libby and Parker are no longer behind us. They're heading toward his car.

"Let them go," my sister says, holding my arm. "I don't want them to change their plans. They're going to the beach. The salt air will do her wonders, and it'll give her an appetite and make her sleep tonight without taking anything."

"I'll take her myself."

"Bobby. Let David do it." Her voice softens. "Besides I want to talk with you."

Parker helps Libby into his car. His movements are protective. He looks back at us and waves. The car starts up with scarcely a sound.

"Bobby, don't!" my sister says, and steps in front of me. I'm suffering the drooly sickness that overcomes a man who's losing blood. I can see the beach, the dunes and the boulders, the wet pebbles and shells, things to collect and bring back with the sea still sticking to them. I look at my sister, for whom I've got a terrific feeling. Hate. Which I've always known has been there but have never cared to examine. There's a banging in my head, messages, like the seasonal shouts to which a tree must respond: *Bud! Blossom! Bleed! Die!* Libby and Parker are gone. My sister and I enter the house.

My sister knows how to do things. The coffee is a special blend, very strong and very good. We sit on, and against, big glaring pillows in a rounded corner of the living room. We sit side by side, as if someone were going to photograph us. We sit silently with our own thoughts. I have thoughts that haven't emerged yet. They're skunk cabbages melting their way up through winter ground. My sister's brown legs are laid out straight. She crosses them, and says, "Would you like to talk about Darcie?"

"No. She's long gone. Another dimension." My hands are tired. For the first time I'm fully aware that I no longer carry a weapon and that if I wanted to commit mayhem I'd have to do so with my bare hands. I drop them.

My sister says, "I don't know how I could have coped with it if it had been one of my boys."

"How are they? Big, I suppose."

"Enormous. Their letters are so intelligent they scare me."

I give a start. There are voices in a distant part of the house, and my first thought is that Libby and Parker never left but simply pretended they had and then sneaked in a side door.

My sister smiles. "I have some house guests. Don't

worry. They won't bother us." She puts her coffee cup to one side and lights a joint. "It's funny," she says, "but these don't really affect me, not the way they should."

"Then why smoke them?"

"I have a few left. Why waste them? You're welcome to one."

"No, thank you."

I put my coffee cup to one side, and she puts her hand on mine. Her face is at once awkward and boyishly pretty.

"Bobby." Her voice is full of concern. "Evelyn phoned this morning. She told me something really wild," I nod. "She seems to think you murdered those men."

I shrug. "She's giving me credit for something I understand was quite professional and slick. Do I look that high-class?"

She studies me for a moment. "If you did kill them you'd be in pieces now. A man can only stand so much." Her hand is back, squeezing mine. She laughs. "Evelyn didn't go into details, but I gathered you molested her. She used the word *humiliate*."

I nod. "Something like that. I guess I've wanted to do it for a long time, but I'm not so sure she was the one humiliated."

"Poor Bobby." She drops her head back. "And poor Evelyn. Her father tightened up all her insides. That's why she's big on the outside. She claims you're in dire need of psychiatric help."

I nod. "Aren't we all." The voices of her house guests can be heard again. They seem nearer, livelier, a little weird. "Who are they?" I ask.

"Just friends, Bobby. Some blacks, and some white boys who try to look like blacks, and some girls. They've been to Mississippi where they saw terrible things. Churches burnt to the ground, little black children tormented by grown men who don't recognize their madnesses, who think they're sane. It never occurs to them they're not."

"What do you do with these house guests of yours?"

"I give them shelter, Bobby. Sometimes we become very pleasant and our conversations become that way. Sometimes we speak without even moving our mouths. Sometimes that's necessary. We live in an age of assassination. Kennedy killed. I could never understand that. King I could. So many others will be killed. The times are horribly medieval."

"Does it bother you that much?"

"Yes, because I'm strong enough to survive and I'll have to see it all."

"You have a nice house here, nice property. You really don't have too much to worry about."

"You miss the point on purpose, Bobby."

I have a smile leaking out of the corner of my mouth, sort of (I suspect) like baby drool. I feel woozy, as if I and not she had smoked the joint. Lack of sleep. I feel like an old person unable to dress or feed himself. A subtle subtraction from reality. It's easy to blot out the whole world. Simply hold your hand before your eyes.

"What are you doing, Bobby?"

Her arm goes around me to provide succor, comfort. I have a yarn to tell but no tongue to do it. I'm a combat soldier nursing his nerves with a woman. My hand touches her raised knee and slides off.

"Bobby, you don't want to do that."

I'm looking for the generous breasts of a pregnant woman but find only my sister's which are hidden in expensive wool. My hand returns for the knee but it sways to one side. At that, she gets up. She covers me with something, and I think of my poor father's optic nerve, of a blanket with cigarette burns and he under it and all his thoughts curled in lonely sleep. I reach for my sister, but her voice is high above me.

"If you really need a woman that bad, I'll get you one."

I'm shaking my head, but I don't mean to.

Head low on the pillow, legs comfortably crossed,

222

blanket pulled up to my chin, I consider my sister's fading presence. She pauses in the distant archway and glances back. Scarcely any light on her face, but a bright haze catches her slim figure which symbolizes serenity or something like that, the way a tree means solidity, permanence, almost foreverness.

Eyes closed, I can't help but weigh the chances for posthumous existence and consider the possibility of an immortal soul. With a summer home tucked away in a remote mountainous range of clouds.

Eyes squeezed, I imagine myself driving my sister's Falcon seventy miles an hour up the state of Maine in search of my father's friend LeBoeuf. A fantastic journey. I'm good at this. The road is edged with flaming brush. In the wind unstable birches cross-examine one another and lose leaves which fly like paper across the road. I've passed Portland, gassed up in Bath, and emptied my bowels in woods outside of Wiscasset. The sun is diffuse and dull, warming nothing, and the wind is unbuckling itself and snapping. Huge blood-leafed trees are hemorrhaging from myriad wounds. Smaller trees put on clownish ceremonies of grief, and naked trees smile fiendishly. The clouds are cold clothes that have blown off the line. In Bangor I discover I'm off my route. A river nearby. Signs: Eddington, E. Eddington one way and Orono and Old Town the other. I remember reading about a legendary man who cried at a crossroads because his shadow had disappeared and it alone knew which road he should take. The Falcon slows to let me get my bearings. The wind lessens, and the dull sunshine spreads messages. The Falcon finds the right route. Relaxed behind the wheel, I'm a reel of film. I'm good at this too. An early representation of my father in a pinstriped suit, a silent man with a cigarette dangling from his mouth. So many evenings spent together saying nothing. The radio playing. He had his programs and I had mine. A clouded picture of my father's father vending vegetables through Liverpool streets, which may not be factual. But I do know that my father was one of many children and the single survivor of a brood of brothers and sisters whose lives were lost early to pneumonia, diphtheria and other miseries. He came to this country as an adolescent, alone and penniless. I don't know when or how he began to make book. There are no records, and he never said.

Woodland colors are rearing up. I've never before seen trees so tall and desolate and so willful and rash. I'm far past Machias and heading into LeBoeuf's territory, where illiterate people have tremendous memories of their past, of their own personal histories, the stunning heat of total recall, like the hundred-degree warmth of the womb. I remember LeBoeuf's jagged face, hollow eyes and long hard teeth, his thoughts embedded in his bones, his single animal-specked hand lying on my father's table. I remember his raising his other arm, gesturing with his partial hand, and telling my father about the shock of separation and how in dreams he searches for his fingers. With whiskey breath and sober voice he tells my father of the woods where one may build a nest and, among dogs (thick-furred mongrels), sleep warm even after the wood fire has died. Sinking into the sour-apple stink of his clothes, he tells my father about the vast protective clutter of trees, the safety of shadows, the sanctity of coves and nooks where a man is a monk, all felonies forgotten, all convictions squashed.

The motor skips with the crazy hops of a beheaded hen. The Falcon sputters into a village where the houses, small and ramshackle, look like sheds, like shithouses, and the trees resemble empty balls of briar. A ghost town. Hello. Anybody home? LeBoeuf hasn't been seen on Ramsey streets in years; the last time was shortly before my father died. He was old then, no longer able to intimidate chiseling horseplayers. Indeed, my father was slipping him money for doing nothing. He returned to the woods. Except for unidentifiable bones which may have been discovered by hunters who stumbled upon his nest, he has vanished without a trace.

There's sweat on my brow and much more on the pillow. And not a sound in the house. Except from me. I'm knocking things over as I get to my feet. My sister shouldn't have left the coffee cups there. The wall rushes to my aid.

A young woman I don't know is alone in the kitchen. She has long frizzled hair and lazy eyes, and she's wearing an old army shirt and tight dungarees. A glass of water in her thin white hand. She's very pale.

"You're Mrs. Parker's brother," she says.

"That's right, and you look high. Are you?"

"Pleasant. That's all."

"How were things in Mississippi?"

"Not pleasant," she says. Her lazy eyes are hazel. She has a gold wedding ring on.

"You're married."

She shakes her frizzy head. "No, I could never submit totally to the will of any man."

"You're a feminist."

"I like to think so," she says.

She runs water for me. I want a cold glass of it.

"Thank you. Where's my sister?"

"She's in her bedroom."

The water clears a crusted tongue. I put down my empty glass.

"She got a nigger in there with her?"

"You don't know your sister very well, do you?"

"No, not at all."

The air is fresh and cold. Much of the sun has vanished. Parker's car isn't back yet, but the Falcon is there. The hood is hot and the fenders and doors are streaked with the grime of hard travel. The windshield is stained with insects. I get in behind the wheel. I know what I want to do, but I'm too tired to make the trip again.

27

"YOU KNOW WHO THITH ITH? I'VE BEEN trying to reach you *all day*. It rang and rang and nobody anthered. Thith ith Louithe."

"No kidding."

"You get the thame conthideration they did. I won't tethtify againtht you. I won't thay anything." I thank her. She goes on: "I don't have any money. They uthed to give me thum but now they're dead. How much can you give me?"

I consider for a moment. "How about a hundred?"

She reverts to French. Swear-words, I suspect. Then her English returns. She wants more than a hundred. She has a winter to get through.

"I can't even give you a hundred."

"You'd better!"

She's weeping, or at least I think she is. She tells me about her childhood and cold Canada, about her girlhood and the nunnery. About an uncle who was a hermit and died alone, and because there was no one to bury him the hard sun took over his body, and so did the wind, and the rain when it arrived, and when those elements had had enough, the maggots appeared. She shudders.

"You don't underthtand what life wath up there," she says. "You can't imagine my life."

I try to. Bitter cold that lingers like a bird with its beak frozen to its food. Wind and rock, the black sky with its solemn slice of moon, a thought for those re-

226

mote forebears whose fingers may have dragged on the ground. The phone is heavy. I nearly drop it.

"I'll mail you two hundred."

"Bring it to me!" she says.

"I'll try."

She tells me about a fear she has had since she left the nunnery, that she would end up murdered in a ditch with her skirt thrown up around her torso. That's the way they'd find her and photograph her, and those pictures would be preserved forever in police files. She tells me about that big silent man who lived with her for a time, a bald spot on his head and a stutter on his lips when he did speak. Once and only once did he take her somewhere, and that was to the beach, from which she returned with her face raw from the sun. One of the few times she has felt alive.

"Ith it fair, I athk you. I have feelingth like everybody elthe. Am I thuppothed to live alone and never have a normal life?"

"I have to go."

"I'm not finished yet!" she says almost in a scream. She's back in Canada and telling me about the metallic howl of the wind, as if it were being blown out of pipes. She tells me that celibacy for men is wrong, and that she knew a priest who couldn't stand it, and she did what she could for him. She was young. He was middle-aged and passionate but not compassionate, and he treated her cruelly.

"Are you lithening?" she says sharply.

"I am."

Her talk reminds me of a drunk who is unaware his skull has been split open.

"You promith you'll bring the money?"

"I promise."

"When?"

"Tomorrow," I say, with a suspicion she has a hidden bank book with an incredible balance.

"It should be more than two hundred," she says.

"It's all I have."

"What if they arretht you?"

227

"You'll still get your money."

"You promith?"

"Yes."

Suddenly I feel genuine sympathy for her. I feel I know what is wrong with her. She has been told too many lies in her life.

28

Rose Mulligan enters my dark house without knocking. I told her the door would be unlocked and I told her where I'd be, but she calls out anyway. "Where are you?" I expected her to be rudderless, but she is steady and direct, guided by streetlight driven like stakes through the windows. With each step into the living room she is struck by intermittent flashes of headlights from the highway. Explosions that don't rock her, merely annoy her. "Christ," she says, "the traffic comes right into your house."

"Draw the shades if you like."

She does, and she snaps on a table lamp. She is wearing a trench coat, which she doesn't take off, and she is carrying a package the shape of a shoe box under her arm. She joins me on the couch, placing the package on the cushion between us. The scar down her nose is red, as if from a crayon, and she has two new front teeth. Her heavy blonde hair has been cut, which makes her face fuller and at the same time relaxed. Matronly. I thank her for coming, and she shrugs, smiles, and says, "It's like being pressed back into service."

"You look rested."

"It's part of the cure."

I pick up the package, open it, and draw out a service revolver by its long barrel. I had a similar one but sold it when I became a detective.

"Will he miss it?"

She shakes her head. "It's not the one he carries around. What are you going to do with it?"

"I just want it for company, not having my own, which is lost."

She puts up a hand. "I don't want to hear about it. I'm really afraid of you now, Southy."

"You don't have to be. But you've taken a risk bringing this to me. What if he finds out?"

"He won't, unless you do something foolish with it."

"How many revolvers does he have?"

"He has a bunch. You know how he likes guns."

"You know, don't you, he shot another kid."

"Southy, please." Her eyes are pure Polish, small and pale and seemingly very vulnerable. "I don't want to hear anything I don't need to know. That's part of the cure too. Southy?" She reaches for my hands. She still likes them. She holds them by the fingers. "He said you were turning yourself in tomorrow."

"I'm not sure what I'm going to do."

"He says you've got no choice."

I smile, reclaiming my hands. "There's always choices. You can always do something or nothing." I take Auntie Wren's envelope out of my back pocket and withdraw three one-hundred-dollar bills. They are to help pay for the work done on her nose and teeth. "I wish it could be more," I tell her.

"You don't have to give me anything."

"That's what's nice about giving. You don't have to."

She puts the money in the pocket of her trench coat. The naked revolver lies between us. I remove it. I shove it under the couch. Then I take her in my arms.

"Forgive me, Southy. I'd rather not."

In her ear I whisper, "That's asking a boy with an empty stomach to keep his hands off the pastries."

"Believe me when I say something?" she asks, remaining in my arms but tightening her trench coat. "I'm at peace with myself. I don't understand it, but I'm not going to question it. I can live with Roscoe

230

without thinking about him, even when I talk to him. I don't need to leave the house like I used to. I can't explain it but it's nice." She smiles like a child, one with strawberry ice cream on her nose. Her poor nose. I kiss it.

"Where's your wife, Southy? She should be here, not me."

"It's important to me you are."

"Southy, I feel like an old whore who doesn't want to be one anymore. I have a son going into the army, probably to Vietnam, maybe to get killed. I have a daughter who's engaged. She's pregnant. She'll be married soon. I've got another daughter who may be pregnant, and she's only fourteen."

She's crying. I try to make her stop with the penetrating eye of a hypnotist. She's not looking at me. I lift her chin and kiss her on the mouth, the kind of kiss I don't believe I've ever given to her before, deep and full and tongueless.

"Oh, Southy," she says, freeing her face. "It's too bad you never had friends. Pals. Guys you could talk with now. So you could settle things in your mind."

I could remind her that ultimately we are each of us alone, which is nothing to be afraid of but merely to be accepted. I could remind her that even being alone can be too much company, the way a fat man is a redundancy of himself and automatically a bore to himself.

I get to my feet and help her to hers. I'm kissing her again and I've got her trench coat open and I have my arms around her under the coat.

"I can't make you understand, can I?" she says, and I can see her mentally placing me, with sympathy, among morose men, solitaries, creatures of lonely habits, their interests morbid in certain directions, their points of view bent.

She has a graceless gait going up the stairs, but on the wall her shadow is nimble. It carries mine. Mine magnifies hers. The bed, which isn't made, distracts her. Together we straighten the sheets and blankets.

231

As she removes her trench coat, her shadow is like that of a soldier. Gravely she says, "No chance she'll come home?"

"No chance at all."

Her blouse reminds me of the fancy cloth that lines old-fashioned chocolate boxes. She drapes it over the back of a chair. We exchange the sort of smile that old friends would. We share the chair for our clothes. We enter a big naked embrace, and then move it to the bed. For my benefit she becomes the phallic-minded female.

29

THE MID-MORNING SKY IS FULL OF COW clouds: time for milking. The grass is brush-stroked from the sun which, by noon, will blaze into the swamp maple whose leaves are already red. Some are on the ground, some are floating in the inlet and some are journeying down the river. Dragonflies dart among the overripe stems to cattails and land on lily pads. Were I to scoop a pail into the water I'd come up with a crayfish. Still bright green, though yellowing in places, are the pickerel-weed, arrow arum and duck potato. They throw shadows on and provide a forest for insects that walk the water. The water scorpion looks too flimsy to hold together. You'd expect a breeze to break it. You'd think the breeze would blow away all the water striders, treaders, measurers and boatmen. At the shoreline a bullfrog stares bulgingly at me like an amiable drunk.

I heave a slow sigh, like a fellow who has fought a good war and now wants peace and a pipe and an old sweater and a newspaper to read. I like where I stand. It's no secret that real estate will become precious in the future, a patch of property where a man can find some privacy, some green, some birds, some sun. Everything else will be city.

If Captain Kilcoyne were not standing near the mouth of the driveway and wondering when and how to approach me, I could easily imagine myself as being utterly alone in nature. I could see myself in that period when life had not crept out of the water but was waiting just beneath the surface, invisible breaths reaching for open air. An exciting time. I could see myself seeking life in the bottoms of pools and ponds, an undemanding job and a richly rewarding one, the sort sometimes available from politicians.

In the house, while drinking my breakfast coffee, I tried to write a little note to Libby but my thoughts died each time the pencil touched paper. I penciled instead elaborate spiderwebs and on another sheet drew circles, worlds with neither beginnings nor ends. At the time the morning was green, still unripe, and the sun was a finger at the window. I scarcely heard it tap. Just as I had scarcely heard Rose when she got out of bed, used the bathroom and left the house.

By the time I finished my coffee, sunshine was fluttering inside the house like lost butterflies, ones that had no business being around at that time of year. The sun: trees rise with it, tower, and then crumble when night falls. I got up and stood in the shine.

Kilcoyne and Jordan are at the top of the driveway, and I suspect some cops are on the other side of the house, though not on my property. So far they're respecting boundaries. Kilcoyne glances at his wrist—at his watch or at the discolored dime that may now be worth a quarter. He has his problems, and I may not be one of them. We may be simply fellow-sufferers. He may be afraid of the stark sunshine as some men are of the dark.

The barrel of Mulligan's revolver, stuck inside my waistband, is biting into my leg. The thing is too big to wear that way. And it's too heavy for my hand. I don't think I even need it. I'd rather take come what may, like a tree in a storm.

I need to swallow to break the swollen silence, the same sort of thick stillness that must have been there when Sputnik was shot off from the steppes of Siberia. Darcie and I waiting for it at the predawn hour the television said it could be seen blinking overhead. I ed Darcie's small hand and pointed, and she said, "That's a star that's moving," and I tried to explain that a star is something else, something more, in existence perhaps when the earth had no green plants and no animals. "And no houses?" Right, only rocks now lying like records beneath the earth's crust, along with skeletons of multicellular life.

Kilcoyne makes a motion with his hand to somebody I can't see. Paul Jordan hitches up his pants. The two could be bankers looking over property somebody wants to buy. They're looking toward the porch which horseshoes my house. I can see more of it than they can. I can see that part which is screened, where I kept the dog when he was small enough to be penned. I can see those places where the screen is damaged and will fly apart one of these days. I'm not handy. I don't fix things.

Kilcoyne is walking down the driveway. I didn't see him when he started.

Paul Jordan is stationary. Like a statue, a small one. The milky sun is souring the sky. I've got spots in front of my eyes, as if from a steak chopped into tidy chewable chunks.

"Southy."

Kilcoyne stands where the stone steps begin, stones that I shoved into the ground myself. Paul Jordan is halfway down the driveway and down on one knee. He has his revolver out and the hand holding it is balanced over his other arm. A man is on my porch with a rifle.

What in Christ is all of this?

Two men are approaching from the direction of the pear tree. Plainclothes and revolvers. Nobody is in uniform.

Kilcoyne comes down the steps. He has no weapon showing. I glance left and right behind me.

"Any more, Cap'n? Any guys across the river?"

"We were hoping you'd come up so we wouldn't have to come down."

He stops a dozen feet from me and positions himself so that Jordan can get a shot at me and so can the

235

others. The man on the porch has his rifle aimed at me over the rail. I don't recognize him. The two that came from the pear tree are vaguely familiar. I think they're from the early-night platoon.

"Where's Mulligan, Cap'n? Why isn't he here too?"

"We didn't ask him."

"You'd have been a hell of a lot safer. He's a crack shot."

"So are these fellas, Southy."

The sun is appearing in bursts now, each time it gets away from a cloud. The clouds appear sharp, like coral. A bird is skimming through the low branches of the swamp maple.

"How come, Cap'n, I'm not one of your own? Why can't you take care of me like the others?"

He stares silently. If there's an answer he's not going to give it, and if there isn't he's not going to say.

"Maybe you think I'm too far gone, Cap'n. Like somebody with bone cancer. It starts breaking out at every joint."

"Open your jacket, Southy."

I touch the button that holds the camel's-hair together. I circle the button with my finger. "Mulligan's a worse case than me. But I guess he's more of a cop. He's a nut but he's predictable, except maybe to me. I know of a newspaper guy who up and quit after the typesetters made a bunch of mistakes in his story that day. You figure I'm that sort of guy but on a different level."

He doesn't say anything. I don't think he even listened.

The camel's-hair falls open. The sun is in my eyes, but I don't want to take the chance of blinking. I'm afraid I might not find my place here again by the river.

"Take it out with thumb and finger, Southy, and let

t mine. It's not even loaded."

s I say, Southy. Take it out and drop it on

236

the ground." His eyes become weary. "You're not giving us much choice."

"What kind of choice are you giving me?"

"A place to rest, Southy. A place to relax and get some care and find your bearings."

"A nuthouse."

"You can call it that if you like."

"I never considered that possibility. That's for dead men without cemeteries."

"A cemetery you don't leave. This place you could."

I'm grinning at him. He's grinning at me. I can't remember his ever doing that before. We have found an angle. We have struck a deal, like two lawyers finding a smooth spot in a jagged situation.

"Well?" he says and waits for an answer, which would be like my signature to something. I've always been afraid of signing things.

I let my eyes stray to the river where I once pulled out a fish that seemed to grin. What the hell kind was it? I didn't know, but it was a big baby. Good fertilizer to make flowers fat, a burst of red roses, like jelly. I carried the fish into the house to show Libby, who said, "Ugh!" She was doing dishes, doing the pans. Roiling greasy water, like a gray and white picture of human blood under a microscope. "Don't leave it here," she said. A luster to her face, as if from a fire. An infinite succession of things I wanted to say to her. About plowing, harrowing, sowing, planting. The good life. The hard life. The impossible life. She turned on the faucet, and water roped out like the muscle of a man.

I grin at Kilcoyne and say, "No such thing really as private property, not in the final analysis, anyway. I mean, you can build a fence or put up a sign saying 'private' but that doesn't mean anyone has to respect it, not if he really doesn't want to. For instance, y~ can't keep animals out. Do you have time, Cap'n? ` like to tell you about a turtle, size of a washtub came out of that river."

"I don't have time, Southy."

"No boundaries to anything, Cap'n, and that extends to people. Nothing a man can't do, or won't do. Do you know what I'm saying?"

"I think so."

"I do, but I'm not saying it right."

"Yes, you are," he says, and seems to hold his breath. No, he's gently expelling it. Suddenly he catches it.

No cause for alarm. I have merely raised my wrist watch to my ear. I have to hear the ticking because now there is no other sound, not even the shuffle of traffic on the road. The sun gives in to the clouds, leaving me as if in the cold silence of deep snow. My dog lifting a leg and drilling a hole into a drift, sniffing around and finding a dead racoon, a handsome thief, even in death, maybe especially in death, its front feet raised stiffly as if to say, "I've had enough." I buried the animal in the snow, and in the spring the body was gone, no traces left, not even bones.

"Southy."

Kilcoyne wants my attention. I do, too. I have a deadly decision to make.

"Living here, Cap'n, I've watched the seasons like a hawk."

"I can see where you would," he says.

"I've fed the ground, made it rich. I can't tell you the satisfaction that gives me. Things growing because of me."

Kilcoyne nods and mentions something about his wife gaining a similar satisfaction from house plants.

"The yard was mine, and the house was Libby's," I tell him. "It was a kind of unspoken thing. I'd come out early in the morning and watch the sun grow on ͏ound. I'd grow, too. What a feeling!"

͏e deliberately coughs. I can't blame him, ͏t things to say.

͏ mad at me once, I can't remember why ͏amed for me to get out of the house. ͏re, but she told me to go play with my fucking flowers. She knew exactly how to hurt me, but usually she would never do it. A good woman, Cap'n, and we had some good times. When we were younger, I'd take her hot from the shower and dry her on me. With her hair wet, she looked just like a teenager. I'm going to miss her, Cap'n."

"It might not be for long."

"How long?"

"That's hard to say."

"Too long, right? A lot of memories in this yard, Cap'n. Too bad. I could do a lot of quiet living here. I wouldn't mind being buried here."

Kilcoyne tenses himself, and there's a small sound from the driveway where Paul Jordan is rearranging a knee and readjusting the way he's balancing his revolver. I figure the others are doing the same. The one I'm worried about is the man with the rifle. He must be good.

"Southy, keep talking if you want to."

"I don't want to." And I ease a hand toward my weapon.

"Southy, don't!"

Thumb and forefinger. That's all. I'm not a madman. I don't want to fight. More to the point, I don't want to die.

I dangle Mulligan's revolver by the butt, and Kilcoyne takes it away by the barrel.

I have a last request, and I hold out my hands. "Cuff me."

A psychopathic killer strikes without warning and with no apparent motive.

Experience chills and terror as the people involved struggle to discover why they are being stalked and who is responsible for these frightening occurrences. Follow the painstaking pursuit of the police as they rush to apprehend the killers, before they can strike again.

_____ 82315 **THE MAJORETTES, John Russo $1.95**

_____ 82233 **FIELDS OF EDEN, Michael T. Hinkemeyer $1.95**

_____ 82326 **THE BAIT, Dorothy Uhnak $1.95**

_____ 82756 **LOVE KILLS, Dan Greenburg $2.50**

_____ 81247 **MICHIGAN MURDERS, Edward Keyes $2.50**

_____ 82871 **LOOKING FOR MR. GOODBAR, Judith Rossner $2.75**

"A girls' boarding school?" Ben said with surprise. "No guys?"

"A lot of guys—three miles away."

Ben thought for a moment. "I guess that makes it a lot harder to date."

"Not for me," I said jauntily. It was the truth—three miles was no harder than three feet away—it all seemed pretty impossible to me.

"Really," he said, interpreting my statement in a different way, smiling and studying me. "Well, at least it cuts down on distractions."

I raised my eyebrows, hoping I looked interested and beguiling rather than bug-eyed. "Do you have trouble concentrating?"

"Right now?" he asked back.

I blushed and he laughed. Then Tim volunteered, "Ben has trouble concentrating on one girl."

"Thanks, Tim," Ben said. It was my turn to laugh. One side of Ben's mouth drew up. "You find that funny?"

"No, no," I said. What was funny was that I, Allison Parker, was trying to flirt with a pro.

Love Stories

At First Sight

Elizabeth Chandler

BANTAM BOOKS
NEW YORK · TORONTO · LONDON · SYDNEY · AUCKLAND

For Jenny and Jessica,
shining more brightly each year.

RL 6, age 12 and up

AT FIRST SIGHT

A Bantam Book / November 1998

Produced by 17th Street Productions,
a division of Daniel Weiss Associates, Inc.
33 West 17th Street
New York, NY 10011.
Cover photography by Michael Segal.

ISBN: 0-553-49254-3

Published simultaneously in the United States and Canada

Bantam Books are published by Bantam Books, a division of Bantam
Doubleday Dell Publishing Group, Inc. Its trademark, consisting of the
words "Bantam Books" and the portrayal of a rooster, is Registered in
U.S. Patent and Trademark Office and in other countries. Marca
Registrada. Bantam Books, 1540 Broadway, New York, New York 10036.

PRINTED IN THE UNITED STATES OF AMERICA

OPM   0 9 8 7 6 5 4 3 2 1

One

"IF YOU PUT off leaving much longer," Miss Henny said to me, "it'll be dark before you arrive in New York."

I peered through the lace curtains of her little stone house at the edge of Fields's campus. Christmas was four days away. My silver Audi was out front, packed with gifts and sports stuff, videos and books, enough to keep me occupied during the long winter vacation.

Miss Henny sipped her tea, studying me. "I believe you'd be more eager to set off with a tent and team of dogs for Christmas in northern Alaska."

"I have a tent. Do you know where I can get some dogs?"

She laughed in that gay, ladylike way of hers that seemed to belong to another era. "Be sure to send my love to Sandra and Julia."

I nodded and drained my cup of tea, the third or

1

fourth I had drunk. Sandra and Julia were my beautiful sisters, twins a year younger than I, who until last year had boarded with me at Fields School in Maryland. Because of our father's job with a mining company, our parents had moved from one foreign city to another. They lived in some pretty exotic locations, but none of them were exactly good places to raise three girls. So for our middle- and high-school years, we were sent to Fields. Then last summer, when our parents came back to the States for good, my sisters bolted for what they considered a "normal" school—the coed public school in the tiny town of Thornhill, New York—our new home.

I'd chosen to finish my senior year at Fields, which to me felt more like home than anywhere else. My sixth-grade teacher, Miss Henny, had become more than an instructor. Over the years she was the one who kept us at her house when the airport was fogged in, who picked us up when we arrived back early from holidays, and who gave us tea and tissue and sympathy when we got the flu. As for the school itself, I loved it. I played on several teams, enjoyed the strong academics, and had a great group of friends. There was only one thing Fields was missing—guys. Not that it really mattered. Unlike that of my popular sisters, my love life was sure to be nonexistent no matter what.

"Allison," Miss Henny said. She always called me by my full name when she was about to say something important. "You know how every New Year's Eve I have a wish for you? Since I won't be seeing

2

you till the term begins, I'll give it to you now."

"Okay." *New Year's Eve,* I thought. There were certain times of the year when my sisters' dating schedule could be tracked only by a computer with extensive memory. Even at Fields their romantic life was legendary. At prom time they'd had so many guys interested in them that they negotiated blind dates for me and almost half my classmates. It was as if the school had put up double radio towers from their dorm rooms, sending out waves to the all-male school three miles away. Now, according to my mother's letters, the twins had taken Thornhill's dating scene by storm. I was dreading having to be the boring, plain-looking sister standing on the sidelines once again. In the small town, where everybody knew one another, the holidays would be full of parties, Mom wrote, "with lots of cute boys for you to meet." That's my mother, ever hopeful.

"My wish," Miss Henny said, breaking into my thoughts, "is that you finally realize all you have to offer others."

"But I do already," I protested. "Fields has been teaching self-esteem since I got here." Hammering it into our heads, actually.

"Then let me be more specific. My wish is that you realize how easy it would be for a nice young man to fall in love with you."

I stared at the thin, gray-haired lady who had never married.

"Your sisters have their beauty; you have yours."

I blinked. How did she know?

3

"Time for you to go," my old teacher said, taking my cup from me and gently pulling me up from the chair. "Don't you have a dinner invitation from your aunt Jen tonight?"

I nodded and put on my jacket. It was the one part I always liked about holidays, seeing my unpredictable godmother.

"I'll miss you terribly, dear. Come back with some good stories." Miss Henny wrapped a wool scarf around my neck and laid her hand lightly against my cheek.

Somehow, without realizing it, I'd grown several inches taller than she. Now she seemed so fragile, like one of her dainty porcelains. Thinking about how she'd aged, I got a lump in my throat. I was halfway down the stone path, lost in dismal thoughts of happy school years slipping away from me, when Miss Henny called out with the howl of a college football coach, "Go get 'em, Al!"

Two hours later I was buzzing up the New Jersey Turnpike, singing Christmas carols along with the radio, when I suddenly realized just how much tea I had drunk at Miss Henny's. I don't know who lays out highways, but it seems they always put rest stops nineteen miles past the moment you figure out you need one—and need it *now*.

I picked up speed. I was close to desperate when I finally hit the exit ramp to the rest stop. By the time I'd circled the jammed lot twice and squeezed my car into a parking space, I was beyond desperate.

I raced across the asphalt, up the steps, and through the glass doors. The foyer was crowded with holiday travelers, and I made the sidesteps and spins of an NFL running back to get to the rest-room area.

Bam! Two other people were also trying to get there, and we all smashed into each other. The three of us spun around like revolving doors—a tall guy, a little boy, and me.

"Whoa!" The guy held the kid and me as we whipped around.

"Sorry!" said the little boy.

"No problem," I responded.

The little boy rushed headlong toward one bathroom entrance and I toward the other.

"Hold up there," the guy called after us.

The kid and I both looked back at him. He was about my age and had dark hair—that's all I had time to notice. He pointed to the signs above the doors, then crossed his hands.

I glanced up at the stick figure of a man. "Whoops." The kid and I crossed paths, each of us finally making it to our right destination.

On my way back out of the ladies' room I glanced at myself in the mirror and saw that my short brown hair had become electric with winter dryness, silky pieces of it flying about. I guess the self-consciousness I always felt when standing next to my gorgeous sisters was already beginning. I frowned at the oval reflection of my face, my lips and deep brown eyes, entirely bare of makeup, suddenly looking very plain. As usual I had nothing but a comb and lip gloss in my bag. I wet down my hair, flattening it against my head, and left.

As I got in line for pizza I thought about delicate Miss Henny bellowing out, "Go get 'em, Al!" I guess I was smiling, for I suddenly noticed the person in front of me watching my face and smiling back.

"Hi," he said. He had beautiful hazel eyes that could melt a girl. Okay, so he was a little short to take to a prom—he was very cute and the right height for a first or second grader. "Did you make it in time?" the little boy asked me.

"Yup. How about you?"

"Just in," he replied.

The guy who was with him, the one who had directed us to the right rooms, turned around. He was tall and had brown eyes with an almost golden light in them, eyes equally capable of turning a girl to syrup. His easy smile told me he knew it. "Close call," he said.

I nodded and smiled a little, feeling awkward around this hunk of a guy, wondering what to say next.

My sisters would've known. Once when they were still at Fields, they gave a flirting seminar in the dorm. It was the most well-attended extracurricular we'd ever had. They demonstrated things like tilting your head and saying something clever, playing off whatever line the guy has just fed you. They spoke in depth about using your eyes to give meaning to what you're saying—you know, flashing them or raising an eyebrow or whatever.

Easy for the twins to say! When Sandra tilts her

head, her streaky blond hair tumbles a little farther down one perfect shoulder. When I try it, with my short, wispy hair, I look like an inquisitive bird. Besides, how do you play off a line like "Close call"? *Yeah, I was never so glad to see an empty stall.*

"Did you wash your hair?" the little boy asked.

My hand flew up to my head.

"That's the style, Tim," the older guy said. "She used mousse."

Tim studied my head with interest.

"Actually," I told Tim, "I just wet it down, trying to keep myself from looking like a mad scientist with a short circuit."

Tim enjoyed my explanation. "Like Doctor Fuzzbuzz," he said.

"Old Porcupine Head," I replied.

"Ms. Fizzy Wig."

"No, no," I said, with mock seriousness, "she's the assistant."

Tim found this incredibly funny. I found Tim, with his mop of light brown hair and dusting of freckles, incredibly charming. "You're pretty," Tim said.

I tilted my head. "You say that to all the girls."

"Just the ones I like." His eyes were round and innocent. This kid was destined to break a lot of girls' hearts. "Would you buy me an ice cream?" he asked. "My brother won't."

I glanced up at Tim's brother, one eyebrow raised. He gave me the exact same look back.

I turned to Tim. "What's *he* got against ice

7

cream?" I asked. Out of the corner of my eye I saw his brother checking me out, his gaze slowly sweeping down and up me. I turned to face him. He laughed, not at all self-conscious about being caught in the act, holding my eyes with his.

Whoa, I thought, *I've been flirting!* Mostly with a seven-year-old, of course, and maybe that's why it seemed so easy. But the guy had noticed. And immediately the old, uncomfortable feelings began to creep in. I wished my sisters were there to pick up the conversation and bail me out.

Then the guy said, "My name is Ben. And what I've got against ice cream is that it becomes liquid. Immediately. We can't stop at every bathroom. I told Tim to choose between a small soda and an ice cream."

It was hard to take my eyes from his—he had the absolute confidence to gaze back at me without blinking.

"I'd suggest the same thing for you," he added, smiling.

"I'm taller than Tim. I can have twice as much."

Ben laughed.

"Want to share a pizza with us?" Tim asked.

"I—uh—"

"Not if she's going to eat twice as much as you," Ben said to his brother.

"I'll pay for my own," I assured him.

"Will you pay for ours too?" Ben asked. "I think you're onto a good thing, Tim. Every rest stop we'll pick up a hot girl and—"

A hot girl? I must've gotten a funny expression

on my face because Ben then touched me lightly on the elbow and said, "Just kidding. *I'll* pay if you'd like to join us."

"Dutch treat," I replied, amazing myself by accepting the invitation.

But then, why not? This might not happen again for another five years, unless, of course, I started frequenting rest stops. Plus I was sure I'd never see Ben again. I could act however I wanted, and who would know? If I made an idiot of myself, I'd never have to face him again. The realization was incredibly freeing.

"What's your name?" Ben asked.

"Allie."

"Allie Cat!" Tim crowed.

I smiled at him.

"Do you like pepperoni, Cat?" Tim asked.

"Anything but anchovies."

"How about goldfish?" Tim asked.

"Only if they're salted."

Tim thought this was hilarious. We finally settled on pepperoni with extra cheese. I forced a couple of dollars into Ben's hand, then Tim and I nabbed a table.

He and I told knock-knock jokes till Ben brought over the pizza and sodas. As we munched we talked about movies, sports, and the gifts Tim hoped he would get for Christmas. Eventually I learned that their parents had divorced last year and the boys were on the way to visit their father.

"And his fiancée. Can't wait to meet the woman," Ben said, grimacing.

The look on his face made me reluctant to ask any other questions related to home. And the truth was, I didn't feel like delving into my family situation either. I did mention Fields.

"A girls' boarding school?" Ben said with surprise. "No guys?"

"A lot of guys—three miles away."

Ben thought for a moment. "I guess that makes it a lot harder to date."

"Not for me," I said jauntily. It was the truth—three miles was no harder than three feet away—it all seemed pretty impossible to me.

"Really," he said, interpreting my statement in a different way, smiling and studying me. "Well, at least it cuts down on distractions."

I raised my eyebrows, hoping I looked interested and beguiling rather than bug-eyed. "Do you have trouble concentrating?"

"Right now?" he asked back.

I blushed and he laughed, winning that round.

Then Tim volunteered, "Ben has trouble concentrating on one girl."

"Thanks, Tim," Ben said. It was my turn to laugh. One side of Ben's mouth drew up. "You find that funny?"

"No, no," I said. What was funny was that I, Allison Parker, was trying to flirt with a pro.

When we'd finished the last bit of crust, we gathered our trash and walked slowly out to the parking lot.

"Where's your car?" Ben asked.

I pointed across the lot.

"This is ours," Tim said proudly, resting his hand on an ancient red Toyota.

"Now you know why I don't want to stop too often," Ben said to me. "I'm afraid it won't start again."

"Do you want me to stay and make sure you get back on the road?" I offered.

"No thanks. Tomato Soup hasn't let us down yet."

I smiled. Tomato soup was an exact description of the car's color.

"Well, it's been nice meeting you," I said, shaking his hand. Ben held on until I looked into his eyes. Until that moment I had no idea that looking and touching could be so dangerous. I felt light-headed and tingly all over. Withdrawing my hand, I quickly backed away and saw a smile touch his lips. He was used to girls responding to him like that. He counted on it. And I was sure that I'd just given myself away as a blushing amateur.

Fortunately Tim reached out for my hand right then. He looked a little solemn, and I gave him a warm hug. As I began to walk away I heard him whisper to Ben, then Ben's quiet reply, "If she wanted our number, she would've asked."

Back on the road again I pressed on the accelerator, putting miles between me and the rest stop as quickly as possible, overcome with embarrassment. One look at Ben should've told me that this was a guy who had "trouble concentrating" on one girl. And surely one look at me must've told *him* that I

11

didn't know how to act around guys. I started punching buttons, searching for a clear radio station, trying to put all thoughts of Ben behind me. Still my eyes darted after every faded red car on the highway. Do you know how many faded red cars drive the Jersey Turnpike?

Get real, I told myself. *And be glad you'll never see him again.*

The romantic holiday songs on the radio were getting to me. I pulled out a Jane's Addiction CD and shoved it into the player, then turned up the volume. Finding my exit, I rushed up the Garden State Parkway. Surely I'd left Ben and Tim miles behind, for there were a million exits to take from the Jersey Turnpike, and Ben and Tim could've been headed anywhere—Pennsylvania, Connecticut, Vermont, Canada. . . . Then I hit the brakes.

Had I really seen it—an old red Toyota stopped on the side of the road?

TWO

THERE COULDN'T BE another Tomato Soup in the universe, I thought as I pulled over to the shoulder, then backed up, my eyes on the beat-up little car in my rearview mirror. I noticed that it had a Blue Heron license plate, just like Miss Henny's; whoever owned the car lived in Maryland. No one was inside. I parked quickly and grabbed my car phone.

I'd barely gotten out of my Audi when Tim called to me. "Allie Cat! Over here!" He was waving his arms at me, standing about forty feet back in the roadside grass.

"Stay where you are, Tim. I told you to stay there," came a voice from under the car.

I walked around to the back of the Toyota. Ben's long legs were hanging out, the rest of him under the car.

"Hi . . . it's Allie. . . . Need help?"

"No. Just taking a coffee break," he grunted.

"Okay. I'm off."

"Allie!" he called, then slid himself out from beneath the car. He looked up at me and grinned. "Nice to see you again."

For a moment I couldn't think of what to say. I glanced down at my hands. "Yeah. Nice to see anyone with a car phone."

He sat up.

"Who do you want to call—Triple A?" I took several steps closer and held it out to him. If he touched my hand and looked in my eyes, would I tingle again or just get grease all over me?

"I think all I really need is a coat hanger," he said, wiping his hands on a towel. "All of ours are plastic. Do you have a wire one with you?"

"Yes," I said. "But I don't think it's going to hold those wheels on."

"It's for the muffler, Allie," he said, lying down again.

"Oh, you mean you have a muffler? It sure didn't sound like it when you left the rest stop."

He gave me a sarcastic smile, then pulled himself back under the Toyota.

"One wire coat hanger, coming up," I said cheerfully.

I fetched it for him, then stood around, watching his feet and listening to him grunt and mutter beneath the car. "What was that you said?" I teased. " 'Oh, fudge'?"

He kicked me, and I laughed.

"Is there something else I can do to help?" I asked after some more muttering from below.

"You can talk to Tim and keep him back from the road. That would be one less worry."

I went and sat in the grass with Tim. "I knew you'd come," he told me.

"How could you know that? You didn't know what road I was taking."

He shrugged and pulled on the coarse winter grass. "Things happen like that at Christmas," he said with a simple faith that touched me.

"Well, it was a lucky thing."

"Where are you going?" he asked.

"New York. My family lives on the other side of the Hudson River."

"Will you be there all of Christmas?" he asked.

"Yes."

"Maybe you could visit me."

"I'd like that, Tim," I answered. "But New York State is a big place and—"

"You have a car," he interrupted. "Do you know how to get to Thornhill?"

For a moment the town's name stuck in my throat. "Did you say Thornhill?"

"That's where my dad lives."

Maybe there was more than one Thornhill.

"It used to be where all of us lived. It's near Elmhurst—do you know where that is?"

I knew, all right. And I knew there was only one high school in the small town of Thornhill, the one in which my sisters had fast become the reigning

15

queens. Ben and my sisters would probably know the same people, be part of the same cool crowd. What if he told a story about a silly girl named Allie who had tried flirting with him on the highway?

"Your cheeks get red a lot," Tim observed.

"It's cold out," I said, though I was warm inside. Despite my embarrassment, a tiny flame started to burn at the thought that I might see Ben again.

"It wasn't cold at the restaurant," Tim reminded me, "and they got red there too. Here comes Ben. He'll tell you how to get to Thornhill."

"He doesn't need to, Tim. That's where I'm going."

"You are? Yow!" He jumped up. "Hey, Ben." His brother was walking with long strides over the grass, looking satisfied with himself. "Guess where Allie's going?"

"In the other direction, hoping to lose us?" he joked.

"To Thornhill."

Ben stopped, though still a short distance from us. "You are?" His easy smile disappeared immediately. "Well . . . great," he said, walking the last few steps to us.

"My parents moved there in August," I told him. "I was only in town for two days, so I don't really know the place."

"There's not much to know." He sounded irritated—almost angry.

"All the friends I have live there," Tim told me wistfully.

16

"It's hard to be away from friends," I replied, turning to the little boy. "All mine are back at my boarding school."

"You'll do all right," Ben said curtly. "It's a small town."

I glanced up at him, mystified by the sudden coldness in his voice. What was his problem? Did he think that knowing no one else, I was going to follow him around like a puppy dog? Did he have such an ego that he thought a little flirting meant I was madly in love with him? Well, I'd set his mind at ease.

"Listen," I said, "I know you must have a ton of friends to see."

"I do," he replied without looking at me.

"All those girls who disturb your concentration," I continued.

He glanced sideways at me.

"But you don't have to worry about me adding to the distractions. I know it's tough. So many girls, so little time." I sighed, my voice oozing with false sympathy.

He stared at me.

"I'm off, guys. Maybe I'll run into you two weeks from now on the turnpike headed south."

Ben didn't reply until I had strode twenty feet away. "Did I say something wrong?" he asked.

"No." I gave them a half wave. "You didn't say anything at all." *Like, "I hope we can get together,"* I thought.

I roared off in my car. When I was a chance

meeting, some girl Ben thought he'd never see again, he was charming. But when he found out we were heading for the same town . . . *Well, he'll be sorry,* I told myself. *When he sees my gorgeous sisters, he'll be begging to visit my home.*

Not that that was any consolation.

"Sweetheart!" my mother greeted me when I walked in the kitchen an hour later. She had the portable phone cradled between her ear and shoulder, a glue gun in one hand and a tumble of wine-colored ribbon in the other. "I have to go, Linda," she said into the phone. "My firstborn is home."

"Mom, couldn't you just refer to me as Allie?" I asked as I took the phone from her shoulder and clicked it off. We hugged. I had become adept at hugging my mother with drapes and paintbrushes and wallpaper rolls in her hands. Every time my parents moved, she redecorated, and if they stayed in the same place for more than two years, she redid the interior just out of habit. "You look great, Mom."

"You too—only a little thin."

She'd been saying that since I was in sixth grade. Maybe she was still waiting for me to get the full, curvy figure she and my sisters had. The three of them had light hair and green eyes. But I was built just like my father and aunt Jen—tall and slim, and sharing their dark coloring as well.

"You're just in time. I have to decide which wreath looks best on the front door." She attached the bow she was holding to a wreath that lay on the long kitchen table next to five others. "I know I can use all of these somewhere."

"You can never have too many wreaths," I replied, smiling. When it comes to decorating, my mother can never have too many of anything—wallpaper patterns, flowered rugs, furniture with carved doodads. Which is why she fell in love with the Victorian town of Thornhill and its wooden nineteenth-century houses painted in a rainbow of colors.

"Can you help carry these?" my mother asked.

I looped one wreath around my neck like a tire and carried two on each arm, keeping my arms outstretched as I followed her out the back door and around to the front. Just as I got to the front steps a BMW pulled into our driveway, its old motor revved too high. The guy driving it saw me and turned to my sisters with a questioning look on his face.

Sandra climbed out from the backseat. "Hey," she called out, "it's a walking Christmas tree."

"Allie, you're home!" Julia said as she got out of the car. "Thanks, Ford." She gave a vague wave as the guy backed his car down the driveway. While I'm a novice at flirting, I'm an expert at reading my sisters. Julia's wave told me Ford was either a new candidate or a boyfriend fading fast—there was no commitment in that wave.

"You look terrific, Al," Julia teased. "But I think you need a little more tinsel on top."

"No, dear, that's my subtle wreath," Mom explained, fingering the decoration that hung around my neck. It was silver, covered with metallic birds dipped in blue and pink glitter.

"Real subtle, Mom," Sandra said, running her hand through blond hair that fell to her waist. Julia's did too, but she usually wore hers up in some way. Sandra smiled at me. "I'm glad to see you, Al."

"Thanks."

"Me too," Julia added. "We missed our big sister. We especially missed you when we had to write papers."

"Everybody at Fields has been asking about you," I told them. "I've got a million messages and cards for you."

"Really?" Julia said, but she didn't sound very interested.

"Miss Henny wanted me to say hello for her."

"That's nice. So which of these wreaths is going on the front door?" Sandra asked Mom.

"That's what I'm trying to decide," she replied.

"Miss Henny's talking about retiring soon," I went on, "and—"

"She should've five years ago," Sandra remarked.

"Come on, Allie," Julia said, "go stand by the door. Model the wreaths for us."

Apparently they were no longer interested in people at Fields. I gave up and dutifully climbed the steps of the porch. My mother and sisters stood a distance back, studying the decorations, directing me to hold each one up at various heights. I did this for three rounds while they argued over which looked best, then I finally got fed up and lined up the wreaths by the door.

"I'm unpacking," I said, heading toward my car, which was parked at the end of the driveway, back near the kitchen.

"I'll help you," Julia volunteered. "How was the drive up?" she asked, trailing behind me.

"Okay." I popped open the trunk. Julia pulled out a basketball and started dribbling to the backboard mounted on the double garage.

"Good shot, Jule!" I called as the ball swished through the net.

She dribbled back to me, then pulled out a lacrosse stick and two tennis rackets. "I'll put these in the exercise room," she said, heading toward the back door.

Sandra circled the porch and joined me. "The wreath with the glittery birds won."

"I thought it would."

She gazed down into the trunk. "Wow—you packed light."

Sandra never went anywhere without several suitcases of clothes. I handed her two bags of gifts, then followed her into the house, carrying my one suitcase and a box of videos. We went through the kitchen and into the hall, then climbed the wide, turning stair in the center of the house.

Sandra stopped abruptly at the entrance to my room. "Oops."

"Oops?" I repeated, trying to see over her shoulder.

"Guess we should leave your stuff right here. *Julia!*" she bellowed.

21

It took the three of us twenty minutes to clear their things out of my room. Why my sisters needed to drape their stuff over my bed and chairs, I don't know, because all three of our rooms were big. Sandra's and mine faced the front of the house, and we both had a bay window with a window seat. Sandra had a private bathroom as well. Julia, whose room was in the back of the house, shared a bathroom with me when I was home, but her room had a door to an outside deck. Our parents have always been careful to balance what they give to each of us. Since I'm away at school, I got to keep our car, but it's understood that when I'm home, my sisters can borrow it and I'm expected to do errands.

With their stuff put away, I opened my suitcase on the double bed. My sisters stretched out on either side of it.

"You don't still wear this?" Sandra said, pulling out a raspberry-colored sweater.

"It's my favorite."

"It was your favorite two years ago," she observed.

"So, I'm loyal." I took it out of her hands and put it in a drawer.

Julia was holding a small blue bag. "Where's your makeup case?"

"That's it," I replied.

"It has one lipstick and a tube of sunscreen."

"That's it," I repeated.

Julia sat up and put on the dark lipstick. It did nothing for her gilt-and-porcelain look.

"Wipe it off," Sandra advised.

"Did you get any good Christmas gifts at school?" Julia asked.

"Some things, but I left them in my dorm room."

"Anything from a guy?" Sandra wanted to know.

An image of Ben's face suddenly flashed in my mind. I quickly forced it away. "Why? Are those the only gifts that count?"

"I was just curious," Sandra replied. "Don't be so sensitive, Al." She played with the beaded bracelet on her left arm.

"That's pretty," I said, hoping to ward off any further interest in my social life.

"Mike gave it to me."

"Mike . . ." I couldn't remember who he was. My sisters and I e-mailed each other about once a week, but I lost track of all their guys.

"Mike Calloway, jock and heartthrob," Julia filled me in. "Basketball hero of Thornhill High. Very, very cute. Very, very stuck on Sandra."

"A basketball player," I said. "You can wear four-inch heels!"

Sandra threw back her head and laughed. "I've bought three pairs this month. But he's not a boyfriend, not yet, and I'm not sure he's so stuck on me." She rolled off the bed and got up to look at herself in the mirror. "Sometimes I think he's more hooked on his sport."

"Well, if you didn't play so hard to get," Julia chastised her. She turned to me. "You've never seen such games—one moment they chase each other

23

down the halls, the next moment they're ignoring each other."

Sandra shrugged—a pretty, sulky shrug.

"How about you, Julia?" I asked, continuing to put things away. "Who was the guy who dropped you off?"

"Ford?" She gave a shrug almost identical to Sandra's, then sighed. Having already noted the vague wave, I figured he was Boyfriend Past.

"He and I starred in *Broadway Revue,* the fall production at school."

"And?" I prompted.

"He's great looking."

"I *saw.*"

"He's got a good voice," Julia continued. "And a lot of ideas for fun things to do."

"But?"

"It's not true love." She picked up a pillow, held it in her arms like a person, then gave it a poke. "Unfortunately he was more interesting when he was playing a role."

"Maybe he's just having a hard time being himself," I suggested, "you know, letting you see who he really is."

"You think so?"

"I don't know what you're bummed about," Sandra said to Julia. "Two other guys called you last night."

"Three," Julia corrected Sandra sweetly.

"No, Jeff's call was for me. He had us mixed up."

"I don't think so."

24

The identical stiff smiles and perfect enunciation of each word warned me that one of the twins' competitive matches was coming on. I'd witnessed enough of them for a lifetime and decided my sisters could battle it out somewhere else. "Listen," I said, "I need to hide your Christmas gifts."

"Okay, we'll close our eyes," Julia replied with a sly smile.

"Out!" I told them.

Sandra laughed.

"Come down for a snack when you're done," Julia said.

As soon as my sisters were gone I put the shopping bags in the closet—where, if the twins wanted, they could easily find their gifts—but hid the three romances I'd brought home to read. My recent switch from Stephen King to gothic love stories was something I preferred to keep to myself.

It took longer than it should have to put everything away because I kept pausing to think about Ben—his smile, the warmth of his voice, his sense of humor. And the way it all shut down when he learned he might see me again.

It wasn't fair! My sisters had an army of guys to choose from while I just wanted to be with one— and he just wanted to be with me . . . when no other girl was around.

Three

BY THE TIME I finished unpacking, two of my sisters' friends had dropped by. My mother, always trying to help along my social life, had been holding back the snacks and sodas, waiting for me to come down. When she asked me to carry them into the family room, I knew she was hoping I'd stay and talk to my sisters' friends. The fact that I was vice president of the senior class and captain of the basketball and softball teams at Fields didn't reassure her; I had to have friends at home too.

When I walked in the room, my sisters introduced me to Caroline, who had a mane of red hair, and Janice, who had silky black hair and incredible almond-shaped eyes. I placed the tray in the center of the group, aware of the two girls studying me.

"Stay," Julia said, catching me by the hand as I turned to walk out. "It's Christmas vacation. Party down, Al."

Before I could reply, Janice said, "So you go to boarding school."

"Yes," I answered, then took a tentative step toward the door.

"An all-girl school," she continued, her dark eyes full of curiosity.

I felt like a strange species she'd just discovered. "The same one my sisters went to," I told her.

Julia yanked on my hand, pulling me down into their circle. I sat on the floor, figuring I could leave as soon as the questions were over.

"I can't even imagine what that is like!" Janice exclaimed.

"I told you what it's like," Julia reminded her.

But Janice shook her head. "Mostly you told me about the guys at the boarding school three miles away."

Everyone laughed.

"Three miles, is it?" Caroline mused, munching on some of the chips I'd brought in. "Well, that's a mile and a half for the girl and a mile and a half for the guy. Do you ever have secret late night meetings in the woods?"

"Uh, no," I responded.

"For that kind of meeting you'd have to get across a river and up a steep hill, almost a cliff," Julia said.

"I tried it once with David Crane," Sandra added, "but he got lost. How is David?" she asked me.

"I don't know." I reached for a pretzel. "I haven't seen him since last year."

"You're kidding!" Sandra sounded genuinely surprised. "But you two liked to talk. You always kept him company for me down in the waiting parlor. At Fields," she explained to her friends, "when the guys came to pick us up, they had to sign in and stay in the waiting parlor."

And guess who used to be sent down to keep all those guys company? While Sandra would finish dressing, David and I would discuss an entire week of sports.

"You know," Sandra said, "I thought with me gone, he'd be sure to date you."

I gritted my teeth. "Guess not."

"Are you an actress too?" Janice asked me, her dark hair swinging forward.

"Janice is going to be the director of our spring production," Julia told me. "She is so, *so* talented."

"Oh, you drama club types," Caroline said, laughing at them. "The way you suck up to each other, telling each other you're wonderful."

"But I *am* wonderful," Janice teased, stretching back into the luxury of a leather chair.

Julia playfully poked Caroline. "At least we're fans of each other and not just the guys' team."

"Caroline is captain of the cheerleading squad," Sandra explained.

"But Sandra *should* be," Caroline told me. "She cheers louder than any member of my squad when Mike takes the floor. What a defection! Our number-one jock interested in someone from the drama club rather than the cheerleading squad."

"But that's not so different from last year," Janice argued from her chair. "Do you remember Ben Harrington?"

My ears pricked up.

"What girl could forget Ben?" Caroline replied.

My Ben?

Caroline combed her fingers through her long, fiery hair. "Now *he* was hot. Too bad he had to leave. His parents got divorced—my mother says Ben's mother was dumped for another woman. He and his little brother moved away," she went on, "to Maryland, I think."

I sat up so straight that Janice glanced at me.

"I wonder if Ben is related to Aunt Jen's friend," Sandra said to Julia. "Isn't his name Harrington?"

"I heard Ben's coming back for the holidays," Caroline continued. "I hope he's driving something better than that red Toyota."

I barely breathed.

"He must've dated every girl on the cheerleading squad," she said, "and in the drama club. The sailing club too—the blondes, usually."

And *I* had tried to flirt with him? My earlier suspicion was right—Ben must've known from the beginning that I didn't know how to flirt and had simply found me entertaining. The final brush-off made more sense than ever.

"The thing about Ben," Janice said, "is that he's truly a nice person. He always had as many guy friends as girls. I guess because he knew he was cool, he could be nice to everyone—people

I wouldn't be caught dead talking to."

Like me, I thought.

"I'm counting on you to introduce us," Sandra said.

"Yeah, well, you're going to have to stand in line," Caroline told her.

"And do it when Mike's not around," Janice advised. "Mike was never as popular as Ben, and it really bothered him. He won't want you hanging around him."

"No guy tells me who I can be friends with," Sandra retorted.

"I could sure use a break from Ford," Julia added.

Déjà vu. I'd seen it all before—my sisters quickly moving in on the most interesting guy around, deflating everyone else's hopes. The thing was, until now it hadn't been *my* secret hope that was squashed. It was a very tiny hope, of course, one I hadn't wanted to admit to myself. But now I knew better. Me and the hottest guy in town? When the moon dropped out of the sky, maybe.

My sisters and their friends went on to discuss other guys and girls in their crowd—who was in and who was out. The names meant nothing to me, though occasionally Ben's name would surface. I found myself wondering if there was a pretty girl at Thornhill High whom he hadn't dated.

It was a relief when I spotted my father standing in the doorway, listening to our conversation, looking perplexed. Sometimes my dad seems like a lost

31

soul in his own household. The others turned and saw him.

"Ladies," he said, nodding at us. He always gets formal when he's uncomfortable.

"Hey, Dad."

"Allison," he said. "Welcome home! May I take you away from your friends for a moment?"

My friends? I got up quickly and followed him through the living room into his study. It was the one room that always felt familiar to me, for the books, furniture, and my father's sculpture collection had followed us from house to house.

"Well, Allie, you look—you look—" Sometimes my father thought too much about his words.

"Like Allie?" I suggested.

He smiled and gave me a quick hug, then retreated behind his wide desk.

"So how's it going, Dad?" I asked, sitting down across from him.

"The Dow fell last quarter, but I'm confident that it'll turn around once stockholders recognize the importance of our new investments in Malaysia. The drilling is almost completed, and the mine samples are positive. It's a matter of getting the right supervisory personnel."

That's my father for you, cuts right to the chase. He's totally uncomfortable with small talk and would've given me the same answer if I'd asked, "How are *you,* Dad?" He is how his work is.

"How about you?" he inquired.

"Well, I sent out the college applications."

"And?"

"I included Harvard and Princeton. I mean, why not shoot for the best? I can deal with rejection."

"That's my girl," he said, looking proud. "Jen called this morning," he added.

"About tonight? She e-mailed me last week, asking if I could have dinner with her."

"Yes, well, there's been a slight change of plans. The dinner is still on, but you'll be meeting later than she'd planned at a restaurant called Candella's."

"Great," I said. "What time?"

"Eight. Aunt Jen has a surprise for you."

"Yeah?"

He nodded. "Quite a surprise."

I got the feeling he didn't fully approve of it, but that wasn't unusual. Jen is my father's youngest sister, an independent type who will go anywhere and try anything. She's single, thirty, and has a very successful law practice in Elmhurst. She's my godmother and with my parents living abroad has been a confidante to me. For the last three years we'd talked about taking a month-long trip to celebrate my graduation from high school. I hoped that was what this dinner was about.

"Candella's is an upscale place, but your mother can fill you in on that," he said, which was the signal that our talk was over.

"Thanks, Dad."

"Thanks, Allison," he said when I was almost at the doorway, "for coming home."

Four

M Y SISTERS SHOWED up in my room the
moment I began to dress for Candella's. The
result was a spread of cosmetics like that in a department store offering free makeovers. I made the mistake of saying that I didn't know what to do with half
the bottles and brushes. The twins went right to
work on me, talking all the time.

"Find out if Aunt Jen's boyfriend, Sam Harrington,
is related to Ben," Sandra told me, squinting at the line
she'd just drawn on my eyelid.

"Is she actually dating Mr. Harrington?" I asked.
Jen hadn't mentioned him to me. Each of us had
our special aunt, and Jen, being mine, usually told
me something important before she told my sisters.

"As much as Aunt Jen dates anyone," Julia answered.

"He's old," Sandra told me. "Too old."

"He's got gray hair," Julia added.

"There!" Sandra said, looking satisfied. Then

35

she caught my face with a light hand. "Don't look yet. Some lips, huh?" she asked Julia.

Julia nodded. "I'm glad you're finally letting us fix you up, Allie. What changed your mind?"

I shrugged. I wasn't sure why I decided to let them make me up that evening or borrow the dress Julia pulled out of her closet with the excuse that it was the wrong color for her. It was the shortest, sexiest piece of velveteen I'd ever put on. Maybe I was making an effort to find some connection with my sisters, or maybe I wanted to feel less like a boarding-school bumpkin who had embarrassed herself flirting with Thornhill's biggest hunk. A half hour later I stared at the dark-haired girl in the mirror and thought that Miss Henny might've been right—I did have my "own beauty."

"Good lord!" my father exclaimed when I passed him in the hall.

"You look beautiful, Allie, just beautiful," my mother said.

"You think I should bring my driver's license so Aunt Jen knows it's me?"

"Chin up. Walk straight," my mother replied, "and don't talk that way."

As I drove the short route to Candella's a new kind of excitement grew in me. I felt glamorous, adventurous. I handed my coat to the guy in the cloakroom and didn't hunch over like a schoolgirl when he checked me out before checking the coat. Aunt Jen came in right behind me. We hugged.

"You look wonderful!" she exclaimed.

I'd never seen her cheeks so pink. "So do you."

She deposited her beaver jacket, then grabbed my hand. "This wasn't what I'd planned for us tonight, but come on," she said, "our table's waiting."

I strutted after my aunt and the maitre d' with an amazing burst of confidence. Maybe it was the attention my family had lavished on me that afternoon or the cute guy at the corner table who turned to look at me and smiled, but for one unusual moment I was feeling so adult and sure of myself, I was ready for anything.

But I never could have been prepared for what happened next. Because one second later I noticed Ben and Tim Harrington across the room—right in the direction where we were headed. Just as I was about to suggest to Aunt Jen that we go somewhere else so I could bolt out of there as quickly as possible, Tim looked up and saw me.

"Hey!" he called. "It's Allie Cat!"

Ben looked up with surprise. His eyes flicked quickly to Aunt Jen, then he turned to the gray-haired man with whom he was sitting. Ben, Tim, and the man, who must have been their father, rose at the same time as Jen and I walked toward them.

Were we sitting with *them?* My legs suddenly felt wobbly. "Hey, Tim," I said softly.

My aunt looked back at me. "You know each other?"

Tim turned to Ben, who was staring at me as if he had just been pinged between the eyes with a rock. Tim nudged him. "It's Allie."

The older man held out his hand to me. "I'm Sam Harrington," he introduced himself in a deep and friendly voice. "You don't by any chance drive a silver Audi and make highway rescues?"

"Uh . . . sometimes."

"Will somebody explain this to me?" Aunt Jen said. "I'm the one who was supposed to be springing a surprise." She playfully flashed a bright, sparkly object on her left hand.

"What's that?" I asked.

Aunt Jen smiled. "I'm getting married, Allie."

I guess I gave her the same shot-between-the-eyes look as Ben had given me.

"Allie?" my aunt asked, leaning closer to me.

"Wonderful," I sputtered out. "Congratulations. That's great. Really."

Not really. My adventurous aunt was settling down. The person in my family whom I most wanted to be like was "the other woman" in a divorce—the woman Ben had told me he wanted nothing to do with. And the guy I'd flirted with because I thought I'd never see him again was going to be connected to me by marriage.

"Why don't we all sit down?" Mr. Harrington suggested.

There was a moment of confusion as Tim crawled under the table so he could take the seat next to me. We seated ourselves around the circle, Tim and Ben on either side of me. At least I didn't have to look squarely at Ben. Instead I studied the strong shape of his left hand and kept smelling his aftershave.

"You look pretty."

I turned to my ardent admirer, Tim. "Thanks. That's a nice sweater."

"*She* gave it to me," he said, with a quick glance toward my aunt.

"Her name is Jen," his father said sternly.

"You already told me," Tim replied. "Twice."

This, I thought, *is not going to be a fun dinner.*

"Tim, did you know Jen is Allie's aunt?" Mr. Harrington asked.

Tim looked at me as if I'd just betrayed him.

"So, Allie," Mr. Harrington said, pulling on his tie, which did not go with his shirt, which did not go with his jacket, "Jen tells me that you attend Fields and you're a top-notch student and excellent athlete."

I stared back at him for a moment, still trying to absorb the fact that this man—Ben's *father* of all people—was going to marry Aunt Jen. I hadn't even known she was dating anyone! Then I remembered that a question had been directed at me. "Yes. I mean, I like school, and I play sports."

"Terrific. So does Ben," Mr. Harrington said.

"Really, you two share a lot of interests," Aunt Jen added.

Just what Ben wants to hear, I thought. I figured his palms were getting clammy at the idea that he might be asked to entertain me over the holidays. *Well, let him sweat. Let him worry that I'm going to join the army of girls who dream of having something in common with him.*

"Ben used to be a basketball player," Tim volunteered. "And lacrosse. And soccer. He was the best and used to get his picture in our paper all the time, and when he was a sophomore, he won All-State Center, and when he was a junior, he won—"

"Tim," Ben said, "give it a rest. She's not interested in all that."

"How do you know?" I asked.

"It's boring," Ben replied. "And it's no longer relevant."

"Maybe it's just boring to you because you already know it all," I pointed out.

"All right," he said stiffly, "we have about ten scrapbooks at home you can go through."

"One will be enough."

He turned and met my gaze steadily.

"Then I'll show you mine," I said.

I heard Mr. Harrington stifle a laugh. He reached for my aunt's hand. "You're right, Jen. She's just like you."

Once again I couldn't help staring at Mr. Harrington. This was going to take some time to get used to.

"Can I see your book too?" Tim asked me.

"Oh, Tim, I was just kidding. I don't really keep things like that."

"When I was in high school," Mr. Harrington said, "the girls always kept dance invitations, party streamers, things like that. A guy knew he'd made a good impression on a date when the girl asked to keep the ticket stub."

"Do you have scrapbooks with stuff like that?" Tim asked me.

When I didn't answer, Ben replied, "Ten of them. Maybe she'll show you one."

I turned quickly. "According to the girls who live here—some of my sisters' friends—ten memory books are *far* less than you've helped to fill."

There was a moment of silence in which I told myself I hadn't said that aloud. But Ben's raised eyebrows told me I had.

"Really," he said, in a tone I couldn't interpret.

"Are you ready to order?" our server asked, arriving at our table just in time. Maybe I should have requested my own bread basket so I could stuff my mouth before I said anything else I'd regret. Now Ben would think I'd been doing research on him.

"Your sisters are the twins," Mr. Harrington said after we had all placed our orders, "the ones who made such a sensation in the school drama production this fall, is that right?"

"Yes, sir."

"Please," he said, "call me Sam."

"Sam," I repeated.

"We carried a story about the Parker twins in our newspaper," Sam told Ben. "Craig took the photos for us."

"Well, Craig always does a good job," Ben replied. His voice held no enthusiasm for the conversation, and I noticed that he wouldn't look at my aunt Jen. I felt bad for her even if she was "the other woman."

41

"I remember now," I said. "Mom mailed me the article."

"Sam is the publisher of the paper," Aunt Jen told me. I could hear the pride in her voice.

"Yeah? That's cool."

Sam grinned. "That's how we met, you know. I interviewed Jen."

Bad move. I saw Ben's hand tense up.

"I thought she was the brightest and prettiest woman I'd ever had coffee with."

I saw Aunt Jen shake her head at Sam. *Shut up*, I silently urged him.

"And tough," he added. "When I asked her for a follow-up interview, she refused. She made me ask her three times."

I knew someone had to change the subject. "I can't wait till you meet my sisters," I said. "You'll really like them."

"Do they look like you?" Tim asked. "Then you'd be triplets." He laughed at his own joke.

I laughed with him. "No, you'd never guess we're sisters. They're gorgeous."

Out of the corner of my eye I saw Ben frowning.

"I need to make a phone call," Aunt Jen said. "Would you come with me, Sam?"

I knew Sam was going to get a lecture on what to say in front of the kids. The last thing his sons wanted to hear was how he fell in love with someone other than their mother.

When Jen disappeared with Tim's father, the little boy asked, "How come your sisters live here and you don't? Did your parents get a divorce?"

"No, it's just that my sisters like to party and date a lot and wanted to go to a regular high school, like the one here."

I caught Ben studying me, almost as if he were sizing up me and my family. "My sisters have always been the most popular girls at school, first at Fields, and now at Thornhill," I boasted, then immediately felt stupid. What did that have to do with anything? But when Ben looked unimpressed, as if he already knew a million girls like my sisters, I became defiant. "Guys can't resist them. You'll see."

"These are the sisters whose friends filled you in on my past?" he asked.

"Yes. Apparently you're a hot topic of conversation at Thornhill High," I told him. "Trust me," I added quickly, "I didn't bring you up."

One side of Ben's mouth pulled up in a mocking smile. Was he laughing at me or the other girls? I wondered. He sure didn't look happy. Nor did Tim, who had begun folding his napkin over and over into the same shape, his chin down low on his chest.

The anger began to drain out of me. There was enough hurt with the divorce and remarriage situation; I didn't need to add to it by saying snide things to Ben. One of us had to make things pleasant—otherwise we'd never get through this dinner or the holidays.

"Tim, did you just see those cakes go by?" I asked, pointing to a cart.

The little boy nodded.

"Go find out what's on there, see what we can have for dessert, okay?"

"You getting rid of me?" Tim asked.

"Yup."

His eyes crinkled up with his smile. He rose and followed the waiter across the room.

"Look," I said, turning to Ben, "we need to straighten out a few things."

"Like what?"

"Well, let's start at the beginning. Back at the rest stop, I kind of flirted."

"Not kind of," he observed.

"It was . . . sort of an experiment. At an all-girls school we don't get much chance to practice, so—"

"I see. I was your guinea pig."

"The good news is that you don't have to worry about me chasing you around."

"I know—you told me that back on the Garden State."

"Moving on," I continued, "I shouldn't have mentioned my sisters or—"

"Why not?" he replied quickly. "I love to know that people are gossiping about me."

"Help me out here," I warned him between tight lips. "You're making me mad."

"Sorry . . . sorry," he repeated, sounding sincere the second time.

I took a deep breath. "I understand that you're not thrilled to meet my family and that you wouldn't like anyone related to Aunt Jen. I'd feel the same way if I were you."

44

He played with his fork, turning it over and over in his hands.

"But I think we should try to make this one meal a friendly one," I told him, "for other people's sake."

"Do you mean for the sake of my father and his fiancée? I don't care how they feel."

"How about Tim?" I asked.

Ben dropped the fork, then sat back in his chair. "You've got a soft spot for him, don't you?"

"Guess so."

"I think you'll go down in *Tim's* scrapbook as his first love."

I blushed. Ben glanced sideways at me, a trace of a smile on his lips.

"Okay," he said, his face growing serious again. "I know you're right. But I'm telling you, I'm in a stinking mood. At the moment I'd like to kill my father, and I don't even want to think about your aunt Jen. So you're gonna have to be ready to change the wrong topics of conversation my father is so adept at introducing and stomp on my foot if I start acting up."

"No problem," I replied. "I'm wearing my sister's spikes."

His mouth softened again, and his eyes got the teasing look I'd seen back on the turnpike. "No, you're not," he said, rubbing the toe of his shoe under the arch of my stockinged foot. "You took them off the moment you sat down."

Five

TUESDAY MORNING WOULD have been dismal in any month other than December. But when I awoke, three hours later than usual, the gray, sleety mix falling outside was warmed by Christmas lights inside. My mother must have tiptoed in and lit the candles in my bedroom windows. In the hall the pine garland that was wrapped around the railing of the second-floor balcony twinkled its way down the steps, leading me from landing to landing. I found my mother in the kitchen, working with her faithful glue gun.

"We're going to have to get you a holster for that," I said, coming up behind her. "G'morning, Mom."

"Morning, sweetheart."

I poured myself some juice and sat down at the table across from where she was attaching little gold horns to some kind of white twig arrangement. "Where are you going to put that?" I asked.

"These are for New Year's, sweetie. We'll be taking them as gifts when we make Christmas visits. For the first time since you girls were tiny, we're just a town away from relatives, at least on your father's and Jen's side."

"How long have you known about Aunt Jen and Sam?" I asked.

"Jen told us this past weekend. I don't think your father is real happy about it, given that Sam is recently divorced, and, well, he is a little eccentric." My mother fussed with the wreath, twisting its leaves. "Anyway, she wanted to tell you in person, and we let your sisters know last night when you were out. Speaking of which—"

"Yes?"

"Could you pick them up from school? It's their last day and early dismissal. I told them to look for you."

"No problem."

"The roads may be icy, and I trust you more than their boyfriends," my mother went on. "Not that they aren't nice boys, every one of them. Now, the one that—"

"I understand, Mom. I'm glad to do it," I said, cutting her off before she went page by page through the current boyfriend catalog.

A few hours later, when I pulled on my old parka, which showed the wear of many camping expeditions, another reason for my mission was revealed.

"You're wearing that?" my mother asked with a frown.

"It's cold out."

"Here," she said, producing a coat so quickly, either she'd learned magic or had fetched it earlier from Sandra's closet. It was made of soft white rain-repellent fabric and had a fur-edged hood that could make Sandra look like Julie Christie in the old movie *Dr. Zhivago.*

"It's not mine, Mom."

"Wear it," she said, pointing her glue gun at me. "And enjoy yourself," she added in a more motherly voice. "Meet some nice boys."

She never gives up, I thought, stuffing the map she'd drawn for me in my pocket.

When I arrived at the school, the lot was filled with cars. I was a few minutes early and feeling restless, so I parked my car and got out to walk. The icy rain had stopped, and a blustery wind was beginning to blow. I was glad I had the hood to pull up over my head.

I strolled along the pavement in front of the school until I reached a long, rectangular wing of the building with a rounded top—the gym, I figured. Suddenly a door opened and Ben emerged. He was wearing a dark gold jacket, the kind a member of a school team wears. His eyes were far away, and his lips held a straight, almost grim line. I took a step back, unsure of whether to speak to him. If he saw me as I turned my back, he might think I was snubbing him. But he didn't look as if he wanted to talk to anyone either.

I turned to retrace my steps and accidentally

kicked a loose stone. He turned his head quickly.

"Hi," I said.

"Hi."

"How are you?" I asked.

"Okay."

"Good."

There was an awkward silence. Ben glanced at his watch.

"I'm here to pick up my sisters," I explained quickly. "It just happens that I keep ending up in the same place as you. My mother sent me."

He laughed. "It's okay, Allie. I know you're not chasing me."

I nodded and turned to continue my walk alone, but Ben fell in stride beside me.

"Were you visiting old friends?" I asked when it was clear he was strolling with me rather than trying to get somewhere.

"I just saw one of my teachers and my coach, Tweeter."

"Tweeter?"

"That's his nickname."

"I bet he was glad to see you," I said.

"How would you know?"

I blinked.

"Sorry," Ben apologized, "I'm still in that stinking mood. Though I faked pretty well last night, don't you think?"

"You did great. Tim actually called Jen by her own name once. Still, faking is hard to keep up for too long."

"Sometimes there isn't any choice," he murmured.

"How's Tomato Soup doing?" I asked, switching to a lighter subject.

"She's being good, hoping Santa will bring her a new engine."

I laughed and so did he, but I could hear the effort behind his laugh. "No one's around," I told him as we walked. "It's all right to be in a stinking mood till your friends come out."

He turned and gazed down at me. For one crazy moment I felt as beautiful as Julie Christie in that fur-lined hood.

"It'll get better," I promised him. "You're back with your old friends now, kids who know you."

Ben looked away.

"I'm sorry it's so hard for you."

"It's much harder on Tim," he replied. "He doesn't understand why any of this happened. I have to keep telling him it has nothing to do with him or me—we didn't make our parents unhappy. But I'm not sure I'm getting through. Our lunch at the rest stop was the first time I'd seen him laugh for a long while."

"If it'll help," I said, "I'll be glad to take him out during the vacation—to a movie or skating, whatever. He'll be a good distraction. Really," I added in response to Ben's curious look, "it's going to be a long two weeks for me. I'd enjoy doing things with Tim."

We had reached the end of the lot and turned back, walking silently for a minute.

"Why is it going to be a long two weeks?"

"Just is."

A gust of wind blew back my hood. I could feel my hair turning into a million feathers and put my hand up as if I could hold them down.

He studied my face. "Because you left behind a boyfriend?"

The school bell rang, saving me from laughing at his guess. I turned with relief as the school doors banged back.

"Benjo!" someone called. Three guys wearing the same gold jacket as Ben came hurrying toward us.

"Harrington! Where have you been, man?" the tallest said.

"Hey, Twist!" Ben replied. They did some macho body banging, one of those things about guys I'll never understand.

"It's Ben!" said a girl who'd just emerged from the school building.

"Hi, Ben," two others called.

"He's ba–ack," teased the tall guy named Twist.

A dozen people headed in our direction. I began to back away as they surrounded him.

"Ben, you look so good!" cooed a brunette.

"How come you didn't come back for home-coming?" another girl asked.

"Yeah, Lenny came back."

"I know," Ben replied, "I've talked to Lenny a couple of times this fall."

"You didn't talk to me, big guy," Twist said. He had a long and comical face to go with his long body. "I'm hurt."

Ben laughed.

They were all around him now. I looked for my sisters and their two friends I'd met the day before, but they hadn't come out yet. From my place at the edge of the crowd I could see that Ben's popularity with the girls hadn't been exaggerated. He was getting a lot of hugs and kisses. A girl with white blond hair and blue eyes attached herself to Ben's side as if they'd been glue-gunned together by my mother.

"What plans do you have for the holidays?" asked one of the guys in a gold jacket.

"Plans? None at the moment."

"To party, party, party," another guy said. "Your name's Ben Harrington, isn't it?"

Ben laughed. There wasn't a trace of the guy with the distant eyes and grim mouth.

"And you *do* have plans tonight," said the white blonde. "You're coming with me to Melanie's party."

"Melanie is having her usual?" Ben asked.

"Of course."

Fifteen people started talking at once, then I heard Ben say, "I just remembered. I can't. I promised Tim I'd take him to the holiday show at his old school."

"You've got to come," Twist urged.

"Someone else can take your brother," the light-haired girl said.

"I'll take him," I said.

Everyone turned around to see who had spoken.

"I told you, Ben, I'd be happy to do things with Tim."

Ben smiled, but I felt as if everyone else was

measuring me and my numbers didn't qualify. A few heads leaned toward each other; girls whispered. *They're curious, not snotty,* I told myself. *They're only looking to see who I am.* But their stares made me self-conscious.

"What if we both take Tim to the show," Ben suggested, "then go late to the party?"

"The problem is," said the girl with the light hair, "it's not my party. I can take a date, but I can't invite others."

"Are you sure?" Twist asked.

"Yeah. It's a closed party," said another girl.

Ben's eyes flicked from them to me. He looked a little embarrassed.

I just wanted to get out of there. "It's no big deal," I said. "I'm not in the mood for partying anyway. Really." I pulled my mother's map out of my pocket. "Write down your address and the time I should be there."

He seemed uncertain.

"Don't be pigheaded."

"Who, me?" Ben replied with a smile. "Okay. Thanks, Allie. You're a pal."

As soon as he'd scribbled down the information I took the map and headed toward the car to wait for my sisters. I pulled up my hood so Ben's friends couldn't see any part of my face. Didn't they know it was rude to stare? And as for their closed party, did I say I wanted to come?

I hadn't gotten far when I heard quick footsteps behind me. Someone caught me by the arm. "Hey, babe," he said. "Come on, slow down," he chided me, catching me lightly by the other arm. "Don't play games."

That was the last straw. I whirled around. I must've had one fierce expression on my face, for the guy stepped back quickly, holding his hands up in front of him. His dark blue eyes traveled down my coat and back up to my face. He was several inches taller than I and athletically built, his hair dark and wavy. "Who are you?" he asked.

"Who am I?" I snarled. "Who are *you*, Cupcake?"

The crowd behind him snickered. Ben laughed out loud. My sisters, who'd finally emerged from the school building, smiled and waved to me—or maybe to the studly guy staring at me.

"Mike," Sandra called out. "That's my sister Allie. She's just wearing my coat."

"Your sister," Mike echoed.

"Sorry," I apologized, "I didn't realize—"

"That's okay. My mistake," he said, continuing to gaze at me with an intensity that made me uncomfortable.

"I know, I know, I look nothing like my sisters."

"That's *very* okay," he said.

"So . . . uh . . . you're Sandra's friend."

"I'm friends with a lot of people," he replied, smiling at me.

"Well, it was nice meeting you," I told him, and extended my hand. He held it gently; I shook his hard, then walked away.

Mike joined Ben's crowd—my sisters' crowd. I

waited in the safety of my car while they all laughed and talked. I didn't want to look like I was watching, but I was dying to, especially as my sisters got closer to Ben. I busied myself by reading a state map of New York but still snuck peeks at them. Sandra was next to Ben, laughing, her golden hair flying loose in the breeze. I turned the map over and explored New Jersey. At last I heard the car door open.

"Thanks for waiting, Al," Julia said, climbing into the front seat.

"No problem," I replied.

"Is Ben ever cute!" Sandra exclaimed, throwing her books into the back of the car, then getting in. "Those big brown eyes. When he looks at you, you feel like he's kissing you."

I glanced at her in the rearview mirror, wishing for a short moment that her golden hair was mine. Then I pulled out of the parking space.

"I wonder . . . ," she said, her voice trailing off, her eyes getting dreamy.

"This is Sandra's latest thing," Julia told me. "She looks at a guy and predicts what it would be like to make out with him."

"How creative," I replied, and tried not to indulge myself in the same fantasy. "Buckle your seat belt."

"Oh!" Sandra cried. I'd taken the speed bump way too fast.

"Tell me," I said as I turned onto the street, "does the prediction ever get tested?"

Sandra smiled and settled back against the seat.

"Sooner or later," Julia responded.

Six

THE HARRINGTONS' HOUSE wasn't far from ours, on a tree-lined avenue just off Hudson Street. When I arrived that evening, Tim answered the door, dancing with excitement. His father, dressed in faded jeans and a jacket with a Grateful Dead insignia, was ready to head back to the newspaper office. Sam was trying to make a deadline for the Christmas edition and had called earlier to ask if I could stay with Tim after the show. Now he thanked me several times, saying that Ben, who was already out, appreciated it too.

"I love Christmas shows," I told him, making sure Tim heard. I didn't want the kid to think he was an inconvenience being passed from person to person.

Actually, the show was fabulous entertainment. Several Christmas fairies forgot their lines, then started quarreling among one another about who should say what. The sign for the North Pole got knocked over—three times. And one of the reindeer danced off the stage. Fortunately he was caught by the pianist, which effectively stopped the music and the other cavorting reindeer so they could get themselves reorganized.

Tim loved the performance, but afterward, when we went for refreshments and he saw some of his old classmates from first grade, he suddenly turned shy. The little kids were still in costume and jabbering to one another. Tim stood on my foot.

"Don't you want to go over and say hello?" I asked him.

"No."

"Would you show me who your friends are? Just point to them and tell me their names," I suggested, trying to help him feel as if he still knew these kids.

Tim pointed out one of the reindeer and said his name was Stefan. Stefan's antlered head kept hitting the noses of two bigger kids who were talking to him.

"He looks like a real nice friend."

"Yeah," Tim said. "Can we leave now?"

"Well, first why don't we go tell Stefan he did a great job?"

"He's the one who fell off the stage."

"Oh," I said. "Well, maybe you can call him tomorrow and see how he is."

We left, and Tim didn't say a word on the way home. I wondered if I should try to get him to talk about his feelings. I didn't know much about him or his family history. To me, he seemed like a kid who'd be popular with his classmates, but under the shadow of last year's marriage problems he might have withdrawn. Stefan might have been his only friend, and not much of one at that.

Tim's mood changed for the better once we got inside his house. The home was smaller and cozier than ours, with just a living room, dining room, and kitchen on the first floor. Each room had long, narrow Victorian windows and plain country furnishings, which I liked. Tim took me upstairs, showing me the two bedrooms on the second floor, one with twin beds where he and Ben were sleeping, then led me up a back staircase to a single room on the third floor. It looked as if it was being converted into an office.

"This used to be Ben's room," he said.

I walked over to a set of bookshelves lined with sports trophies. "Are all of these Ben's?"

"Yup. I can read them now," Tim told me proudly, and worked his way down the line. Soccer, basketball, lacrosse, most valuable player, scholar-athlete. Ben had done it all.

I picked up a photograph that showed Ben and another guy grinning at the camera, their arms around each other's shoulders, both of them holding lacrosse sticks.

"That's Lenny," Tim told me. "He was Ben's best friend, but he's in college this year. That book has more pictures," he said, pointing.

I lifted down the scrapbook and paged through, recognizing some of the guys I had seen in the parking lot, especially Twist—he always stood out.

"Why did Ben leave his trophies and pictures here?" I wondered aloud.

Tim shrugged. "He said there isn't enough room in our new house, but there is."

I put down the book and ran my hand over the cool metal of a basketball award. "Well, I guess he's displaying trophies from his new school now."

Tim shook his head. "He doesn't play sports anymore."

"He doesn't?"

"He does homework with me in the afternoon, then, when Mom comes home, goes to work at a store."

What a change from his previous high-school years, I thought.

"He still goes out like he used to," Tim added. "Girls call him all the time."

Just what I wanted to hear. "Well, it's nice that some things don't change. You ready for a game?"

We went down to the living room and played three hands of fish. Then we looked through the Harringtons' library of videos. "Let's watch this one," Tim said. "It's a Christmas movie."

He'd selected *It's a Wonderful Life,* with Jimmy Stewart, which seemed to me a little bleak for a seven-year-old, but Tim thought Clarence the angel was funny. We settled down on an old love seat across from the television.

"I might need some tissues," I said, moving a box to the coffee table in front of us.

"You cry at movies?"

"I do at this one."

"I do whenever I watch *Toy Story*," Tim confessed, then clicked on the video.

Twenty minutes later, after scrunching himself closer and closer to me, he fell sound asleep. He looked younger than seven, his eyelashes curling softly against his cheeks. I lifted my arm and draped it around his shoulders so he'd be more comfortable sleeping against me.

About halfway through the movie I heard a key being inserted in the front door lock. I glanced at my watch, surprised; it was about ten-fifteen, and Sam had said he wouldn't be back till after eleven.

The front door opened, and Ben walked in. He glanced at me and Tim in the living room, then disappeared for a moment, hanging up his jacket. I stopped the video.

"Hope you didn't come back early for me," I called softly to him.

Ben stepped back into my line of vision.

"I told your dad to work as late as he needed to," I continued. "There's plenty of videos to watch. Tim and I are doing fine."

"I can see," he said, coming into the living room.

"So go back to your party," I told him.

He sat down on the other side of the love seat, which made it a tight squeeze with Tim in between. "I guess I'm not in the partying mood." He picked up the cassette case to see what we were watching, then noticed the tissue box. He started to smile. "Do you cry at movies?"

"At this particular movie, yes," I replied, prickling a little.

"But it's got a happy ending," Ben pointed out.

"Sometimes you can cry on the way to a happy ending," I told him.

He looked at me silently for a moment. I remembered what Sandra had said about how by just looking at you, Ben could make you feel as if he were kissing you. I looked away. "I should go."

"Not if you want to see the end of the movie," he said, making himself comfortable, putting one leg up on the coffee table and his arm across the back of the love seat.

"I've seen it several times."

"Me too," he replied, "and I've never cried. But that other one with Stewart, *Mr. Smith Goes to Washington*? My nose turns into a faucet."

I laughed.

"You think that's funny?"

"Yeah, I do," I said.

"Stay, so I can laugh at *you*. Will you?"

I shrugged. "Okay."

He picked up the remote and clicked on the movie. I settled back against the love seat and slid down a little so I could rest my head against the upholstery rather than Ben's arm. Ben glanced sideways at me, smiled, then reached for an old quilt and tossed one end to me so it was spread over the three of us.

I watched the film, wrapped up in a warm and

golden feeling. Tim shifted around between Ben and me, opening his eyes just long enough to look from one to the other, then fell back asleep. Never in my life had I felt so blissfully content. When—without laughing—Ben handed me a tissue and our hands brushed, that content feeling fizzed into an incredible tingling.

Part of me wanted the movie to go on forever, while another part wanted to get the heck out of there before I got truly hooked on a cool guy with a million girlfriends—makeup and big-hair girlfriends who were nothing like me. What had Ben said earlier? *You're a pal.* So what else was new? I'd been a pal to all the guys who fell in love with my sisters.

Of course, the movie did end. Ben hit the rewind button. "I guess I'll have to add tissues to the shopping list," he teased.

"Excuse me? I used two."

He grinned.

"Let's watch another."

We both looked at Tim, surprised. "You're awake?" I asked.

"Come on, buddy," Ben said, "we've got to get you to bed."

"I want to watch another," Tim protested.

"It's too late. Come on, now. Allie will come up with us to tuck you in."

We got Tim upstairs and into his pajamas. He was so tired that he kept walking into things. Ben and I couldn't help laughing. Finally Ben pulled up the covers and tucked them under Tim's chin. Then he leaned down and kissed him gently on the forehead. If the girls at Thornhill High had seen such tenderness, they would've turned to putty.

"Next," Ben said, glancing up at me.

You or him? I was tempted to ask, but I leaned down to Tim, and two little arms wrapped around my neck. "Sleep tight," I whispered.

We headed downstairs without speaking. When we reached the first-floor hall, Ben touched me lightly on the elbow. "Thanks, Allie."

"I wish you'd all stop thanking me. He's a great kid."

Ben leaned against the stair railing. "I'm glad you like him because I think he's got a major crush on you."

"Well, I always wanted a kid brother, you know, somebody to toss a ball to."

"You don't have any brothers at all?"

"Just my two sisters."

"I saw one of them at the party tonight. She—" He hesitated.

"Is nothing like me?"

Ben smiled. "I guess everyone tells you that." He sat down on a step across from the front door, leaving room enough for me, but I remained standing. "I talked to her for a while."

"Which one, Sandra or Julia?"

"The blond one," he replied.

"They're identical twins, remember?"

"Oh, right." He leaned back on his elbows. "I guess that's why it seemed as if she was always around."

I didn't tell him that he might have seen just one who *was* always around.

"It was the sister who came with Mike. You know, Cupcake?"

I grimaced. "You enjoyed that scene, didn't you?"

"It was good for Mike. I like him, but he can get a little cocky around girls."

"Something you would never do," I added.

"I didn't say that." Ben laughed.

"Sandra is the one who's interested in Mike—at least she was as of yesterday. It changes from day to day." I lifted my parka from the hall coatrack. "Julia's seeing someone named Ford."

"If-ever-I-would-leave-you Ford?" he asked.

"Who?"

"He played Lancelot in *Camelot* last year," Ben explained. "When he sang that song, all the girls in the audience fell in love. The thing is, Ford does leave them—flat."

"Well, I'm not too worried. Mike and Ford have met their match. Sandra and Julia know all the games. They always get whatever guy they want."

Ben stood up. "How about you?"

"Me? I play in a different league."

"I should've guessed," he said.

I struggled to get my arms in the holes of my jacket. Ben stood in front of me but didn't try to help. He simply watched me as if he knew he had eyes that could silently hold and kiss a girl. *No big deal,* I thought. *If you don't look at them, they can't kiss you.* But I did look right into those golden browns, and for a moment I stood planted like the hallway coatrack. Then from somewhere deep and scared inside, a voice warned—*Hurt City, Allie. Get out of here!*

"Have to go," I told him quickly, opening the front door.

"Allie—?"

"Hey, here comes your dad." I rushed through the door. "Hi, Sam. All done? I was just leaving. Tim's asleep. Ben got home early," I chattered as I passed him on the walk.

"Ben came home early?" Sam repeated with disbelief. "My Ben? Is he sick?"

I stopped and glanced back at Ben, who was still standing in the lighted doorway, his hands on his hips. "Seems all right to me," I replied. "Maybe he's just tired."

Ben disappeared into the house without a wave.

"Call it a father's intuition," Sam said, "but I think he's caught something. How are you feeling?"

Light-headed, tingly, confused.

"Fine," I replied. "I rarely get sick, and I've had a flu shot."

"That's always a good idea," Sam said.

Yeah, I thought as I hurried to my car. *It's just too bad they can't immunize against hopeless love.*

Seven

THE NEXT MORNING I got up early and trailed my mother around the house, carrying a cup of cocoa and a stepladder, fixing curtain swags and rearranging ornaments at the tops of our three Christmas trees. Aunt Jen called to see if I could meet her at her office in Elmhurst for a run and a quick lunch afterward. At school I ran as part of my training for other sports, but my aunt had done marathons, and I always liked to be challenged by her. I was heading out the back door in my Lycra pants and jacket when Julia came down for brunch.

"How was the party?" I asked, pausing at the kitchen door.

"Great!" Julia replied. "Some college guys came."

"Anybody who was anyone was there," Sandra added, walking in behind her.

"How you'd know who else was there is beyond me," Julia remarked to her twin, "the way you kept orbiting around Ben." She filled a mug with water and put it in the microwave.

"Just for an hour," Sandra replied. "Ben left the party at ten o'clock," she explained to me. "Everyone was wondering why."

Both of them looked at me expectantly.

"Well, why?" I asked.

"I was hoping you'd know," Sandra said.

I lifted my car keys from a hook. "Nope."

She wasn't dragging me into *this* campaign. This time I wasn't helping her out—getting information, carrying messages. If Sandra was in serious pursuit of Ben, the only way I'd survive the holidays was to distance myself from their affair. I started out the back door.

"Did you see that hissy fit Meg threw when Ben left?" Sandra asked, grinning at Julia.

I hesitated. One question, *then* I'd distance myself: "Is Meg the girl with white blond hair?"

Sandra nodded.

"That hissy fit was brought on by you, Sandra," Julia pointed out, "long before Ben left. Meg seemed to think he was her date."

"Well, Ben didn't."

"How was Mike?" I asked, my resolution weakening again. I couldn't help wondering if he'd thrown a macho hissy fit when he saw his "babe" flirting with Ben.

"Funny you should mention him, Al," Sandra replied. "He asked about you." She gave a little shrug. "I told him we didn't think to bring you because you weren't much for partying, and anyway, you were baby-sitting."

"Allie, are you sure you didn't see Ben last night?" Julia pressed.

"I left the Harringtons' house when Sam came home." Technically it was the truth.

Julia removed her cup from the microwave and dunked a tea bag, studying me.

"I'm headed over to Aunt Jen's," I told her and Sandra, then walked out the back door.

As I drove to Elmhurst, I wondered about Sandra's plans. Her show of interest in Ben might have been nothing more than a strategic move in her game with Mike, a ploy to make him jealous. But if the prize really was Ben—and I had the terrible feeling it was—all other interested girls might as well forget it.

When I arrived at Aunt Jen's office, she was dressed in an aqua running suit but still doing business on the phone. She waved at me, and I started pushing back oak chairs, clearing a space in the room. As soon as she finished the call we did warm-up exercises.

"I haven't been running as much as I should," Aunt Jen admitted as we bent our right legs back and stretched. "Men can be such a distraction."

"Tell me about it."

"Oh, really?" Aunt Jen turned her head sharply. "You tell me about it—tell me about him."

"Who?" I said quickly. "There's nobody."

I could tell she didn't believe me, but she let the

subject drop and continued the stretches. "Okay," she said, standing up and patting her jacket. "I've got money for the deli and keys."

"I've got tissue," I told her, rising to my feet.

"Lip gloss." She slipped it in her pocket. "That's it. Let's go."

As was our custom, we didn't talk much the first mile and a half, just cruised along, finding our rhythm. It was forty-something degrees, but the air was still and the sun bright and warm on our backs. By our second mile we were outside the small town, running a hilly road next to golden winter fields.

"Allie, thanks for being such a good sport the other night," Jen said. "I'm sorry our dinner for two turned into a party of five."

"Well, things always get crazy during the holidays," I replied.

"I told Sam he should have time alone with his kids," Aunt Jen continued as we shortened our stride to take a steep hill, "especially when they first arrived, but he decided otherwise. And I didn't want to seem like I wasn't happy to join them." We crested the hill. "Anyway, thanks for making it easier, especially with Tim."

I didn't know what to say. I loved Aunt Jen, but I cared about Tim and Ben too, and I knew this marriage was upsetting them.

"There are a lot of people who don't approve of what Sam and I are doing," my aunt went on. "There are people who make me responsible for his divorce."

"Are you?"

She laughed. "I can always count on you to be straight with me. And to be straight with you," she said, "the love between Sam and his wife died shortly after Tim was born. But they'd decided to continue as partners in raising their children. That arrangement did not become difficult for them until I came into the picture. For that, Sam and I are jointly to blame."

We ran another half mile in silence. "I want to be really happy and positive about your engagement," I said at last.

"But you've already seen the other side of it, the effect on Tim and Ben," she replied.

"Yes."

"Which is the proverbial good news–bad news for me," she added as we reached a flat stretch of country road. "The bad news is your aunt is a villain to your two new friends. The good news is I now have a wonderful link to them, especially to Tim, who has obviously taken to you."

I nodded.

"I asked Tim if he wanted to go ice skating this afternoon and bring along a friend or two," Aunt Jen continued. "I told him we could go to the video arcade or a movie."

"He didn't want to," I guessed.

"Right. The problem is, I need to keep my hand extended to him, but I also have to respect his feelings about me. He has every right not to like me. I'm afraid this is going to be a miserable holiday for him."

"I already told Ben I'd do some things with Tim."

My aunt reached for my hand as we ran and squeezed it hard. "Thank you." She sounded relieved. "I didn't want to impose on you, but I was hoping you would say something like that."

"Love can sure get messy," I said.

"Tell me about it."

I arrived home about two-thirty in the afternoon and found my sisters finishing up batches of homemade cookies. My mother had exchanged her glue gun for an icing brush and was working at the kitchen table.

"Did you see your friend waiting for you on the veranda steps?" she asked. "He wouldn't come in."

"My friend?"

"He's really cute, Allie," Julia said, smiling, "but you'll never be able to wear heels."

"Tim?" I guessed, backtracking to the door. "Tim Harrington?"

"Could be," my mother replied. "He said he's not allowed to tell strangers his name."

"Harrington?" Sandra repeated. "You mean he's Ben's brother?"

I opened the back door and called Tim's name. Sandra immediately got out a plate and started piling cookies onto it.

At my third call Tim came streaking around from the other side of the garage. "Allie Cat! You've got a basketball hoop. Wanna play horse?"

"Okay. But come in for a minute," I told him, "so you can meet my mom and sisters."

He paused just inside the kitchen door, looking shy for about twenty seconds, then said, "I could smell those cookies outside."

"Really?" Sandra replied. "I was just making a batch for you and your brother."

Tim walked over to her and studied the plateful that she was arranging. "We like the chocolate ones best."

Anything that wasn't chocolate was quickly removed and others piled in their place.

"Does your family know where you are?" I asked Tim.

"I told Ben I was out playing."

"Did you tell him where?"

"I didn't know where. Craig, who lives next door, had to show me."

I handed him the phone. "Call home and tell Ben you're here. I'll go get the ball."

When I returned to the kitchen, Tim was up on the stool next to my mother, watching her paint a Christmas-ball cookie into a basketball with a big *T* at the top. Julia was listening to Sandra talk on the phone.

"Oh, it's no problem at all," Sandra said. "I love having Tim here."

I? Was *she* going to shoot baskets with him?

"Tim says he likes chocolate," Sandra went on, "and I could never eat all these cookies on my own."

73

"Good thing the rest of us are here too," Julia said loudly.

"Look," Tim said, pulling on my sleeve. "Your mom does good art."

My mother glowed, totally charmed.

"Cool," I replied. "Ready, champ?"

"Let me give you our phone number and address," I heard Sandra say as Tim and I headed out the door, "just in case Tim disappears again."

Yup, that's the reason, I thought.

I let Tim start our game to see what kind of shots he could make, if any. Athletic talent must have run in the family, for he had a sweet little layup and was amazingly accurate from about ten feet out.

"Where were you today?" Tim asked as he dribbled around, deciding on his next shot.

"In Elmhurst, visiting my aunt Jen."

He didn't say anything, just got a look of stony concentration on his face, then launched the ball.

"Good one! Go again," I said.

He missed and tossed the ball to me.

"She and I went for a long run together. It was lots of fun," I told him, wanting him to know I liked Jen but being careful not to talk too much about her. "Should we spell *horse* or something longer?" I asked.

"Can we practice layups instead? I need to work on dribbling after I catch the ball."

"Okay."

Tim did layups from both sides, determinedly

working off every kind of pass I threw. After a while we changed places.

"Ready," I called, then sprinted toward the basket. Tim threw the ball too far ahead of me and I had to lunge to get it. I didn't see the tall guy coming hard from my right side—not until after we slammed into each other. But when I realized he was trying to intercept the ball, my game instincts took over. I struggled with him, wrenching it out of his hands.

"Jeez, you fight like a cat!" he exclaimed.

"That's because she's Allie Cat," Tim said, laughing at us.

I glanced up at the dark-haired guy, recognizing him. "Hi, Mike."

"Hello, Allie." He stared at me with those brilliant blue eyes.

I dribbled away from him.

"Do you remember me, Tim?" Mike asked. "I played with your brother last year."

"I remember. You're a forward."

Mike smiled. "Can I play with you guys? Two against me."

"We take it out first," Tim replied quickly.

Mike nodded, then looked at me. "I have one rule."

"Let's hear it," I said.

He touched my hand. "No fingernails. No claws."

Now that annoyed me. I mean, I don't have to resort to such things. Of course, what Mike didn't know is that I always play better when annoyed. And when someone plays me man-to-man and too close, well, as my coach says, "Allie's plugged in." I fake, I run, I rebound like I'm on springs. I was determined to make this guy sweat a lake.

Tim kept up a constant chatter, playing as well as calling our game like a radio announcer. I continually fed Tim the ball, and we were winning by a few points. I thought that Mike's ego might get the better of him and he'd start squelching Tim's two-point tosses to the basket. I even admired Mike for choosing to stick close to me and allowing Tim to succeed.

Which probably shows how naive I am about guys. After all, it was pretty obvious that Mike was playing basketball like a heavy-contact sport, moving with every move of mine, teasing me by dribbling foolishly close. He made a lot of hand fouls that a varsity player wouldn't. But I was so focused on winning, I didn't stop to think about it—not until the game was over and Tim was hopping around victoriously.

"Did you see my last shot, Ben?" he called out.

I turned around to see Ben sitting on the porch with Sandra and Julia, bundled up in their winter jackets and eating cookies. "I saw five of them. They were super," Ben called back. "Hey—coat on, keep your coat on, Tim. You'll catch cold."

"He's strong from the left side, just like you," Mike said to Ben as we walked over to the veranda.

"I know. We've got to work on that right side."

Ben glanced at me and smiled. "You've got to work on the left."

"That's what Coach says."

"Are you coming to the holiday game, Ben?" Mike asked. He stood very close to me. I moved over, but then he moved over.

"I wouldn't miss it."

The two guys started talking about the team's season. My sisters listened with that interested tilted-head look girls get when bored. As Mike talked, *bragged* actually, he draped his arm casually around my shoulders, like we were old sports buddies. I wished I could duck inside and clean up. Julia and Sandra must've known that the guys were coming over, for they had brushed out their hair and applied some eyeliner and mascara. I felt self-conscious next to them. I knew my face got beet red when I played, and I could feel my bangs drying in little salty sticks on my forehead.

"Do you think I can convince Allie to stay in Thornhill?" Mike asked Ben. "We could use her on the team."

"Why not?" Ben said, meeting my eyes, then glancing at my shoulder.

Mike was massaging it now. His hand began to move slowly down my arm. I stood there like a statue, wondering what the heck he was doing. He slipped his fingers between my arm and ribs, still moving his hand downward until it came to rest at my hips. His fingers curled around my waist, pressing against my thin Lycra suit. I saw Sandra watching and suddenly figured things out: He and Sandra were playing a new game, and I was his prop. Well, he really was a cupcake if he thought he could make her jealous of me!

I moved away from him and folded my arms in front of me, rubbing them with my own hands as if I could wipe off Mike.

Ben noticed. "You're going to catch cold," he said, removing his gold jacket.

"No, I'm plenty warm. I wear this suit for sports all winter long."

"But you've got goose bumps," he replied, touching my arm where I'd pushed up one sleeve.

"I don't think so."

He put his team jacket around my shoulders, holding it there for a moment. It was warm, warm from him wearing it. I shivered.

"You don't think so?" He laughed lightly, then turned back to Sandra. "Maybe we should finish the cookies in the kitchen."

"Of course," she said, reaching for his hand to lead him inside.

How could he know—I'd never tell him—that my shivering wasn't due to the weather?

Eight

THE GUYS MADE a big dent in our cookie collection that afternoon. Afterward Sandra headed off with Mike to do some Christmas shopping, and Ben and Tim left to buy a tree. Julia borrowed the Audi so she could meet some friends at the mall up the highway. With my father working in Manhattan that day and my mother keeping a hair appointment, I had the house to myself for a few hours.

I took possibly the longest shower in history, enjoying every minute of it. Then I spread my Christmas gifts out on the floor of my room and began to wrap them. I was fussing with one for my mother, struggling with an overly ambitious bow, when the phone rang. I grabbed the receiver with one hand, the fingers of my other hand having somehow become part of the ribbon I was trying to loop and knot. "Hello?"

There was silence at the other end.

"If this is an obscene call, you're going to have to breathe louder than that," I said.

"Sandra?" a voice asked.

"No."

But before I could identify myself, the guy rushed on. "This is Craig. Craig Smythe. I think you know me, but I'm not sure. I'm in your English class. What am I saying? I mean Spanish. Third row. But I take English right after you do. We pass each other at the door. When I get out of calculus in time, that is. Well, anyway. I've got light hair. Does that help?"

"Help what?" I asked.

"I take pictures for the paper. I took a lot of you in the fall production."

"I think you've got—"

"Which, maybe, you'd like to see sometime," he hurried on. "I mean, I'm sure you already saw the ones printed in the paper. I have a feeling I'm not making too much sense."

You're right about that, I thought.

"Anyway, I was wondering if you'd like to see a movie, maybe after Christmas? Or before? Whenever."

"Listen," I said, "I have to put down the phone for a second. I need to cut the ribbon off this present I'm trying to wrap or else cut off my hand and let it stay as part of the decoration. But don't hang up—I'll be back in a moment."

I laid down the receiver, then extricated my hand from the ribbon and snipped the package free from its tangled-up mess, thinking as I did—*Poor guy, he hasn't got a chance.*

"Hi, I'm back."

"Hi," he said shyly.

"I'm not Julia. I'm her sister Allie."

"Allie? I didn't know Julia had another sister. I'm sorry. You must think I'm crazy."

Yeah—crazy in love. "Not really," I told him, and measured out some new ribbon. "I've answered the phone for my sisters before."

"Maybe I lucked out getting you," he said. "I wasn't making any sense, was I?"

"Well, if I were the president, I wouldn't hire you as my spokesperson." I gathered up loops of the bright red ribbon. "But I have trouble saying things right when something matters a lot to me. Everybody does." I almost had the ribbon under control and was ready to wrap the metal twist around the perfect bow.

"Thanks for saying that," Craig replied. His voice was lower and much mellower now that he was relaxed.

"Well, it's true," I told him. "Darn this ribbon!" I exclaimed as the loops sprang out of my hand. "It looks perfectly tame on its roll, then fights me like a cobra when I try to make a bow."

Craig laughed. It was a warm and friendly laugh. He sounded nice, but I knew he'd have to be cooler—much cooler—for Julia to give him a chance.

"I just buy the ready-mades and stick them on a package," he told me.

"That's because your mother's not Martha Stewart," I replied.

"Your mother's Martha Stewart?"

"No, no, I was just—"

He laughed. "It was a joke. I'm only slow and confused when I try to talk to Julia. I wish I could just e-mail her."

"That doesn't work," I advised him. "Not with Julia, at least. But I'll tell her you called," I added, "and you should call back. She expects guys to do that."

"It took me a month and a half to work up the nerve this time," Craig replied. "Tell her I'll call, oh, sometime around Washington's birthday."

"What if I give you a specific time to call back," I proposed, "and I make sure I answer the phone first. We can talk a little before you talk to her. Will that help?"

I didn't usually volunteer my services, especially since I'd been unwillingly drafted into them so many times at Fields, but he seemed truly sweet, and I could see myself in his shoes. More easily now than I could have last week.

"I'll think about it," he replied. "But thanks. Did you say your name was Allie?"

"Yeah. You better give me your last name again and your phone number."

I scribbled down the information, then clicked off the phone. After tossing aside the uncooperative ribbon, I carried my mother's gift downstairs and searched the Christmas trees till I found a ball that matched. I tied it with a simple bow to my mother's package, snapping off a piece of tree and adding that for the final touch.

When I'd finished all the gifts and placed them under the tree, I returned to my room and slipped out one of my gothic romances from the space between my mattress and headboard. Wrapping a quilt around me, I snuggled into my window seat, enjoying the mystery and the heroine's secret longing for the dark, possibly wicked man she had fallen hopelessly in love with. Except it wasn't hopeless; these stories always ended happily. I needed to be part of a story I knew would end happily.

The afternoon faded around me. I didn't notice that I was reading by purple twilight until a pair of bright headlights swung into the driveway that curved below my window. Sandra was being dropped off. But it was the guy named Twist, not Mike, who was helping to carry her packages.

Not long after, I heard my mother and Julia come in. I stuffed my paperback behind the mattress and joined them down in the kitchen. Both of my sisters were pulling boxes out of shopping bags.

"I was just as glad Mike had to help his father," Sandra was saying to Julia. "Sometimes he acts weird—hi, Al. And I don't need weird when I've got a lot of shopping to do. Twist, at least, is good for laughs."

"As well as a close friend of Ben's," Julia added slyly.

"Oh, that's right," Sandra replied lightly. "I'd forgotten."

"Did you two leave anything for other shoppers?" I asked.

"Tissue paper," Julia said, grinning at me.

My mother came in from the dining room, her hair a new light blond shade, making me think of hay in the manger, which, of course, I didn't say.

"Let's see what you've bought, girls. Oh, my!"

Julia and Sandra pulled out all of their purchases except for what they had gotten for my mother and me. We tried on scarves and bracelets and hair stuff, smelled men's cologne and women's perfume, and handed around CDs. My mother was holding up a pair of glittering panty hose, an arm in each leg, making them dance, and Julia was modeling a red lace bra she'd bought for herself, wearing it over her shirt, when my father came in. He made a hasty retreat to his study.

"You know, Mom," Sandra said, "sometimes I can't imagine how you and Dad ever got together."

My mother smiled. "You girls don't know everything about romance."

"I mean, I can't imagine him asking you for a date," she persisted.

"I asked *him*," Mom replied. "Twice before he asked me back." The three of us contemplated that silently for a moment. *Speaking of impossible matches,* I thought—"Julia, a guy called you this afternoon." I pulled the scrap of paper from my pocket and handed it to her.

"Craig Smythe," she read aloud. "I don't know anybody named Craig Smythe."

"A Craig from your Spanish class?" I prompted. "He sounded really nice."

She shook her head. "What did he want?"

"To see a movie. He sounded really nice," I repeated.

"I know who he is," Sandra told Julia, "and he's nothing to get excited about. You've seen him around— reddish blond hair, medium height, so-so dresser. He's always taking pictures for the paper."

"Maybe I'd better be busy," Julia said.

"Why don't you call him back and find out what movie he wants to see?" I suggested. "What do you have to lose if it's a good movie?"

My mother looked at me with surprise.

"Well, if you think he's so nice, why don't *you* go with him?" Julia asked.

"Really," Sandra remarked, laughing. "This is a hoot coming from a girl who was busy whenever I went out of my way to arrange dates for her."

"I had a full schedule," I defended myself. Besides, I'd gotten tired of being the consolation prize for the guys Sandra turned down. I had begun to suspect that she used me to keep track of them in case she wanted them back.

"Well, if you don't want this guy's number, Allie," Julia said, "I'm throwing it away."

I watched Craig get dropped in with the morning's banana peels. My sisters went back to examining and comparing their purchases. When the phone rang, I was glad for an excuse to leave. I answered it in the hall.

"Julia? Sandra?" the guy asked.

"No," I replied wearily. "Guess again."

"I'm glad I got you," the guy said, his telephone voice soft and deep. "How are you?"

"Fine. Which twin do you want?"

"I want to talk to you."

"I think you're confusing me with my sisters."

"What did you do this afternoon?" he asked.

"Wrapped gifts. Read. If you'll hold on for a minute," I began.

"If *you* will hold on for a minute," he countered.

"Mike?" I asked, suddenly recognizing his voice, though he was making it sound lower than usual, as if he thought it was enticing or something.

"Yes."

"You've got the wrong sister."

"Maybe," he replied, his voice husky. "Maybe."

"Sandra!" I hollered, not bothering to cover the phone. "*San-dra,* pick it up!"

Then I left the receiver lying off the hook and walked away. I had better things to do than be a pawn in their stupid game.

Nine

O N CHRISTMAS EVE, I went for a run by myself, heading away from the last minute shoppers in town. I could have run for miles on that crisp, cold day and kept wondering what it would be like to have Ben beside me. I imagined matching his long footsteps with mine, striding in perfect sync, not talking, just being together. And then I remembered that Sandra was imagining what it would be like to make out with him.

When I arrived back home, Aunt Jen had come over and was getting a Christmas tour from my mother. I could hear them walking from room to room, Aunt Jen exclaiming over the decorations. Sandra and Julia were in the downstairs hall, Sandra standing in front of a mirror, holding her hand up close to her face, gazing at her image. She smiled at me in the mirror and wiggled her fingers, making her left hand sparkle with Aunt Jen's engagement ring.

"Come on, Sandra," Julia said. "You've been wearing it for five minutes."

"Okay," Sandra finally agreed, then slipped off the ring. Julia put it on and held out her hand, watching the diamond catch fire.

"My turn," Mom said as she and Jen joined us.

Aunt Jen glanced at me, but I shook my head. I'd been trying to squelch ridiculous romantic dreams that, since I'd met Ben, were popping up like dandelions. I didn't need to see how an engagement ring looked on my hand.

"Aunt Jen," Julia said, "have you picked your bridesmaids yet?"

"How about Sam's best man?" Sandra asked.

"We're going to think about all that after the holidays," our aunt replied. "Right now we're focusing on my getting to know Sam's family."

My mother admired the flashing diamond on her finger, then handed it back. "Jen has invited us over to the Harringtons' tonight to help trim the tree," she said.

"I don't want to interfere with your plans, girls," Aunt Jen added. "But if you're free, we'd love to have you." She looked at me hopefully, and I nodded.

"Of course we'll come," Sandra said. "What's Christmas Eve without a little kid? And Tim is so cute. I love being around him."

Julia glanced at me and rolled her eyes. I had to laugh.

My mother insisted on bringing food, and Aunt Jen gave up trying to persuade her not to. After Jen left, I was sent to Jim Danner's, an old grocery store on Main Street, to purchase some snacks.

I spent ten minutes circling the crowded lot behind Danner's, then parked the car and walked around to the front entrance. I unzipped my red parka, put a basket over my arm, and started up the first aisle, picking up cheeses, dropping them in.

"Hey, Little Red Riding Hood!"

I turned around. "Hey, Mike."

"Picking up some goodies for Grandma?" he asked. "Mmm."

"Don't get your hopes up, Wolf," I told him. "Both grandmas are dead."

He laughed.

I selected two more cheeses. "What are you up to?" I asked, when he continued to hover about.

"Just picking up some butter." He held it up.

We reached the end of the aisle. "Well, good luck in choosing the fastest cashier line. And have a great holiday if I don't see you."

He took the basket from my hands.

I looked at him funny and took it back. "I have more shopping to do."

He pulled on the basket's handle until I let go, then dropped in his butter. "I figured that. I'm helping you."

"Oh. Well . . . thank you."

Mike laughed. He really was good-looking, his black, wavy hair and dark lashes making his eyes even bluer. He had a movie star face, the kind with very chiseled features—but having nothing particularly interesting about it. He was a good match for Sandra.

"And I'll be seeing you tomorrow," he said as he carried my basket down an aisle of crackers and chips. "Sandra invited me over."

I picked up some multigrains and water crackers, then handed them to him.

"What do you want for Christmas this year?" Mike asked.

"Hiking boots. A sleeping bag. And a pair of good cleats for lacrosse."

He smiled. "No perfume?"

"It makes my eyes water."

"Mine too," he said, "when I get close to a girl." He stood close and looked at my neck, which is long—one of my better features, according to Sandra. I put one hand on it self-consciously, and he laughed.

"You're really kind of shy, aren't you?" he remarked, following me up the next aisle.

"No."

"Well, you're shy around me," he replied with a persuasive smile.

I looked into his eyes. "The word is *uncomfortable.*"

"Why? I don't want you to be." He sounded earnest. "You sure are hard to read, Allie."

"I'm not trying to make it difficult." I put two jars of olives in my basket, lifted it out of his hands, then headed for the deli counter.

"Listen," he said, "I've dated more girls than I can remember the names of."

"That's impressive."

"What I'm saying is, I've had experience. And you're not like the others."

I grimaced. "I think the next sentence is, *I've never felt this way before.*"

He pulled me back by the arm. "No, the next sentence is, I don't usually bother with girls who make it hard to talk to them. I don't have to."

"Unless it serves your own purposes," I replied. "Your strategy is obvious to me." I hurried toward the deli.

"Okay, Allie," Mike said, catching up with me. "Tell me what's so obvious that I'm missing it."

Customers, who were waiting for their numbers to be called, turned around, gazing at us with mild curiosity. I took a ticket and tapped my foot.

Mike faced me, his arms folded in front of him. "Are you going to tell me?"

"I don't like it when people play games with each other. I don't want any part of your and Sandra's game."

"What game is that?" he asked.

"What game?" I repeated, my voice breaking high. I took a breath and lowered it. "You know what I'm talking about. You're not the first guy who's tried it. Though you're probably the first who thought you could make her jealous of *me.*"

"Your sister may be playing games," Mike said. "But I'm not."

"Well, you're not exactly acting like a devoted boyfriend."

"What'd she say?" an old man asked.

"He's not exactly acting like a devoted boyfriend," his wife answered loudly.

"I think it's her sister's boyfriend," another customer added.

Oh, man, I thought. *Call number twenty-nine, please.*

"For a good reason—I'm not her boyfriend," Mike insisted.

"Listen," I said, "Sandra's not here, so what's the point? I'm not going to tell her about the way you flirt with me. I'm not going to help you make her jealous."

"What makes you think that's what I'm trying to do?"

I turned away, shaking my head. Mike reached for me, turning me back toward him. "Why are you so sure that's what I want?"

"This is better than the soaps," the old man said.

That did it. My mother was going to have to live without her goose liver pâté. I crumpled up my number and headed to the cashier lines. Then I remembered sodas and made a quick detour, picking up two six-packs.

Mike followed and tried to carry them for me.

"Please, give me a break," I said.

"I've given you several, but you don't seem to catch on."

"I caught on two years ago, when my sisters' boyfriends started hanging around me so they could get information about the twins."

"But I'm not one of your sister's boyfriends," he

argued, "and I think she's made that clear."

"You only have to *want* to be," I said, then got in line.

I guess that point hit home. We stood in line silently through several checkouts that were ahead of us. I started putting my purchases on the belt, and he began to help but didn't meet my eyes.

After I paid for my purchases, Mike caught me by the coat and held on tight while the clerk rang up his. I stood there, unwilling to make another scene. When he let go, I quickly lifted my two bags, which were heavy with jars, bottles, and cheese. He tried several times to get ahold of one.

"This is getting old, Allie," he said as we walked around the building and across the parking lot, still struggling for control, each with a hand on a bag. "Just let me carry one of them. It would make me feel better."

"It makes me feel better to carry them myself," I replied. Then I thought, *Oh, chill out, Allie. He knows you're onto his game now; he's just being polite.*

We relinquished our hold at the same time.

"Oh!"

We quickly grabbed for the bag, knocking our heads together. The slippery plastic slid past our fingers and we tried to catch it again, wedging it between my thigh and his knee. We started laughing, then I lost my grip on the other bag. We both bent at the waist, grasping at the bags, our heads together, laughing uncontrollably. Mike finally grabbed one and straightened up. I got the other and leaned back against red car—a dusty-looking red car. A Toyota the color of tomato soup.

Then my eyes met Ben's. His friend Twist was standing next to him.

"Need help?" Ben asked.

"No," Mike replied, still laughing. "But thanks. And be careful, you guys. Assisting Allie is a dangerous sport."

"Really," Ben said.

Twist grinned at me. "I'm Twist. Neither of these jerks are going to remember to introduce me."

"Hi. I'm Allie Parker."

He nodded. "I know. You're already famous around these parts."

"Famous for what?"

The three guys laughed.

I looked from one to the other. There I was, standing in a parking lot with three cool guys smiling at me. *If only the girls at Fields could see me now,* I thought. Except that I ruined it by blushing, letting everyone know that I wasn't used to this kind of attention.

The guys talked for a minute more, mostly about basketball and the upcoming holiday game, then Mike helped me carry the packages to my car. As he and I walked across the lot I heard Twist say, "You're right, Ben. It's hard to believe they're sisters."

Ten

"DON'T MAKE ANY sudden stops," Julia told my father.

She, Sandra, and I sat in the back of the sedan, holding our hands up in front of us, trying to dry our nails. And for the second time in four days I was wearing a full face of makeup. Maybe I was morphing. I hoped it wasn't an irreversible process. While we got dressed, I'd wanted more than anything to tell the twins about the events at the store and parking lot. To boast, actually. But I didn't because I thought Sandra's feelings might get hurt. And to be honest, I thought mine might too if my sisters treated it all as no big deal.

It is no big deal, I told myself, *unless you go to an all-girls school.*

"Are the Harringtons on Walnut Street?" my father asked.

"Yes," I replied. "Turn at the next corner."

"Slowly," said my mother. Her nails were dry, but she had been glue gunning on the way out the door, making Tim a wreath with little plastic basketballs. Now she held it carefully in front of her.

We pulled up in front of the tall blue-and-white house and made a parade up the Harringtons' walk, carrying food and decorations. Sam greeted us at the door. "Merry Christmas! Merry Christmas!"

Tim popped out from behind him. "Hey, Allie Cat!" Then he saw the wreath my mother was carrying. "Awesome!" he said.

My mother beamed. "It's for you."

Ben came out from the kitchen area, followed by Aunt Jen and a guy with strawberry blond hair.

"Isn't this cool?" Tim asked, holding up his wreath.

"Very cool," Ben replied. "Hi, Mr. Parker, I'm Ben. This is our neighbor, Craig."

Craig the photographer? The same guy who'd called Julia? I didn't have to wonder for long. He gave me a shy smile but could hardly look at my sister when introduced.

"Craig's parents own the Card & Party Shop on Main Street," Ben told us.

"Which is lucky for us," Sam said. "Every Christmas Eve, while his parents are finishing up at the shop, Craig comes over with everything I've forgotten to buy, like wrapping paper, tape, ribbon, tinsel. . . . It's become a tradition."

I glanced sideways at Julia to see if she recognized Craig as the guy whose number she'd dropped in the trash, but she gave no sign.

"Well, let's take everybody's coats," Sam said.

With the skill of an actress who never misses a blocking tape, Sandra positioned herself perfectly for Ben to help her with her jacket.

I shoved Julia ahead of me so that Craig got a chance to take her jacket. Julia had to help him along, and when he finally saw her in her red silk blouse with a deep V neck, I guess it was too much for him. He took two steps backward into Ben, letting the coat drag on the floor. Then he swooped up the coat, looking distraught, as if he'd been dragging a person. *Poor guy,* I thought once again.

"I'm so glad you're all here," Aunt Jen said as the coats were hung up. "Come into the kitchen. We have cider warming."

We proceeded toward the rear of the house, but Tim held back. "I want to hang this," he said, holding up his wreath.

"Later," his father replied. "Let's get some drinks."

"I want to hang it now."

Ben gave his brother a warning look.

"I'm going to put it on the front door," Tim went on defiantly.

"We already have a wreath there," Sam said with strained patience.

"But I want this one there."

I wondered why he was acting bratty, then Aunt Jen volunteered, "We can put Tim's wreath on the door. It'll look good."

"No," Sam said sternly, turning to Tim. "I like

the one Jen picked out, and it's going to stay right where it is."

My mother looked uncomfortable, as if she'd caused a problem.

"How about your bedroom door, Tim," I suggested, "since it's your own wreath?"

Tim looked at me sulkily. I stared back until he changed his stubborn little expression.

"There's a nail already in the door," Ben said. "I'll get you some string."

A few minutes later Tim and I were hanging up the wreath.

"This looks great," I told him.

"You like her." Tim sounded resigned and unhappy.

"You mean my aunt Jen? Yes. I like her very much," I said, laying my hand on his shoulder.

"Oh," he mumbled.

We'd just turned to go downstairs when the phone rang. The call was immediately picked up by an answering machine in the bedroom. I heard Sam's recorded voice followed by a beep, then a girl's voice: "Hi, Ben, this is me. Come over as soon as you get rid of your guests. Tap on the den window—my parents will be asleep."

"They just keep calling," Tim told me.

Now both of us were resigned and unhappy. We returned downstairs to the living room.

The tree had been put in its stand before we arrived and decorated with strings of big-bulb lights. Jen and Sam were opening up dusty boxes of ornaments, laying them out for us. Tim went over to watch, standing by his father's side, away from Jen. My own father was sitting in the corner, reading the Christmas edition of Sam's paper, and would probably move on to Sam's book collection next. My mother was fussing with the Harringtons' curtains. I wondered if Sam knew what kind of family he was marrying into. Good thing he was a bit eccentric too.

The guys and my sisters were seated on the floor around the hearth, which crackled and snapped with a warm fire. Ben stood up when he saw me. "Can I get you some cider, Allie?"

"Not right now, thanks," I said, joining the group. Ben returned to his seat on the rug next to Sandra, who casually dropped her hand so that it rested lightly on his knee. If I videotaped her, I could have run a sequel to last year's flirting seminar.

"So you and Twist played together even in grade school," Sandra said to Ben. "He's such a nice guy."

"He's a clown." Ben smiled. "We started out in first grade together. Craig too. Craig's family moved next door when he was—how old?" he asked, turning to his neighbor.

"Uh, three."

Ben waited quietly, having provided Craig with an opening into the conversation. "Three," Craig repeated, then fell silent.

"On which side of the road do you live?" I asked Craig.

Before he could get out an answer—and admittedly he was slow in response—Sandra said, "Twist and I went shopping the other day. You ought to see what he bought for you, Ben."

"Some joke," Ben guessed. "He always does."

"I could give you a hint," she said with a teasing look—another video moment.

"You could."

"The west side," Craig finally responded. "I live in the gray house with the rust shutters."

"Do you have a darkroom at home?" I asked.

"Down in the basement," he replied, warming up a little. "I built it myself. I'd be glad to show it to you sometime."

"What's there to see if it's dark?" Sandra asked.

Maybe she was just teasing him, but it shut him down cold. Julia hadn't said a word yet, which was unusual. Maybe she had figured out who he was.

"Okay, everyone," Aunt Jen said. "Time to deck the tree."

"Dig in and throw it on," Sam added.

My mother looked horrified. "Don't you have some kind of decorating plan?"

Sam shook his head. "Just make it stick."

Craig stood up and offered Julia a hand. She looked so graceful rising to her feet that she made Craig look good. His blue eyes shone and caught hers for a moment. I realized then that people can become incredibly attractive when their faces are lit with affection.

"Is it all right if I help myself to some cider?" I asked Sam.

100

"Sure thing. You're family."

I had headed out to the kitchen when I heard footsteps behind me. "It's okay, I can get it myself," I told Ben.

"You could, but I'm feeling competitive. Is assisting you really a dangerous sport?"

I grimaced, and he laughed. "I've got some questions for you," he said in a low voice, giving me a light push toward the kitchen.

I hoped the questions weren't about his chances with Sandra. At Fields, I had spent a lot of time answering such queries.

As soon as the door swung shut behind us Ben asked, "Is it hopeless with Julia?"

"For you or Craig?"

"Come on, Allie," he said, making a face at me. Then he turned on the stove and began to stir the cider.

"For Craig," I said, "it's going to take a miracle."

Ben glanced over his shoulder. "Do you believe in them?"

"Miracles? At Christmas, I do . . . sometimes."

He turned and smiled. "So do I . . . I think." His dark eyes warmed me like embers. Then he turned back and continued stirring. "I'm not sure whether to encourage Craig. I hate to see him get hurt. You know, he and I didn't really hang out together in high school, but before that I spent a lot of time at his house. He's a nice guy, a guy with a good heart who'd do anything for anybody. That counts for me, much more now than it used to."

Ben stared into the steaming cider as he talked.

"Craig is funny and imaginative," he went on. "But he has a hard time being himself until he knows a person, until he trusts a person—especially when he's got a major crush. And does he ever have one!"

I sighed. "I wish I knew how to be his angel and help him along."

"You already have your angel assignment," Ben replied with a smile. "If there's one thing Jen and I can agree on, it's that you're getting Tim through this holiday. Besides, you've helped Craig already." He picked up a cup and ladled in the cider. "He told me he talked on the phone with the nicest girl in the world."

Even though it was Craig's compliment, I loved hearing Ben say it. He handed me the warm glass, and I lowered my head to take a sip.

"Whoa!" His hand caught my chin, lifting it up. "You're going to burn your tongue, Cat."

"Smells good," I told him.

"It's Danner's—you know, the place where you and Mike shopped this afternoon." He looked as if he were going to say something else, then decided against it. "Anyway, as I was saying, you've been helpful enough. Driving up here, I was worried about whether I could still fit in with my old friends. It never occurred to me I'd find a new one. In a way I've found two—you and my old buddy, Craig."

"Good," I said, demonstrating the same large vocabulary as Craig.

"Well, we'd better get back in there and make sure my buddy hasn't tangled himself up in tinsel while watching Julia hang an ornament."

I nodded and followed Ben through the door. Buddy feelings were a long way from the passionate desire I'd been reading about in my paperback romance. I doubted the girl whose den window Ben would be tapping on later was considered a buddy. *Reality check,* I thought. *Just like Craig, you too can get hurt.*

A further reality check came an hour later, when we'd finished hanging the balls. Sandra picked up her earlier conversation with Ben about mutual friends, and Julia joined in. Craig knew who they were talking about but like me was on the outside of that crowd. So we just listened and hung icicles on the tree, one shiny strip at a time. Tim helped us.

"You know it was rude of you," Sandra said to Ben, "to have left Meg at Melanie's party an hour after she brought you."

"She didn't actually bring me," he defended himself. "I drove to her house, and we walked from there."

"But Meg is the one who invited you," Sandra pressed him.

"I would've been asked anyway."

"Oh, really," she teased, "you're awfully sure of yourself. I guess all those stories about you are true."

I looked over my shoulder at them.

"Depends on what stories you mean," he answered. "I've heard a few about you as well."

"You tell one, I'll tell one," she proposed.

He raised an eyebrow. "Ones we've heard about each other?"

"No," she said slowly, thoughtfully, moving closer to him. "Tell me one about yourself that no one else knows." Sandra had the magic of narrowing a room—or an entire gym—to a world holding only her and a guy. She did it with her eyes. I'd seen it all before, but I'd never felt so pushed out. I turned back to my work, just in time to catch Tim climbing the unsteady ladder on the other side of the tree.

"Tim, be careful!" I said.

At that moment he lost his balance and slipped off the ladder, flailing his short arms as he landed and sending two balls flying across the room. A silver one smashed against a table. Tim stared at the broken ball, his face turning pale.

"I didn't mean to. I didn't!" He looked from his father to Jen to his father. "I didn't mean it!"

He seemed panic-stricken. I wondered if the ornament was one of Aunt Jen's.

"It's okay, Tim," she said. "I know it was an accident."

But he still looked upset, as if they wouldn't really believe him.

"Glad you did that, Timmy," Craig said, walking over to him, resting his hand on the ladder. "I've been trying to knock off ornaments all night."

Tim glanced at Craig.

"I've tried three times to crash into the Christmas tree but just keep missing."

The corners of Tim's mouth turned up a little.

"Maybe I'll climb up this ladder and do a one-and-a-half tuck into the tree. Remember how you liked them?"

"Into the pool, not into the tree," Tim said, smiling.

"Just watch me." Craig climbed up several steps, then stood on the edge of one, balancing on his toes so well that I knew he really was a diver.

"No!" Tim said, giggling.

"Didn't you know it's bad luck for the new year if the tree isn't knocked over at least once?"

"No way," Tim told him.

"In fact, my uncle Dave says it's bad luck if you don't throw the tree out the window—from the second story," Craig went on. "You've seen our tree lying out there in the yard, haven't you? That man flattened beneath it is Uncle Dave. Unfortunately he usually goes out with the tree."

Tim laughed and snuck a peek at his father and Jen, who smiled back at him. Then Aunt Jen winked.

Craig climbed down the ladder, not realizing he'd done more than help Tim out of a bad moment. Julia had been watching and laughing quietly and was still smiling now. There is something very appealing about a guy being kind to a child.

An hour later, when my family was leaving, Ben helped me on with my coat. "Maybe there is hope," I whispered to him.

He gazed down at me, his dark eyes glimmering. "For who?"

I pulled my eyes away from his. "You know," I said, and left.

Eleven

CHRISTMAS MORNING I was dragged out of bed by my sisters. We hurried downstairs with as much laughter and excitement as we did when we were little and Barbie dolls were waiting under the tree. My father sat back and watched, looking happy and bewildered: little doll clothes or teenage girl clothes, it was all strange to him. We gave my mother a pile of pretty gifts and my father a stack of books—biographies, history of science, history of anything. I knew he wanted to take his "toys" off to his study and read, but first my mother shepherded us to a church service.

As soon as we arrived home again we were back at our gifts, trying things on, listening to new CDs. I was thumping through the front hall in my heavy-duty hiking boots when the doorbell rang. I opened the door.

"Merry Christmas," Mike said. "I hope all your Christmas wishes came true." His eyes traveled down me, past the hem of my short skirt, down my silver mist stockings to the heavy boots. "I see one has. Nice outfit."

"Thanks. Come on in. *San-dra!*"

"Do you always have to shout?" he asked, but he was laughing. He laid several wrapped boxes down on a table, and I took his coat.

"I think she's upstairs, trying something on."

"Then I'll just go right on up," he said.

"You can try," I replied, hanging his coat on a hook, "if you don't mind my mother lassoing you with a string of Christmas lights, dragging you downstairs, then deciding you look nice next to the hearth—permanently."

He grinned. "This wouldn't be a bad place to live."

"You might not think that when my mother plugs you in."

"Three girls my age," he went on.

"Two. January third I'm out of here."

"That's too bad. Do you have to go back?"

"Sandra!" I called again, but he anticipated it and put his hands over his ears before I opened my mouth. "Faker," I said. "Your fingers were spread out."

He smiled impishly, then took a step closer to me, his eyes an intense blue. He stood close enough to slow dance. "Allie, why do you want to go to a school—"

"Well, here she comes," I said. "I heard her door open."

A moment later Sandra leaned over the second-floor balcony, her golden hair tumbling down. "Be right there!"

Julia came down the steps with her. Both of them wore new skirts and cropped sweater tops. They modeled them for Mike, who turned to me with another of his devilish smiles. "Anytime your mother wants to get out that lasso. . . ."

"I'll let her know," I replied, grinning.

"Lasso?" Julia asked.

"Just a joke," I said.

Sandra frowned a little. "I have your gift under the tree, Mike."

"These are yours," he replied, picking up his wrapped boxes, "one for each of you."

Julia looked at him, surprised. *He's playing games,* I thought. *He's letting Sandra know she's not the only girl in the world.*

"Well, how nice," Sandra remarked without a trace of a smile.

"It is nice," I said, trying to turn the game around, "and clever—scoring brownie points with the rest of us."

Mike blinked.

"Well, let's go open presents," Julia said.

As we walked toward the family room we passed my mother in the living room, fussing with a strand of lights she'd wrapped around a fig tree. Mike glanced sideways at me, and we burst out laughing.

"Same dumb joke," I explained to the others.

Sandra retrieved Mike's gift from under the tree, and Mike had the good sense to sit next to her as she unwrapped the gift from him. Julia and I both waited so Sandra could be the center of attention.

"Oh, Mike, thank you," she said, lifting out a bottle of perfume. "I've been wanting this."

"I know, you wrote down the name for me."

She removed the pretty glass stopper and dabbed her wrists. "Want to smell?" she asked Julia and me, then reached across to us.

"I love it," Julia said, sniffing.

"Mmm," I responded, careful not to breathe in. "It's wonderful."

Mike started to smile, and I bit my tongue so I wouldn't laugh at another private joke. Then he unwrapped his gift, a sports watch, and put it on immediately. Julia and I each opened a pair of earrings. I counted on Sandra to notice that she received something different from our gift, something she'd asked for, so she was special. Julia and I thanked Mike and made a hasty exit, leaving him and Sandra to work things out between them.

"Allie," Julia said to me when we were in the hall, "do you have any idea what Mike's up to?"

"Playing the same games Sandra's playing. Making her jealous, keeping her guessing. Don't you think?"

"Maybe," Julia replied thoughtfully. "There's something else I've been wondering—do you have any idea when a guy finds you attractive?"

"What do you mean?"

"Well, that answers my question," she said.

"What do you mean?" I demanded again. "Julia!"

But she headed upstairs without responding.

*   *   *

"Time to strut our stuff," Julia said two hours later.

In years past, when we joined our parents for the holidays, our Christmas celebration was just a dinner for five. But now, living in an area where my father had grown up and my mother attended college, we were going "visiting." After making two brief stops in town, leaving behind my mother's New Year's wreaths and bottles of wine, we drove to a country estate where some banking CEO lived, someone with whom my father's company did business.

The house was a big yellow stucco structure, built in the eighteenth century. Inside, chandeliers hung with greens and long tapered candles doubled their flames against mirrors and paned windows. Men in tuxes played music while others walked around with little silver trays. After my father introduced us to the host and hostess, he and my mother moved on to talk to some business associates. My sisters and I were on our own and stood in a tight circle in the center of a high-ceilinged parlor.

"I don't see anyone we know," Julia said, glancing around.

"Well, it's time we expand our horizons," Sandra replied. "Thornhill is getting a little too small for me. Let's take a tour. There must be some interesting guys here."

The party was spread over the first floor, and we moved from room to room. "Until we've checked out everyone, don't stop, just look," Sandra directed.

"Not even for food?" I asked since we were now in the dining room.

Julia giggled. "This girl stops for chocolate."

She and I let Sandra move on while we snatched up some chocolate creams. When we caught up with Sandra with an extra cream wrapped in a napkin, we made her beg for it.

"Hey, there's Ben and Sam," Julia said, pointing to the doorway across the center hall from us.

Ben was wearing a dark suit and sharp tie. The sophisticated manner in which he nodded and spoke to an older couple made the guys I knew look like Little Leaguers.

"You know the rule," Julia teased, "can't stop till we've checked out all the rooms."

"This girl stops for hot guys," Sandra replied.

Ben and his father didn't notice us staring, but the silver-haired guest did. "Excuse me," he said in a gravelly voice that carried. "I'm sure these pretty girls are waiting for their chance to talk with me."

The man's wife laughed. Ben and Sam turned around, then Sam called us over and introduced us to Mr. and Mrs. Strott. The couple was friendly, asking us how we liked living in Thornhill, what we thought of the shops, the school, et cetera. Despite their interest in us, Sandra kept saying quiet things for Ben's ears only. I did my best to keep up the conversation and cover her rudeness. The result was that I ended up discussing camping areas accessible to senior citizens with a seventy-year-old couple while Sandra led Ben off to the chocolate creams.

Julia and Sam moved on to find Jen and Tim. Mr. Strott and I finished up our comparison of hiking trails, then I wandered on alone. I wanted to find Ben and Sandra, but I was almost afraid to. I didn't want to see them flirting, him becoming another one of her guys, she another one of his girls.

I stopped in a room full of skylights and red poinsettias, a garden room with big windows built onto the back of the house. Except for the flowers and one bench, the room was empty. I could hear the music from across the hall and sat down on the bench to listen. Through the doorway I caught a glimpse of Tim tagging after my mother and waved at him. He changed directions, joining me on the bench.

"What did Santa bring you?" I asked when he sat down.

"I know there isn't a Santa, Allie."

"Me too," I replied, "but he still leaves me stuff."

"I got a cool computer game and a new glove because my hand's getting big. And a boom box. And skates. *She* gave me the skates."

I figured *she* was Aunt Jen. "Sounds like a pretty good haul," I said.

"It's okay." He swung one foot back and forth. "Mommy has other stuff for me in Baltimore."

"Did you call her today?" I asked.

He nodded. "We used to come here with her. I didn't like it because she always made me dance with her."

"She likes to dance?"

"Yeah, and Dad doesn't. He's got a lot of left feet."

"I think two are enough to make it hard," I said. There was a long silence.

"If Mommy was here now, I'd dance with her. I wouldn't whine."

"When you get home, tell her that." Then I had a wild hunch. "Want to dance?"

"Okay."

We rose together. Tim put one hand up between my elbow and shoulder and held the other straight out. "The person with the biggest feet leads," he told me.

"Guess that's me."

Natural athletes move well, even when they're seven. I adjusted my steps to Tim's boy-size ones and danced around the room with him.

"Do you wanna turn?" he asked. "Wanna twirl around?"

"Sure."

We turned in opposite directions, colliding, then pulling apart. Our laughter echoed in the big room.

"Try again," Tim said, "this way." We whirled— once, twice, three times. "Again!" he cried. We spun to the music till I was dizzy.

"Whoa! Stop," I told him.

"Are you going to throw up?" he asked.

"Don't sound so hopeful."

Tim chortled, and a deeper laugh joined his. We turned around to see Ben sitting on the bench. I put a hand out to Tim to steady myself. "How long have you been here?"

"A while." He smiled and stood up.

"So, what do you think—are Tim and I ready for ballroom competition?"

"As soon as you figure out which one is leading," he said.

"The one with the biggest feet," Tim and I responded at the same time.

Ben came over and looked down at our feet. "I win. Can I have this dance?"

I hesitated. "You mean with me?"

"Why would I want to dance with my brother?"

"You have before," Tim said. "You taught me how to do teenage dances."

"Right," Ben replied. "But this is a slow, old song. It's easier to dance to with someone who's almost the same height."

Tim shrugged and went to sit on the bench. Ben slipped his arm around me. I felt his left hand press warm against my back. His right held mine gently, letting my hand rest in his.

"I—I don't really know how to dance this way," I told him.

"It's easy. Just move with me."

Okay, I told myself, *okay. Dance is simply movement and balance.* Only I wished he'd stop looking down at me and start moving.

"Relax, Allie," he said.

Breathe, I reminded myself as we started to dance.

The awkwardness slipped away with the music. We moved all the way around the room, my feet matching his, backward and forward, sideways and around, me always in his arms. I forgot all about being just a buddy, Tim's pal, a funny highway pickup. I wanted to dance close to him. I wanted to be always matching my feet to his, backward, forward—forever in his arms. I wanted to bury my face in the warm place between his neck and shoulder. I heard the slow, romantic music—could hear it inside me.

Then Ben started laughing. "I don't know what song you're dancing to, but the one from the other room stopped," he said.

"Oh. Oh, yeah." I let go and backed away, embarrassed.

He laughed again and pulled me toward him. I resisted, but he held me even tighter. With one hand he gently laid my head on his shoulder. "Come on, Allie Cat," he whispered in my ear. "Hum a song, and we'll dance."

Twelve

WE DANCED UNTIL the music started up again. It was a fast sleigh song and I thought Ben would let go of me, but he held me close and danced even slower than before. I could feel the strength in his arms, the roughness of his jaw and neck against my cheek.

I saw Tim fidgeting, then he rose and left. The realization that I was this close and alone with Ben did strange things to me. My heart started skipping crazily, like the sleigh bell music, but we moved together so slowly now that we'd almost stopped.

"What song are you dancing to?" I asked, trying to laugh, hoping it would cover my trembling.

"The same one you are," he answered, his voice deep, melting me.

He says that to all the girls, I thought. *He knows all the lines, just like my sisters.* And just like their gullible guys, I was close to believing the words were reserved just for me. I pulled back suddenly, afraid of being hurt. "I—I don't think so."

He pulled me to him. "I know so," he replied, his mouth so close to mine, his words felt like kisses. "Close your eyes, Allie."

"Why?"

He laughed quietly. "So you don't go cross-eyed staring at my nose."

I was staring at your mouth, I thought. I glanced past him, struggling to get back to the real world, the world where I belonged. In the room across the hall I saw my parents, Julia, and Aunt Jen looking around as if they were trying to find someone.

"I thought you wanted to be kissed," Ben said.

"Kissed? By you?" If my mouth touched his, I wouldn't be able to hide my intense feelings. My parents and Aunt Jen would see, my sisters would know, and worst of all, Ben would realize I wasn't just another girl to fool around with but a hopeless, head-over-heels case. If my mouth touched his, I might never recover. "No."

Ben gazed down at me, his eyes narrowing.

"My family is looking for me," I told him.

"You know, I thought you were different from other girls," Ben said, keeping me close so that I couldn't avoid his eyes. "But Mike was right—you play as hard to get as your sisters."

I pushed him back, stung by his words. "You think I'm playing hard to get? I think you've got the wrong girl!"

He stared at me, his dark eyes turbulent.

"There she is," my mother called. "Hey, Allie, Ben, time to go."

There was nothing he and I could do except act as if we'd been in the middle of a friendly conversation. I heard him take a deep breath and let it out again. We met my family in the center hall.

Sam, Tim, and Sandra stood at the other end of the hall, putting on their coats. "Sandra's coming with us for the rest of our visits," Aunt Jen told me cheerfully. "Why don't you come too, Allie?"

I wondered who had invited Sandra and glanced at Ben.

"Tim would enjoy it," he said stiffly.

"Thanks, but no thanks," I replied. "Tell Tim we can do something tomorrow."

Ben nodded silently and headed down the hall, Aunt Jen following him.

My family and I left soon after. Julia and I rode to the next two destinations in silence, turning on our friendliness at each visit, then sinking back into our own thoughts once we were in the car again. At last we arrived home and wordlessly plodded upstairs to our bedrooms. Then both of us forgot to knock, entering our shared bathroom from opposite doors at the same time.

"I'll use Sandra's," she said.

"No, I will," I offered. "Julia, are you okay? You've been quiet."

"And you haven't?" she countered. She pulled her hair up into a ponytail and began to wash her face. "I guess I've been thinking a lot."

119

"Should you be doing that on Christmas?" I teased.

"Christmas is what has gotten me thinking." She dried her face, then put cream under her eyes and wiped away the mascara. "All the tinsel and stuff. Do you ever feel like you're walking around with a smile plastered on?" She wiped off her lipstick. "Like you're tired of faking it, tired of acting the way everyone expects you to, but you don't know how else to be because you're no longer sure what's real for you?"

"In certain places I feel that way."

"So what do you do?" she asked.

"I leave. I run back to a place where I know who I've always been."

"Fields," she guessed.

"But that's not a good solution," I went on. "I should be able to be anywhere with anyone and be myself." I glanced at my own made-up reflection. "But I'm not. Especially when it counts." She met my eyes in the mirror. "That makes two of us."

About six-thirty that evening Julia put on casual clothes, then drove off to exchange gifts with Ford and meet up with some friends. She asked me to come, but I told her I was tired. Can a person's heart feel tired? Mine did. All the feelings I had developed for Ben that would never come to anything were taking their toll. I was drained.

My father finally got his chance to read, and my mother went up to their bedroom to watch *My Fair*

120

Lady on TV. I poked through the videos I'd brought from school, trying to find one that would sufficiently distract me from the fact that Sandra had not yet returned. She and Ben must've been having a really good time. I imagined him putting his arms around her, saying, "I thought you wanted to be kissed." She wouldn't get scared the way I had.

I'd just picked out a foreign film from my collection, counting on the fact that reading subtitles would keep my mind off other things, when the phone rang.

"Julia, Sandra, Allie?"

"One of us."

"Allie," he guessed again, "this is Craig."

"Hey, Craig, how was your Christmas?"

"Great!" he said. "I got the Nikon I've been wanting for three years and have been shooting film all day—rolls of aunts and uncles. I can't wait to do some night photography—it's supposed to work well in minimal light conditions."

"I'd like to see your photos," I said. "Especially the ones you took of Julia. Speaking of her—she's not here right now."

"Does she sense I'm going to call and make a quick exit?"

"Just bad timing," I assured him.

"Ben's been giving me a lot of encouragement," Craig said, "and a lot of advice about girls."

"Nothing like getting it from the expert," I remarked, unable to keep the sarcasm out of my voice.

"He's a nice guy, Allie. I know him better than

anybody does—know the part of him that kids at school have never seen. You won't find anyone more decent than Ben."

I didn't need to hear this.

"And it has to be tough on him, coming back," Craig added. "He had everything going for him if he'd stayed for his senior year—sports, girls, popularity with teachers. He was the golden guy of Thornhill, you know? His parents knew that and let him choose where to live. But he felt like Tim needed him, so he went to Baltimore."

This talk of Ben and what a great guy he was made me too upset to say anything.

"Are you there, Allie?"

"Yeah," I replied, my voice a little quivery.

"What are you doing tonight?" he asked.

"Watching a German movie with English subtitles about Berlin in the 1930s."

"Alone?"

"How many other people do you think want to see something like that? Sandra's out with Ben," I added.

Then Craig surprised me by asking, "I'd like to see the movie; could I? I won't stay late. I'm helping out at the shop tomorrow morning—it's a big sale day."

I didn't know Craig that well, but what the heck? He seemed like a good guy, and I didn't feel like being alone. "Sure, come on over," I said. "Dress down."

It turned out that we dressed almost identically, in flannel shirts and jeans. I carried a huge platter of chips and dip into the family room while he loaded up the VCR. We kicked off our shoes and sprawled out on the sofa recliners with the chips and remote between us. I felt like I was back at the dorm—stopping the video, munching, talking, starting it again.

I was slipping another video into the machine when I heard the front door open and Sandra's heels clicking across the foyer. "Anybody around?"

"We're watching a movie," I called to her, settling back onto the sofa with Craig. "Second show is ready to begin."

Her footsteps grew muffled by the living-room carpet, then she stood in the doorway. "Oh, hello," she said, seeing Craig. "I didn't expect you to be here."

She sure is good at being rude, I thought.

Then Ben entered the room. My whole body tensed up at the sight of him. He looked just as surprised as Sandra to see the two of us sitting there.

Craig grinned at him. "Hey, Ben! Up for a sci-fi?"

"Whatever you're watching," Ben replied. He wouldn't look at me.

"I don't like sci-fi," Sandra told Ben, as if it were his house and he should do something about it.

"Well, here's what I brought from school," I said, showing them the box, "and here's our home collection."

We ended up watching *Excalibur.* To be more accurate, they ended up watching it; I watched Ben and Sandra. The two of them sat on the love seat. Sandra conveniently leaned back against Ben, turning her head now and then to make private comments, laughing quietly with him. I was about ready to take a sword to her. *Chill out, Allie,* I told myself.

I don't think I was ever so glad to see King Arthur get it through the gut. I stood up at the first movie credit.

"Well, I should be getting home," Craig said, rising with me. "Thanks a lot, Allie. It's been fun."

"Do you need a ride?" Ben asked.

"No thanks. I'm parked on the front street," Craig replied.

I needed some fresh air, so I led him back through the kitchen, picked up my parka, and escorted him outside. We passed Tomato Soup and were striding side by side down the driveway when a car turned in, coming fast.

"Yikes!"

Craig jumped sideways and yanked me out of the way, holding on to me as Julia hit the brakes. She screeched to a halt and quickly lowered her window. "Sorry! Sorry, I didn't expect anyone to be there," she said.

"Don't worry about it," I replied, walking over to her. "We should've been looking where we were going instead of talking away." I had to reach back and grab Craig's jacket to pull him up to the car window. Julia gazed at him with those starry green eyes of hers.

"Hi," he said.

"Hi."

Silence.

"How was your Christmas?" he asked her.

"Okay."

"I hope you got what you wanted and a surprise too. Surprises are important," he rushed on, "because when something good and unexpected happens, it gives you hope."

"Unless it's the wrong kind of surprise," she said.

He looked at me quickly, needing help.

"Craig and I watched one of the weird videos I brought back from school," I said, "and *Excalibur* after that. He was just headed home."

"I thought you were tired, Allie," Julia remarked, sounding a little irritated.

"I was. But when Craig suggested we get together and watch videos, it seemed like a good idea."

"Well, I didn't actually—," Craig began.

I kicked him. "Come on," I said, starting off, "I'm getting cold."

Craig followed me. When we reached his car, I apologized for cutting him off like that. "But I had a reason," I said. "It doesn't hurt for Julia to think you have various girls to call up and hang out with."

"I guess you're right," he replied, "but I've never played those kinds of games."

"Neither have I," I said, "and look where it's gotten me."

"Where?" he asked.

"Nowhere," I told him, and he smiled. "Well, it was fun, Craig. Really. You're a great guy—don't forget that. G'night." He drove away, looking thoughtful.

When I stepped back into the warmth of the kitchen, Sandra and Ben were there, talking to Julia.

"Glad to see you and Craig are hitting it off," Ben remarked to me. "He's a great guy."

"Yup," I said.

Julia looked miffed again, and I was miffed as well. It was bad enough that Ben was getting snared by Sandra; he didn't have to make it worse by pushing me toward his old buddy from next door.

I excused myself and went upstairs. After changing into my nightshirt I turned off my lamp and opened the curtains over the window seat. The electric candle in the window along with the moonlight made me feel a little more peaceful. My gifts were piled onto the window seat, and I looked at each of them again, finally picking up the box from Mike. *Poor Mike,* I thought, opening it, *there's no hope for him till Ben goes home.*

I removed the earrings, then noticed that the tissue had been taped down beneath them in an odd way. With my finger I pulled it loose. Under the tissue lay a chain dangling a small gold heart. A note had been placed beneath that.

"Hope you find this before you throw out the box," I read. "See—I'm not trying to make your sister jealous."

I held up the heart, gazing at it with amazement, letting it sparkle in the candlelight. The hidden gift was very romantic but crazy. I could barely imagine Mike and me as friends, let alone a couple. We both liked sports, but that was it; his idea of a great foreign film was probably one starring Arnold Schwarzenegger.

I slipped the heart and chain back in the box, then heard footsteps and voices on the driveway below my window. I knew it was Ben and Sandra. I didn't want to watch, but I had to.

Ben leaned back against his car, talking with Sandra. She laughed and put her arms around him. There was more laughing, more talking—she was enjoying being in his arms—I knew how that felt. Her hair shone pale gold in the moonlight. I'd never met a guy who could resist her golden hair or laughing green eyes.

And Ben didn't. It was a long kiss—I think. How long's eternity? That's what it seemed like to me.

At last Sandra returned to the house. Ben started to get into his car, then suddenly turned and looked up, gazing right up at my window. Afraid that he might see my face illuminated by the candle, I quickly put my hand over it. Ben stood up straighter. What a stupid thing for me to do! Now he knew for sure that someone had been watching.

I let go and slid down to the floor beneath the window frame, fighting back the tears, losing that battle, feeling like a fool. I guess this was how King Arthur felt, getting it through the gut.

Thirteen

WHEN I AWOKE the next morning, I made a mental list of things to do: Clear things up with Mike, help Julia and Craig, entertain Tim, and—somehow—get over Ben. I had another week left at home. I could moon around and feel sorry for myself or do some things I'd be glad for later.

I called the Harringtons first and was relieved when Sam, not Ben, was the one who answered the phone. He was delighted at my offer to take Tim and a friend ice skating that afternoon. The next item on my list, talking to Mike, wouldn't be quite as easy to handle. Face-to-face was always better, but Sandra was home, so I couldn't invite him over. While my sister was eating breakfast, I snuck into her room, found her red address book (she'd already entered Ben!), and copied down Mike's number and street. Then I pulled on my running togs and headed off, conveniently passing by the Calloways' house on my route.

Actually, I passed it twice while trying to decide what I would say. If his flirtation with me was just a way of getting to Sandra, it was no big deal. Sandra's actions in the last two days had extinguished any concern about hurting her feelings. As for my old rage against guys who might be using me, I was tired of being angry; a guy who'd use me wasn't worth getting all wound up about. But the little gold heart hidden in the box, *that* worried me.

When I'd first met Mike, I readily pegged him as an egotistical jock. Now I wondered if I was guilty of the same thing as some of my sisters' crowd— judging too quickly. Looking back, the scene in the grocery store and the tug-of-war with the bags *had* been pretty funny. I suspected that when Mike's ego didn't get in the way, he was a nice guy.

I had also come to realize that unexpected feelings can spring up between the most unlikely pair—Julia and Craig, for instance. Though last week I would have thought it impossible, what if Mike was actually getting a crush on me? I didn't want the heart of anyone to get as bruised as mine felt right now.

I stood before the Calloways' large green-and-white house for the third time, then sprinted up the driveway and rang the bell. The door opened, and I was confronted with a pretty girl who looked about eleven and had Mike's dark hair and bright blue eyes. The startling thing was there were four younger versions standing behind her. They couldn't stop giggling when they saw me.

"Do you want Mike?" the oldest girl said. Before I could answer, she yelled for him, just like I yell for Sandra.

A minute later Mike came down the steps. "Allie!" he exclaimed. "I didn't know you were coming."

"I guess I should've called first."

"No, I like surprises."

Another chorus of giggles.

"This is Allie Parker," Mike said to the girls.

"I thought her name was Sandra," one of them replied.

"They're sisters," he said shortly. "Don't you all have something to do?"

They gave me mischievous grins and reluctantly headed toward a room in the back of the house, disappearing one by one.

Mike led me into the living room. I'd noticed from the outside that the house had a turret at one corner, and I immediately walked over to the circular area with windows and deep-pillowed benches. Mike smiled. "Girls always like this corner," he said, joining me.

He sat on the floor, then reached up for two pillows, placing one behind his back and one next to him—for me, I figured. But I took a seat on the floor across from him instead. He laughed and scooted over to me. "Lean forward," he said, placing a pillow behind my back. He smiled. "No, you're not shy at all," he teased.

"I'm not," I insisted. "I came over here, didn't I?"

131

He nodded. "And I'm glad. I get tired of girls playing hard to get."

"Mike, I'm not playing at all."

"Good, then I won't have to," he replied. "Chasing a girl is tough enough without having to wonder whether she wants to be chased."

"I don't want to be chased," I told him.

"It can be fun for a while, as long as it doesn't take too long to get to the kissing." He gazed at me intently.

"I don't think you understand," I said, trying to figure out another way to explain. "I found the chain and heart last night. It's very pretty."

He glanced down at my throat. "How does it look on you?" he asked. "Did you put it on?"

"No."

"Why not?" He sounded hurt.

"Because . . . because I'm not going out with you," I replied.

He laughed and put his arm around my shoulders. "How could you be? I've only known you four days, and for the first three of them I was after your sister."

"Then why did you give it to me?"

"I wanted to. I didn't know there had to be another reason to give a gift."

I was silent for a moment. The idea of giving a gift just because you want to—not because it's expected, and not to get something back—touched me. But still, this gift was a heart. I tried to explain one last time. "Here's the problem. If you've ever fallen for someone—fallen hard—and that person doesn't fall for you, it can really hurt. It can hurt as bad as anything you've ever known."

"I know, Allie," he said, "and I can't promise anything. But I hope you'll take the chance anyway. I don't intend to hurt you."

Hurt *me?* He had it all backward! Or else I did.

"I was wondering," he said, "are you coming to the game tomorrow night? Everybody will be there—we're playing our biggest rival, Elmhurst."

I pulled up both knees and wrapped my arms around them, wrestling with the strange idea that he really could be interested in me.

"Would you come and see me play?" he asked with the earnestness of a little boy. "Allie? It would mean a lot to me."

The things I did that meant a lot to Ben were giving him a hanger to fix his car, taking care of his brother, and helping out his old friend. It was nice to think that simply *being there* for Mike—rather than assisting in some way—really meant something to him.

"Uh . . . sure. Why not? I love basketball."

He grinned. "For once I'll have a girl watching who really knows the game."

I straightened up. He meant it as a compliment, but it always annoys me when guys assume girls know little about sports. "Afterward everyone usually gets together at Bingo's Café," Mike went on. "I'd really like for you to come with me."

I hesitated, then nodded. Why not go where I was wanted?

"It's funny. You can be real quiet," he observed. "You're not big on flattery. But somehow you give me more confidence than other girls do."

"I didn't think you needed any confidence."

"It's a good act, huh?"

"Better than the one I usually put on," I said, smiling. "I guess none of us are sure of ourselves." I stood up. "I better get going."

"I'll see you tomorrow night, then." Mike rose and walked me to the front door. He placed his hands on my shoulders, holding me still, and moved his face toward mine. If I turned away, would he say, "I thought you wanted to be kissed"? I closed my eyes and hoped for the best. *Maybe sparks will fly,* I thought; *maybe the moment Mike's lips touch mine, all my feelings will change.*

He kissed me softly. I stood still as a statue, wondering how the mere brush of Ben's hand could make me tingle all over while Mike's lips did nothing.

Mike smiled. "No, you're not shy," he said for the umpteenth time.

"God, Mike! Just because I don't come on to you doesn't mean I'm shy!"

He laughed, and I hopped down the steps and sprinted off.

I arrived home sweaty and confused. Music came from the living room—ripples of sound that I recognized as piano exercises. I was standing in the hallway, listening, when Sandra hurried down the steps.

"You may want to run a few more miles," she

said, snatching up her coat. "Julia just got started."

"I like hearing her play."

"You always were our best audience, Al." She pulled open the front door. "See you later."

"Sandra!" I called after her. "Wait! I need to ask you something."

She turned back. "Can you make it quick?"

The quicker the better. "Mike, uh, mentioned tomorrow night's game—and Bingo's afterward. He was wondering if, uh, I was going."

"I hope you told him yes," Sandra replied. She didn't bat an eyelash. "I'm sure Julia and Ford can give you a ride to the gym, and Mike will give you one home. I'm going with Ben."

"Oh. Oh, okay." Obviously this new arrangement was just fine with her.

"Well, I'm out of here. I've got to find something incredible to wear for New Year's Eve."

I wondered if she and Ben had already made plans for the big night. I thought about rushing back to Fields and spending New Year's Eve with Miss Henny. But that would be retreating, and I had done enough of that in my life. The best thing I could do was keep myself too busy to think or hurt.

The next item on my list was Craig and Julia. I stuck my head into the living room, and after a moment Julia paused in her playing.

"What's up?"

"Just listening," I said.

"Have a good run?"

"Pretty good," I replied, entering the room. She

had music books spread all over the piano. "This looks like major composer stuff. Are you working on something?"

"Schubert."

"Really?" I said. "I thought you were tired of practicing classical works."

"I thought so too. Just like I thought Miss Henny was a teacher too old to know anything. But she was right—talent is not enough. I'm taking lessons again, and in January I'm starting voice as well."

"That's terrific! I can't wait to tell her."

"I'm glad you think it's a good idea," Julia said. "Sandra says I'm crazy, and Ford gets mad because I spend so much time practicing."

"Yeah, well, that's guys for you," I replied. "They expect girls to stand around waiting for them to finish a ball game but get offended when we have our own practice and competitions."

Julia nodded. "Ford doesn't play sports, but he works out in a gym every day. I'm supposed to want to go with him and see how many pounds he can press. But he doesn't want to hear me play, so I don't see why I should watch him push and pull machines."

I sat down on the bench beside her. "I get the feeling Ford's not going to be your one true love."

My sister sighed. "Maybe I want too much."

"What do you want?" I asked.

"Someone I can love and like too, if you know what I mean. I want someone who is really romantic but a real friend as well."

"Maybe you don't want too much—just looking for it in the wrong guys."

"Maybe," Julia replied, her fingers playing silent notes the length of the piano. "So how is it with Craig?" she asked.

"What do you mean?"

"Do you like him?"

"A lot," I said. "He's easy to talk to—"

"When he's with *you*." Realizing she'd cut me off too sharply, she added quickly, "I think it's great he's so comfortable with you. What kinds of things do you talk about?"

"Oh, everything," I said. "He's observant, the kind of person who's very interested in other people. That's probably why he's a good photographer, and it also makes him fun to be around. He knows all kinds of things."

"So, has he asked you out?" she asked.

"You mean on a date? No."

I debated whether to divulge Craig's feelings for her. She must have figured he liked her enough to have called her for a date a few days ago. But she'd chosen to ignore him, and I knew he would seem more interesting if she wasn't so sure where she stood with him now. I decided to give her the all-clear sign from me but not make winning him seem like a sure thing. "Craig and I are friends—buddies," I told her. "You know me; romance isn't really my thing."

"Then why are you reading those paperbacks?"

I stared at her accusingly. "Julia!"

"Well, Allie, you've been hiding stuff in the same place since you were eight years old. Of course, I'm going to look."

"And I trusted you."

"You didn't answer my question. Why are you reading romances if it's not your thing?"

I took a deep breath. "I wish it were my thing, just once." *Like right now,* I thought, *with Ben.* "But all I ever do is make friends with guys or become their consolation prize." I started playing "Chopsticks."

"I've always envied the way you make friends," Julia said. "And I've always admired the way you are with guys—direct. You know how to be yourself, and they really like you for who you are."

I stopped playing. "I've always envied the way you make guys fall hopelessly in love with you. I can't even imagine it."

"Yeah, well, don't bother. Most of the time they're in love with what I add to their image of themselves. They create in their own minds the perfect girl to go with the face, a girl who isn't real—not me. And the terrible thing is, I've let them." We sat side by side, staring down at the keyboard. "I don't know if this is a really depressing conversation or a really hopeful one," I said. "We both want the same thing, so maybe it's not crazy—maybe it's really possible."

"To be ourselves? To have both love and friendship?"

I nodded. "Heart and soul."

"Want to play it?"

We did.

Fourteen

I'D FORGOTTEN ALL about Stefan, the dancing reindeer who fell off the stage, until I took the little boys skating that afternoon. Stefan didn't have much more luck on the ice, and Tim struggled to get used to his new skates. My old, nicked-up blades glided like I'd attached kitchen forks to my feet. We were a dangerous trio. It didn't take long for other skaters at the rink to move out of our way when they saw us coming.

Eventually, despite protests from Tim, I sat down and watched. I knew he needed to have fun with a kid his own age without a "grown-up" between them. Tim and Stefan met two other kids from school, and the four of them became a squadron of planes that didn't always know where they were flying. I let them skate and laugh and shout to the point of exhaustion, then drove the boys home, dropping Stefan off first.

When we arrived at Tim's house, he told me,

"You've got to come in. I have a present for you."

"I would even without a present."

"You'll like it," he said as I trailed him up the walk. Tim pushed open the front door and dropped his skates with a clatter. "I'm home!"

"No kidding," Ben called from upstairs.

"Did you bring back both legs?" I recognized the voice as Craig's.

"Yeah, and Allie too."

I hung my coat over the banister and followed Tim into the living room. "Let's look at my gifts first," he said, then showed them to me one by one, explaining how to use them. I kept missing the details, distracted by the presence of Ben in the house. When Tim tried to explain some mixed-up rules for a board game, I had to focus as hard as I did in math class.

"Get it?" Tim asked me. "Get it?"

I stared down at the colored squares, listening to footsteps on the stairs. "Sort of."

"Hey, Allie," Craig greeted me, coming into the living room. "Hi, Tim. Hi, Ben."

I wasn't sure what I'd see in Ben's eyes. The turbulent, angry look they held after we had danced on Christmas? Or laughter because he'd caught me spying when he kissed my sister? "Did you give Allie her present yet?" Ben asked.

Nothing. There was nothing in his eyes, which was worse than what I'd imagined. I was just a person visiting his little brother.

Tim crawled under the tree, then squirmed out again and handed me a box.

"Wow! Did you wrap this yourself?" I asked.

He nodded. The paper, which had footballs and cartoon characters all over it, didn't quite make it around one end of the box. A stick-on bow had been placed in the bare spot and another one on top.

"I taught him all my wrapping tricks," Craig said, grinning. He and Tim stood next to me as I tore the paper. Ben kept his distance.

I lifted the lid and pulled back pieces of tissue. A furry leopard head emerged—two of them—slippers in spotted fake fur with big leopard heads on the toes.

"Wow!" I said, pulling them out. "These are . . . incredible."

"You like 'em?"

"Of course!"

"Leopards are cats too, Allie Cat," Tim told me. "That's what Jen said. They ran out of Garfield."

"Leopards are much cooler," I said, removing my shoes and pulling on the slippers.

"Jen said you have the same size feet as her."

"I do. These are perfect." I got up to model them for him, doing some fancy turns, then wriggling my toes. "They feel real comfy," I told him, sitting down again to take them off. "Thanks, pal." I held out my arms and gave him a big hug. He squeezed me tight. Over Tim's shoulder I saw Ben watching, his face expressionless.

The phone rang, and Ben turned away to answer it. A moment later he said, "It's for you, Tim. Who's J. R.?"

"A kid from my class last year. He was at the skating

rink. I'll take it upstairs," he added, in what I thought was Tim's imitation of Ben wanting his privacy.

When Tim had disappeared, Ben said, "He saw some kids he knew at the rink?"

"Yes, J.R. and his friend Kevin."

Ben sat down across from me and stretched his long legs out in front of him. "I was hoping something like that would happen. I appreciate you taking him, Allie."

"It was fun," I told him. "Tim mentioned Jen twice. Is that going better?"

"I think so. When he decided to get you a gift this morning, he let her drive him to the mall."

"Great!" At least I could still talk to Ben about Tim. Nothing would change that.

Craig sprawled comfortably on the rug between Ben and me, leaning back, propping himself up on his elbows.

"Craig just showed me some pictures of Julia—photos he'd taken at the fall production," Ben said.

Craig and Julia, another "project" we shared. "Yeah?"

"They're terrific," he added, then glanced at Craig, who looked as if he were going to deny it. "Don't argue," Ben told him. "They are some of the best I've ever seen. They have—I'm not sure how to put it—a sense of a real person behind the face."

"A person with heart and soul?" I suggested.

He nodded.

"I could give them to you, Allie, to give to Julia," Craig offered.

"Not yet," I told him. "And you should be the one to give them to her. Just not yet."

I saw Ben tilt his head, one side of his mouth curling a little. Had I said something funny?

"The thing is, I don't know what to do next," Craig said. "I don't have a good excuse to see her. We can't decorate the tree again."

"We can take down the tree," I replied. "Or you can come over for another of my strange videos from school. You can show me how to shoot good pictures—I'll make Julia model. We can, I don't know, there must be a million ways to get you two together. I just have to figure out which is best and in what order."

I heard Ben laugh.

"Julia is getting back into classical music again," I went on, "and taking it seriously. She's practicing piano and is starting voice lessons in January. File that away for future reference."

The sardonic smile on Ben's face was getting to me. "What?" I asked him, prickling. "What's the problem?"

"The Parker sisters should open a dating consulting firm," he replied. "You and your sisters know all the maneuvers. You can coach the rest of us."

"The practices would be fun," Craig noted cheerfully.

"I don't know if guys would have the endurance it takes," I commented.

"Oh, I think we would," Ben answered smoothly. "At the end you could test us at rest stops on the Jersey Turnpike."

That stung.

"You know what, Ben? You know what would do you a lot of good?" I said. "To fall head over heels with a girl you can't have."

The smile on his face disappeared.

"To fall in love—I mean really, incredibly in love—with someone who isn't interested in you, and see how that feels." I forced myself to meet his eyes steadily, making him look away first.

"Well." After a moment Ben stood up. "Can I get anybody a soda?"

"Uh . . . I'll take one," Craig said when I didn't reply.

Ben went out to the kitchen. I rubbed my head, then felt Craig patting my foot.

"Got a little intense, didn't I," I murmured.

"A little," Craig said gently.

We sat quietly, which was something I could feel comfortable doing with Craig. If Julia and he ever got together, she'd find out how nice that was.

"Craig," I said after a few minutes, "will you be photographing tomorrow night's basketball game?"

"I cover all of them."

"Julia will be there. Afterward everyone's going to Bingo's. Julia's going with Ford, but don't let that bother you. He's sinking fast."

"Bingo's is where the team hangs out," Craig said.

"Right. I'll be there with Mike."

"You're going with Mike?" he repeated, clearly surprised.

Ben had just come back into the room. "Yeah, well, it's a long story," I muttered.

Ben set down three sodas. "I brought an extra

144

in case you wanted one," he told me.

"Thanks. Can I take it with me?" I asked, rising. "I really have to get going."

"Sure."

"Anyway, you should come, Craig," I told him as I walked to the hall to get my coat. The guys followed me, Ben carrying my soda. "A lot of kids will be there, and I'll hardly know anyone."

"Allie," Craig said, "Bingo's is where the team and their friends hang out."

"Yeah, so?"

"I'm not part of that crowd."

"Like I am?" I laughed. "I've never been part of a cool crowd in my life."

"You are now," Ben interjected, handing me the soda can. "The captain of the basketball team has made you part."

He sounded angry, as if I'd been given a free pass to a social scene where he didn't think I belonged.

"Mike invited me to join them for one night," I said. "And I agreed. Lucky *him!*"

I opened the front door, strode down the walk to my car, and drove off with my head held high.

Oh, I was cool, I was a girl who knew what she was about and where she was going. . . . I just didn't happen to notice right then that it was snowing like crazy. A blizzard was blowing, and I didn't even turn on the windshield wipers, not until I pulled into our driveway and realized I couldn't see three feet past the hood of my car. I flopped against the steering wheel, my heart aching, wishing like anything it was January third.

Fifteen

IGH WINDS AND snow made it impossible for anyone to go out Saturday night. As the snow fell, Julia shifted from piano exercises and Schubert to love songs—long, sad love songs that made me crazy. Then Sunday morning Sandra put me in an even better mood by modeling outfits she might wear New Year's Eve. Sometime the previous evening, while I was finishing my paperback romance, Sandra had called Ben and asked him to go with her to Twist's big year-end party. He, of course, said yes.

By noontime Sunday the storm had tapered to flurries. I spent the afternoon clearing the walk and driveway and would have happily shoveled all the roads in town as an excuse to be away from the house. But the basketball game was that night, and I eventually had to come inside to take a shower.

At dinner my mother passed around overcooked chicken and said how delighted she was that I was going to the game with my sisters. Then I informed her I would be meeting Mike and Sandra was going with Ben. She looked confused.

"That's a terrible arrangement," she said. "When the holidays are over, you'll all end up miles away from each other."

"It's safer that way," my father remarked.

"I already have Ben's e-mail address," Sandra told everyone. "And I can stay with Allie on weekends."

I choked on my chicken, then gulped down some water. "You can stay with Miss Henny."

She smiled at me. "You don't really mean that."

"I do mean it. My room's small, and I've got my own life at school now."

"How fortunate for you," Sandra said coolly, "that I didn't try to keep you out of my life at my school. You sure managed to land yourself in the middle of things."

"I didn't try to."

She gave a little shrug. "Well, in the end you did me a big favor, getting me off the hook with Mike. Not that I ever really encouraged him," she fudged, "but I hate to disappoint guys who want to date me."

"One of the tragedies of your young life," I muttered under my breath.

"Funny how things turn out for the best," Sandra said. "All's forgiven, Al." She breezed upstairs to make herself more beautiful, if that were possible.

"You don't look too happy for someone who's just been forgiven," my father observed.

I glanced up from my plate, blinking away my

miserable mental image: Ben and me in Fields's waiting parlor, making small talk, while Sandra finished dressing. Out of the corner of my eye I saw Julia shake her head at Dad. The subject was dropped.

Ford picked up Julia and me at seven o'clock. I hadn't gotten a good look at him my first day home, but I could see now that with his blond hair, gray eyes, and high cheekbones, he was a guy with a future in soaps.

When we arrived at the school gym, a mob had already gathered for the traditional holiday game. In small towns like Thornhill, not just students but adults and little kids show up to cheer on their team. People had brought homemade signs. Foil streamers and pom-poms in Thornhill's gold and Elmhurst's scarlet floated, shook, and shimmered. Music blared. The game hadn't begun, but the place was already rocking.

Both teams were warming up. As the three of us made our way along the sidelines, looking for an empty space in the stands, Caroline, the twins' friend, caught me by the arm.

Her red hair looked like a lion's mane tonight. A big *T* stretched over the chest of her cheerleader sweater and narrowed down to her waist, where a short gold skirt with blue pleats flared over full hips. "Hey, girl," she greeted me.

"Hey, Caroline! You look terrific."

"Thanks. You know we'll do our best, Allie, to cheer him on."

"Him?"

"Everyone," she called to the other girls on the squad, "this is Allie. Allie Parker." They gathered around.

"Julia and Sandra's sister," I explained.

"Oh, really?" a dark-haired cheerleader replied. "I didn't realize that."

"We wrote a new cheer for Mike," another girl told me.

"Well, that's nice," I said. It wasn't until I walked away that it sank in: I was not being introduced as the twins' sister but as Mike's date.

Julia and Ford had gone ahead and claimed part of a bench in the stands. I climbed up after them.

"They got a great turnout," I said.

"Everyone in this town shows up for sports," Ford remarked. "It's the one thing they can all understand."

I glanced around the gym. "There's Craig," I said, standing up and waving to him, but he was busy taking pictures. Tim, who was sitting with his father and Aunt Jen, saw me and waved back from the next set of stands. Before he could squirm his way over to us, his father collared him.

As people squeezed into the packed gym it was becoming more and more difficult to hold on to seats for Sandra and Ben.

"Isn't your sister ever on time?" Ford complained.

The teams lined up to be introduced. The announcer called the names of the visiting team first and for each team the bench players before the starting lineup. When everyone on the home team but Mike had run out to the center and high-fived his mates, the announcer finally called out, "Starting at forward, Thornhill's team captain, senior, number ten, Mike Callowaaaay!" The gym erupted.

It was weird, totally weird, feeling the bleachers vibrate, having hundreds of fans cheering around me, drums beating, girls waving their pom-poms for the guy who would be driving *me* home tonight. I felt as if I'd taken over some other girl's body.

We stood for "The Star-Spangled Banner," facing toward the flag that hung at the far end of the gym. Julia elbowed me as the anthem started. "Mike's looking for you."

Mike and I turned and saw each other at the same time. He continued to gaze up at me, and I flicked my head in the direction of the flag, signaling to him that he was supposed to be looking that way. He just smiled.

Then Ford twisted around next to Julia, searching the rows behind us. "Why does that photographer keep looking up here?" he asked.

"Do you mean Craig?" I replied, glancing sideways at Julia.

She shrugged.

The anthem ended, and the starting players took their positions. Caroline and her squad raised their pom-poms. *Jump ball, jump ball, hey hey hey!*

I knew most of the cheers and was in the mood for hollering. A few minutes later Janice, the striking, dark-haired girl from the drama club, scrambled up beside the three of us. "What a mouth you have!" she said to me. "We could use her in the spring production, Julia."

It was a good game, the score seesawing back and forth. Mike played well—not exciting basketball but very solid. Twist turned and faked and spun with the ball, demonstrating where he got his nickname. I was really enjoying myself, and only Ford seemed annoyed by my cheering, which had become contagious.

Then the ref made a bad call, a real stinker against our team.

"Go see an O.D.!" I called out.

"An O.D.?" Janice asked.

"An eye doctor—in Latin, I think."

"Go see an O.D.! Go see an O.D.!" the chant went up from our section.

Janice and I were swinging our hips, leading the crowd, when all of a sudden Ben came up beside me. Sandra was on the other side of him.

"Having a good time?" he asked me.

"Oh, yes!"

"You'll go deaf," Sandra warned Ben. "Allie cheered for me the year I went out for JV basketball."

"I wasn't cheering for you, Sandra, I was yelling directions."

Ben laughed.

"We were afraid you wouldn't find us," Julia called over the roar of the crowd. "When did you get here?"

"The national anthem," Sandra replied.

"That's how we found you," Ben added. "I saw Mike and Craig turned this way and turned with them, thinking Old Glory was hanging up here."

We got back into watching the game, and I continued to cheer. I had to if I wanted to stay sane. Each bump of Ben's arm sent sparks through me, and being squeezed together there on the bench, we bumped a lot. Sandra wanted the seat on the end so she could run up and down the bleachers, saying hello to friends. Every time she left, my heart started thumping the way it had when I realized Ben and I were dancing alone. Somehow the eight hundred other people in the gym didn't seem to matter.

"Calm down, Allie," I mumbled to myself.

"Did you say something?" Ben asked.

"No. No."

"Yes, you did," Janice whispered to me from the other side.

"I just don't get it," Ford said. "What is it that makes girls so crazy about jocks?" He was watching the girls two rows in front of us checking out the players. "We make heroes out of a group of guys who bounce a ball and throw it through a hoop. I mean, look at our school photographer." He pointed to Craig. "You'd think he was covering the NBA play-offs."

Craig had been snapping pictures energetically during the first two quarters, getting down on his stomach, up on a stepladder, oblivious to everyone and everything but what he was shooting.

"That's how a photographer works," Julia said. "He takes lots of pictures to get one or two perfect shots."

153

"Craig covered us in the fall production that way," Janice reminded Ford, "and got some great photos."

"And covered the kids in the town's Halloween parade that way," Ben added, "and the shop owners at Christmas. It's not only jocks Craig pays attention to—he finds anyone an interesting subject, except maybe himself."

"Which is why I find *him* interesting," I said.

Having finished the sales pitch, Ben and I glanced at Julia, then at each other. He smiled a little. We were still connected by our hopes for her and Craig. But I let the momentary connection go too long; Ben must have seen something else in my eyes, for as he looked at me his eyes changed. The gaze, the warmth that made them like embers, was suddenly there again.

Then the halftime horn blew and we both looked away.

I guess everybody in high school dreams of making an entrance with either the school hero or hottest girl around. After the game I achieved that dream at Bingo's Café, and frankly, it's not all it's cracked up to be.

Maybe the self-esteem stuff Fields's teachers have been pounding in our heads has given me a false sense of my own importance, but it really annoyed me to be viewed as nothing but "Mike's new girl." Why wasn't he "Allie's new guy"? Of course, his crowd knew him, not me, but what bothered me was that no one there wanted to know me. Everything I was asked that night related to Mike:

What did he give me for Christmas; what did I think of the game he'd just played; what were his and my plans for the rest of the vacation?

Bored, I picked up my soda and french fries, hoping to have a real conversation with Craig. Ben had convinced his old friend to come, but he was sitting at a booth on the edge of the in-crowd gathering, talking to people who weren't part of the group. I started in his direction, then Mike caught me by the arm.

"Allie," he said, "are you going with me to Twist's New Year's Eve party?"

I gazed down at him with surprise. Maybe this was dream number two of high school, being asked on the big date by the school hero in front of others. But I felt trapped. Ben, who was sitting at the next table with his arm draped around Sandra, was watching and listening for my answer—a lot of people were. Why would Mike risk rejection in front of them? Unless, of course, he was sure I would say yes.

And the truth was I wouldn't embarrass any guy by turning him down in front of his friends, especially on his big night. "Sure," I said.

Mike took my soda and fries from me and pulled me down into the seat next to him. Ford sat across from us. "I've hardly had a chance to talk to you since the game," Mike said.

"That's okay," I replied. "You're the star tonight and have lots of friends to see."

He put his arm around me. "You're a sweet girl."

I grimaced, and he laughed. "Okay," he said, "pretend you're not."

"I don't have to pretend."

"Did you ask Allie about Tuesday night?" Julia asked, coming over to our table. She sat down next to Ford. "I couldn't remember if you had something to do, Allie."

It was an old warning system devised by my sisters and me, a way of giving the other person advance notice in case she wanted to wiggle out of an invitation. Usually, however, *I* wasn't the one who needed time to think up an excuse.

"Julia and I are going up to Windhaven for the Boat Light Parade," Ford told us. "It starts at six o'clock. Afterward we can walk through Windhaven Park. My parents have a cabin there, and we can hang out. They won't be around, of course."

"Sounds cool," said Mike. "We're free Tuesday night."

"How do you know I am?" I asked.

Mike laughed. "Because I haven't asked you to do anything else yet."

"That only means *you're* free."

He looked confused for a moment, then grinned. "You're right. You're not sweet."

"So are you coming, Allie?" Ford asked.

I thought for a moment or two, longer than I needed. "Okay."

Ford glanced over at Sandra and Ben. "You guys are welcome too," he said.

"No thanks, we already have plans," Ben replied, which made me feel both relieved and miserable.

For the next hour I tried to keep my focus on

Mike. After all, he was the one who wanted me around. As he drove me home from the café we talked a little, then lapsed into silence. I figured that the hard-played game was catching up with him.

"You look tired, Mike," I told him when we pulled into the driveway. "I can walk myself to the door. Don't get out in the cold."

He unbuckled his seat belt. "Stay here where it's warm," he said, and put his arms around me. He pulled me close to him, turning my face toward his.

His eyes were an incredible blue, his mouth as sensuous as a guy's in a cologne ad. He sure would have looked good hanging in a gym locker at Fields. *Maybe this time,* I thought. *Maybe this time I'll feel something.*

We kissed. A short kiss, then a longer kiss, then one that felt as long and wet as the Mississippi. I waited for fireworks. I would have settled for a glowing cinder. Nothing.

Right when I was about to pull away, the two of us were frozen like two deer in the headlights of a car.

Mike drew away, laughing as the headlights were quickly extinguished. "Guess we've been caught," he remarked.

"Yeah," I said, laughing with him. "Well, good night."

I kept a smile on my face all the way to the back door. The headlights that had illuminated us belonged to Ben's car, and if I didn't keep laughing, I'd cry.

Sixteen

MONDAY MORNING WAS one of those blue sky, white snow days, when the sun is brilliant and the snow dazzling and you can hardly wait to get outside. Tim called, asking if I wanted to go sledding. An hour later I found him waiting on his front steps, holding the ropes of an old runner sled and a snow tube. "I know the best hill. It's a long walk, but we can make it."

We walked three blocks to the end of Walnut Avenue. I dragged the sleds while Tim ran ahead and slid on every gleaming patch of sidewalk ice he could find. The street ended in a field of snow that was about eight inches deep, a gradual uphill climb stubbled with high grass. Tim pointed me in the right direction and told me to go first. "Ben always goes first so I can walk in his footsteps."

"There are some footprints over there." I pointed.

"Those are Ben's from yesterday, when he

mashed down the snow to make a good run for my sled. But he went the long way."

At the end of the field we walked through a stand of windblown pine, then looked down over a long sweep of hill. "Perfect!" I said. "It's absolutely perfect!"

"Do you want the runner sled or the tube?" Tim asked, dancing around.

"How about if we switch back and forth?"

He plopped down in the tube. I gave him a push and listened to him screech and holler all the way down. When he stood up and signaled that he was clear of the path, I set the runner sled in the track. I felt like a little kid again, getting a running start, flying down the hill on my belly, the wind and snow in my face.

"Your eyes are really shiny," Tim told me six or seven runs later. "And there are snowflakes in your hair."

"Then we look alike," I said, pulling my ski hat down over my ears and pulling down his too.

We rode the runner sled together several times, sitting toboggan style, racing each other up the hill after every run, panting and slipping and throwing snow. On one of those trips uphill the snow tube zipped past us.

"It's Ben!" Tim exclaimed happily.

My heart quickened. When the tube reached the bottom of the run, Ben turned to wave at us. Tim sidled close to me, forming a snowball in his hand.

"Don't let him up the hill," he whispered.

"Right," I said, and scooped up some snow.

160

"Make as many as you can. We'll need extra power."

I packed three more snowballs. "You give the signal, sir," I told him.

We watched Ben making his way up the hill toward us. He must have known what was coming, but he pretended not to.

"Ready," Tim said. "Aim." He lifted his arm. "Fire!"

We pelted Ben with snowballs and snow blobs, hastily making more as he dropped the snow tube and armed himself. He was a good shot, and Tim and I had to duck and skip despite the advantage of being uphill.

"Fire! Fire!" Tim kept shouting.

When Ben was about fifteen feet away, he got me with a snowball hard on the arm.

"Yow!"

"Don't give up," Tim cried.

"I have not yet begun to fight!" I exclaimed, quoting somebody or other.

Ben laughed and leaned over to scoop up more snow. I reared back and threw. Bull's-eye! It wasn't really what I was aiming for, but I got him—right on the butt.

Ben straightened up slowly.

"Oops," I said with a smile.

Tim laughed hysterically.

Ben just looked at me, then started to walk slowly toward me, not saying a word, shaping a huge snowball in his hand.

161

"I think it may be time to retreat, sir," I said to Tim.

"Retreat!" Tim shouted.

We scrambled up the hill, tripping in the heavy snow, trying to pull the sled with us. I felt my feet go out from under me. Ben had ahold of my ankles.

"Help, Tim!"

Tim ran over and tried to pull me uphill by the arms. I went down on my stomach in a mound of snow.

Ben flipped me over on my back—a little too gently for a guy bent on revenge—and began dragging me down the hill. I held on to Tim and dragged him. He laughed all the way.

At the bottom of the hill Ben dropped my ankles and stood over Tim and me. "Now try to get up," he said.

"Conference, Tim." I squirmed around on my back so I could whisper to him. "We'll have to fake him out," I said, cupping my hands over my mouth. "Pretend to go for Ben's ankle, and when he starts to react, jump up. Then I'll get his other ankle."

"Then we'll smother him with snow."

"Right."

Tim executed the plan perfectly, snatching at Ben's ankle, then springing to his feet. I gripped the other ankle, hanging on like a mad dog, and pulled. Ben went down on his rump. Snow flew. We were like three people splashing in a pool, making waves, with fountains of snow shimmering down on us.

I laughed till my sides ached and lay back in the

snow exhausted, still laughing. The brilliant sunlight seemed as if it were dancing in my eyes. I listened to Ben's deeper laugh and Tim's bright giggles till the three of us finally quieted down. Staring up at the high blue sky, I was content to the tips of my toes.

A minute or two later Ben stood up and pulled Tim and me up with him. "You're nothing but trouble," he said, "both of you."

"There wasn't any trouble till you came," I replied.

We climbed the hill, retrieving our sleds on the way.

When we arrived at the top, Tim wanted to ride double decker on Ben's back. I gave them a push-off, then took the snow tube down by myself. We made the same run several times, and I experimented with shifting my weight to make the tube spin. When Tim saw me whirling around, he wanted to try it.

Ben and I launched him, then Ben held the runner sled in position. "Do you want to go by yourself or with me?" he asked.

I hesitated, then told myself not to make a big deal out of nothing. All he'd asked was if I wanted to share the sled. "I'll go with you."

"Double decker?"

I nodded.

He lay down on the sled, and I lay down on top of him.

"You're going to have to hold on tight, Allie," he said. "The upper deck always gets the bumps and turns worse. Can you loop your feet around mine?"

My legs were shorter, so I hooked them just above his ankles. I was glad that there was enough fiber fill between us to keep him from feeling my beating heart.

"You're not afraid to hold on to me, are you?" he asked. "If you are, I'm going to lose you halfway down the hill."

I pulled myself forward two inches, rewound my feet, dug my fingers into his shoulders and jammed my chin down on his neck. "How's that?"

"Better," he said, laughing. "Just keep your mouth closed when we start. I don't want to get bitten."

He pushed off with his strong arms.

"How can I keep my mouth closed when—whoa—*ooo*—*oah!*"

We went flying down the hill—I think he was steering crazily on purpose—swerving left and right, hitting a big bump.

"Ow!" I screamed in his ear but hung on tight.

We swerved past Tim, who was pulling his tube up the hill, and shot over an icy patch.

"Cripe!" I exclaimed.

"Hang on!"

We swerved again and at the bottom of the hill whipped around in a hockey stop that threw us sideways off the sled. Ben tumbled after me, rolling on top of me. For a moment neither of us spoke.

"Are you okay?" he asked.

Having Ben on top of me, gazing down at me with his face six inches from mine, had a devastating effect on my memory of English. He slipped one arm under my back and a hand under my head, pillowing it in the snow. I had lost my hat somewhere, my toes were frozen, and the skin between my jacket sleeve and glove was stinging, but I had never felt so warm, so wonderful, cradled by him.

"Allie, are you okay?"

I nodded.

"Did you have the breath knocked out of you?"

Not in the sense in which he meant it.

"Say something," he persisted.

"I'm okay."

He looked at my mouth as I spoke. I looked at his—I wanted to take off my gloves and trace the curve of his lips with the tips of my fingers. His head lowered. I lifted one hand and very lightly touched his cheek. He was so close, I could feel his breath.

"Allie?" His voice was soft, his face so near.

Just one kiss, that's all I wanted. A centimeter more and our lips would touch. There was no sky above me, just Ben. All I wanted was Ben.

"Hey! You guys okay?"

Tim. I had completely forgotten about him. I wrenched my head around and saw him about forty feet up the hill, running toward us.

Ben rolled off me. "We're fine," he said, "just fine."

We sat up like two people awakening from a strange dream, then stood up slowly and dusted the snow off ourselves. "Thanks for checking, little brother," Ben said as Tim reached us.

"Some ride!" Tim exclaimed.

"You've got that right." Ben picked up the rope

of the sled and started up the hill, followed by Tim. I straggled behind, needing time to recover.

For the rest of the runs Tim rode with either Ben or me. When he wanted to do the hill alone, Ben and I took turns on the remaining sled rather than riding down together. I didn't know what he was thinking, but I was sure I couldn't get that close again without kissing him.

I no longer felt warm—in fact, my frozen toes no longer felt anything—and Tim, having endured a lot of tumbles, was soaked straight through. We finally headed home.

On the way to the Harringtons' house both Ben and I were silent, which allowed me to lapse into dangerous daydreams. How would it have felt, his lips against mine? What would it be like if he wanted me, only me? I imagined us returning to his house after a kiss in the snow. We'd build a fire together, and snuggle in front of the hearth, and—

I should have left out the fireplace part. An image of Sandra on Christmas Eve, sitting by the hearth, her gold hair catching the firelight, her hand resting on Ben's leg, suddenly popped into my mind.

"Allie? Allie?" The real Ben was speaking.

We'd reached the Harringtons' walk, and I saw that Jen and Sam were up on the porch.

"There's something we should talk about," Ben said.

"I think you're in trouble," Tim observed. "That's how he begins whenever he's going to tell you what you've done bad."

"Allie hasn't done anything bad," Ben assured him.

"Yet," I added, laughing nervously. I was afraid Ben had sensed that my feelings ran deep. Now he was worried things had gone too far and wanted to make clear that there was nothing serious between us. He probably thought he needed to set the story straight before I saw Sandra, before I said something that might ruin his plans for just the two of them tomorrow night.

"It's about tomorrow night," he began.

I frowned and said nothing.

"The boat parade at Windhaven that you're going to with Mike, Ford, and Julia. Remember?"

"Oh. Oh, right. What about it?"

"I've been to that parade," Tim interjected. "It's pretty. All the boats have lights. And Santa Claus rides in one."

"I want to make sure you know what you're getting yourself into," Ben said.

I didn't like the tone of his voice, the sound of a big brother warning his little sister.

"I'm not planning to get myself into either a boat or the river, but I can wear a life preserver if you think it's advisable."

"It won't help you in the woods," he replied.

"What do you mean?"

"You're going to Ford's cabin in the woods." His voice cracked with frustration. "And his parents aren't going to be there."

"So?" I challenged him.

"I don't like to stick my nose into other people's business, Allie. But your sisters haven't been here that long, and Julia may not know about the stories Ford likes to tell—the things he brags about to other guys. That cabin is a favorite place for his . . . his . . . conquests."

I laughed at Ben's old-fashioned language. But actually, I'd already thought about the possibility. Aunt Jen had a cabin at Windhaven, a camping area about forty minutes from Thornhill, and I knew most of the dwellings were isolated, surrounded by dense woods. My main reason for saying yes the night before was to make sure that Julia didn't go alone.

"Mike's no angel either," Ben added.

"Excuse me?" Now he was treading on dangerous ground.

"Mike's got a reputation."

"So do you," I reminded him. What a jerk—trying to destroy my thin little hope for romance, my only hope for getting over him!

"Not the same kind of reputation," he replied, his jaws tight.

"What kind do you have?" Tim asked.

Ben glanced down at him. "This conversation is between Allie and me, okay? Dad and Jen are on the porch. Go tell them about sledding."

Tim pretended to start off, then circled back, standing behind Ben, listening. To me, Ben said, "Mike likes to brag about what girl he's been with and what he's done, what *they've* done—"

"You're assuming I'm just another girl to Mike," I said angrily. "You wouldn't want me to assume that Sandra's just another girl to you, would you?"

He turned away.

"What gives you the right—"

"Listen to me," he said, turning back. "Mike's very competitive."

"Like you're not?" I replied.

"Leave me out of this!" Ben exclaimed, color rising in his cheeks.

"I will," I replied, "just as soon as *you* leave *my* life alone!"

Jen and Sam turned, hearing our heated conversation. Tim wasn't going anywhere.

"I'm only looking out for you," Ben told me. "I'm warning you, Allie. Mike is competitive, and since he can't compete in drama and Ford can't compete in sports, they compete with each other in something else."

"What?" Tim asked.

Ben glanced behind him. "Crazy Eights. Scram!"

"Well," I said, "maybe I haven't had as much experience as you and all the other macho guys of Thornhill High, but no guy talks me into anything. I know who I am." *An idiot who has fallen in love with you,* I thought. "And I know what I want. And the last thing I need right now is you acting like my big brother."

"Fine," he said.

"Fine," I said.

We stared at each other, then I turned on my heel and stomped home.

Seventeen

I LOVE THE woods. Add a river and a cabin, and I'm one happy camper. Five P.M. Tuesday, I eagerly pulled on my new hiking boots. Despite Ben's warning I was looking forward to our trip to Windhaven.

Sandra, who was getting ready for her date with Ben, came to my room, hunting for a pair of silver earrings to go with a new outfit. "If you don't mind me giving you a little advice," she said, looking down at my heavy boots, "Mike likes really feminine stuff."

I shrugged. "Okay with me if he wears high-heeled ankle boots."

Julia was in the bathroom, and her laugh echoed out from there. "Can I borrow your old hikers, Allie?"

"Sure. I've got some extra warm socks too."

We needed the wool socks when we reached the docks of Windhaven Marina on the Hudson. The night was clear and very cold. Boats sailed past with thousands of colored lights twinkling in the wind, each boat a starry constellation shining against the black night. Mike stood behind me, his warm arms around me, bending his head close to mine, the two of us oohing and aahing at the passing boats. It was a scene sparkling with romance and possibility; maybe that's what convinced me it was time to give up. As hard as I tried, I still felt nothing for him.

After the parade we returned to the marina lot to pick up backpacks that the guys had stuffed with blankets and snacks.

"I thought we'd leave the car here and take a moonlight hike to the cabin," Ford said as we put on our packs. "It's about a half mile from here."

"Sounds good," I replied. I wished we could hike all night.

Ford led the way, followed by my sister and me, with Mike last in line. The path was winding, but the moonlight guided us, breaking through the leafless branches, glistening on old stumps and sprawling logs that were sugared with snow. The walk would have been perfect if only Ford had shut up. Instead of listening to the gorgeous silences and mysterious night stirrings of wood creatures, we got to hear him talk about himself.

As we walked I noticed that Ford's backpack was coming unzipped. I stared at the shiny cans inside: He had brought a six-pack of beer. "Did you guys bring any sodas?" I asked.

"Lots," Julia said, pointing to Ford's pack, then she saw the beer.

Ford glanced over his shoulder and removed his pack so he could zip it up. I opened mine to check the contents. More beer. "I hope we have soda," I said, "because I don't do alcohol."

"You'll be thirsty when we get to the cabin," Ford replied. "The beer will taste good."

"We're underage," I reminded him.

"Lighten up, Allie," Ford said. "No one's around."

Mike glanced from him to me.

"That's just it," I told Ford. "If we were legal, I still wouldn't drink when I'm in an isolated place with someone I don't know very well."

"She's your date," Ford told Mike. "What was it you said last night—you like a challenge?"

"Excuse me?" I said.

"It's okay, Allie," Mike answered quietly. "I packed one soda. We can split it."

"Three ways?" Julia asked.

"She's your date," Mike told Ford.

"They'll change their minds when we get to the cabin and it feels like a meat freezer," Ford replied.

"Don't count on it," I said.

"You can't just turn up a thermostat," he went on. "It takes a while to build a good fire."

"I know. I was a Girl Scout."

"Still are," Ford remarked. To Julia he said, "My parents keep brandy there. You'll like it. It'll warm you all the way down." He pulled her back against him, running his hand down the front of her.

Before she could react, there was a loud crash in the brush. We all jumped. It sounded like a large animal, a deer maybe, and had come from the path behind us. Ford took advantage of the moment, holding on to Julia tightly, his hands moving over the front of her, sculpting her. I saw her pull forward, trying to loosen his grip.

There was another crashing sound, then a shout. "Allie! Allie, help!"

Tim's voice. For a moment I stood frozen with amazement, then I raced back over the trail. Julia was right behind me, the guys following her.

"Tim, where are you?"

"Over here," he called back to me. "Here."

We found him in a small clearing along with someone else. "Craig!" I said, surprised.

Tim's neighbor was standing on one leg, leaning up against a tree, his hand gripping a low branch. "Hey, guys," Craig greeted us, as if we were passing by in the school cafeteria. "What's up?"

"Are you hurt?" I asked. There was snow all over his jacket, and I noticed he wasn't putting weight on one ankle.

"Just resting," he replied.

"He's hurt. He stepped in a hole," Tim said.

Mike shook his head, his mouth pulling tight in a look of disgust. Then he crouched down and began to probe the sore ankle. Craig winced. "Really, I'm okay," he insisted.

Mike didn't buy it. "I think you've done some damage. You need to get it checked out. Allie, give me your scarf and hold his foot off the ground, will you?"

I knelt down and supported Craig's foot while

Mike bound it in my scarf and his, twisting them around the foot and ankle like bulky athletic wraps. Ford sat down on a log and watched, looking as if he wanted to strangle Craig. Julia remained standing, though Ford had brushed off a wide space on the log for her.

"What are you doing here, Tim?" she asked.

"Um . . ."

"I was taking pictures at the boat parade," Craig answered for the little boy, "and brought Tim along."

Ford narrowed his eyes. "Where's your camera?"

"In the car. I used up all my film."

Mike rested back on his heels, studying his finished work. "It'll do."

"Thanks, Mike," Craig said. "It feels better already. Have a good hike, everyone. Tim and I are heading back to the lot."

But Tim shook his head. "Craig," he said.

"We're leaving, Tim," Craig replied, as gruffly as I'd ever heard him speak. He tried to walk, then stopped and sucked in air. I knew he was in agony.

"Don't put weight on it, stupid!" Mike said sharply.

"Okay. No problem," Craig replied. "You all go ahead with your hike. We're not far from the car. Tim will find me a walking stick, right, Tim?"

The little boy didn't budge.

"Put your arm around me and lean on me," I told Craig. "I'll walk you back."

He refused. "I don't want to ruin your night."

"I find that hard to believe," Ford said with a sarcastic smile. "In fact, I find you hard to believe."

"I'll take his other side, Allie," Mike said. "We can move faster."

"I'm sorry about this," Craig told us as we helped him along.

"When you can walk again, I'm going to kill you," Mike replied.

"Why not put me out of my misery now?"

"Because I owe you for some good newspaper photos."

We made our way back to the parking lot. Since Craig's car had a stick shift and clutch, which required him to drive with both feet, Mike had to play chauffeur for Craig and Tim. Julia and I followed them in Ford's car. The six of us met up again at a hospital ER about ten miles from Thornhill. As soon as we arrived I called Sam from a pay phone. He said he'd contact Craig's parents, then come out quickly to take care of matters.

By the time I got back to the group, Craig had been registered and given a wheelchair, so there was nothing for us to do but wait until he could be seen.

"There's no reason for you guys to hang around," Craig told us. "Someone's coming from home."

Ford and Mike glanced up at the clock. A few minutes after eight—there was plenty of time to continue the date.

"I'm staying," I said.

Julia still wasn't talking, but she'd chosen a seat next to me, as if to say, Whatever Allie's doing, I'm doing.

"You know what I'm wondering," Ford said to

Craig, "how come you kept looking our way at the basketball game—at Bingo's too—but won't look at Julia now?"

I wanted to punch him in the nose, but Craig replied calmly, "It's a standard reaction when you've made a fool of yourself."

"It's a standard reaction when you're really hot for a girl you can't have," Ford said.

Craig met his eyes straight on.

"If I didn't know better," Ford persisted, "I'd think you were following us tonight."

"We were," Tim volunteered, "to make sure Allie and Julia were okay."

"What?" Mike said. "Why?"

"Ben told Allie that she shouldn't go because Ford did things in his cabin," Tim replied. "He said you would too, Mike, because you're repetitive."

"Competitive," I corrected quietly.

Mike, Julia, and Ford turned to me—Ford with a look of disbelief.

"That's what happens when you go around bragging," I said.

"Allie wanted to go anyway," Tim continued. "And Ben wouldn't come with me to make sure she was okay. So I asked Craig because he was going to take pictures of the parade."

"Allie," Julia said accusingly, "how come you never mentioned any of this to me?"

I shrugged. "I figured it was just stories. Besides, I knew we could take care of ourselves."

Ford swore softly under his breath. Mike looked

uneasy. Craig focused on the registration desk, his mouth set in a grim line. Julia watched him for a minute, then rested her chin in her hands, her fingers covering her face up to her eyes.

That's how Ben found our cheerful little group. He and Sandra had been sent to the hospital while Sam tried to contact Craig's parents.

Ford was the first to see Ben. "Thanks," he said sarcastically. "Thanks a lot."

Ben looked uncertainly from one person to the next. "Tim, what were you and—"

"You wouldn't come with me," Tim cried defensively. "I asked you to, but you said Allie's friends were none of our business."

"Oh, jeez," Ben murmured, figuring out the situation. "What a mess I've made."

Ben took charge then, saying he'd stay with Craig and Tim. Julia looked as if she were going to cry and asked Ford to take her home.

"Me too," I said.

"And me," Sandra chimed in. "Hospitals are so depressing." She was the only one in a cheerful mood. "I just don't know how anyone stands them."

"People don't come here to have a good time," I snapped.

She shrugged and a few minutes later squeezed in Ford's car, seating herself between Mike and me. Sandra and Mike talked all the way home, though what they said, I wasn't sure and didn't care.

My mind was on Craig . . . and Julia and Ben and me, and what a huge mess we'd made.

Eighteen

SANDRA THOUGHT IT was extraordinarily lucky that we'd come across Craig when he was injured. I didn't enlighten her. Julia said nothing that night until I met her in the bathroom. She was brushing her teeth fiercely.

"Want to talk?" I asked.

She showed me a mouth full of foam.

"I guess I should've warned you."

She spit into the sink and rinsed. "You guess right."

"I—I guess I didn't want it to be true," I explained.

"So you could prove a point to Ben? So you could be out while he was out?"

Her words hit home.

"I'm sorry, Al," she said quickly. "I'm mad, and I'm all mixed up."

"Mad at me? At Ford?"

179

"At both of you—and myself. I must've been crazy when I decided to date him."

"I hope Craig's doing all right."

"Me too," she said, but volunteered nothing more.

The next morning I called Craig's house and left a message for him to call back when he was up to it. Then my sisters and I were corralled by my mother for a major housecleaning event. At lunch Sandra asked to borrow my car so she could go shopping.

"You mean there's still an outfit in the mall you haven't tried on?"

She grinned at me. "If there is, I'm going to find it."

As soon as Sandra left, Julia started practicing piano. She was playing up a storm and didn't hear the light knock at the back door.

"Hey, Craig," I said as I opened the door. "How are you doing?"

"Good." He leaned on a pair of crutches. "Good."

"I can see that," I said. "Tell me, are you slowly turning into a mummy, or is that a new-style boot?"

He laughed. "The foot's broken, but not too bad."

"Come on in."

"I won't stay long," he said, hobbling into the kitchen.

"Does it still hurt?" I asked.

He shook his head. "They gave me lots of painkillers."

"Yeah? Do they work for the heart too?"

"Not so far," he said, sitting on the edge of a

high stool. "I'm really sorry about last night, Allie. I came to apologize."

"You don't owe me an apology," I replied. "Ford had those backpacks loaded with beer. I was just as glad to get home."

He nodded. "I'd hoped that something good would come out of it for you. I thought maybe you'd stay at the hospital so you could have some time with Ben."

"Why would I want time with Ben?"

He just looked at me.

"I'm that obvious, huh?"

"Maybe I can see it because I'm in the same boat." He set his crutches aside, then pulled off his backpack. "I brought Julia's pictures," he said, reaching into the sack. "Double prints, one envelope for her and one for you in case you want to take some photos back to school. In your envelope I added pictures of Sandra and Tim . . . and Ben. Okay?"

"It's the best present you could give me," I told him. "Thanks."

He glanced toward the living room, where the piano music was reaching a crescendo. "I also bought a pair of tickets to the opera for Julia."

"I'll go get her."

"Allie, wait!" he said. "Would you stay around when I apologize to her? I feel like a real jerk."

"I'll stay," I promised, "but you are *not* a jerk."

I hurried off and caught my sister at a half-note pause. "Got a minute?" I asked. "Craig's in the kitchen."

Julia's hands hovered above the keys. "Craig?"

She got up and bumped into a leg of the piano, which was unlike her. As we passed through the hall I saw her glance at herself in the mirror and tuck up a piece of hair. There was hope.

"Oh, no!" she said as soon as she saw Craig's cast.

He gave her a crooked smile. "It's no big deal. And I won't stay long. I just wanted to apologize."

"For what?" she asked.

"Screwing up your date last night. Making Ford mad. Embarrassing you. Acting like an idiot. Did I leave anything out?"

"No big deal," she repeated back to him.

"I thought you might like to have these," he told her, handing over the pictures. "They're from the fall production. I'd be glad to make more if you want to give some to Ford."

"Thanks," she said, and opened the envelope.

I peered over her shoulder. Ben was right about the photos: The picture on top was more than a snapshot of a pretty face. Craig had caught the energy and spirit of Julia. She pulled out another photo, one he'd taken backstage before she went on. You could see her excitement, the effort to focus, the fear and the hope, all bundled inside her.

"This is wonderful!" I said, taking it from her, holding it up for Craig.

He nodded and smiled. "It's my favorite. Used a telephoto."

Julia slid the pictures back in the envelope. "I want to look at these by myself if you don't mind."

"Sure, I've got to get going anyway," Craig

replied, pulling on his backpack. "One other thing: I have two tickets to a concert given by the Hudson Valley Opera Company on New Year's Eve."

Julia's eyes opened wide. "New Year's Eve?"

He nodded and reached into his pocket. "The company is local, but I think they're good. And it's early in the evening, so I thought you and Ford could fit it in before Twist's party."

"Oh," she said, sounding disappointed.

"I can't fix last night," he explained. "I hope these will make up for it in some way." He handed her the tickets and pulled himself up on his crutches.

Julia gazed up at him with her round green eyes, standing close to him so he had to bend his head to look down at her. I'd seen that ploy before.

"The problem is," she said, "the only kind of operas Ford knows are soaps. I think he'd be disappointed."

"Well, I was trying to find something you'd like. It's the thought that counts."

"So you don't want to go?" she said, sweeping him with her long lashes.

"I'm sure somebody will enjoy the concert," Craig replied. "Maybe Allie and you could go together," he suggested, "then meet up with . . . whoever, I don't know. I'm not good at these things."

Julia flicked the tickets back and forth against one wrist, then rested her hand on Craig's. "I thought *you* liked this kind of music. You said the company was good."

"I like all kinds," he replied, swinging himself toward the door as soon as she removed her hand. "And this company really is talented. Well, I've got to return my father's car. He doesn't like to drive my stick."

Julia watched him hobble out onto the porch, then hurried after him and grabbed his crutches from behind. "I'm *not* letting go," she said.

Craig looked over his shoulder at her, surprised.

"Want me to hold up a sign?" she asked, frustrated. "Come on, Craig, I was hinting for you to ask me out."

"When?" he asked.

She blinked, then burst out laughing. "Turn around," she said, letting go of one crutch. "Please?"

He faced her, looking uncertain.

"I was rude when I didn't call you back," Julia told him. "Rude and wrong about you."

He studied her face as if she were speaking a foreign language.

"I'm sorry, and I'm asking for another chance. Okay? What time is the concert?"

"Seven."

"Ask me, Craig! Ask me if I'm doing anything New Year's Eve! I know it's stupid and old-fashioned, but I'm one of those girls who likes to be asked out by the guy."

"I like being invited by the girl," he replied.

Julia chewed a finger, looking nervous.

Craig's eyes crinkled a little, a shy smile forming on his face. "Want to go out on New Year's Eve?" he asked.

"Yes."

Can the way two people look at each other really be equal to a kiss? Their lingering gaze was. I quietly closed the back door and retreated to the family room, figuring it would be a while before Craig's father got his car back.

That look haunted me all day—the long gaze between a girl and a guy who were falling in love. That night I tossed and turned, barely sleeping. Having seen the real thing, I knew I couldn't fake it anymore.

And I couldn't face all those parties. I'd come to like some of my sisters' friends, like Janice and Caroline, but a night of partying with the fast crowd and pretending with Mike was not the way I wanted to start the new year. Julia told me that she'd delivered the bad news to Ford as soon as Craig went home Wednesday. Thursday it was my turn. Unlike Ford, however, Mike wasn't a bad guy, and I felt like a louse backing out the morning of New Year's Eve. But he took the news pretty well. When I called Mike to explain, he interrupted my long apology and said, "It's okay, Allie, I understand. Don't worry about it." I was thankful that he didn't give me a hard time.

My mother, on the other hand, was not pleased. Just when she thought her duckling was turning into a swan, I announced I was staying home on *the* big party-and-date night.

"Wish I could stay home," was all my father said.

An hour later, when everyone was out on errands,

Aunt Jen showed up, dressed as if she'd just left work, offering no explanation except a sudden impulse to "visit."

"This is about tonight, isn't it?" I asked suspiciously. "Did my mother call you?"

"Your father."

"Traitor!"

"He says the two of us are alike."

"Well, if we are," I replied, "then you know there are times when you're happiest by yourself. Cripe, *he* knows that!"

She held up a white box tied in string. "I stopped at a bakery. It's almost lunch. Want to add inches to our waistline and talk a little?"

"No."

She slipped off the string and opened the box. I surveyed the pastries.

"Oh, why not," I said. We started with two crullers and an account of what had happened at Windhaven. I guess I repeated myself a couple of times.

"I think I've got the part about Julia, Craig, and true love," Aunt Jen finally told me, wiping some powdered sugar from her mouth. "What's really on your mind?"

Ben. He'd been on my mind since the day we met.

"Want me to guess?" she asked.

I glanced away.

"Ben Harrington," she said. "What went wrong between you two? Something was very right when you started."

I could feel the tears building up. "I went wrong."

"What do you mean?"

"I realized it yesterday. I was watching Craig and saw how he kept missing his opportunities. He was so sure he didn't have a chance that he couldn't see it—not even when Julia was batting her eyes at him like a pair of butterflies in distress. It got me thinking. I had a chance with Ben, but I didn't go for it. I let Sandra take over—I didn't even try."

My aunt nodded.

"The thing is, in sports and academics I'm a fighter. But I got myself so wrapped up in who was in what crowd and how a guy could be interested in me when my cool and beautiful sisters were around—I just wimped out."

"Now and then we all wimp out," Aunt Jen said.

"Yes, but I . . ."

She waited patiently for me to go on.

". . . think I love him. I couldn't help it—I fell for him." I tried to blink back the tears; it was useless. "Picked a great time to wimp out, didn't I? I know, I know, I'm young, and there are other sea horses in the ocean."

Aunt Jen smiled and touched my cheek gently. "I think you mean starfish in the sea."

"I wish I'd stop wanting him so much. And I wish I hadn't been such an idiot."

"Allie, one thing I know about love is that you can't love another person well until you love yourself. Both of you have to believe you have a lot to offer each other. I think you do believe in yourself now. Next time you get a chance at love, you'll be ready."

"Will it be as good as I think it could have been for Ben and me?"

"Oh, just you wait, girl," she said, smiling, "just you wait!" She gave me a hug.

"You brides," I teased her, "you're all so starry-eyed."

"Maybe . . . maybe. As for tonight, how does this suit you?" She held up a string, dangling a key.

"Your cabin?" I said, reaching for the key. "I can finish that moonlight hike and test out my new sleeping bag. I'd love it."

"You mother will worry that it's too lonely for you."

"I've camped by myself plenty of times," I assured her, swinging the key on its string. "My father will talk her into it—after you talk him into it."

She laughed.

"Happy New Year," I said, smiling through my tears.

"Happy new you."

Nineteen

M Y MOTHER PACKED a freezer chest full of my favorite food. My father carried it out to the car and checked the battery on my cellular phone. It was their way of parenting, and I appreciated the fact that they did those things instead of asking a lot of questions.

I was sorry I wouldn't see Julia and Craig dressed up for the concert that evening. I was glad, however, to miss Sandra's New Year's Eve outfit, which I knew would be breathtaking. I was on the road by four o'clock and arrived at the cabin at sunset.

For a long time I stood outside and watched the sky give its last amazing color show of the year. Then after a quick dinner I went for an evening walk. I thought a lot about Ben and wondered what it would be like to take a moonlit hike with him. I remembered every second of our almost-kiss in the snow and found myself close to tears again, hanging on desperately to Aunt Jen's wisdom. *Next time,* I thought. *I know myself better now. Next time I'll be ready.* Though how there could be a time when I'd love anyone but Ben, I sure didn't know.

It was only eight-thirty when I got back to Jen's place, but I was tired. I lugged armloads of wood inside the one-room cabin, stoked up the fire, and put on my Fields Follies nightshirt. The shirt, which was left over from our senior class performance, reached to midthigh and was decorated with glitter and tiny feathers in pink, purple, and orange. I pulled on the leopard slippers Tim had given me, laughing at my New Year's Eve outfit. With my sleeping bag unzipped and spread out in front of the hearth and the lights extinguished so I could enjoy the flickering fire, I took out a new paperback romance and lay down to read.

I didn't make it past page eight. At least, that's what page I found myself facedown on when I awoke some time later. I jerked up, having been startled by a noise, though my head was too foggy to recall clearly what I'd heard. Snow sliding off the roof, I told myself. The fire was nearly out, and the room was chilly. I rose to put on a log, then heard another noise: crunching snow, footsteps outside the cabin.

As if the person knew I was listening, the footsteps stopped. I waited in the silence, barely breathing. Maybe I'd imagined the steps; maybe it was just another moonlight hiker.

I tiptoed over to the window and peered through the heavy curtains. My skin prickled.

From that angle I couldn't see anyone, but a car was parked out front—one I didn't recognize. My Audi was around back. I wondered if I could slip out the front door, which was the only door to the place, and run around the cabin to my car. No—better to exit through the back window. The tiny back window? *Calm down, Allie.* This was just another camper, maybe someone who was lost, I told myself. But I was scared. Remembering I'd left my cellular phone on the kitchen counter close to the door, I hurried to get it. I was about to punch 911, then realized that by the time the police found a cabin in Windhaven, I could be wearing an ax in my back.

Just then the door handle rattled. I watched in disbelief as someone standing on the other side of the door turned the knob. The door remained bolted closed; though Aunt Jen rarely locked up in the country, I had done so that night.

Then I heard metal scraping inside metal. How easy would it be to pick the old lock?

I reached for the only weapon close by—a big iron skillet that hung above the stove. I stood back against the wall, my arms raised, ready to come down hard on the intruder.

The lock clicked, and the door swung open.

"Ben!"

"Allie!"

We stared at each other for a long moment, then he said, "Could you lower that thing?"

I dropped the skillet to my side, feeling foolish

and suddenly angry, having been frightened for no reason. "What are you doing here?"

"I was going to ask the same thing of you."

"I was given a key."

"So was I," he said in a voice as icy as mine.

Then his eyes traveled down me, noticing the glittery nightshirt, my long bare legs, and the big leopard slippers.

"You're supposed to be out celebrating," I told him. "Sandra will be waiting for you. She's spent the whole week putting together an incredible outfit."

"I think yours wins the prize," Ben replied, one side of his mouth drawing up.

My cheeks burned, and I quickly walked away from him.

He followed me. "Listen, I'm sorry," he said, "but Jen and my father never mentioned you might be here."

"*Might* be? She *knew* I was! I can't believe she tried to fix things this way!"

"I honestly didn't know you were here, Allie," he said, then leaned down and picked up my paper-back. "You read these kinds of books?"

I snatched the romance away from him. "You had to see smoke coming out of the chimney. You had to know someone was inside."

"I was thinking about . . . other things. I didn't even see your Audi, much less chimney smoke."

"And furthermore," I said, as if I'd caught him in some kind of trick, "that's not your car."

"It's my father's. I lent mine to Craig since he needed an automatic."

I tossed down the book. "When I see Aunt Jen," I muttered to myself.

"What was she trying to fix?" he asked.

I glanced up at him, and his dark brown eyes held mine. Would there ever be a time when he looked in my eyes and I didn't feel as if I were falling under his spell? I looked down quickly at my furry feet. I'd rather have taken a double set of exams than answer his one question. But I knew if I wanted to move on and be ready for the next time, I had to be straight with him.

"Aunt Jen knows I, uh, kind of . . . sort of . . . fell for you. Big time." My voice was shaking. "Of course, you're used to that. Anyway, I missed my chance with you, and she was trying to give me another. That's all."

I felt his hands on my shoulders. "Allie, look at me," he said.

"Thanks, but I've looked enough."

He cupped my face in his hands, lifting it up until I had to meet his eyes. "Here's what I'm not used to: waking up able to think of nothing but seeing one girl. Going to sleep, thinking about that girl. Hoping that when I turn a corner, that girl will be there. Driving and hoping like crazy every time I see a silver car go by. Listening for anything anyone—including her sister who I'm supposed to be dating—might say about the girl. Cheering at a basketball game, aware of every time the girl brushes against me. Being jealous of a seven-year-old kid when the girl puts her arms around him. That's what I can't get used to. Big time."

With one finger he gently traced the shape of my mouth. "I was just trying to survive the holiday," he said. "I never expected to fall in love."

"You too?"

"I love you, Allie."

He cradled my head, and his lips touched mine. There was sweet fire in them, and it swept straight through me. I started to tremble. His arms came around me and pulled me close. We held on tight to each other, and he rocked me a little. "I can't believe you're actually in my arms," he said, "and that you want to be. I'd stopped hoping."

I pulled back my head and reached up to touch his face. "I want to be. You don't know how much!"

I could feel his heart beating fast beneath his jacket. He pulled my face toward his, and we started kissing again. Then the phone rang, making both of us jump.

"It's my cellular."

We watched it from across the room, staying wrapped in each other's arms. "I guess I'd better answer it," I told him. He let go of me, and I hurried over to pick it up.

"You had me worried," Aunt Jen said before I spoke a word.

"Well, you should be," I replied into the phone. "Because a few minutes ago I was ready to kill you—right after I nearly walloped Ben on the head with your skillet."

"You didn't."

"Came close," I said, laughing. "Who do you think you are? Cupid?"

"It wasn't planned," Aunt Jen explained. "It just evolved after your mother called in a panic saying Ben had broken his date with Sandra."

"Sandra! I forgot! It's New Year's. She'll never speak to me again."

"She's out with Mike, according to the latest bulletin from your father. You girls are making your parents crazy."

Ben was standing next to me now. "Sandra's out with Mike," I told him.

"I counted on that," he said.

"Anyway, dearest niece," my aunt went on, "I'm calling to warn you that Sam, Tim, and I are on our way with our sleeping bags."

"First you play Cupid, now you're a chaperon."

"Exactly."

We signed off, and I told Ben they were on their way. "I suppose I should change out of my sparkles and feathers."

He laughed. "Before you do, let's dance."

I glanced around the cabin. "All I brought was a disc player with headphones."

"Who needs music?" he asked.

"Not me," I replied, smiling. "I proved that once before."

He took off his jacket and wrapped it around my shoulders, holding me warm in his arms. Then we danced slowly to what had become "our song," the music we heard inside us.

Do you ever wonder about falling in love? About members of the opposite sex? Do you need a little friendly advice but have no one to turn to? Well, that's where we come in . . . Jenny and Jake. Send us those questions you're dying to ask, and we'll give you the straight scoop on life and love in the nineties.

DEAR JAKE

Q: *My boyfriend, Pete, never pays much attention to me when we're in school. When we go out on the weekends, though, he's great. What's going on? Is he embarrassed to be seen with me?*

RK, Plainfield, NJ

A: There are several possible explanations for Pete's behavior. Maybe he's unsure of how to treat you around his or your friends. He could be shy about showing his affection in front of people who could tease him later, or he could feel awkward around your friends if he doesn't know them too well. It could be that Pete's very focused on his studies and doesn't want to be distracted while he's in school. Basically you're going to have to confront the guy if you want a straight answer. Try to pose the question without any anger or resentment—that could put him into a defensive mode. Instead let him know that you're feeling hurt and wondering why he doesn't talk to you much during the week. Once you know what's motivating his silent treatment, you can work on a compromise that will make you both happy.

Q: *My ex-boyfriend Aaron is dating other girls, but he doesn't like that I'm dating other guys. He's told all his friends not to go out with me even though one of them, Jason, likes me. I don't want to hurt Aaron because I do still care about him, but shouldn't I be able to date anyone I want to?*

AT, Des Moines, Iowa

A: Even if Aaron decided to join a monastery and never date again, the fact that you two are broken up means that he has no say in your current dating life. He's trying to control you, and that's not okay. It's understandable that you still worry about his feelings, but you have to put yourself first. Aaron has no right to tell other people that they *can't* date you or to tell you that other guys are off-limits. However, you did mention that Jason is a friend of Aaron's, and that can be a dangerous area. Would you want Aaron to go out with one of your close friends? I'm guessing no. If you and Jason have a real connection that you think could lead to something serious, don't give up on it. But if it's just a crush, try to find someone who isn't friends with Aaron so you can truly have a fresh start.

DEAR JENNY

Q: *I decided to break up with my boyfriend, Steve, but then he found out his parents are getting divorced. He's going through such an awful time that I can't imagine hurting him, but I just don't want to be with him anymore. What do I do?*

PH, Oxford, MI

A: Your motives are very kind—you want to spare Steve additional pain. However, what you're doing will actually make things worse for him in the long run. Eventually you'll have to be honest, and the news will hurt a lot more after you've been together for even longer. Watching your parents separate is really tough, and it can take a lot of energy to stay strong. What Steve needs now is your support. Tell him that while your romantic feelings have changed and you no longer want to be his girlfriend, you do want to be there for him as a friend. Instead of being the girl who stuck around out of pity and then ditched him once the divorce was final, you'll be the one who never lied to him and helped him through a rough time without making false promises.

Q: *I have a major crush on the son of my mom's best friend. When he comes to our house with his mom, he always flirts a lot, but he's a couple of years older than me, and I can't tell if he's just teasing or if he really likes me. How can I find out without making a fool of myself in front of someone I'll have to see all the time?*

TH, Jackson, TN

A: I know exactly how you feel—when I was thirteen, my mom had this friend with a gorgeous, incredible son who I would have died to go out with. I never told him how I felt, and I always wondered what would have happened. Like you, I was afraid of the potential embarrassment factor of being turned down by someone who knew my *mom*.

But you know what? I never realized that there are ways to be subtle in these situations. So I advise you to do what I should have done—go for it. Flirt back, encourage his interest, and try to talk to him alone, without your parents around. It can be tempting when you like a guy to get supershy around him, but you must do the opposite and be your friendliest. This should give him the opportunity to know that you're interested and to give you more information about how he feels.

Do you have questions about love? Write to:
Jenny Burgess or Jake Korman
c/o Daniel Weiss Associates
33 West 17th Street
New York, NY 10011

Don't miss any of the books in *Love Stories*
—the romantic series from Bantam Books!

You'll always remember your first love.

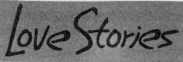

Looking for signs he's ready to fall in love? Want the guy's point of view? Then you should check out the *Love Stories* series. Romantic stories that tell it like it is— why he doesn't call, how to ask him out, when to say good-bye.

SUPER EDITION

Daring, irresistible... totally necessary. Meet Rob Barden.

It's Different for Guys
Stephanie Leighton

Nothing's worse than having to spend every day with someone you hate ... unless you hate the thought of spending even one day without him ...

Who Do You LOVE?
Janet Quin-Harkin

I wanted to be with Matt every minute of every day. Then I got my wish.

24/7
Amy S. Wilensky

The *Love Stories* series is available at a bookstore near you.